PRAISE FOR YVONNE JOCKS AND *THE RANCHER'S DAUGHTERS*!

FORGETTING HERSELF

"A tender, sweet story that carries a powerful message readers will not be able to ignore."

—*Romantic Times*

"A wonderful, can't-put-it-down read, *Forgetting Herself* is a welcome addition to my keeper shelf."

—*Amazon.com*

"Ms. Jocks shows promise, and she obviously did her research."
—*All About Romance*

BEHAVING HERSELF

"Yvonne Jocks has written an engaging novel with warm, wonderful characters her readers will give their hearts to. Nicely done, Ms. Jocks."

—*Amazon.com*

"Compelling characters and rich description add up to a savory read."

—*Romantic Times*

THE QUESTION

Papa cleared his throat, startling them. His amusement had darkened to something more intense. "You want this Englisher to call on you, Laurel Lee?"

This was the moment of truth, the point where he would guess their charade. And yet, smelling Cole's clean scent of soap and leather and shirt starch, with his hand warm around hers, the words came easier than she'd feared. "I . . . I think so," she admitted, as if it really were the truth. "I'd at least like to find out."

Collier squeezed her hand in approval.

Papa scowled at him. "You employed?"

"One definition of a gentleman," Collier offered, "is a man who need not work for a living. I receive a quarterly allowance from my inheritance."

"A remittance," clarified Papa in disgust.

Collier stiffened, but conceded, "If you like."

Papa shook his head, as if he'd seen everything.

Unwilling to let Collier make all the effort, Laurel said, "You always did want me to be a lady, Papa."

Her father looked like he might just argue with her, then shook his head and simply turned to leave. "You two got enough rope to hang yerselves, anyhow," he offered. And with that, he stalked off to talk to Laurel's mother.

Frances — who proves
herself every day. Thank
you for everything!

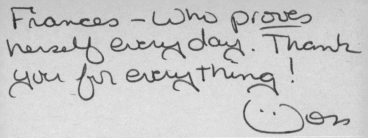

THE RANCHER'S DAUGHTERS:

PROVING HERSELF

YVONNE JOCKS

LEISURE BOOKS NEW YORK CITY

A LEISURE BOOK®

November 2001

Published by

Dorchester Publishing Co., Inc.
276 Fifth Avenue
New York, NY 10001

ISBN 0-8439-4910-4

The name "Leisure Books" and the stylized "L" with design are trademarks of Dorchester Publishing Co., Inc.

Printed in the United States of America.

Visit us on the web at www.dorchesterpub.com.

To those people brave enough to carve their own place in the world, no matter the obstacles or expectations, and who are kind enough to do it gently.

In memory of Davey.

Prologue

London, 1897

Collier Pembroke had never seen his brother so frightened.

Excusing himself to Lady Vivian, he made his way across the ballroom, past sombreros, feathers, war paint, and fringed shirts celebrating a Wild West theme. When he reached his older brother he asked, "What happened in France?"

"I need to marry," said Edgar.

Collier stiffened, as if struck by an arrow from one of the brightly painted bows being bandied about. They'd had a deal!

Rather than discuss this publicly, he steered his brother to the terrace, away from the heart of the party. Several guests nodded as they passed, particularly ladies. Despite his relative youth, Collier had managed his family's estate for two years; people knew him. Besides—blond and charming, the two eldest of the Viscount of Brambourne's sons made an attractive pair, even with slashes of aboriginal "war paint" decorating their cheeks.

"You *are* joking," he accused, once outside in the not-so-fresh air of the London terrace. "And I hardly find it amusing."

Edgar sank onto a balustrade. "I need a drink."

When Collier signaled a waiter, Edgar asked for bourbon instead of his usual Courvoisier. "What I'd really like is absinthe," his brother admitted once the waiter left. As if anyone drank absinthe in polite company!

But societal acceptance rarely influenced Edgar's preferences.

"You have to marry *whom?*" More than a little curious, Collier felt only relief when Edgar said, "Anybody."

"So you've not put some innocent in the family way, then?"

"Good heavens, no! I could if I had to, though." Edgar's frown matched his war paint. "Really. I'm rather sure of it."

Collier's eyes narrowed. "And ruin your life, as you so often put it?" *And ruin mine, too?*

His only hope of inheriting rested on his older brother's never marrying, never siring heirs. Until now, Edgar's particular tastes—and distastes—had complemented just such a plan. Lord Edgar Pembroke wished to neither work, marry, *or* inherit more than he needed for his amusements. Collier, though, wanted it with a determination beyond his twenty-six years.

But clearly something had changed.

"That was before I saw him!" insisted Edgar. "He was so . . ."

Collier waited.

Edgar clenched and unclenched his gloved hand, shaking his golden head. "Broken," he whispered.

"Your . . . friend?" tested Collier. "The one in France?" To mention the notorious playwright's name at a ball, even in assumed privacy, could be social insanity. One did not openly consort with convicted "deviants."

No, one traveled secretly to France to visit them after their release from jail, instead. At least, one did if one was Lord Edgar Pembroke, heir to Brambourne.

Collier had stayed in England, done most of the work, and tried, as ever, to keep his brother out of trouble.

Proving Herself

When the waiter brought their drinks, Edgar downed his far too quickly for a man of his upbringing. "They ruined him," he repeated. "Auctioned his possessions, banned his work. His wife sends him a hundred and fifty pounds a year. Who can survive on that? He's not seen his children since before the trial. Good Lord, Collier! I thought if anybody could maintain his spirits through two years in prison it would be he, but he didn't, not really, and now . . ."

Collier, accustomed to his brother's histrionics, waited.

"I mustn't take that chance," insisted Edgar, shaking his head. "I have to undo some of the damage I may have dealt my own reputation. Our *family's* reputation."

"And you think defrauding some poor woman into marriage will help?" Collier could not keep the disgust from his voice.

Music from inside nearly muffled Edgar's reply: "Yes, I do."

"Your friend's marriage hardly helped him."

Edgar wasn't listening. "I'm sorry. We had an understanding, and I'd not have broken it if this weren't so consequential. But I—I've turned over a new leaf. I *will* marry. I will sire heirs. And . . . and I've told the guv'nor as much."

Edgar's vehemence unnerved Collier even more than had the thought of his getting some woman with child. "Father?"

His brother, eyes begging sympathy, handed him the letter. "I told him I'd like to start managing our properties myself."

Collier did not have to break the wax seal or unfold the crisp paper to know what it said. Everyone knew what happened to second sons who got in their older brother's way. They vanished, exiled to the ends of the earth.

Though some fathers would tell them so in person.

"We'll say you're traveling on business," continued Edgar. "That we're sending checks for expenses, not remitt—"

"Bastard." Collier interrupted one ugly word with another. From overseer of Brambourne to "remittance man," just like that?

"You can go to America," suggested Edgar, gesturing through the open doorway toward society's mockery of the

13

Buffalo Bill show that had so delighted Her Majesty. "Have adventures."

Adventure? From across the room, Lady Vivian Fordham peeked coyly at them both from behind a fetching purple bandit mask. She too was part of the future Collier had built—in England.

"I'm sorry," repeated Edgar, wincing at his betrayal.

He blanched when Collier said, "You will be."

Chapter One

Wyoming, 1898

When she left the land office, Laurel knew to seek out her father and confess. Jacob Garrison would frown on any of his girls riding alone into town, much less what his second daughter had just done there. Best that he hear it from her.

But love tempted her away from her good intentions.

Halfway to her family's ranch and the battle that awaited her, she reined her bay gelding off the worn track. Snapper responded with ears up and head high. Together they escaped for the treeline, up inclines of varying steepness, past large boulders and small meadows—running away, and yet going home. The same wildness that had gotten Laurel into so much trouble throughout her eighteen years spurred her on toward sanctuary.

She didn't stop until she reached the high pine grove.

A one-room plank shack slumped in disrepair, testament to four years of Wyoming's harsh winters. To Laurel, it held heaven. Swinging her knee up and over the top pommel of her sidesaddle, she hopped to the ground with more agility than elegance, rubbed Snapper's broad forehead, then hurried to the rough-hewn door.

She had to brace her shoulder and push. Her booted heels dug into the dirt, and she heard a rip from her shirtwaist. The door, dragging the ground on worn leather hinges, slowly opened.

Wide enough for a woman, anyhow.

Eagerly she slipped into shadows lit by one small window—into peace, belonging . . . happiness. She drank in the afternoon coolness, planned where to put a bed, a table. Relaxing into the enormity of what she'd done, Laurel knew she'd found the love that could endure her entire life.

As of today, this abandoned shack in the foothills of the Bighorn Mountains was hers. Not her father's, or some husband's—hers! So were the trees, a stretch of creek, and the columbine that misted blue across patches of meadow. She'd just joined a growing number of girl homesteaders populating the frontier, and she now owned a quarter section—a whole hundred and sixty acres—of Wyoming.

For this, she would risk her father's reproach. Still, her head came up when she heard her horse nicker a clear greeting outside. Along with everything about ranching, her father knew his second daughter too well.

Taking a deep breath of *her* air, Laurel squeezed out through the barely open door and squared her narrow shoulders. Time to face the consequences.

As usual, judgment sat a worn California saddle, double-cinched atop a tall buckskin.

One of the first ranchers in the Sheridan area, Jacob Garrison had earned every white hair on his head, every deep crease in his bearded face. And he would stop at nothing to protect his ranch and family . . . whether they wanted his protection or not.

As he drew his buckskin to an easy stop, his gray eyes shining with disapproval from the shadow of his black Stetson, Laurel felt more acceptance from the land than from her father.

"I guess you heard," she admitted, awaiting his certain reprimand. "I filed on the claim."

"So they say," he drawled. He didn't dismount.

"I didn't outright lie," she assured him. She cared what he thought. "I didn't say I was twenty-one. I just swore I was as old as Clarence Perry and Stubby Harper. And that's true."

She hadn't liked doing even that. But when this beautiful stretch of land came available for a second time—after she'd thought it lost forever—what choice did she have?

Nobody had balked at Clarence or Stubby filing claims!

Her father grunted, noncommittal, and his gaze swept across the shack, the trees . . . the thick wilderness of the area. His silence worried her. He was not a talkative man, but neither was he ambivalent—especially when his daughters bucked him. Laurel had known that even before her older sister had shocked the family by marrying up with a sheep farmer. Her father was no less ambivalent now.

"Don't you have anything to say to me?" she asked.

"Nope."

And in that simple answer, she felt her peace with this place drain into uncertainty. "Why not?"

"Won't last."

That knocked the wind out of her, sure as pitching off a horse. Her response—"*What?*"—did not carry the confidence she would have liked.

"Hard enough for a full-grown man to prove up a claim," her father said, "much less a girl. Not alone." Was he referring to the man who'd just quit this claim to go east? She had more mettle than him!

"I can work hard," she insisted. "I'll start small, just a few head! I'll have hay cut for them before autumn, for the horse, and . . ."

She faltered to silence.

"Maybe you could." It wasn't the praise she longed for, but

it soothed her some. Then he added, "But you ain't hazardin' winter up here. Not alone."

Too late, she realized just what she faced. Papa's disapproval she could ride out; his fear for her safety was a different matter.

Nobody could stand against that, especially with the truth about Wyoming's deadly winters on his side. Even cowboys who wintered in line camps did so in pairs.

"There are residency requirements," she reminded him. "To prove up this land, I have to live off it. I can't leave for the winter. I can't leave my cattle!"

From the height of his saddle, her father said, "Best not buy any, then. You'll be home this winter, where you belong."

With one final nod to punctuate his decision, her father reined his buckskin in an easy circle, then rode off downhill toward the ranch—the empire—where he'd filed his own claim twenty years earlier. In that time cities had been born, railroads had moved in, and most of the free land worth working was taken. Folks said the frontier was vanishing.

Laurel meant to keep at least a piece of it for herself.

Despite a lifetime's conviction that her father's word, like God's, finished the matter, she shook her head.

"I need my *own* place," she whispered as he rode into the trees. "My own life. It's time."

She still had three good months before winter would sweep down the Rockies to terrorize her claim. In three months of hard work, who knew what she could accomplish?

"I'll prove it to you," she insisted softly.

Maybe if she said it often enough, she'd make it true.

The ends of the earth, for Collier Pembroke, turned out to be somewhere in northeastern Wyoming. The train that carried him there had its comforts, thank the Lord. He could still travel in first class, instead of crowding onto an immigrant-class cattle car, despite his own alien status.

But hell with burnished walnut fittings, plush brocade seats, and a dining car was still hell. And accepting charity from his only relative on this side of the Atlantic surely placed him in its third level, at least.

"It's a lovely residence." Mrs. Alexandra Cooper, his older cousin, spoke the first proper English Collier had heard since New York City. "We often hire it for the summer, while the Garrisons are in the countryside, and it offers a great deal of room."

"Garrison is your partner?" clarified Collier, glancing at her American husband. A stylish, dark-haired fellow with graying temples and a thick mustache, Benjamin Cooper had dancing blue eyes that belied his advancing age and distinguished position as a gentleman rancher.

"Now, Jacob might say I'm *his* partner," corrected Cooper pleasantly, with that odd familiarity that Americans so often adopted. Jacob, indeed. "Or his *segundo*—his second. He figures doing most of the work puts him on the moral high ground."

"If you'd not provided financial backing, he'd have nothing with which to work," assured Alexandra loyally.

Her husband laughed. "Could be the Circle-T wouldn't exist, darlin', but Jacob Garrison will *always* find work to do."

Cooper had come from a good family, Collier understood, before that foolish war had ended America's Southern aristocracy. His background showed in his ability to leave labor to the laborers, as well as in his choice of a wife . . . if not in his speech.

"Perhaps you could suggest some investment opportunities in the area," asked Collier, forcing the words out. They all knew his traveling on "business" was a pitiful excuse for his expulsion. And if the desiccated wasteland rolling past the Pullman palace car window was any indication, Wyoming held no more opportunity than had the heat of Texas.

Or hell.

The red dirt, exposed rock, and occasional bits of rolling brush called tumbleweeds certainly fit the description.

"Well, son," drawled Cooper, "I'll be honest with you. The beef bonanza's 'bout over. Most of our foreign investors pulled out after the Die-Up—that's when a lotta cattle just up and died back in the winter of '86—and I can't say as folks wept to see those investors go. You'll have to do some lookin' for your opportunities."

The Coopers' young son, who until now had managed to be seen but not heard, spoke up. "Uncle Jacob says there's always opportunity for a man who's willing to work hard."

"Hush, dear," said his mother. "Mr. Garrison is a lovely man, but he is decidedly middle-class."

"He's as rich as Father!"

Alexandra flushed. Collier glanced quickly out the window to hide his own amusement at the boy's gaffe, while she explained why true gentlemen never mentioned money in public.

How often had Collier heard the same speech? In the last half year he'd found the lesson came more easily when one *had* money. His own remit—rather, expense account—barely provided.

Hell. At least in Texas they'd played polo.

"So you see," finished Alexandra, "if we did not employ people to do the work *for* us, where would they be? It's the natural order of things."

"You haven't been reading that Darwin fellow again, have you?" teased her husband.

"Benjamin!" Alexandra turned away, properly put out.

Collier asked, "You're familiar with Darwin's theories?"

"Ever' once in a while," admitted Cooper, eyes dancing, "you Brits smuggle one of them newfangled books over here."

"May I ask what you think of his theories on survival of the fittest?"

Alexandra protested—"Collier, *really!*"—and put her gloved hands over their son's ears.

"I *think*," conceded Cooper, with excellent aim, "that it's about as far from that primogeniture business what's sent you out here as an idea can get."

Exactly. Collier decided not to underestimate this man's intelligence, despite the thick drawl.

The Cooper boy, even with his mother's hands for earmuffs, asked, "What's prime . . . primo . . . ?"

"Primogeniture," explained Alexandra, "is a law in Britain that allows only the eldest of a nobleman's sons to inherit. It keeps our estates from being parceled into tiny, useless plots."

"No matter how competent the eldest son may or may not be," Collier added grimly. But if he could prove himself the fittest . . .

"Can't say as a law like that would stand a healthy chance in these parts," Cooper noted. "Nor the fellow who proposed it."

Though the thought cheered Collier, Wyoming was still hell.

During her first month homesteading, Laurel Garrison felt like the luckiest person in the world.

Her sister Victoria, always hungry for adventure, could not fully grasp it. Not even after roughing it alongside Laurel for the whole month—one reason Laurel had managed as well as she had.

"I admire what you're doing," Vic insisted, rubbing liniment into her sister's sore shoulders. "So does Mama." That had been a second reason. "And this is better than helping at the law office. But . . . do you really want to do it for *five years?*"

Forearms braced wearily on her knees, Laurel watched the silhouette of aspens swaying between her and the stars through a second window that she'd cut for herself. From a ridge, farther up-mountain, she'd caught a distant glimpse of wild horses today, and she'd felt free.

She smiled. "Guaranteed."

When Vic dug into a particularly tender spot, even that was fine. Laurel had strained those muscles working her claim.

The two girls had cleared the cabin of brush and empty cans from its previous claimant, and even shot a few snakes. They'd blocked gaps beneath the walls with rocks and mud,

21

and built their own bed of logs and rope. Vic's callused hands on Laurel's shoulders proved that the younger girl had provided more than just companionship.

Laurel's own palms felt like rock. Her left thumb was swollen purple from a blow with the hammer. She'd scraped her knuckles raw and torn a fingernail nearly off. Laurel did nothing but work, stopping only when nighttime forced it.

She had so much to do! Irrigation ditches to dig for her late-season garden. Shingles to lay for the roof. Wood to chop—always more wood to chop, whenever she found fallen timber to drag home on horseback. During a Wyoming winter, firewood meant life over death. And she just *had* to stay the winter.

"If I write about our experience homesteading, I've got to explain it," insisted Victoria. She lightly slapped Laurel's sore shoulder, then wiped her hands on a flour-sack apron. Water was too dear to wash in, what with toting it from the gravel-bottom creek . . . and who knew? With all Vic's scribbling, perhaps the younger girl's hands could use some liniment, too.

Laurel drew her wrapper back around herself, against the mountain chill, and rolled back onto their bed. She'd cut the straw that filled their tick mattress herself. It crunched beneath her, smelling of her very own mountain meadow.

"Laurel," prompted Victoria at her silence. "Is it really worth all this? *Look* at you!"

Even avoiding their stained mirror, Laurel knew her face had sunburned, peeled, and burned again. Her brown hair had lightened on the ends, where her hat didn't cover it. She'd strained and sweated until her dresses hung too big on her.

"I'm not trying to win a beau," she pointed out midyawn. As if she ever had! "I'm trying to start a ranch."

"We already *have* a perfectly good ranch!" But Vic's voice seemed to recede beneath the whisper of aspen leaves, the haunting call of an owl. A tiger moth fluttered about their coal-oil lantern, throwing odd shadows.

Proving Herself

The Circle-T isn't ours, Laurel wanted to protest. *Papa's leaving his half to Thaddeas.*

But she must have fallen asleep instead, because she woke to predawn gray. Only the *rat-tat-tat* of a woodpecker, then the call of a jay, broke the stillness that wrapped itself like a blanket around her.

She crawled wearily over her sleeping sister to abuse her body and feed her soul some more, fortunate beyond measure—with only a few problems.

"I'm sorry, Miss Laurel," said Mr. Harper from behind his big, glass-covered desk. "Your, er, *ranch* simply is not a feasible investment for us at this time."

"Why not?"

His smile faltered. "Pardon?"

She'd been within the hallowed walls of the First Bank of Sheridan only a few times in her life, usually with her mother. In fact, her mother was the only other woman she'd ever seen in here. It unnerved her to come alone. But Laurel did know, from previous experience, that questions were permitted.

"Why is my ranch not a feasible investment?"

Mr. Harper glanced nervously out his office door, which he had properly left ajar throughout their interview.

Laurel felt the pull between her eyes that meant she was turning obstinate. She hadn't wanted leave her claim to come here. She hadn't enjoyed letting Victoria style her hair, powder her face, lace her into this bolero-jacketed, gored-skirted, green-serge excuse for a suit. And she despised asking for help.

But as a landowner, she had responsibilities beyond cutting wood and digging ditches. So she tried again. "Why isn't—"

"Our criteria are rather complicated," Harper assured her.

"Maybe you could explain them."

His smile tightened. "Miss Laurel . . ."

"Garrison." He would not call her brother Mr. Thaddeas!

"Miss Garrison." Somehow he made even that sound like

23

a pat on the head. "It might be easier for all involved if you sent your brother or father in to discuss this with me."

"It's not their ranch!"

"I am unsure," said Mr. Harper, "if it qualifies as a ranch at all until you've purchased some livestock."

"That's why I need the loan."

"Now, Miss Garrison," chided Harper. "I've been patient with you because of your family's ties to Mr. Connors." Mr. Connors owned the bank. "But I have real business to conduct. If you want cattle, your family has plenty. As far as the First Bank of Sheridan is concerned, however, you are simply not a feasible—"

"Clarence Perry was a feasible enough investment," she pointed out. "Why did you approve *his* loan?"

"I refuse to debate this with you." Mr. Harper stood and went to the door. "Good day, Miss Laurel."

"Is it because he's a man?"

"I said *good day*, Miss Laurel."

She reached down and grasped the back legs of her chair, then raised her chin. "I'm the same age as Clarence," she reminded him. "And I advanced further in school. So if there's any other reason—"

"*Yes*, Miss Lau—Miss Garrison." Harper changed the appellation only when she glared at him. "We *did* approve Mr. Perry's loan, in part, because he is a man. Men have business sense that ladies do not, as I believe you've just demonstrated. Men do not let their emotions override their judgment. Men have valid work experience, as does Mr. Perry. And men, might I add, reach their majority sooner and so are less likely to be evicted from their homesteads by their fathers before they prove up. *Good day*."

She stared at him, furious and mortified. It wasn't fair that men got special opportunities. It wasn't fair that the whole town knew Papa meant to keep her off her claim this winter. And that he could do just that wasn't fair either!

"Must I send someone for your father?" threatened Mr. Harper. So she stood. This was *her* interview, about *her* loan application, for *her* ranch. She would *not* be carried out the same way her father had once carried her away from a roundup she'd refused to leave.

But she wished she had worn her cowboy boots under her skirt, the way she normally did, so that she could stomp on Mr. Harper's cloth-topped shoe as she walked by. In these foolish, button-up *girl* shoes of hers, she'd damage her own foot as surely as his.

But she had to strike out somehow. So once she'd passed him, crossing into the marble-floored foyer of the bank, she spun back to him and announced, "When I succeed with my ranch, Mr. Harper, I guess I'll do my banking elsewhere. Good day!"

"Good day to you, Miss Laurel," said the banker wearily.

Stalking to the door, Laurel nearly collided with a gentleman who was entering.

"Pardon. Quite my fault." And he stepped out of her way to hold the door open. He had an accent; in her mood, even that annoyed her. Probably this *foreigner* would get a loan before she ever would, and for no better reason than that he was a . . .

Man.

And he was that.

When she actually *looked* at the stranger, the worst of Laurel's rancor drained right out of her.

The fellow holding the door open for her had to be the prettiest man she'd ever set eyes on.

His golden hair caught late-morning sunlight like an archangel's halo, and he had full lips, and the brightest eyes she'd ever seen—lash-fringed eyes, silvery eyes that reflected the blue Wyoming sky. Darned if he didn't even outshine pretty.

She'd never seen so beautiful a man in her life.

When he gazed back down at her, she felt oddly as if the rest of the world faded off, as if nothing mattered more to him at that moment than her. He cocked his head gracefully, and his smile hinted at dimples in his perfect cheeks.

"Miss?" he prompted, his British accent as thick as honey. "Are you quite all right?"

Flushing, she looked quickly down . . . but couldn't keep from noting his fine configuration as she did. The man had a sleekness about him, like the line of a thoroughbred horse. The cut of his tailored coat, from the width of his shoulders to the slim tapering of his hips, complemented it beautifully.

But he wore pricey, cloth-topped shoes, like the banker's. Impractical. And he smelled of soap, as if sweat had never touched his handsome brow. Even his suit, a spotless tan linen, showed him unfit for actual work.

What a waste.

Laurel looked back up at him. "No," she admitted. "I'm not all right. I wasn't born a man, so I must be incompetent." She moved to pass him, then paused to add, "Though I guess I'm a better rancher than *you* are."

He smiled, with real dimples this time. Despite his strong jaw, the smile itself pulled lopsided, boyish. It nearly lit up the afternoon. "No doubt," he agreed amicably.

Beautiful. What a waste.

Laurel stalked away to figure out how to get cattle, any cattle, without asking her family—or more men—for help.

The man behind her entered the bank.

26

Chapter Two

Quite the shame, thought Collier as the little suffragette flounced off with a swish of green skirt. She had the potential to be pretty, with all that gleaming brown hair and those flashing blue eyes. She even dressed well enough, though with a bolder carriage than her fashionable suit merited. But her high flush could not disguise the warm tones of a face too much in the sun. And her brazenness, though amusing, was beyond the pale.

Odd that he would think about her at all . . . except for how her determined stride made those skirts sway. And yet within an hour, his encounter with the rancher girl lingered in his thoughts as the most amusing part of his errand.

"The banker was insufferably rude," he told his cousin and her husband that evening, enjoying an after-dinner brandy in the parlor. The home the Coopers had leased was indeed fine, though sparse in decoration for a fashionable residence. Of particular luxury were the modern conveniences—gaslights, indoor plumbing, even a telephone oddly situated in the kitchen pantry.

The parlor where they sat had a simple, light wallpaper and striped, fabric-covered seats. The chairs made up in comfort what they lacked in true dignity.

"This is still a rough country," drawled Cooper. "Folks don't always savvy finely mannered types like yourself."

Rough, Collier could understand. But . . . "Do local women really work as ranchers?"

The Coopers looked at him blankly enough to answer his question in the negative.

"A young lady I noticed at the bank, who seemed agitated, said she was a better rancher than I."

"Laurel?" Alexandra seemed taken aback.

Cooper, however, grinned broadly. "I'll bet you're right, darlin'. Now did this gal have brown hair, like coffee without cream, and fine blue eyes? 'Bout seventeen . . . no, eighteen years old now, I reckon?"

"Yes." Collier put down his empty snifter, intrigued.

Cooper's eyes were dancing to match his grin. "Well, isn't that a caution? You met up with Laurel Garrison."

Garrison. "Related to your business partner?"

Cooper nodded. "She's gone and filed on a homestead; I'd forgotten she means to run cattle. She'll do it, too, if her papa doesn't set himself against her. That girl's a pistol."

Pistol seemed to be a compliment.

"I wonder," mused Alexandra, "why she was at the bank?"

At the same time, Cooper chuckled. "When she was a little thing, learnin' to crawl, Laurel ran her poor mama ragged. Jacob took to tying a stake rope 'round the baby's waist, so's Lillabit could take a rest from chasin' after her."

"Oh?" Collier, who had a younger sister he rather liked, found the image nowhere near as amusing as Cooper clearly did.

"She had a nice, roomy spot to play in," defended Cooper. "No cactus or chips. And Jacob braided the rope out of rags, so no real hemp touched her soft skin . . . except once or twice, after she'd started two-footin' it. She'd wriggle loose and jackrabbit off so fast, her papa had to rope her." Again Cooper laughed.

Good heavens. In light of all this, the girl's conduct today might be thought exemplary!

"Either she was depositing or withdrawing," mused Alexandra. "That *is* how banks work, is it not?"

"Banks?" Benjamin Cooper blinked back his memories, as if surprised to find his wife talking to him. "That's correct, darlin'. More or less."

"If the bank cooperates," added Collier dryly. Neither this bank nor the town's other two had suggested useful investment opportunities . . . within his limited means, in any case. To prove himself worthy to return to England, Collier knew full well that he, unlike true remittance men, must actually *do* something.

As long as he did not embarrass the family by lowering himself to labor, service, trade, or journalism.

Increasingly depressed, he said, "I believe I should take some air. Where is the best place for amusements around here?"

He refused to say "these parts," even in jest.

"Try the inn," said Cooper. "It's a fine establishment, and you might even find some other remittance men—"

"Mr. Cooper!" scolded Alexandra, even as Collier flushed.

The American looked from one of them to the other, clearly ignorant of his insult.

"A remittance man," clarified Collier slowly, "is a rotter, sent away to spare his family the embarrassment of his scandals. I have evaded such scandal. I am merely a second son."

"My apologies," said Cooper. "Around here we don't always see that fine a difference. But if you visit the Sheridan Inn north of town, you might find some other *second sons* making use of Bill Cody's saloon. I recommend you try the Wyoming Slug—instead of a soda mixer, the barkeep uses champagne."

Collier had so many protests to that bit of information, he

could not organize them all, so he simply said, "Thank you. Good evening, then. Alexandra."

He bowed politely to them before escaping to "the inn."

Alexandra had a rather sly expression on her pretty face, one that Collier did not wholly trust. Looks like that could indeed drive a man to drink something called a "slug."

Standing knee-deep in mud and thigh-deep in water, exhausted from her struggle with a bogged heifer, Laurel feared her father was right. What if she couldn't do this on her own?

When Snapper lifted his head toward still-unseen company, Laurel even thought, If they offer help, I won't take it!

But that would be foolishness. Cowboys accepted a hand when they needed one. She couldn't endanger a cow for mere pride.

Darn it.

The big, rawboned heifer lurched weakly and bugled out a cry for help that tore at Laurel's heart. Heaven knew how long it had struggled here, exhausting itself, before she'd ridden over to check the water hole nearest her claim. An hour had passed since then, to judge by the slant of the sun, and she'd barely managed to free and tie two of the bogged cow's legs.

While she waited, Laurel pulled another rawhide strip from her filthy dungarees, under her tied-up skirt, then set about fighting the cow for possession of its right leg. Dodging the animal's overlong horns when necessary, she kept watch for a rider to appear over a swell of the rolling foothills.

When someone did, she squinted to clear her vision.

This was no cowboy, but the man from the bank. He rode a white thoroughbred, rather than a mustang, and sat one of those useless Eastern saddles with no place to tie a rope or hang a canteen. And the closer he came, the prettier he got.

Today he wore riding pants, not dungarees, and a jacket that looked to be split-tail. Even under his straw boater, sunlight glowed from his tawny hair.

Proving Herself

Laurel felt mixed relief and disappointment. Maybe she would free this cow herself, after all.

The stranger cocked his head as he rode closer, and even confusion looked good on him. "Good Lord," he murmured, sounding just as British as she remembered. "You aren't . . . yes, I see that you are. What *is* she playing at?"

Laurel stood there in the mud hole, feeling not only frustrated but stupid and dirty, and not liking it one bit.

"Excuse my boldness," he added quickly—and just in time. "But . . . you *are* Miss Laurel Garrison, are you not?"

She nodded, still eyeing his white jacket, white hat, white horse. Was it humanly possible for any man to be so *clean*?

Beautiful or not, he should *not* have laughed.

Follow the track past the aspens, Alexandra had insisted. *The view is quite singular.*

Faced with a girl in a mud hole, Collier marveled at his cousin's misdirection. She wore a sweat-stained cowboy hat. Her scrawny excuse for a pony sported a cowboy's saddle—one of those heavy monstrosities with fat leather stirrups, a wide saddle horn, and a cantle so high as to rob riding of any skill whatsoever. And she'd been wrestling with a bovine beast that surely outweighed Collier five times over.

A casual observer might think he'd come across a boy, with her being waist-high in water. When it came to women, though, Collier was no casual observer. He recognized this one's heart-shaped face, small nose, narrow chin. Curves beneath her frock's soaked bodice confirmed her femininity quite as thoroughly as had the sway of her green serge skirt outside the bank.

As a gentleman, Collier tried not to stare. As an *exiled* gentleman, he did not try too hard.

A singular view indeed—local flavor, like an Italian maiden stomping grapes or a Spanish boy running with the bulls—but not at all what he'd expected. Alexandra had so clearly contrived the meeting, and likely at Collier's expense, that he had to laugh.

31

Then, at a wet *spat*, he stopped laughing.

A glob of mud stuck to, then dribbled off of, the shoulder of his coat and onto his borrowed mare. And Laurel Garrison, her hand especially muddy from her volley, eyed him murderously.

"You threw mud at me," Collier accused—stating the obvious, true, but quite an unexpected obvious.

"You were laughing at me." As she waded out of the mud hole, he saw that she not only wore a filthy calico dress, which might once have been red, but had on drenched dungarees under gathered folds of her skirt. Sloshing, heavy with muck, to her pony, she turned modestly away from him to untie the wet knots in her skirt, so that it fell in filthy folds to cover her pants. *More's the pity.* The denims actually showed her figure to better advantage.

"I did not laugh *at* you," he defended—as if she deserved explanation. Who knew what was *in* that mud?

Mounting her pony, the girl retrieved a length of rope off her saddle and shook out a loop. "I'm what you were looking at."

"And I suspect you are what—who—my cousin sent me to see," he admitted, intrigued by how easily she swung the loop over her head before tossing it toward the cow. That she missed hardly lessened the show. "I expected buffalo, or an Indian village, or perhaps an unusual rock formation."

Dragging her wet rope back to try again, the girl squinted at him from beneath the shadow of her soiled hat.

"No matter," he insisted, taking refuge in good manners. "If I insulted you, please do let me apologize."

Instead of accepting his apology, much less returning it, she tossed her rope again. In the meantime, he wondered what his cousin could possibly be up to. The rope landed neatly around the cow's horns, and it so impressed him that he said, "Good show."

The cowgirl secured the rope around her saddle horn, then clucked her horse into backing up, starting to pull.

Dividing his attention between her, the trussed cow, and

his soiled lapel—a handkerchief made little headway against the stain—Collier realized her goal. "Pardon me," he called, "but did you mean for *all* the animal's feet to stay tied?"

She glared at him, remarkably threatening for such a small young woman.

"I only ask," he added, "because your cow just kicked one of them loose. Likely it's of no consequence . . ."

"Whoa!" Immediately seeing the truth of it, Miss Garrison rode her pony back toward the pond to create slack. She closed her eyes for a long, tired second, then dismounted and trudged back into filthy water.

In that moment she seemed even less suited for so grueling a task. Likely the cow was tame, but it still sported the longest horns Collier had ever seen.

"Does your father not *hire* people to do this?" he asked. Then again, the man had allegedly leashed her, when she was a child.

"I'm not doing this for my father," she said.

"But can't I fetch someone to help you?"

She stopped, as if his voice grated on her—despite the fact that it had been called by many ladies "delicious." Then, as if she'd made a decision, she turned. "Once I tie off her foot, you could back Snapper up while I guide her out."

What? Him?

"Snapper being the pony," he clarified, eyeing the shaggy little horse with its mud-smeared excuse for a saddle.

"Never mind." The girl went back to cow wrestling.

Was there truly nobody else to summon? Collier looked around him at the sloping, tree-strewn wilderness that was northeastern Wyoming. From town he'd ridden an hour, mostly uphill across boulder-strewn, ditch-cut fields. The aptly named Rocky Mountains loomed ahead of him.

Perhaps there was nobody, at that.

Blurring class divisions weakened the fabric of society . . . but Miss Garrison *was* a young woman, from a marginally good family. Passably pretty, even, under the mud.

Bloody hell. At least, thought Collier as he dismounted, nobody would oversee and report his social lapse.

The girl's shaggy bay pony had a longish head, a deep body, and short legs. Collier offered it a gloved hand to sniff, scratched behind its shaggy ears, then blew gently into its nose to introduce himself. Only once "Snapper's" ears signaled wary acceptance did he wipe some of the mud from the creature's saddle with his ruined handkerchief.

Miss Garrison did not actually clear her throat, but Collier sensed her impatience at the same time the pony's ears flickered in her direction. Giving up on the mud, he stepped into the fat leather stirrup and swung onto the little beast.

"Don't we make an inadequate pair?" he murmured as he patted its withers. How one ever posted a trot in a saddle like this, he could not imagine.

"There!" Miss Garrison raised both hands, empty, as if in victory. "Now back Snapper away slowly; he knows how to do it. Lean away from the rope so it won't cut you."

Delightful. Doubting that so small an animal could do such heavy work, Collier nevertheless drew back on the reins and touched the pony with both heels. As it slowly retreated, the rope drew taut. With a great slurping noise, the cow pulled free to be dragged, thrashing and bellowing, to freedom.

As soon as the beast made dry land, the pony stopped on its own. It was not stupid at all . . . and stronger than it looked.

Wading from the water, Miss Garrison tripped slightly, muttered something under her breath, then turned around and plunged her hands into the muck to retrieve her boot. She limped the rest of the way out, dumped the boot's muddy contents, then balanced on one foot to pull it back on.

"Would you like some assistance—" But Collier bit back his offer to help when she managed the task, stomped her foot to secure the fit, then scowled up at him. He remembered her bright blue eyes from the bank. They were flashing now, too.

You are very welcome, he thought darkly.

"There's too much slack," she said, once more approaching the struggling cow. "Back up again, just a little . . . please."

Since he'd not had to demand that small courtesy, Collier did as she requested. Miss Garrison then untied the cow's feet.

The miserable animal, ribs heaving, still did not rise. To Collier's amazement, the girl took it by the tail and hauled upward with what must be all her strength.

Then, as it suddenly scrambled to its feet, she ran for his thoroughbred.

Good Lord. The long-horned cow was nowhere *near* tame!

It lunged after the girl. The rope, still around its horns, pulled Snapper and Collier forward before slowing the beast's charge. And Collier's borrowed mare, clearly wanting nothing of muddy locals or charging cattle, danced back with rolling eyes well before the girl could reach it.

Stranded, Miss Garrison spun to face her cow, wide-eyed, and whipped off her hat as if for defense.

The cow lunged at her again.

The rope held.

Annoyed, the beast turned with a snort and charged Collier.

Snapper leaped back so nimbly that Collier grasped the oversize saddle horn, lest he lose his seat. Miss Garrison shouted.

The huge, horned monster swung in her direction, dragging Collier and the horse with it for several feet before the pony regained traction.

Collier whistled sharply between his teeth.

Laurel shouted again and waved her hat.

Only when the cow slowed its angry charges and merely glared, turning its heavy, once-white head from Collier to Laurel, then back, did Collier even remember to breathe.

"Good Lord," he marveled, and moved to wipe his brow with his handkerchief. Then he laughed, for it was a muddy mass. "Good Lord. Are you even marginally sane?"

"Sane enough to wish your mare hadn't bolted," admitted Miss Garrison, low, and Collier's slowing heartbeat sped again.

She wasn't yet out of danger.

Eyeing the cow, and noticing how angrily it still eyed both of them in return, Collier mimicked her low, feigned calm. "Shall I come get you, then?"

Now he heard the tremor of uncertainty beneath her tone. "That would be a help, yes."

"You needn't resort to sarcasm," he murmured, edging the pony carefully toward her. It responded beautifully.

The cow watched them evilly.

"I wasn't being sarcastic," she protested through her teeth, smiling at the cow as if to disguise her true intentions. Then she said, still not looking at him, "But if I insulted you, please *do* let me apologize."

Mocking him, too! Did Americans even understand common courtesy, or did they merely scorn it?

"Saucy," he chided, now close enough that the slack rope could not protect her. "P'raps I should let the cow have you."

"I'm not so sure you won't," she challenged. Still not taking her gaze off the horned beast, she reached out one small hand toward the pony, toward Collier—so close, as if to touch safety would attain it. . . .

And with a strangled bellow, the cow charged them both.

Chapter Three

So *this* was what Papa had tried to protect her from!

Laurel felt the ground shake under the cow's hooves while she dove—too far, too *far!*—toward Snapper and the greenhorn.

She felt herself miraculously caught and lifted, one strong arm hard around her, up and against the man's side. Mud thrown from the cow's horns spattered across her, even as Snapper half wheeled, half leaped out of the beef's way.

Her feet flew out from the force of the turn, but amazingly the Englishman kept both his seat and his tight hold on her. When her mustang dove nearly sideways, he held firmly with his thighs—she felt one of them clench under her—and leaned so far over that she practically lay on top of him.

He could ride! And he smelled very good, too.

Embarrassed, Laurel tried to swing a leg over Snapper, behind the cantle. Her foot caught in her wet skirts; when Snapper lurched awkwardly, she nearly fell.

"Do stop wriggling," commanded the Englishman.

"Give Snapper his head!" she commanded right back, despite his forearm cutting across her ribs.

"You must be—"

"He's trained for this!" Though Papa hadn't seen the sense.

The Englishman must have believed her, because Snapper's movements became more natural then, more his own, as he faced off against the cow.

The cow snorted, still furious over its perceived mistreatment. But though it had considered charging Snapper's flank, some herd-animal instinct made it hesitate to approach the mustang face-on. Laurel drew a deep breath and realized that the Englishman's arm, around her middle, also circled scandalously beneath her bosom.

Worse, it felt rather . . . nice. Nicer than it should.

Maybe the thrill of facing danger made her giddy.

"Help me turn," she asked, again trying to swing her leg over the horse's rump. *Damn these skirts!*

"Here," he offered in that thick voice of his—but instead of slinging her behind him, he pulled her up into his lap. At least she was no longer dangling.

But thank goodness they knew each other's families!

When the cow moved to circle Snapper, Snapper blocked its way. The cow snorted.

Momentarily distracted from her compromising position, Laurel called, "You're welcome, you old bag of bones!"

"Clever," complained her rescuer. The word breathed across her temple, rumbled against her shoulder, in his chest. "Taunt it. Wise choice. Shall we insult its mother?"

Who knew Englishers could be funny? "We could do that."

"Your mother," he called, "was a cow."

Laurel laughed up at him, even as his bright eyes—a silvery blue, or maybe gray—sparkled down at her. He seemed even prettier the closer he got. Overwhelmingly so.

Maybe that tingling sensation *was* the excitement of escaping the cow, but Laurel didn't think she'd normally notice a fellow's jawline, his cheekbones, his lips, or even how his gold-streaked hair brushed against his collar and clean-smelling neck. Or how increasingly surprised he also appeared as neither of them turned away.

No. It wasn't just the cow.

He felt warmer and stronger, more solid beneath her, than his fancy clothes hinted. And he rode remarkably well.

Laurel had been warned often enough to know exactly what was happening to her. She'd just expected to feel it with a cowboy.

He's foreign, she argued weakly with herself. *Those full lips!* He should look sissified with such a gentle mouth. Instead he just seemed sincere.

And so beautiful it dizzied her.

He's a dandy, she told herself as he leaned nearer. But his hard arms, his thighs, didn't feel like a dandy's. She couldn't breathe.

And it didn't matter. Against all sense, she wanted nothing more than to linger close to him, admire that handsome face, let him kiss her the way she felt sure he meant to.

The way she hoped . . .

Which was why it annoyed her that he suddenly, firmly, closed his eyes. He had very long, thick eyelashes for a man. He pursed those full lips . . . and opened his bright eyes, only to look away. "Ah," he murmured. "Well."

Well?

She sat there on his lap, huddling into his warmth against the summer breeze on her wet clothes, and he said *well?*

Laurel reached up, wove her fingers into his hair to draw his face back to hers—and only then saw just how filthy her mud-caked hand looked beside his clean-shaven cheek.

Oh, no. No! How must the rest of her appear?

But before she could drown in embarrassment, the Englishman's eyes shined down at her.

"Pleased to meet you; my name is Lord Collier Ellis Pembroke." His voice sounded thick and rich enough to lick from a spoon, despite his hurry.

Then he kissed her.

Collier had not intended to kiss Miss Garrison. She was soaking wet. She'd covered him in muck. She smelled of dirt and water and disturbingly like cow.

And despite that, he found her lack of artifice somehow as refreshing as he found her clinging clothes sensual.

Perhaps he *had* wanted to kiss her. But a gentleman could rise above his baser instincts, and he was one. And she came from a marginally good family.

But then she'd touched his face and hair, the most intimately he'd been touched in weeks. He'd looked into those true blue eyes, that fey, if muddy face, and he kissed her anyway.

Clearly Laurel Garrison had not been kissed a great deal, but when Collier gave a gentle nibble on her lower lip, she quickly softened into willingness beneath him. *Ah . . . much better.* Not surprisingly, for a girl bold enough to challenge horned beasts, she met his dare, mimicking his entreaty on *his* lower lip—which made him all the more aware of her warm, wet curves in his arms. When Collier changed the slant of his mouth on hers, she sighed in approval. Her fingers dug into his back through his riding coat, as if to keep purchase . . . and *he* was not the slippery one! He found himself curling down and over her, felt the earth move.

He nearly fell when her horse, with a shake of its head, took several steps that nearly rid the beast of them both. Collier grasped a handful of the gelding's coarse black mane. Laurel, still in his arms, grabbed a handful of him. "Oh!"

"Whoa," soothed Collier at the same time, and drew back on the forgotten reins in his hand. "Whoa, boy."

Appropriate advice, that.

What was he doing?

The girl blushed, then readjusted her hold on him and slid partly off his lap, stretching for the stirrup to escape him. At that sensation, Collier blushed too. He quickly slid his foot out of the way of her smaller, filthier boot.

Then, when she slipped, he found himself with an armful of cowgirl yet again. The cow itself was now grazing at the end of its lead, looking as docile as a beast with such demonic horns could . . . but it was better that they not push their luck.

Miss Garrison's hair smelled lovely. Like pine trees, mountain flowers, and rainwater—and mud. Only slightly like cow.

Clinging to him, all damp curves and warmth, she finally found the stirrup. Then she swung behind him, as proper as they might manage at the moment, despite one of her arms being draped loosely about his waist.

Not as improper as they'd been.

That she said nothing in the face of their transgression nodded either toward her upbringing or her unease. Collier owned that responsibility. "Please accept my apology for my boldness. I do not normally behave so."

The voice behind him asked, "You think I do?"

Was there any way he could *not* insult this girl? "No. I could tell you do not."

He felt her shift, felt her fingers press slightly against his waist and her chin brush his arm as she leaned around him. "You could? How?"

By turning his head and slanting his gaze, he could glimpse one of her curious, suspicious blue eyes.

He wanted to see her mouth. Thinking it better that he did not, he turned forward again. "Trust me."

"I don't *know* you, Mr. Pembroke." He did feel the fool, not introducing himself for so long. "Or is it Lord Pembroke?"

He liked the way her words felt, so near his spine. "Lord Collier, actually. But only as a courtesy."

"Really?"

"Yes." He noticed that she'd not agreed to trust him.

"Well, my word. *Lord* Collier."

"For all that Americans claim to abhor aristocracy, you certainly are impressed by the most token of titles."

"Did I say I was impressed?"

So impertinent! So why did Collier want to laugh? Other than the unbelievably blue, sunny sky above him and the mountain air crisp in his lungs at midsummer? Other than how lovely this girl's kisses had tasted, no matter how improbable or unwise?

"So are we stranded here, tied to a cow?" he demanded,

as a distraction. "Or do you know how to end this little stand-off? You being the better rancher than I."

"Hand me the lariat," she said. "Please."

"The what?"

"Tied to the saddle horn. Connecting us to the cow."

"Ah. The rope." When he didn't untie the rope fast enough for her, her two muddy arms wrapped around him and fumbled at it too, getting in his way. "Excuse me. I know a few knots."

"Fine." And she accepted the lariat as he freed it. "Now ride closer to the cow."

He waited.

"Please."

So he did, and she began the job of jiggling the loop loose from the cow's horns, which, unfortunately, jiggled her against Collier's back as well. He desperately searched for distraction. "So what *does* impress you?" he asked. "If not titles."

From what time he had spent in America, he'd met far more young ladies with Cinderella dreams than not.

"I hadn't given it much thought." A particularly violent shake of the rope rocked her against him. He gritted his teeth. "A hard worker, I guess."

"A *laborer?*" That seemed about as far from a Cinderella dream as one could imagine.

"And an American," she added archly. "Preferably from Wyoming, though I could make an exception for a man from Montana, I suppose. Maybe Idaho. As long as he knows cattle."

"Then why ever did you kiss *me?*" he demanded.

"I don't know," she admitted. "You *did* help rescue me." To his relief, she at last slipped the lariat off the cow's long horns. Then she began to reloop the rope, which incited more wiggling. "I hope not to need rescuing in the future."

"You will if you fraternize with beasts like this," he noted. "How many of them do you own?"

She said nothing. She even stopped looping the rope.

"Aren't you starting some sort of ranch?" At her continued stillness, he even twisted around in the saddle to look at her.

She ducked her head, then mumbled, "None."

"Excuse me?"

"*None.* I don't have any cattle yet."

"Not even this one?"

"It's my father's. I just have my horse and my land."

"Even I know that one needs livestock to produce *more* livestock," he pointed out, an attempt at delicacy.

"And I will," she insisted. "Once I can afford some. There. Now we can go get your mare. If you please, Lord Collier."

Guiltily, he remembered the beautiful, borrowed thoroughbred Alexandra had offered him. Refusing it as anything other than a loan took almost more self-control than he had, so he called the mare Foolish Pride.

Thoughts of Alexandra distracted him even from Miss Garrison's sarcasm as, finally, he figured it out. "Good Lord."

"I am *not* calling you Good Lord Collier."

What? "No, of course not. I believe I know why Alexandra sent me to see you."

"She sent you to see me?"

Collier guided the pony down the hill, glad to spot his mare watching them warily some distance away. "She sent me here. I assume you're the person I'm most likely to have met. So . . ."

"She really sent you to see me? But why? That's not proper, is it? I mean, *we* weren't, but . . . ." Wisely, she fell silent.

"Yes, that bit was wholly unexpected," he agreed. Enjoyable or not. "No, I believe she wants me to invest in your ranch."

The prettiest man Laurel had ever seen had kissed her.

And she'd sure kissed him.

And now . . . "You're investing in ranches?" she asked warily. She'd already used up her savings repairing the cabin, which was why she'd needed the bank loan. But banks weren't people. . . .

43

"I hope to do business during my time in Wyoming."

"I thought you were just a remittance man."

He stiffened but said nothing.

She'd taken his help. She'd kissed his soft lips. But somehow, this time Laurel summoned the willpower to do the right thing. "Well, I appreciate Lady Cooper's kindness, but if you were hoping to invest in my ranch, I can't accept."

"I wasn't," clarified the Englishman—rather rudely, she thought—as they reached his horse.

She scooted back on Snapper's hindquarters, transferring her grip to the saddle's cantle, so that the Englisher could dismount without kicking her. "You *don't* want to invest in my ranch?"

"Of course not. You *are*, after all, a woman."

Only her father's strict training around animals kept Laurel from grasping the fancy boot that went by her and pushing the Good Lord Collier off her horse headfirst. Then, when he reached the ground properly, caught his mare's reins, and glanced back up with those bright, bright eyes, she realized he was teasing her.

She flushed—but she kind of liked it. It was almost as if he agreed how foolish such ideas were. Who would've thought?

Silly saddle or not, he was clearly a horseman, too. Pembroke murmured to his mare, held her bridle, and drew her attention patiently back to him even when she stared, startled, off toward the mountains. But Laurel didn't like admiring him.

She pulled herself forward and into her mustang's empty, warm saddle. She took satisfaction in thrusting her boots into the stirrups again, taking the reins. "Well, I couldn't accept."

Not as long as Papa threatened to pull her off the claim.

"I do not believe I offered." Pembroke swung himself onto the thoroughbred with far more grace than should be possible, especially with the stirrups hanging so short.

Laurel winced to see just how muddy she'd gotten his suit. "*Would* you have offered? If I didn't say no first?"

"Really, I couldn't say."

More courtesy. She preferred the banker's honest condescension. "Try some honesty," she suggested, too bold with this man but unable to stop herself. He wasn't like the fellows who'd started mooning around her ever since she went to long skirts. His clothes and speech and posture and saddle made him something wholly apart from her world, somehow not as threatening—on the range, anyhow.

Kisses aside.

Looking slightly down at her, saddle to saddle, he said, "I am sorry, but I'd hoped for a better-established business."

There. Was that so hard? "I'd turn you down if you did."

His eyes flared, but otherwise he kept that unruffled air about him. "Then everything is as it should be."

She nodded. But it didn't feel as it should be.

"Shall I escort you home, Miss Garrison?" Laurel guessed he asked from some misplaced, gentlemanly duty.

"No," she assured him. "But thank you for helping with the cow. I'm not sure—" Oh, this was hard. "I'm not sure I would have managed alone."

"You might surprise yourself," he said, then ducked his head. "In fact, for the sake of reputation, it might be best if we weren't to speak of . . ."

Oh, golly. She'd *kissed* him! "I'll forget it if you will."

"Perhaps it's for the best," he agreed.

"Papa doesn't take real kindly to things like that."

Lord Collier blinked at her, as beautiful in confusion as in his other expressions. "He dislikes gentlemen assisting you?"

Now she stared—until he shut his eyes in realization. "Ah! You meant the, uh . . ."

"What else should we keep on the quiet other than that?"

He squinted at her. "That I helped with manual labor."

Surprised, Laurel laughed aloud. "Can't let *that* get abroad!"

He looked relieved. "Exactly."

But she thought, as he reined his thoroughbred away from her, that she wouldn't be forgetting either the kiss *or* the help anytime soon—even if Lord Collier *wasn't* the sort of man to impress her.

Despite how he seemed to float on horseback.

*   *   *

Alexandra's head came up in surprise when Collier passed the parlor en route to the stairs. "Good heavens! Did she throw you?"

For a moment, Collier wasn't certain whether she meant the mare or the cowgirl.

"Yes," he answered, choosing the latter for his own strained amusement. "She did."

And he climbed the stairs for a change of clothes.

Chapter Four

When he'd first arrived in the United States, Collier traveled to San Antonio, in Texas, to meet a college friend and play polo in San Pedro Park. Capt. Glynn Tourguard had offered him a position on his ranch—all of his trainers were Englishmen. Collier, though oddly flattered, had turned him down. If he hoped to convince his father to accept him back to Brambourne, he had to. Pembrokes did not work for wages.

Eventually, though, inertia had begun to drain him as surely as did the ungodly summer heat. As desperate to reclaim his sense of purpose as to escape the Texas summer, Collier had accepted Alexandra Cooper's invitation to Wyoming.

But that inertia had begun to creep up on him again here.

By mid-July, Collier stopped telling people he was in Wyoming for business, for fear they would ask after his success. By late July he sought legal help to locate even a modest investment opportunity, since the bankers proved of no use.

A modest opportunity was all he could afford.

"Not that you're impoverished," insisted the lawyer. He was

Miss Laurel Garrison's older brother. A family photograph hung on his wall. Collier tried not to stare at the pictured sister—one of many—with the intriguing tilt of determination to her chin.

"I've had dealings with other remittan—second sons, over the last few years," explained Thaddeas Garrison. "Generally they get more than this."

"The rest is to live on," Collier reminded him evenly. Unlike some British expatriates, he understood at least the rudiments of budgeting. Once the Coopers moved on, he would do well to afford a boardinghouse. How many lonely, degrading weeks would it take before he, like many true remittance men, started living from check to check, seeking solace in drink, and reducing himself to squalor?

Garrison nodded with something that looked like grudging approval. "The problem is, most operations that could use what you're offering are one-horse spreads. Small ranches . . . maybe some mining claims, which are even worse investments. They won't earn enough to survive on for a few years, much less pay dividends."

Collier had gathered that much. "What about without expecting a profit?" Once, the idea would never have occurred to him, much less firmed itself into words. This was Brambourne's money, after all.

But it was also his reputation. Better to lose every pound than to report an inability even to invest it . . . to admit that the money from home was, in fact, nothing more than a remittance.

Even to himself.

Thaddeas Garrison exhaled—almost a snort—and shook his head. "This is about saving face?"

"As I said, what if turning a profit were not my main criteria?" prompted Collier evenly.

For a moment he thought the lawyer would order him out. But apparently he overcame his prejudices—with effort.

"Well, you still have to start small. And find someone trustworthy. I'm guessing you don't want the reputation of being defrauded, even if you don't care about the profit. There are people around here who wouldn't mind cheating an Englishman."

"Do you have any suggestions?"

"Pembroke, I am *not* going to help you lose money."

Then what in bloody hell am I supposed to do? Collier took a long, deep breath. He would not embarrass himself further. "Thank you for your honesty," he said, then pushed his chair back. "How much do I . . ." But even as he began the question, Collier again noted the portrait on the wall, the girl with the heart-shaped face, big eyes, wide mouth, and mischievous determination.

A desperate choice, true.

"Pembroke?" asked Thaddeas Garrison. "You okay?"

No. He was desperate. "How much do I owe you?"

"I didn't do anything," protested Garrison.

"You gave me almost an hour of your time." Collier frowned. "I am not ready for charity quite yet."

"I don't know how you do things in England," warned the young lawyer, leaning forward. "But in Wyoming we charge for honest work, not for talking."

Bemused, Collier spread his hands to show the matter finished. Americans took offense at the oddest things. "If I insulted you, I apologize. I meant only to pay my own way."

"If you're going to last around here," warned the lawyer, "you'll pay your own way, all right."

As if lasting *around here* were high on Collier's list of goals. But having something about which to write home—something that sounded hopeful, no matter how hollow—*that*, he wanted.

And he knew where to get it.

Laurel almost refused Lady Cooper's luncheon invitation. Not that she disliked the woman. Didn't understand her, maybe, nor Uncle Benj's reasons for marrying up with an Englisher, no matter how pretty. But disliked?

Well, Laurel disliked her world of tea parties, fancy gowns, and high manners. But that was because she always felt big and clumsy in that world, no matter how small she really was.

Sitting across a white tablecloth from Collier Pembroke, she felt all the clumsier. His white summer suit, complete with starched collar, was as fashionable as his neatly slicked-back hair. *Duded up like a mail-order catalog on foot*, her father would say, but on him it looked somehow sleek and attractive. His heavily lashed eyes seemed particularly bright in the sunny dining room. When he smiled, he lit the room.

How did one make small talk after having kissed?

Apparently Lord Collier knew the secrets of making small talk after even the most inappropriate of kisses. Or warnings.

"Has anybody attended the theater recently?" he asked, his voice richer than the fine soup Laurel was careful to scoop *away* from and not toward her. Her mother had taught her the rudiments of polite dining, after all!

"Why, just the other month, in Denver, we saw a fine performance," drawled Uncle Benj. And, as Laurel's father often pointed out, once his partner started talking, everyone else could give their jawbones a holiday. While Uncle Benj described the play, Laurel sneaked another peek across her mother's dining room table at Lord Collier, and she felt inadequate.

She might be the better rancher, but he was clearly the winner at polite soup eating.

"Why don't you tell us about this ranch of yours, darlin'?" asked Uncle Benj, as the maid showed up to clear their dishes. When Lady Cooper cleared her throat he added, "After we retire to the parlor like civilized folks, that is."

Young Alec said, "Yes, do tell us, Laurel!"

Even Lord Collier looked interested.

But Laurel couldn't think of what she would say, other than that she had a month, maybe two, before she would lose her land.

And that hurt too much to think, much less put into words!

In the parlor, Lady Cooper played piano, Uncle Benj told Laurel how wonderful she was, and Lord Collier mainly watched. That unsettled her more than anything else.

"I wish I could file on *my* own claim," announced Alec, swinging his feet. "I love the Circle-T, but it's already . . . *done*."

"Is that a bad thing?" asked Lord Collier.

"Laurel gets to create something all her own."

"And you get something solid," the Englishman replied. "Something created by your father, and his father before him, and—"

"Just me," Uncle Benj interrupted, grinning. "And Jacob and Lillabit. The Circle-T's only existed twenty-odd years."

Laurel tried to turn the conversation. "I suppose that your family's estates are pretty old then, Co—Lord Collier?"

"Yes," he echoed, an odd bitterness in his voice. "Pretty old indeed."

She flushed and looked away.

After what seemed like forever, Lady Cooper finished her piano piece and said, "Benjamin, would you be so good as to have our horses saddled, so that we might all take some fresh air?"

"I can help," said Laurel quickly, gratefully.

"No need, dear," insisted Lady Cooper.

Lord Collier added, "The Coopers hire stable help for that."

"The help can't have *all* the fun," teased Uncle Benj.

But Lady Cooper sat up all the straighter. "I will not have my guests helping with chores. Nor will I accept *you*"—she fixed her husband with a glare—"allowing it. Am I understood?"

This was why Laurel had almost refused the invitation!

Uncle Benj kissed his wife's cheek, grinning at Laurel as if they hadn't committed some sort of crime against etiquette. "I do believe we're outnumbered, Laurel, darlin'."

She tried to smile, but she had a sudden feeling of being trapped.

"Alexander, you may go too," consented Alexandra as her husband left. The boy bolted from his chair and after his

51

father, toward the back of the house, like a spring colt. But then Collier's cousin made a misstep.

She said, "I'll stay and chaperon the young people."

Laurel Garrison's blue eyes widened in shock. Collier felt similarly.

From the hallway, they heard Alec say, "Ow!"

Then Cooper reappeared in the doorway, hand on the sill, and rasped, "You'll what?"

Miss Garrison stared from Collier to Alexandra and back, something of a snared-rabbit look about her. *Good Lord.* Did she think this was about courtship?

Only when Alexandra said, "One must maintain propriety, no matter how unnecessary," did Miss Garrison sit warily back.

Cooper shook his head and blew out his breath forcefully enough to ruffle his salt-and-pepper mustache. "Now, darlin', Jacob hasn't recovered from his *first* daughter's courtship. Let's not be helpin' any of the others on to theirs just yet."

"That," said his wife primly, "is why I'm acting as a chaperon." When her husband simply stared, she stared coolly back.

"Right you are," he finally said. Then he winked at Miss Garrison before vanishing, again toward the back of the house and the stables.

The cowgirl looked doggedly at her hands in her lap. She clearly lacked training in social conventions. Not that she'd slurped her soup, or blown her nose on her sleeve, but . . .

Courting, marveled Collier again. *Her?*

Compared to that, asking what he meant to ask did not seem quite so distressing. As soon as the screen door at the back of the house closed, he moved to the settee, beside their guest. "May I speak frankly, Miss Garrison?"

She stared up at him, again like a rabbit in a snare. Or perhaps a fox: rabbits were less apt to bite. "Frankly?"

He did not realize his desperation until he found himself taking her gloved hand in his. "Please?"

She hesitated, searching his eyes. Whatever she saw in

them must have eased her mind at least a little, because she nodded.

"Remember last month," he prompted, "by the waterhole?"

Only when she flushed and jerked her hand free of his did he realize his mistake. The Chinese laundry had cleansed that afternoon out of his suit, but his blood still remembered her in his arms, wet and amazingly willing. Cheating danger, and how they had celebrated.

"That is to say . . ." He closed his eyes, but that only brought the images more clearly into his mind. "I mean . . ."

Alexandra began to play Chopin again, and even had the nerve to smile. "What *do* you mean, Collier, dear?"

Miss Garrison warned, "What *about* the water hole?"

"During our *conversation* by the water hole," he clarified, "you would not accept my investment in your ranch."

"You didn't offer," she agreed slowly. "I'm just a woman."

She was that. Even in the same room as Alexandra, Laurel Garrison exuded intense, if unpolished, femininity.

"You would not have accepted anyway," he reminded her. "However, in the time that has passed, circumstances have changed. I mean to say . . . perhaps we could both reconsider."

Miss Garrison looked wary. "Reconsider?"

"My investment in your ranch, of course. I would very much like to buy you some cattle."

She opened her mouth—quite an attractive mouth; no wonder he'd kissed it—but nothing came out.

He leaned nearer, elbows on his knees. "You need cattle. Let me buy . . . ten head. Fewer, if that's too many."

"But why *would* you? What do you get?"

"Ultimately, if you sell the cattle at a profit, I get back my initial investment plus some of that profit. It's a simple proposi—" He stopped himself. "Business arrangement."

Miss Garrison shook her head. "No, you're getting something else out of it, or you wouldn't have changed your mind."

Laurel Garrison *was* intelligent—for a girl who wrestled cows. And something about her, be it her earnest day suit or

53

the youthful simplicity of her pulled-back hair, invited honesty in return.

Perhaps it was that he had kissed her. Thoroughly.

Collier leaned close enough to smell the mountain pine in her hair. "What I get is the ability to say I've invested. Tell me how much you need, and I'll write a check."

She met his gaze with hers, watching his eyes very closely. For a moment he imagined she could see his hopes for a future.

When she shook her head, it unsettled him all the more.

"You can deposit it at the bank and have your cattle by the end of the week," he insisted.

"I can't."

"Of course you can. You would have taken the money from the bank, wouldn't you?"

"It's not that; it's—"

"Three head of cattle," he repeated, then took her hand again. "It's more than you have."

She shook her head.

God help him. *"Please."*

He did not expect her to cry.

"I *can't*," insisted Laurel, yanking her hand free of Lord Collier's gentle, soft-gloved grip. To her dismay she felt tears burning her eyes. To be so close to what she wanted—the cattle, of course. To have someone actually show faith in her, and to have to refuse . . .

It hurt. It ached in her chest, tightened her throat. "It's not that I don't want to, but I *can't*. I . . ."

Lord Collier's silvery gaze seemed needful somehow, as if this meant as much to him as it did her. But how could it? It was her life, her dream.

And now she had to face the truth about it.

"I can't keep the ranch," she heard herself admit. "My father won't let me."

Lady Cooper had stopped playing the piano.

"Pardon?" asked Lord Collier.

He'd helped her once. She guessed she owed him the truth—and herself, too. "My father won't let me winter alone. And if I don't meet residency requirements, I'll lose the homestead."

He blinked at her, leaning back, and for a moment she wondered if he understood—*really* understood—the effort that admission had taken her, the pain and loss that she faced.

But he asked, "Then why on earth are you even trying?"

What? She pushed back from him and stood. She could not feel so trapped, so frustrated and not even *move*. "To *try!* I kept thinking that somehow I'd prove I could do it, but . . ."

But it was almost August. She folded her arms, almost hugging herself, and said, "You'd be throwing your money away."

"Ah." Lord Collier sat still, calm and lovely as ever. Then, cocking his head, he said, "If you are to fail anyway, does it matter whether you fail with a few more cows?"

She took a step back from him. *"What?"*

"You won't be endangering the animals, will you? If you must, you can sell them in a month or two at a loss, and—"

So much for his faith in her! "And be a laughingstock?"

He blinked. "Pardon?"

She began to pace. "Bad enough that nobody lets me work cattle because I'm a girl. If I lose money in just a month or two, they won't let me work cattle because I'm *bad* at it!"

"At least," said the Englishman coolly, "we—you—could claim to be doing something."

"Something *stupid*."

He narrowed his eyes, clearly annoyed. But they were discussing ranching, and Laurel no longer felt inadequate. She saw she'd been lured in under false pretenses. Worse, this man had chosen her with no interest in her qualifications as a rancher. He didn't think she could succeed; he just didn't care.

Buying cattle knowing full well that he would lose money on them? No wonder folks ridiculed remittance men!

Then he asked, "What if I could help you keep your ranch?"

Laurel stopped so suddenly that her skirts brushed a chair. *What?*

No. Surely not. Just because she wanted something to be true didn't make it so. But she looked at the Englishman sitting so neatly on her mother's settee, his eyes silvery-bright, his hair like an archangel's, and somehow, with him looking so beautifully determined, she couldn't help hoping. "How?"

"I have no earthly idea," he admitted, and she spun away so that he wouldn't see her frustration. This was why she ought not have hoped—much less put hope in *him*!

"But I've known your situation only five minutes," he added. "I might think of something. I *am* a businessman . . . when permitted."

What if . . .

Laurel pressed a gloved fist against her mouth. "You don't know my father like I do."

"Perhaps if we offered him financial incentive."

She spun on him. "A bribe? You really *don't* know him!"

Even Lady Cooper laughed at the idea.

Lord Collier frowned. "You say his main concern is your safety. Perhaps we could hire a companion for you."

"No woman in her right mind would spend a Wyoming winter on the mountain," she warned him, then scowled when he quirked an amused eyebrow at her. "Except me."

"Quite. And I imagine it would have to be a woman—" He spread a hand to fend off feminine outrage when she glared at him at the same time Lady Cooper huffed. "Unless you can hire some sort of proxy to replace you on the homestead during the winter months. An overseer of sorts. I would have to see the homestead law, but do you suppose that's permitted?"

She shook her head.

He stood, pressing his full lips together in thought. She found it almost breathtaking to watch someone think so fast—even if he was doing it for his own purposes, and not really hers at all.

Collier paced a few steps, then turned and faced her again. "You're not yet twenty-one, are you?"

She shook her head.

"I didn't think so. And twenty one is the age of majority?" She nodded.

He clasped his hands behind him. "If you were to marry, you would become your husband's legal concern instead. I don't suppose you've got a beau who might be rushed, have you?"

"No!" Did he think she would have kissed him the way she did, down by the water hole, if— Darn it, they were supposed to be forgetting that. "No," she said again. "And I don't want one! It's *my* ranch!"

He took a quick step back. "Merely inquiring, I assure you. Let's see, then. Who has your father's ear, who might intercede on your behalf? Your mother? Cooper?"

But the more possibilities he suggested that she dismissed, the worse she felt. "It's no use."

"What happens if you default on this homestead, but leave the cattle on the range? Next spring you file again."

"Not on this land. I only got it because the fellow who filed four years ago moved east. Anything available next year will be out past the deadline—"

He raised an eyebrow. "Deadline?"

"Sheep country," she clarified. "It's got terrible grass."

"I'm sure the sheep ranchers appreciate that," he mused, then waved her annoyance away. "Pardon. Just thinking out loud."

"Thank you for trying," she told him. "No matter why it is you want it so badly. But it's no use."

Instead of giving up, he crossed to her, took her hands in his larger ones, and ducked his head near hers. "Miss Garrison. Look at me please."

Even with the *please*, she did not like the command. She studied their gloved hands instead and, past them, their feet. He still wore those foolish, expensive, cloth-topped shoes. But she wore foolish girl-shoes herself today, for etiquette's sake.

57

Even their gloves had little use beyond the decorative.

Then Collier lowered his voice into a sugary dare. "Laurel."

A dare she would answer. She looked at him.

"I shall think of something," he insisted, and with the intensity of his eyes, the strength of his jaw, she had a hard time doubting him. "I promise I will think of something."

She shook her head slowly, unwilling to risk hoping.

"When I do," he insisted, "tell me you'll let me invest."

"You won't."

"Then you shan't have to make good, shall you?" He looked very much as he had before kissing her: focused, fervent, incredibly engaging.

Not that she ought to remember the kissing.

"If," she said slowly, finally.

"When," he agreed. Then he raised her gloved knuckles to his lips. She hadn't expected that either, nor the steamy warmth of his breath through the thin, useless cotton.

Perhaps, from the way his eyes widened over their hands, neither had he. But he recovered quickly enough, even grinned that slightly lopsided smile, the one that kept his beauty human.

Laurel had the sinking feeling she'd just done something very, very foolish—even before Uncle Benj returned to the parlor.

Chapter Five

Laurel wrenched her gloved hands free of Collier's when she heard the kitchen door slam shut. Somehow she managed to turn away from him and the hope he offered before Uncle Benj's cheerful, booted stride reached the doorway.

But her father's partner still saw something.

"What's wrong, darlin'?" he demanded, coming immediately to her side and shooting a dangerous look toward Lord Collier.

"I'm fine. Really." She attempted a smile that, to judge by Uncle Benj's clear suspicion, did not succeed. "But I would like to go home now, I think. If Lady Cooper doesn't mind."

"I'll ride with you," agreed the rancher.

"Really, Uncle Benj. I got here just fine on my own."

"And I'll see you get back just fine," he insisted.

So they rode back to her claim together. He even gave her a fair piece to compose herself, during which he merely commented on the unseasonably warm weather, the flowers, and her beauty.

Then he asked. Sort of. "A man marries a woman," he

mused aloud as they left the track to ride cross country. "He lives with her, travels with her, has his only child with her—only one he knows of for sure, anyhow. . . ."

She did not smile at his attempt to shock her. She was busy remembering Lord Collier's words. *Not if*, he'd said, *when*.

Did she dare hope?

"It seems a fellow owes his lady certain courtesies, after that," continued her adopted uncle. "Like the chance to do some schemin' now and again. But Laurel darlin', you are special to me. I won't have even my beloved wife causin' you distress. So why don't you tell me what the hell that was about?"

His insight startled her even more than the curse. Relieved, she smiled. She should have known he would not be fooled. "Nothing, really."

"I don't owe you near as much schemin' time," he warned.

But what was there to keep secret? Beyond what she'd been keeping secret for over a month, anyhow: the water hole.

"Lord Collier wants to invest in my ranch, that's all."

Uncle Benj laughed. "The boy must be gettin' desperate."

Laurel stared at him until he realized what he'd said.

"Not that you don't likely have a fine establishment, darlin'," he added quickly.

"But Papa doesn't mean to let me keep it," she finished.

"I am aware of his resolve there, yes," he agreed. "Can't even say I'm against it."

Him, too? "Uncle Benj!"

He held up his right hand to ward off her dismay. "If I could figure a way to let you have that land but winter in town, I would most certainly do so. I reckon your pa would, too, for all that he'd prefer you settle down properly instead. But you winterin' alone in them mountains . . ." He shook his head.

"Maybe it will be a mild winter," she pointed out.

"Maybe not," he countered. "I would be as loath to see harm come to you as your own father is. He loves you enough to risk your hatin' him for it. Reckon I can do no less."

I might be able to keep you on it, Lord Collier had said. But he had no reason to worry about her her safety.

"May I ask you something?" Laurel ventured as they reached the leaf-dotted shade of the treeline.

"You may ask me anything, darlin'. I told you that years ago." And he had. Uncle Benj had been the one to confirm for her that people made babies pretty much the same way she'd noticed animals doing it. He'd let her try a cigar once—one puff had been enough—and had slipped her sips of beer and even whiskey over the years.

But this was a different kind of question. "Why'd you marry Lady Cooper?"

Uncle Benj stared at her, his eyebrows high. He was a slim man, still dark-haired except for his sideburns and some gray in his mustache. But today he looked almost as old as her father.

Which, she realized with some surprise, he was.

"Anythin' except that," he decided finally, pleasantly, and pointedly. "Well, looky there. See that there bird's nest?"

"I didn't mean . . . I don't mean to question that you *did*. She's clearly a wonderful person."

"Tendencies toward subterfuge aside," agreed Uncle Benj.

"And beautiful."

"As a Texas sunset. First thing that drew my eye to her."

"I guess you must have fallen in love with her."

"Helps the marriage immensely," he agreed.

"But . . . she's English."

Uncle Benj looked amused. Clearly he knew that.

"And you're a rancher. An *American* rancher."

"I'm a rancher by necessity, darlin'," he reminded her. "If life worked out how I once figured, I'd be a plantation owner on a spread to rival that Brambourne Cole's always talkin' about."

Cole! She could only imagine how the Good Lord Collier would react to the nickname, and liked it immediately.

"So you married her because she's from the kind of life you once thought you'd have?"

61

Uncle Benj looked down at himself. He dressed like a rancher—a well-off one. "Seems I came close. In no small part due to your folks."

"Oh."

They rode on in silence until he finally prompted, "But?"

"Then why *did* you marry her?" Laurel guessed he could refuse to tell her again, as easily this time as before.

But instead Uncle Benj winked and said, "Because your mama was already taken."

The next morning Laurel opened her eyes to a woodpecker's hammering. She took a deep, happy breath, surprised by how warm the air felt. Surely it would be a mild winter, with a summer like this, wouldn't it?

Crawling out of bed, she didn't bother with a robe. She washed quickly before pulling on a simple workdress.

"Mmm," protested Vic into the pillow. "What?"

"Nothing," whispered Laurel at the thatch of curly dark hair that hid her sister's face. "Go back to sleep."

"Good." Vic sighed, and Laurel sat back on her packing-crate stool, picked up her boot . . . then sat there in the shadows. Why wasn't she still asleep? It was dark!

Maybe Victoria and Lord "Cole" had the right of it. Maybe no woman in her right mind would homestead, much less on a mountainside. Was she in her right mind?

She looked at the cowboy boot in her hand. She loved wearing boots, their comfort and protection and sure step. The ground never felt so solid when she was wearing girl-shoes that couldn't even ward off a decent dew, much less rocks or thorns or cow chips. Was she really the only girl who'd ever noticed that?

Among her sisters, it seemed she was.

If she decided to behave as a woman ought to, to give up the hard work and ride out the winter safe in town, then what did she have to look forward to? New winter fashions? Parties and dances? Services in the stark white church every Sunday?

She agreed with Mr. Thoreau and Miss Dickinson about having a better cathedral right here in the woods.

Courting?

Fellows had been sniffing around Laurel since she'd turned sixteen, and a sillier process she'd never seen. A cowboy who looked just fine in his baggy shirt and butternut trousers would spiff himself up like a parlor decoration, hair slicked back, jaw shaved, and mustache waxed, just to request the chance to sit on her folks' porch swing with her and say nothing.

And after they had such good sense about footwear, too!

She'd quit that foolishness after the first few tries—men she'd considered friends, who'd managed to embarrass both of them so badly that she couldn't ask them for roping lessons or horse advice ever again. But if she moved back to town, there they'd be again, those otherwise capable fellows who didn't see her as anything but a potential bride.

Laurel shuddered and pulled on her boots, enjoying the firm *thunk* of her foot into each solid leather heel. She guessed it didn't matter whether she was sane or not. She wasn't styled for the same niceties her sisters were. She didn't enjoy them—like at Lady Cooper's luncheon the other day, they'd downright spooked her. Which left building a life of her own, one she did fit.

Which meant finishing her woodshed, on sheer faith that she would need to keep wood dry come winter. Not that she put too much faith in the Good Lord Pembroke, no matter how pretty he'd looked trying to convince her.

Digging holes for corner posts, she wasn't surprised to look up and see her father, astride his buckskin, watching her from the trees. The last pinks of sunrise had barely left the sky, and her skirt hem hung dark with dew. He must have gotten up as early as she had, to already be here.

Papa nodded a mute greeting and rode into the clearing. Wiping her hands on her skirts, Laurel met him halfway.

"Laurel Lee." Her papa's gray eyes surveyed her morning's

work from beneath the shadow of his Stetson. "Buildin' a shed."

Even his questions came out sounding like commands.

"Yes, sir," said Laurel, reaching out to stroke Casper's blond neck, his whiskery nose, as she looked up at her father. "You always told me wood's no good wet."

Instead of answering, he eyed the garden, then her corral. Likely he thought her a fool too, to do so much work for something she'd have to leave. "Where's your sister?"

"Still asleep." Laurel relaxed when a smile briefly creased her father's face.

"Takes after her mother."

And I take after you. Did he even know that? Everything Papa did, she'd wanted to do, always. Even this.

"Light a spell," she invited. "Stay for breakfast. I'm sure Vic will be out soon. She just stays up later than me, writing in that journal of hers."

"Takes after her mother," said Papa again. With a creak of leather he swung stiffly off Casper. He loosened the horse's cinch, then left the animal to forage while they talked.

"Mama keeps a journal?" asked Laurel, fetching him some water from the pail hanging by the door.

"Obliged." He took the tin cup. "Sometime back."

"Why did she stop?"

"Raisin' a family's hard work. Honest work."

"I never said otherwise," Laurel protested.

Papa glanced at the cabin, then back at her.

"*You* started a ranch without implying any of that!"

"Different for me."

"It shouldn't be," she insisted.

"Husband might disagree."

"Then thank goodness I don't have one!"

Only when her voice echoed to silence in her little pine clearing did Laurel realize how she'd raised it. No matter how she tried, it seemed she and Papa always ended up fighting.

At least, they had since she'd turned twelve and he started treating her like a lady.

Her father returned the cup to its pail. He stopped, dead still, when Victoria appeared in the doorway in her cotton nightgown, dark hair curling everywhere. "What are you yelling— *Oh!*"

Then she ducked back inside before their father recovered enough to turn away. "Hello, Papa!" she called.

Jacob Garrison looked accusingly at Laurel, as if it were *her* fault her younger sister was gallivanting half-dressed about the foothills. Still screwed up tight from their argument, and embarrassed by her temper, Laurel went back to digging holes.

For a few minutes Papa just watched. Then, as incapable of standing still while someone worked as he was of flying to the moon, he strode over to the garden. He caught up the hoe on the way, and began to hack at weeds.

Unlike some cowboys, Papa did what needed doing, not just what he could from horseback. That was the only reason she guessed he'd agreed to the town house—for the girls' schooling. Laurel wondered if he ever felt as if he were suffocating after too many weeks in town. Better this, the smell of freshly turned soil, the strain of her arms reminding her that she was alive.

The soft chopping of the hoe into the dirt stopped. She looked up, caught her father's eye, and followed the encouraging tilt of his head.

Just past the cabin, amid the trees, stood a doe and her fawn. The baby stood almost as large as its mother, its speckling long gone beneath a shaggy brown coat. Both creatures stared back, dark-eyed and free.

Then, quick as a wink, they bolted.

Laurel looked at her father, pleased to have shared that moment with him. He nodded as if he understood, then returned to the garden. But instead of doing more weeding, he lowered himself onto one knee—stiffly, as befitted an old cowboy—and pulled up one of her onions. He knocked the soil off it, then turned it in his callused hand.

It seemed an odd thing for him to do; the stalks had just

barely begun to droop into a request to be harvested. Misgiving tightened in Laurel's stomach as she watched him. She didn't want to ask. Maybe if she just ignored him . . .

But that would be cowardly, and she took pride in never being a coward. Besides, it was her garden, on her homestead. So she crossed the yard to him while he retrieved the knife from his belt, cut a section off the onion, and shook his head.

"What is it? Have pests gotten to it?"

"Thick and tough," he told her, then tossed her the onion.

She caught both the vegetable and the reference he'd just made. *Onion skin very thin, mild winter coming in; onion skin thick and tough, coming winter cold and rough.* And the skin of this onion was by no means thin, despite the warm weather.

"That's an old wives' tale," she protested weakly.

"Bees are buildin' their nests high," he noted. Another wives' tale. "Woolly bears are near to black."

"You can't predict the winter, Papa. Not even with onions and bees and woolly-bear caterpillars to go by." And the shaggy coat on the fawn. She didn't want to remember that.

Her father stood again, slowly, to his full height. He was not a tall man, but she'd realized that only a year ago. He didn't have to be. "Won't have you stayin' past snowfall."

No. That was all she really had to say to test his resolve, wasn't it? *No.* She'd said that to his face only once, as a child, with dire results. But she wasn't a child anymore.

What would he do if she dug her heels in, once and for all?

Victoria reappeared in the cabin doorway, fully dressed this time. "Papa! Why are you here? Is everyone all right?"

"Family's well, Victoria Rose," he assured her, then flung the bit of onion he still held across the clearing, toward the wood, before turning to receive a hug from his third daughter.

"You're just making sure we're behaving ourselves, right?" When Papa held Victoria back to study her, clearly remembering how she'd been dressed when she first came out of the cabin, she only grinned. Vic had their mother's knack for laughing off Papa's solemnity. "Well, aren't we fortunate I've got a job at the newspaper now—maybe I can keep our scandals out of it!"

He was not amused.

"Stay for breakfast, Papa," said Laurel. This was still her land. She was still hostess. "Tell us what brings you here."

He nodded in the polite response he would give any settler and followed them into the shadowy, one-room cabin, taking off his hat. Putting on the beans she'd soaked the previous night, Laurel tried not to see the cabin's interior through his eyes: no whitewash, no nice furniture. She'd gotten by with packing crates, the bed, the table, and the new camp stove. And she was proud of her stove.

Homesteaders couldn't prove up without one.

"You don't mind beans, do you?" asked Vic, as if they could have offered him eggs or meat. They didn't have either just now—but Vic had, Laurel could smell, put biscuits on.

"Nothin' wrong with beans," he assured them.

Especially flavored with new onion. "Sit a spell."

He settled himself carefully on a packing crate and told them what he'd come to tell them. "Kathryn's birthday is next week. Your mother expects you at the ranch."

"Is she going to have school friends over?" asked Victoria.

"Jest family," insisted Papa. "Mariah's sheep farmer and the Coopers."

Family? The Coopers? Not surprising, since her second youngest sister Kitty and Alec were good friends. And Uncle Benj *was* practically kin. But . . .

"Did you hear?" teased Vic. "Lord Collier might be there." She knew full well Laurel had dined with him and the Coopers.

What was there to do other than concentrate on chopping onion—minus the thick, tough skin—and pretend not to notice her father's darkening interest?

"Lord Collier," he repeated, his drawl making a mockery of the title. So much for pretending not to notice.

67

"Lady Cooper's cousin," she clarified. "He's staying with—"

But when she glanced back, his distaste made it clear he knew exactly who the Englishman was. Papa wasn't as susceptible to bright smiles and dimples as were other members of the Garrison family, she guessed. Especially not on men.

"What is he to you?" he asked, his very tone a warning.

As if she were looking for a beau, much less a foreign one! Laurel wondered exactly how she would torture Victoria for this. "He isn't anything to me," she insisted, wishing that sounded more true. It *was* true. Especially if one forgot the kissing . . . and the business they'd discussed earlier this week.

Laurel realized she had too many exceptions to convince Papa, even if she was innocent. Practically. So she added the onion to the beans and tried a little more truth.

"I dined with Uncle Benj and his family last week," she explained. "Lord Collier wants to invest in my cattle ranch."

At Papa's expression of disbelief, she lifted her chin. "He *does!*"

"Only got that one cow," Papa reminded her, incredulous. And that one had been a maverick.

Not if I let him invest. "Well, I turned him down, of course!" But that was treading toward untruths, so she turned back to the stove and stirred the pot.

"He must be a hard fellow to say no to," teased Victoria.

"Maybe for you." Laurel felt far too aware of her father's gaze to laugh. "*You* think he's the shiniest thing Sheridan's seen in years."

At least attention shifted momentarily off her. "He *is*," insisted Victoria to their father. "And he's interesting—from a whole nother country! That doesn't mean we can't behave around him. It's just that some of us are around him more than others."

Papa's gaze slid back to Laurel.

"Well, maybe you can swoon at his cloth-topped feet at Kitty's party, then," she challenged, annoyed.

"That wouldn't be any worse than asking cowboys to

please show me how to throw a lariat," countered Vic, taking
affront at Laurel's tone. As if Laurel had used that merely as
a ploy to flirt with cowboys.

"They did show me how to throw a lariat!" she retorted.

Then it occurred to her that her father had never given her
permission to spend time with any of his hands. "Like perfect
gentlemen," she added weakly.

Which was mostly true.

Papa shook his head and muttered, "Losin' my appetite."

Which apparently reminded Victoria to check on the rolls
in the Dutch oven. "All I'm saying is, a fellow like that would
be hard to refuse. Doing business with, I mean."

As if anything else would apply to Laurel!

Papa said, "Been askin' 'bout homesteads." It came out
sounding like an accusation.

"*You* have?" asked Victoria, uncertain.

But Laurel knew whom he meant, even before he clarified,
"His Lord God Pembroke."

She just wasn't sure whether to be embarrassed that her
father knew that much, or pleased that Lord Collier was keeping his promise . . . trying to, anyhow. *I shall think of something*, he'd said, and he'd kissed her knuckles. Well, her dress
gloves—another reason to dislike that useless fashion!

"Do you think he'll try filing a claim?" asked Victoria.

Both Laurel and her father snorted at the very idea—then
looked at each other, startled. To her relief, his eyes warmed
with humor. Any man whom Laurel couldn't imagine homesteading, he seemed to figure, was a man he didn't have to
worry about.

And she *couldn't* imagine Lord Collier doing anything so,
well . . . laborious. So perhaps Papa was right.

They managed to enjoy their breakfast together anyhow.
Things didn't get strained again until Laurel walked with him
back to Casper, his buckskin, as he readied to leave.

He swung himself into his saddle, set his heels, and stared
down at her. "First snowfall," he warned, in case she'd forgotten.

She stared up at him and thought: *No.* But she'd lost the desperation to say that just now. She would prove it to him instead.

Then he said, "Best not set your heart on such as can't love you back, Laurel Lee." He nodded at her and reined his buckskin back toward the Circle-T.

Laurel could only hope he meant her ranch.

Chapter Six

Collier received the letter, in Edgar's hand, the day before Miss Kathryn Garrison's party. He tossed it unopened onto the desk.

"You and your brother are close, then?" drawled Benjamin Cooper, who'd brought the missive.

"Increasingly less so." And Collier turned the page of the book he was reading, called *The Beef Bonanza*.

"I do believe that book was written afore you were born," warned Cooper. "There's not much of a bonanza left to be had."

Collier looked up only from basic courtesy. "I'll bear that in mind."

"Especially not in the one-horse operations." Cooper's eyes, particularly bright, confirmed Collier's suspicions of a warning. Heaven forbid he tread into the life of Laurel Garrison! "If you really want to invest in somethin', I hear tell the automobile has a fine future ahead of it."

Collier looked deliberately back down at his book. It seemed the more polite choice than telling the man to sod off. Only once Cooper left the room did he glance toward the letter. Likely it would be bad news.

But he opened it anyway.

Because she was late for Kitty's party, Laurel rode in along Goose Creek, where the trees would hide her, taking time to catch her breath. She'd gotten late through foolish concerns over her tanned skin, her rough hands. It would be equally foolish to tear in so fast, pouring sweat, that she scared the guests.

Not that the guests meant anything to her.

When she rode through a sweep of willow leaves, near the family's old claim cabin, she was surprised to see an old friend. Nate Dawson, her father's ranch hand, sat on the rock where they used to meet when she wanted to learn how to cowboy . . . or when she ran late. More than once he'd taken her horse in himself while she made for the house, to sneak in the back way.

He stood and palmed his hat off when he saw her, as if she were still living at home, as if they'd never fought.

"Same old Laurel." And he reached up to help her dismount.

"I'm not awfully late, am I?" she asked as he lifted her to the ground. But he didn't step back from her very quickly.

The last time they'd fought, it was because Nate wanted to be more than friends. He hadn't insulted or compromised her, but it had made things awkward between them all the same.

"Only a little after two," he told her. "I think your sister's saying you're already upstairs, getting ready."

Laurel groaned. "Victoria?"

"One and only." Nate still hadn't stepped back.

Darn it!

If Laurel wanted a beau, she could do worse than him. Lean and tanned as most cowboys, he had shaggy brown hair and a ready smile. He'd proved his loyalty more than once, especially during last year's family scandal—Mariah's marrying that sheep farmer.

But Laurel didn't want a beau, certainly not one who didn't understand why she couldn't just marry a fellow with a homestead instead of proving up her own.

"You ought not be out here," she protested reluctantly. "I'm sure Mama has refreshments set up for the hands."

"Let me see to your horse," he insisted. "You get inside before the boss knows you weren't there all along."

And although Snapper was *her* horse, *her* responsibility, Laurel knew Victoria was running a risk by covering for her.

"Thank you." She put a hand on his arm. "I owe you."

Nate looked at her for a long time, as if maybe she did, which worried her. "Miss Laurel, can I ask you something?"

Miss Laurel? "What is it, *Mr.* Dawson?"

As she'd hoped, her return formality teased a ghost of a grin out of him, but he avoided her gaze as he asked, "Are you sweet on that Marmaduke what's been bedding at the Coopers'?"

Then he looked up, and she could see how much the thought had troubled him. It troubled her, too. *"What?"*

"Well, folks have been saying . . ." He kicked a tuft of grass. "Not that I listen much."

"People think I'm sweet on a remittance man?"

"Not a lot of people, but you did go to the Coopers' t'other week. Well, I told 'em they were liars," he assured her vehemently. "I said, 'Miss Laurel has too much horse sense to let some fancy-pants Englisher charm *her*. And they saw as I had a point. But, I figured I should ask you direct."

Which, she realized, was very much what her father had recently done. Who else thought she was sweet on Collier Pembroke?

Don't be ridiculous, she thought—but it didn't come out of her mouth. Maybe the not-to-be-remembered kisses by the water hole silenced her. Or maybe the fact that Pembroke was doing her a favor, no matter his reasons. She couldn't just dismiss him as she would a . . . a sheep farmer.

73

"Thank you for asking me," she said, and Nate nodded. "Maybe you could tell people it's none of their business."

He frowned impatiently. She hadn't said what he wanted her to say. But she wasn't sure she could say more and still be truthful or fair—a situation she liked no more than he did!

"Are you sure you want to see to Snapper?" she asked now, a desperate change of topic. "I ought to be the one doing it. . . ."

Nate scowled. "Get along now."

So Laurel did, circling to the two-story ranch house from the river, on the kitchen side. Though they had shade trees, Papa had refused to plant any too near the house. But by tucking her skirt up into her belt, so that its folds hung as high as her stockinged knees, Laurel managed to shimmy up a post to the veranda's roof, then through her younger sisters' gabled window.

"Laurel!" Victoria's exclamation startled Laurel so that she fell, with a thud, onto the wooden floor. "It's about time. You nearly got me into very big trouble."

"I didn't ask you to lie for me," said Laurel, untucking her skirt as she sat up. She'd just sort of hoped.

"I told Papa we were fixing your hair—" Victoria made a face—"and trying to smooth your elbows."

"You said 'elbows' to Papa?" Their father considered the mention of any noninjured body part to be somehow brazen.

Victoria nodded. "And your knees."

Stifling a laugh, Laurel peeked out of Kitty and Elise's bedroom, into the upstairs hallway, then darted into the bedroom she'd always shared with Mariah and Victoria. It felt strange to see her sister Audra's things there. But Mariah had left to marry, and Laurel *did* have her own home now.

Until first snowfall, anyhow.

She peeled off her dusty dress, then hurried to the washbasin in her unmentionables to splash scented water onto her face, her neck, her bared arms. She refused to ask if her elbows looked so terribly bad. "Are the Coopers already here?"

"The Coopers?" When Vic handed her a flour-sack towel, Laurel snapped it at her, and Vic laughed. "Yep. *All* of them."

Which meant Lord Collier, too. Had he thought of something?

Vic handed Laurel her blue party dress. Laurel pulled it over her head in a rustling confusion of bishop sleeves and lace bertha, then spun to have Vic button it. "Nate Dawson thinks I'm sweet on him." Where there was gossip, could Vic be far behind?

"You've always liked Nate," admitted her sister.

"No, sweet on *Collier*." Laurel grinned, now that it wouldn't be such a betrayal of her English . . . friend? Co-conspirator? Partner? "Dawson called him a Marmaduke."

"Well, Marmaduke or not, who *wouldn't* be sweet on him?" countered Vic, which made Laurel feel somewhat better.

"A cowboy."

"Well, you may be a rancher, sister, but you are never going to be a cowboy. Sit down." Laurel sat, and Victoria quickly combed her hair, then began braiding it.

If Papa had his way, Laurel wouldn't be a rancher either. Not this winter, anyhow.

How far had she fallen, that her only hope for a solution was a handsome blond Marmaduke?

Collier didn't have a solution. The news from Edgar had stunned him so, he was having trouble reasoning at all.

Still, somehow he suspected seeing Laurel Garrison would help him figure the rest of it out. But she had still not come down to her sister's lawn party at the Garrisons' country home—if one could call a wooden farmhouse, no matter how nicely kept, a "country home."

Laurel's mother—introduced to him as Elizabeth Garrison—had done a nice job of setting up trestle tables with pink bunting decorations in the shade of some nearby trees. She was showing Benjamin Cooper wax gramophone cylinders that, Collier could only assume, were newly acquired.

The cheerful strains of "Hot Time on the Old Town" soon sang
out into the summer air.

Laurel's father, the dour rancher himself, looked even
more like a judge, with his white whiskers and terse way of
speaking. No, he likely would not be bribed. Alec Cooper
dogged the man's heels as Garrison exchanged words with
some ranch hands who'd come up to the house for lemonade
and biscuits. Alexandra sat on a wooden folding chair, discussing something with a strawberry-blond daughter and the
lawyer Thaddeas. Mr. and Mrs. Stuart MacCallum, newlyweds, from what Collier understood, stood very close to each
other, speaking in tones nobody else could hear.

Still no Laurel.

"Where the hell is she?" muttered Collier under his breath.

Only then did he feel a gaze on him, and he slanted his
own downward to see the smallest Garrison girl watching
him. She had cascading blond hair caught back in an oversize blue bow, a picture of innocence. And she asked,
"Where the hell is *who?*"

Collier sank into a crouch to put himself more at eye level
with the child. "I beg your pardon," he said seriously. "I
should not have said that word."

She shook her head in solemn agreement.

"You know not to repeat it, don't you?" he asked.

She nodded.

"What's your name?" he asked.

"Elise."

He made an abbreviated bow. "Pleased to meet you."

"You're pretty," she said.

Collier widened his eyes. Starting a bit young, wasn't she?
"Thank you," he said, resisting the urge to smile.

Elise rocked back on her heels. "Where the hell is who?"

Collier scowled at her, then heard a screen door slam shut,
and slowly stood. Was that Laurel?

Having only seen her in a day suit—and mud—he barely
recognized her in a fashionable party dress. Gray lace overlay
a lawn gown of blue, in a Gibson-girl style that slimmed her

hips and raised her . . . complemented other womanly attributes. She wore her hair braided into a crown, sleek and sensible.

Good Lord. She was . . . attractive!

Her gaze seemed to sweep across the rest of the company, then caught on Collier's, even as he stared. For a long moment Laurel stared back. Then she flushed and went to the sister whose birthday it was, the brown-haired, bespectacled girl.

Her next-youngest sister—Victoria?—stood for a longer moment on the porch, watching him with interest that a true Englishwoman would never venture.

But he was not in England anymore. And with the letter from Edgar still rustling in his pocket, Collier was currently disenchanted with the women of his mother country, as well.

How are the business ventures progressing? Edgar had written before closing, as if any news Collier offered would approach the import of his own. Collier wrote back, *I am part-owner of a Wyoming cattle ranch.* Just to see how it looked, should he mail it.

It did not look half bad . . . if he could only make it true.

Laurel Garrison, hugging her younger sister, glanced toward him again. Somehow they would find a way to discuss this.

"Collier, dear," greeted Alexandra, coming to his side. "Are you surviving the heat? Let Audra fetch you some lemonade."

"Please," agreed Collier, and smiled at the strawberry blonde, who seemed to be Audra. "Thank you."

She all but ran toward the house.

"I *do* wish you would tell me what has upset you," coaxed Alexandra, once they were alone. "I'm quite certain it pertains to that letter from Edgar, so you might as well tell me the rest."

Collier said no more than when she'd started asking him, last night. He was unsure he could force the words out to so sympathetic—so *British*—an audience without embarrassing himself.

77

"One mustn't keep these things to oneself," she insisted. Then she groaned when little Elise raced screeching by them, pursued by Alec and two dogs. Unlike Mrs. Garrison, however—who only called a warning about the phonograph—Alexandra had too much breeding to raise her voice at her son.

"I'd best speak to Mr. Cooper," she decided, instead. "Are you *quite* certain—"

Miss Audra returned, carrying two glasses of lemonade from the kitchen. Collier said his thanks, then waited until the girl backed away from them before he told his cousin, "Please go on."

With clear reservations, she did.

He found Laurel again; she was talking to her older sister and her sheep-farmer husband, MacCallum. She met his gaze, then averted her eyes. Both MacCallums looked over their shoulders at him. Collier noticed Thaddeas Garrison scowling in his direction as well. *Lovely.*

At this rate he would never get the chance to speak to Laurel in private; everyone would be watching for him to make some sort of romantic overture.

Alexandra had moved and was speaking quite seriously to her husband until Cooper caught her waist and swept her into an impromptu dance to the Spanish instrumental playing on the phonograph. Alexandra protested, but clearly with little conviction. Mrs. Garrison laughed at them. Little Elise dragged the birthday girl—Kathryn?—into a dance of their own.

Collier decided a better opportunity would not come. He strode to where Laurel still stood with her sister and brother-in-law, and bowed. "May I have this dance, Miss Garrison?"

She hesitated, eyes widening. Surely they danced in Wyoming!

"I promise not to tromp your feet," he insisted.

"It's not that." She pressed her lips together, nodded, then looked quickly toward the phonograph, almost startled, when "La Media Noche" scratched to an end.

Was her distressed glance toward the suddenly silent machine relief or disappointment? Either way, Mrs. Garrison replaced that wax cylinder with another, and cranked the handle.

"Go on, Laurel," insisted Mariah MacCallum.

"All right," said Laurel, as the announcement before the song identified it as "And Her Golden Hair Was Hanging Down her Back."

Collier did not miss the soft look that the MacCallums exchanged, as Mariah had golden hair. He, however, had more interest in the brunette who reluctantly placed her hand in his.

She wore no gloves, but he still did. The latest recording had a cheerful beat to it, and Collier found it easy to swing his pretty little rancher into step with him.

Miss Laurel matched him step for step. "We don't normally dance here," she admitted, her gaze skipping between his chest and his eyes, down and up. "Uncle Benj was just being . . ."

"Himself?" suggested Collier. She laughed, and they both relaxed slightly. "I could think of no other way to speak privately with you," he admitted over the music, leaning his head toward hers. "Without endangering our reputations, that is."

For some reason she laughed at that idea. When he quirked an eyebrow, she reined her gaze back to his chest and he could see no answer through her eyelashes.

"You've been asking about homesteads," she told him without looking up.

When he turned with her, she easily followed his lead. "It hasn't done me a great deal of good."

Her gaze rose to his again, stricken. "No?"

"Unfortunately not, but I'm not done," he assured her. "I'm rather desperate to announce some progress to my family. Thus far, your ranch is the closest I've come to anything of worth."

She rolled her eyes. "I feel so very special."

79

This time he spun with her. Clutching at his arms, she rode out the spin beautifully, her gored skirt flaring behind her, and she laughed up at him. Unseemly or not, he had a hard time not grinning at her clear enjoyment of the maneuver.

"Why is it so important that you announce progress now?" she asked him.

Remembering the letter in his pocket, and so many very different dances back in England, Collier frowned.

"Cole?" she prompted—and when he started at the nickname, she flushed. "I mean," she corrected teasingly, "*Lord* Cole."

They held each other's gazes in playful challenge. Never would Collier have thought he'd find it so easy to talk to either an American or a woman about things that truly mattered.

"I received news yesterday." He admitted to her what he'd not yet told Alexandra. "My older brother is engaged."

"Congratulations," she said, but must have read his expression, because she added, ". . . is what I would normally say, but clearly that isn't the case?"

He shook his head. "He once agreed never to marry. That way my children would inherit. But he's broken his agreement."

She snorted. He blinked, startled to hear such a sound out of so pretty a face. "I'm sorry you won't inherit, but really—he has the right to marry if he wants!"

Collier did not, of course, mention Edgar's reasons for thus far avoiding marriage. Instead he offered more acceptable reservations. "He does not love her, and I doubt she loves him."

"How can you be so sure?"

"Two years ago she promised to marry me."

Her eyes widened, and they danced in silence until the last, scratching notes of the song. Well, at least he'd said it. His onetime flame, the Lady Vivian—who *did* have golden hair, though only once had he seen it hanging down her back—no longer had him suffering in silence. For that, he felt grateful to the less polished, more candid Miss Laurel.

"That's—that's terrible," she said finally, as they stepped back from each other. The dance *had* ended, after all.

He shook his head. "Vivian wanted to be mistress of Brambourne. I should have realized."

"No wonder you want to have good news of your own."

"There must be a way," he insisted. Then, at a tug on his coat, he turned to see the little blond she-devil with the big blue bow. "Hello again, Miss Elise," he greeted warily.

"Can *I* dance?" she asked.

"That's not how you do it, Elise," corrected Laurel. Then, instead of instructing her sister on the true etiquette of dancing, she said, "You bow, like this, and say . . . What was it you say, Lord Cole?"

He narrowed his eyes at the nickname, but consented to demonstrate both bow and request to her sister, one hand neatly behind his back. "May I have this dance, Miss Elise?"

Instead of agreeing, the little girl bowed back. "May I have this dance, Mr. Cole?"

This was very much not Brambourne, so Collier scooped the little girl up into his arms. "Only if you watch your language," he cautioned dryly as another tune, "Mockingbird," whistled out of Mrs. Garrison's phonograph. "And my name is Lord Collier."

The little girl leaned dramatically back and forth to the music. "Oh." But she did not correct herself.

Instead she asked, "Are you going to marry Laurel?"

Collier stopped dancing. "Good Lord!"

"Elise, really!" protested Laurel. She and Collier glanced at each other, mutually amused at the foolishness of the young. . . .

And stared.

It was a ridiculous idea. Even if it would remove her from her father's legal authority. Even if it would give him something quite startling with which to counter Edgar's missive. Even if it would provide him a place to live when the Coopers left Sheridan. It was . . . It was . . .

Laurel was not yet flatly denying it. Neither was he.

81

Their eyes widened in something akin to mutual panic. "No," Collier managed to say finally, at the same time she did.

Laurel laughed an uneven laugh. "Of course not."

"Not in the least," added Collier.

"Goodness, no," agreed Laurel. But from the way she glanced at him, she wasn't thinking as resolute a *no* as he would have thought.

"Stuart married Mariah," insisted the little girl he held, still swaying to the music even if he did not.

"Stuart and Mariah," corrected Laurel, "were in love. Lord Collier and I are not."

That, at least, they could agree on. But when Elise, clearly disappointed, said, "You could still marry, couldn't you?" he could not help, well . . . considering it. If only to dismiss it.

It was sheer folly, of course. Desperate they might be, but this?

No, he thought grimly.

But from the depths of his desperation, against all wisdom, wrenched the word *maybe*.

Chapter Seven

Laurel's mother led an easier life than many frontier wives. The family had a large stove, a crank washing machine, an indoor pump, and the help of Mrs. Sawyer, their latest housekeeper. But still . . .

Drying a plate, Laurel looked longingly out the window toward the corral and wondered what the menfolk were saying.

The women, not surprisingly, were talking about men.

"I'm happily married, Alexandra, so I don't mean anything improper." Mama directed her next comment to Victoria. "And I'd never want this to leave the room. But—" As if she didn't have the words, she whistled a long, descending note. "Your cousin has got to be the most handsome young man I've ever seen."

"Mother!" Mariah said in a gasp. Even Laurel stared. She was younger than Papa by perhaps fifteen years, though Mama's hair was still a luxurious brown, and she'd kept a good figure. But she was in her *forties!*

Even if she could still whistle pretty well.

Vic, taking another plate from Mrs. Sawyer to dry, said, "You can't mean to deny it, Mariah!"

"I *do!* True, Mr. Pembroke is . . . pretty," their older sister admitted. "But not handsome. Not like Stuart."

Victoria and Laurel exchanged amused looks. Stuart MacCallum wasn't unattractive. He had a solidity about him, an earthiness some women might like. But handsome? Not like Lord Collier.

Lord Collier drew the eye, then rewarded it for coming.

"Pretty, then," said Mama diplomatically. "And I've seen a lot of pretty men. Men who made a career of being pretty."

"Oh, really?" Lady Cooper laughed.

Mama winked and took a washed cup. "In my wild youth."

But Mama often teased about her mysterious "wild youth."

Were the men discussing the next wild-horse roundup? Laurel wondered. The government had put a bounty on mustangs. Laurel would like to be down there, arguing that . . . but she was avoiding Lord Collier ever since her sister had embarrassed them both. *Married?*

Besides, she was one of the women.

Mariah sat down, as if disgusted by all of them, and Mama got out a candy stick for her. "Are you sure you don't want some fresh air?" she asked.

She didn't offer Laurel or Victoria candy or fresh air. It seemed Mariah and Mama had grown even closer since the marriage. If Laurel never married, would she lose that? Much though the idea pained her, she looked out the window again, and noticed Lord Collier strolling toward the creek. Maybe he did not feel part of the men's conversation, any more than she did the women's.

"That's a very pretty dress, Laurel," offered Mariah.

"Thank you." Laurel put her last dish back in the cupboard with more force than necessary. *Yee-haw.* Now they got to talk fashion. "Mama had it made while we were in Denver this spring."

"Under protest," her mother teased. Laurel had to admit she did fancy how the material swished around her ankles, how the gray lace traced a leafy pattern over the blue lawn. At least Mama hadn't chosen flowers. But she still hated the shoes.

"Perhaps she can go to the same couturier for her new winter gowns," suggested Lady Cooper.

Laurel wiped her hands on the flour sack that, tied behind her, made an impromptu apron. "I don't need new winter gowns."

Mariah shook her head in that know-it-all way of hers. "You always say that, and you're always wrong. There will be parties for Christmas, and dances. You might as well look stylish."

"I won't be going to parties and dances," Laurel reminded her. "Likely I'll be snowed in on my ranch."

Mariah looked helplessly toward their mother, so Laurel did too. "I'm old enough to get married like Mariah did, but I'm not old enough to risk my claim cabin in the winter?"

"I wouldn't want *anyone* I loved wintering alone," said Mama. And Laurel had hoped that if she would find support from anyone . . .

She tore off her flour-sack apron. "Are we finished?" She didn't want it said that she shirked her work—even woman's work.

Mama hesitated, then gave in. "Go ahead and enjoy the sunshine, sweetie. While you can."

While you can. Laurel all but fled for the creek, almost turning her ankle on the uneven ground in those girl-shoes. Only when she reached the sheltering trees that grew along the creek could she slow down and take a breath. Here in the grass and trees, by the rush of water, she could be herself. And here she could find the Englishman who might yet have a solution for her.

She expected to find Lord Collier.

She just didn't expect to find him in the willow grove, looking young and lonely on Nate Dawson's rock.

*   *   *

85

Collier rested an arm on his knee, staring at the creek and feeling useless. Then Laurel Garrison appeared through a curtain of willow leaves to pull him out of his sulk.

She did look attractive in that gown—the shape of leaves, dappling the clearing, blended with its lace pattern, and in the shadows her own eyes glowed somewhere between blue and gray. Her braided crown of dark hair showed off the angle of her heart-shaped face, the slant of her pretty jaw, even her ears.

She had surprisingly ladylike ears.

Collier looked past her for companions, but he saw none. He doubted convention would condone so private a meeting in Wyoming, any more than in England, yet their privacy relieved him.

With Miss Garrison and her little homestead, he still had at least a chance to grasp at something that mattered.

Apparently she felt the same. "You've got to think of something."

"Other than our marriage, you mean?"

Her stricken expression, before he could smile his insincerity, did little to soothe his self-esteem. Less so her response. "I don't want to marry you."

"So I assumed," he assured her. "Never fear. I've cherished no romantic intentions toward you either." He tried not to remember the feel of her wet curves in his arms and on his lap, the taste of her mouth opening under his own . . .

Well, they had agreed to forget that. Apparently she had done so.

He felt somewhat less bruised when she frowned. "Why not?"

Because I have no future. Because I have been exiled from my past. Because Fate has conspired to make me into so hollow a shell of the man I thought I would be, I've no heart with which to love anybody. Especially you, leaf shadows and liquid eyes or not.

Because I have allowed you to see me too desperate to make any pretense of glory or allure.

He made do with, "What gentleman would want a wife he could not impress? I am, after all, no laborer. And I hail from neither Wyoming, Montana, *nor* Idaho."

To judge from her startled expression, she remembered her own words from the water hole. "That's not fair. You never told me what would impress *you*."

"I'm not sure I know anymore." He tossed a pebble toward the splashing, gurgling creek.

She smiled that wide, forthright smile of hers. "So it's not just me that has you bucking our marriage."

"Oh, it is you," he assured her solemnly. Only when her eyes widened did he return her now fading smile. "But not just you."

When she came to the boulder, he pretended to feint, as if she might throw more mud. She studiously ignored that. "Well, it's not just that you're an immigrant man-of-leisure that would make me decline," she conceded haughtily.

When he saw that she meant to climb onto the rock, Collier stayed her with a gloved hand, then shrugged out of his suit coat and laid it, lining up, to protect her gown. Sir Walter Raleigh he was not. But he'd not been absent from England *that* long.

Miss Garrison eyed him oddly, then carefully sat on the coat instead of the stone. They still had a marginally respectable foot of space between them—not enough to make this conversation proper, of course, but perhaps enough to protect him from injury, should her father or brother discover them.

Permanent injury, at least.

"Actually," she said, "it's been nice *not* worrying that you might be sweet on me. I mean, other than . . ." She blushed.

Collier looked quickly away. "Yes."

"But that was just a . . ."

"Quite," he agreed, and cleared his throat. "An anomaly."

"A *what?*" When he glanced back, she looked more annoyed than flustered.

"An exception to the norm," he clarified, amused.

87

"Oh." She remained wary. "Exactly. So I haven't worried."

He cocked his head. "Were I . . . sweet . . . it would worry you?"

"All I ever wanted to be was a rancher." She flopped back on the silk lining of his coat and stretched her arms out over her head, as if celebrating her own reach. Did she have any idea how improper such a pose was? Or how erotic? Her bosom fought the restraint of its bodice, and the way her back arched and her hips slanted downward reminded him of nothing so much as—

Well, of things he ought not be thinking around any woman of good breeding. Or supposed good breeding. It did perhaps explain the water hole, though.

"Everyone assumes I want to settle down, marry, have children," she explained, relaxing from her stretch. When she pillowed her head on her arms, he judged it politic to look elsewhere. "No matter how often I tell them different. It's not that I disapprove of those things, but . . ."

Collier watched a butterfly float by, more intrigued by her words the less he watched her body. "But?"

"Hard enough to be a rancher without being a wife. Look at what happened after dinner. The men went to talk livestock, and the women stayed behind to clean. And why don't the men stay behind? The kitchen isn't their job, that's why. They work outdoors, chopping wood or building fences. But I've been chopping wood and building fences, too. Did you see *me* out by the corral smoking cigarettes?"

Well, wasn't she the suffragette? "I should have noticed if you had," he teased.

"Sometimes it seems the whole world is crowding me into behaving like some *woman*," she admitted. "And every time I reject another beau, or . . . or wear my cowboy boots under my dresses, where nobody should be looking anyway, it feels like I'm bucking the world all over again. I don't like feeling that way. I don't mean it wrongly. But it's not my fault I was born female."

After that little speech, Collier had to look back at her. He managed to focus on her face, her eyes. "No, I suppose not."

"So as soon as you opened your mouth, out by the—that is, when we met . . ." she clarified quickly, and blushed again.

He looked away again. They'd do best to avoid remembering their first meeting or open mouths.

"I figured right off that we had so little in common, you had to be safe," her voice explained.

Safe? He might not be the scapegrace his brother was, but neither had Collier ever held the reputation of being safe around single women. Or married ones. Did she think him a gelding?

But when her gaze met his, her blue eyes widened, as if she realized the true impropriety of lying beside him, where he had only to lean over her, lower himself onto her. . . .

She scooted herself quickly back up, bracing herself with her arms splayed out behind her. It still showed her bosom in good form, but held less invitation. And he did still need her more for other purposes.

"Can't you think of any other solutions?" she pleaded.

"Other than what?" he challenged, perhaps too innocently.

She lifted her chin in a dare. "I refuse to even say it."

"Yet you *do* admit that marriage would be a solution?"

"A *bad* one!"

"Well, yes. That goes without saying." And it did. His level of desperation—even to *consider* the suggestion of a six-year-old—humiliated him.

Not that he needed to maintain a facade around this little rancher woman. Perhaps he understood what she meant about feeling safe, at that. "Unfortunately I've thought of no *good* solutions."

She wrapped her arms around her skirted knees. "Oh."

"I *am* still willing—even eager—to invest," he insisted. *Part-owner of a Wyoming cattle ranch*. Even if he had to admit, some months later, to the investment's failure, he could survive several months on the esteem of such an announcement.

Laurel shook her head. "The only thing worse than losing

the ranch would be knowing I had lost someone else's money, too."

"Even if I don't mind losing it?"

"You *should* mind."

"At this point," he admitted, "I consider it a payment on the remnants of my pride."

"Then you have a pretty strange kind of pride, and I won't be party to encouraging you."

No lady in England would ever have spoken so directly. But he was no longer in England—might never be again.

That, however, did not bear considering.

They sat in dappled sunshine, listening to the birdsong and the creek, until she said, "I don't understand a pride that comes from what folks think of you, instead of who you really are."

Which suggested something quite fantastic. "You yourself do not care what people think of you?" he asked carefully.

She sat up straighter, as if alert to a suggestion she might resent. "I care what my family thinks of me. And what folks think of them. But I guess I care about the homestead more, or I never would have caused as much talk as I already have."

Not to mention meeting him here, unchaperoned.

"You let the land office misconstrue your age," he reminded her. "For land that's available only to people twenty-one or older." Or head of a household. Or a military veteran. He had done his reading. But she was neither of those, either.

The little homesteader nodded slowly. "But I'm not alone."

"So you are not *wholly* against certain . . . duplicity."

She narrowed her eyes. "I'm more against it than not."

"Even if it would allow you to keep your homestead?" So now he was corrupting honest young country girls. That he did not feel ashamed only proved the depths to which he had sunk.

"Why?" she asked, wearing that dangerous, mud-throwing look.

In for a penny . . . "What if we should pretend to marry?"

*   *   *

Lord Collier had looked so pretty this afternoon, in Laurel's favorite spot by the creek, that she'd found herself not listening to him so much as watching him. But she heard his foolish notion clearly enough. "What?"

"A marriage of convenience," he clarified. "But less permanent, and only you and I the wiser. You must admit, half of Sheridan seems to fear us mere steps from the altar already."

"They do not!" But when Lord Collier only held her gaze, Laurel had the grace to look down at the lace across her lap. Even Papa had wondered!

"How do folks pretend to marry? We would have family there." A horrible thought occurred to her. "Unless you meant to elope, and we couldn't do that. It would break my parents' hearts!" As if lying would not? She was loco to even consider it!

"The marriage itself would be legal," admitted Collier. "We need not bribe the judge or minister. We need only see it as a business arrangement, and treat it thus."

"But why?" *Loco!*

"You keep your ranch and do on it whatever you originally meant to do. I have quarters for the winter, and something to write home about, and may invest as much as I wish in the . . . what is the name of your ranch, anyway?"

Of course he had to ask that. "It doesn't have one yet."

He shrugged, as if even that did not matter. "In the ranch. This continues for two, perhaps three years."

She looked toward the mountains. She loved it out here. The higher she went into the foothills, the happier she got. To spend another winter in town, with barking dogs and crying children and trolley bells, would be terrible.

The surge of determination that swelled her chest surprised even her. So instead of laughing in Lord Collier's lovely face, she heard herself echo his words. "Two or three years?"

"You come of age," he explained. "The ranch may even start to turn a profit. Should we succeed—as a business, I mean—I could finance my own return to Brambourne in some semblance of triumph."

"And then?"

He blinked, as if startled from a fine fantasy. "Then?"

"At what point do we tell people we've annulled it, so it's not a real marriage, and we were just living together without the benefit of clergy?" She winced to imagine it. *"Papa, you know how you fussed about that Englisher and me marrying up, a while back?"*

Then Collier said, "I suppose we could divorce," and the original idea seemed saner from pure contrast.

"You think I'd disgrace my family with even a *pretend* divorce?"

"Perhaps, if they dislike me enough, they might not mind so terribly." Bracing his weight on a hand between them, he leaned nearer. "Or if I succeed in England, I could desert you."

Her mouth fell open. "Well, thank *you* kindly!"

Only then did his dimples show. "Merely being courteous. That way I'd be the villain—with some safety provided by the Atlantic Ocean—and you'd have everyone's sympathy."

As if she wanted anyone's sympathy. Or as if something so minor as an ocean would stop her father—or her mother!—from hunting down anyone foolish enough to hurt one of their girls. Even *pretend* hurt.

It all seemed so complicated it made her head hurt. Then he said, "And you would have your ranch."

Maybe her head didn't hurt so much, after all.

Her ranch. For all his archangel hair and perfect features, Lord Collier could have sprouted horns and a tail, for the temptation he'd placed before her. Laurel braced herself to argue him out of ever suggesting anything like this again.

But then he went and said, "Perhaps you're right." And he leaned back. "It is a desperate idea, of course. I apologize."

Confused all over again, Laurel slid off the boulder and went to the creek's edge, folding her arms around herself, droopy sleeves and all. She was desperate, too.

Lord Collier said, "It was rude of me even to presume—and after your family's hospitality, as well as Benjamin Cooper's—"

"I can't decide right away," she interrupted.

Now he sounded oddly frightened. "What?"

"I . . . I need to think about it." She turned back to him, longing for guidance, afraid to take it. "May I think about it?"

"Certainly," said Collier. "Business decisions ought never be rushed."

And that was all this was: a business decision.

It frightened her less that way.

"Or pretend marriages?" She attempted a smile.

His laugh sounded nervous, despite the boyish brash of his angled smile. "Quite. Except . . ."

Another exception? She wasn't sure she could take many more.

"It is August," he reminded her. "Even were we courting already, marriage before winter would be something of a scandal."

He was right. Again. "Oh."

"Not impossible," he assured her. "But if we are even considering this, we should let people know our intentions, or they shall never believe us when the time comes."

Oh. Looking down, Laurel kicked a rock into the creek—then tried not to hop from a hurt toe. *Darn shoes!* "What does that mean, exactly?" she asked. "Letting people know our intentions?"

"It means us courting." Lord Collier spoke from so close that she spun and nearly fell in the creek, but he smoothly caught her arm. "And me asking for your hand in marriage."

"Oh." Surely pretend courting would not be so terrible as the real thing, would it? She thought she would scream if she found herself trapped on another silent porch swing!

"We needn't actually marry, when the time comes," he assured her. "But if we should choose to do so . . ."

"The longer we've been engaged, the better," she agreed.

"Exactly. For the sake of plausibility, we shall have to . . . that is to say . . ."

She felt as if her head would explode. *"What?"*

"We must pretend romantic feelings toward each other." *Oh.*

Lord Collier looked down at her, smelling of soap and saddle leather. Without his wearing his coat, his suspenders defined the angle of his chest and the width of his shoulders under a fine white shirt. And his hair lapped golden at his cheekbones, at his neck. How many women could only dream of such a man talking marriage to them, even pretend marriage? *What a waste.*

Laurel's voice sounded strange to her own ears. "We could do that."

His gaze searched hers; then he nodded, offering his arm. "Shall we start now?"

Now? She stared at his starched white sleeve with a mix of fear and longing. But fear was something she'd never meant to live by. This was practically, she decided, a dare.

"Now," she agreed—but offered her hand first. They shook. They walked back to the ranch house together.

Chapter Eight

Victoria Garrison caught up with Collier and Laurel before they reached the house. "You met up? Don't you know what folks will think?" She cocked her head. "Why *did* you meet up?"

For some reason Laurel seemed to relax at her questions. "You're the one who's been teasing me about Lord Collier," she said.

Collier eyed the younger girl more closely. Had she?

"That's because it seemed so silly." Victoria cast Collier a quick glance. "No offense, your lordship."

"None taken," he assured her. Best to start with their fiction now, after all. "It took us by surprise as well."

Laurel looked quickly up at him. He smiled determinedly back—*Remember the plan?* Stricken, she nodded and looked away.

Would these little boosts to his ego never end?

Miss Victoria looked from him to her sister and back several times. "What took you by surprise?"

Cole held Laurel's arm a little closer to his side, tucked under his own. "Our feelings for each other."

Laurel stiffened. And how would *she* have phrased it?

The younger girl's gray eyes widened. "Your what?"

"By surprise," agreed Laurel pitifully. *Good Lord.*

Her sister glanced quickly toward the house, where family had gathered on the porch. "You can't be serious!"

"Well, we are," said Laurel firmly. "And what's more, you've been suspecting it all along, *haven't you*?"

Collier searched the face of his new, supposed lady love. *Good Lord!* Why not just wink and nudge the younger girl with an elbow? But the sisters were busy reading each other's eyes.

To his qualified relief, Miss Victoria nodded. "Right," she agreed slowly. "You know, I *have* sensed something between the two of you, even before you did yourself."

Laurel nodded sharply. "I thought you had."

Then the younger girl ran ahead to the ranch house, where other curious faces had turned toward them.

"She would have guessed anyway," defended Laurel, as if he'd spoken. "Vic can ferret out a lie faster than anyone I know. Better to have her on our side."

Vic? "And yet I cannot help but fear that you are not particularly deft at this."

"Lying?" she demanded. "No. No, I'm not deft at lying."

"Then learn," suggested Collier. "If you do wish to try this, learn quickly. And smile. People are watching."

"That's something else I hate about courting."

"You do realize," he warned, "that if you confess this ruse to the wrong party, I may lose more than a chance at middling respectability."

"I won't tell anyone but Victoria," Laurel promised.

"Good," he said.

"Good," she returned, and wobbled slightly, as she'd done more than once on their walk back.

"Is something wrong with your feet?"

"I hate these shoes."

He arched an eyebrow. "You seem to hate a great deal."

She grimaced. "*Smile*, Lord Collier. Folks are watching."

He deliberately smiled down at her as if she truly *were* his special love. Women more worldly than she had fallen prey to that smile. Collier knew quite well that he had dimples.

But Laurel only flushed and looked quickly away. Perhaps this was a truly terrible idea.

That he had none better almost frightened him.

"Did you have a good walk?" asked Mama, as Laurel settled herself on one of the porch steps. But the older woman's wandering gaze noted Lord Collier before returning to her daughter.

Unsure how she could lie to her mother, Laurel just nodded. It had been a good walk, more or less. Now she had some hope.

That was what she had to remember: the hope of keeping her ranch. Maybe, against the threat of her marrying up with an Englisher, Papa would be glad to let her winter alone.

She doubted it.

Later, when the sisters clustered together to bid Mariah good-bye for the day, Audra asked, "Is Lord Collier really sweet on you, Laurel? He looked at you like he was sweet."

"I've suspected it for weeks now," insisted Vic firmly.

After a quick hug, Mariah fixed Laurel with a teasing look and said, "Well, he certainly is ornamental."

"May God go with him," murmured MacCallum fervently, muscles bulging as he lifted his wife into their buckboard.

All of which felt embarrassing enough. But when Laurel saw Collier drawing her father aside, clearly requesting a private word, that was when she panicked. Nobody could lie well to her father . . . except maybe Victoria.

She took several horrified steps in that direction, as if drawn against her will. Papa would see their lie, and then what?

But as she got closer, Collier's words somehow sounded honest even to her.

"I assure you that neither of us intended this. As soon as

97

we suspected our regard, we determined to ask your permission."

Papa stood silent as ever, but Laurel thought she detected a hint of emotion under the shadow of his hat. What surprised her was that the emotion was amusement. *He doesn't believe it either!*

Should she feel relieved or indignant?

"Permission," Papa echoed, challenging the word.

"We," said Collier. "That is, *I*, would like your permission to pay court to your daughter Laurel."

Papa noticed Laurel even before Collier did, and studied her steadily before scowling back at the Englishman. "To what end?"

Looking over his shoulder, Collier saw Laurel and reached for her. Reluctantly she went to his side and put her hand in his. He'd taken off his gloves, and his palm felt warm, steady.

"Should your daughter prove willing," he said, "then toward the only respectable end of any such attachment."

Papa folded his arms and shifted his weight, looking from one of them to the other with suspicion. Their joined hands, in particular, seemed to hold his attention. He wasn't as surprised by the request, Laurel realized, as by her going along with it.

"I would consider it an honor," insisted Collier, looking at her as if she were, indeed, special. "Sweet Lorelei."

She said, *"What?"*

"A Lorelei is an enchantress who bewitches sailors with her song." Collier smiled as if he found her reaction more charming than annoying—although a glint to his eyes said differently.

"Bewitches 'em to their deaths," added Papa, surprising them both. "If I recall rightly."

To their deaths? Laurel stood straighter. "Really?"

"Ah," said Collier, somewhat flustered. "I forgot you've a German background, Mr. Garrison."

"You're comparing me to some witch who sings folks to their deaths?" Almost too late, Laurel remembered their charade. Could the Laurel she was pretending to be have found that romantic?

Collier squeezed her hand a little too tightly. "The sailors under her spell no longer care for their own safety, Miss Garrison. It is that part of the legend to which I refer. If you were to deny me this chance to prove myself . . ."

"You'd *die?*" No, she couldn't find romance in that.

He narrowed his silvery eyes, urging her to play along. "Perhaps not. But I might feel as if I had."

The longer he held her gaze, the more she did like that he could create such a fancy for her, silly or not. "Oh."

Papa cleared his throat, startling them. His amusement had darkened to something more intense. "You want this Englisher to call on you, Laurel Lee?"

This was the moment of truth, the point where he would guess all. And yet, smelling Cole's clean scent of soap and leather and shirt starch, with his hand warm around hers, the words came easier than she'd feared. "I . . . I think so," she admitted, as if it really were the truth. "I'd at least like to find out."

Collier squeezed her hand in approval.

Papa did not look happy. "And if it takes?"

"Excuse me?" asked Collier.

"He means, if we *do* want to . . . if we decide we're well matched," she explained. "What then?"

Papa scowled at him. "You employed?"

"One definition of a gentleman," Collier offered, "is a man who need not work for a living. I receive a quarterly allowance from my inheritance."

"A remittance," clarified Papa in disgust.

Collier stiffened, but conceded, "If you wish."

Papa shook his head, as if he'd seen everything now.

Unwilling to let Collier make *all* the effort, Laurel said, "You always did want me to be a lady, Papa."

Her father looked as if he might just argue with her, then shook his head and simply turned to leave.

"Mr. Garrison," prompted Collier, surprising her with his grit. "I would have your answer, if I may."

So Papa pivoted back to face them, brow low, mouth set. Laurel found herself holding her breath as tightly as she was holding Collier's hand.

"You two got enough rope to hang yerselves, anyhow," he offered, then stalked off to talk to Laurel's mother.

Laurel stood very still. They'd done it. The very hardest part of the charade, and they—Collier, really—had done it!

"Enough rope to hang ourselves?" he echoed, uncertain.

"That means yes. He thinks we'll come to our senses faster by keeping company than staying apart—but it's a yes!"

"Ah." And he took a particularly deep breath, as if he'd felt less confidence than he'd shown. "Good show, then."

Pleased, she elbowed him lightly in the ribs. "Lorelei?"

"You may well be leading me to my doom," he explained.

She laughed. Collier cocked his head at her, his hair molten in the late-afternoon sunlight, his eyes somehow golden too.

"Permission to call on you is hardly permission to marry," he reminded her, as if afraid she would become over-confident.

She shook her head. "Stuart didn't even get *this* far."

"Then congratulations." But Collier had to add, "Lorelei."

"And you," she returned. "Cole."

They studied each other somewhat warily, then returned to join the party as an actual courting couple.

"She's a *Yank*," insisted Nigel Graham, the third son of Lord Hunstanton. The four Englishmen had gathered at the bar as a fitting end to a splendid—if bastardized—game of polo. They had half the necessary players, and but for Collier's thoroughbred the horses had no real training. But they'd enjoyed themselves, even so.

Unfortunately they were now enjoying themselves at Collier's expense. "Really, Pembroke. What good could possibly come of wooing an American?"

"Perhaps marriage," suggested Collier, to try the idea out.

From the nearly identical stares of his countrymen, the idea fared poorly.

"You don't mean to stay here forever, do you?" demanded Taylor Worthing, second son to the Baronet of Carlisle.

"Not forever," agreed Collier.

"Then think of what an embarrassment she'd be in London!"

Luckily he had no intentions of finding out—although he could not tell them that.

John Baines yawned. "Please." He was in fact heir to a duchy, but had incited his own exile through his enjoyment of drink, gambling, racing, and a married countess. "I thought you had something to prove to your old man. Marrying a Yank will hardly show you in a better light. Or . . ." His eyes gleamed behind a pair of wire spectacles. "Or are you *not* planning to marry her at all? Is this merely a way to get to know the girl better?"

"Now that would be the ticket," agreed Nigel.

Accepting his drink from the scowling bartender, Collier wondered if he truly belonged with his fellow countrymen— at least these examples, here and now. They made for sympathetic companionship, a chance to hear the Queen's English spoken correctly, and a good game of polo or cricket or tennis.

But they also represented much of why neither the English nor the Americans particularly respected remittance men. Worthing and Baines were blighters, full through, and Graham seemed intent on learning to be. If he were being punished by exile, why not commit the crime?

Collier sometimes felt that way himself. But *he* had a plan.

"My only intentions," he insisted, low, "are marriage."

"Drinks on me," called Baines loudly. "My allowance came in, and I insist. Here's to mixed marriages!"

Other men in the bar made agreeable noises, and why not? Americans liked free drinks, even if they did not always like the men who bought them.

Collier covered his shot glass with his hand when the bartender came by. It wasn't evening yet. "Thank you, no."

Baines and Worthing rolled their eyes at each other.

"You," said the bartender, surprising all four by speaking directly to them. "These parts, we don't discuss respectable ladies in drinking establishments, savvy?"

"Ah," said Collier. "Thank you for the advice."

The redheaded bartender held his gaze suspiciously, then continued to pour drinks for his suddenly thirsty clientele.

The other three gentlemen stared at him.

"When in Rome," reminded Collier, and finished his drink.

"I've a splendid idea," said Baines, brightening. "Let's the four of us head to the third floor to celebrate Pembroke's new love in a more fitting way. My treat."

The better prostitutes in town did business on the third floor.

Before he'd realized his own intentions, Collier had the man's lapel in one hand and his forearm across Baines's throat as he lifted him smoothly back onto the long, shiny, imported-from-England bar.

"I do not imagine," he warned, "that one should discuss a respectable lady in that context, either." He smiled. "Savvy?"

Worthing and Graham pulled him away quickly enough. And when Baines brushed himself meticulously off, glaring at Collier, they hovered nearer him. Baines was, after all, a true heir. As soon as his father died he could return to England—no matter how bad his behavior, damn him.

"Do not forget where you are from, Pembroke," he warned. "Or just how little this godforsaken place truly counts." Then he stalked off, toward the elevator, his lackeys in his wake.

What the hell am I doing? wondered Collier, staring at his hand. He'd come to fisticuffs before, true, but he'd been drunk.

He did know how little Wyoming counted. He'd not forgotten that this was hell.

He just didn't know to what level he'd now descended.

*   *   *

"Your remittance man's runnin' late," noted Papa, stepping onto the porch. With her little sister Kitty, Laurel sat on the ranch house steps in another pretty dress . . . and cowboy boots. She still disliked courting. It meant time spent away from the very homestead she meant to save.

And now Papa was going to ride her about Collier.

"I don't think he likes being called a remittance man."

Papa snorted again. "Lives off remittances." But he didn't look quite so threatening without his hat.

"I think it means something worse in England," she said.

"Ain't no compliment here."

Kitty shifted beside Laurel. "Why does courting make people so unhappy?"

"What?" demanded Laurel, and even Papa pushed away from the wall to squint at his second-youngest daughter.

"Last year when Mariah took up with Stuart, everyone got angry," she insisted, pushing her spectacles up more securely on her little nose. "And now you and Papa—"

Laurel looped an arm around her skinny sister and gave her a hug. "Don't be silly, Kitty-kat. Papa and I always fight."

Now Papa squinted at *her*.

"We do so!" she insisted. "Ask Mama."

"Ask me what?" Mama stepped out the open door onto the porch, wiping her hands on her apron.

"Thinks we fight," explained Papa, looking somehow sulky.

Mama blinked. "You and me?"

He inclined his head toward Laurel.

"Oh." Mama slipped her arm comfortingly around Papa's waist, leaning into his side. "She's right, Jacob. You two fight like cats and dogs. It doesn't mean you don't love each other."

Papa squinted at her. Mama wrinkled her nose at him.

Kitty bounced and pointed. "Look! Here he comes!"

At least, they assumed the one-horse buggy that topped the rise was being driven by Collier. When it stopped, then started again in a lurch, Laurel covered a laugh with her hand. "I do believe you're right, Kitty."

Even Papa began to grin. "Ain't never drove his own horse before," he guessed, maybe because Collier was English.

"Or someone gave him a bad horse," added Mama, trying to hold back her own smile. That seemed much more likely.

Laurel stood to better see. "Oh. Poor Collier."

Not only was the horse stopping and starting on its own, it also kept trying to stray off the track into nearby pastures. Each time the driver got it going in the right direction, it found a new way to disobey him.

The occasional side view confirmed that this was Uncle Benj's phaeton. Laurel cocked her head, making out the bald face on what looked to be a sorrel—and understood. "It's *Firefly!*"

Papa clarified everything in one disgusted word: "Cooper."

Not that he likely minded seeing Collier embarrassed by an unruly two-year-old colt. But he'd likely object to Uncle Benj subjecting a two-year-old colt, barely harness-broken, to Collier.

"Ooooh," said Mama. "Now that's just mean."

Laurel bit her lip, trying to will Firefly to pull steady. She knew Collier was good on horseback . . . but how would she convince people she'd marry a man who couldn't drive a buggy?

Then Kitty said, "He sure must want to see you."

Suddenly Laurel saw the situation from a different direction.

One did not ride a carriage horse—certainly not while it was pulling! That was the only thing that kept Collier from leaping onto the demon beast's back, instead of struggling from the phaeton. No matter how the untrained sorrel exasperated him, neither would he risk ruining its potential by using the whip or sawing the reins. He considered simply leaping to safety past the vehicle's oversize wheels and letting someone else deal with horse and buggy both. A hike back to town, even in the August heat, seemed preferable to continuing this madness all afternoon!

But he was to see Laurel this afternoon. The facade of courting gave them perfect opportunities to deliberate their business arrangement. He would buy cattle as a wedding gift. She would sit for a wedding portrait to send to his family.

But Collier's disagreement with the heir to Bracknell brought up one particular topic they had not yet discussed, one that definitely required privacy.

Two to three years was a very long time to require celibacy of a healthy young Englishman, after all!

So he braved the track to the Circle-T, and the vexation of this animal, long enough to reach the two-story white farm-house.

"I may be a moment helping you—" To his surprised relief, Laurel leaped into the phaeton's box with a flash of petticoats and boots before the horse even saw her coming.

Of course, the demon then bolted, nearly pulling Collier's arms from his shoulders before he'd set for it.

Laurel, however, wore leather riding gloves. Taking her own seat, she opened her hands to him. "May I? Please?"

He doubted she could handle so contrary an animal, but they were on the plains; where was the risk? He handed her the reins. "Just be careful—"

To his surprise, Laurel stood in the box, her booted feet braced. "*Giddap*, Firefly!" And off they went!

Chickens, a dog, and one startled cowboy leaped from their path as Laurel drove the horse in a wide turn around the outbuildings, then back toward the track to town. Long, dark strands of hair already flying free from her coif, her skirt flapping in the wind, she laughed out loud. "Let's see if we can't run some of this wildness out of him," she called to Collier, clearly delighted with the very unruliness that had him wishing he carried a flask.

He tried not to hold on to the seat rail too tightly. "All right," he agreed, lest she was daring him. He supposed they did have more room to run than he was used to. "Let's."

She flashed him a beautiful, blue-eyed smile, for all the world like Boudicca charging the invading Romans in her chariot—but in a better mood. Perhaps she could drive this villain of a horse because she understood it. Perhaps running the wildness out of *her* would work better than reining it back, too.

Collier wondered if she might prove more amenable to certain arrangements in their marriage than he'd hoped.

Chapter Nine

Laurel liked driving. She liked careening away from the ranch behind a feisty two-year-old, frightening jackrabbits and what looked to be a badger. The sky made an endless huge blue bowl over her. The great plains stretched forever to the east—a direction she hoped never to travel very far—and the Bighorn Mountains loomed, rocky and powerful, to the west.

Courting or not, she felt happy.

By the time Firefly let up on the bit, settling into a fairly steady trot, Laurel also felt ready to settle back and simply breathe. So she turned to hand the reins back to Collier.

That was when she truly remembered him.

He took the reins politely enough, and he even flashed her that incredibly bright, slightly lopsided smile of his—at least she had not frightened him! But, brushing a leather-clad hand across her face, and the hair that fell across it, she realized that she likely did not look like the kind of woman an English gentleman would be wooing. She felt her face heat with a blush.

Collier's dimples deepened. "I will admit," he said, "never

have I seen a woman look mussed quite as well as you do."

Her cheeks burned hotter. "This sort of thing is the reason Papa always chides me about being ladylike."

"Is it not normally your habit, then? Ladylike behavior?"

"No. I'm surprised that a blueblood like yourself is even willing to pretend to marry me."

The idea of pretending to marry Collier Pembroke wasn't nearly as frightening as the idea that nobody would believe it.

Driving more easily now that Firefly had been given a chance to kick up his heels, Collier said, "I believe any man would be fortunate to get you."

She stared at him, then twisted away toward the mountains. In the distance, pronghorn antelope turned their white tails and bounced past the horizon. "I don't want any man."

But the familiar words sounded oddly hollow.

"Perhaps that is why he would be so fortunate."

Unsure how to react to that, Laurel tugged off her gloves, tucked them into her dress's belt, and began to pull pins from her hair. She'd let her sister Audra style it earlier. "I should look more presentable, in case anyone comes across us."

"Here," he said, and turned Firefly off the main track, toward the treeline that marked the creek. On purpose!

"Collier Pembroke! We're supposed to stay in plain view!"

"You don't think that, after such a run, this demon horse deserves a drink of water?"

Her hand full of hairpins, she studied him for any sign of artifice, but she got distracted just studying him. He surely was an attractive man, especially with the sun reflecting off his halo of hair. "Where's your hat?"

"The wind took it," he confessed. "I dared not leave the buggy to take chase."

Since he'd probably have worn a boater or a derby anyway, she decided she liked him bareheaded. "I . . . suppose we can let Firefly have a drink," she said slowly. They *were* practically engaged.

"And I shall help you put your hair in order," he offered. "While we are stopped."

"You know how to style a woman's hair?" She laughed, but Lord Collier regarded her solemnly.

"Perhaps better than I can drive," he said.

That was when Laurel felt it the first pang of something unnamed, unfaced. She stoically ignored it.

When they reached the cottonwood shade by the creek, where Firefly could wade in still harnessed, Collier tied the reins and said, "Now turn away from me. Yes, like that."

And his fingers swept her hair back from her shoulders.

Laurel tried not to shiver. The urge to do so only increased when he sighed in something close to frustration. "No, this shan't work. Would you . . . I know it's rather improper, but might you kneel in the footwell, so that I can better reach?"

Drawing her skirt out of dirt's way, she did, and Collier drew one of his high-booted legs up under him, on the seat.

Laurel became increasingly aware of his other thigh, so close to her shoulder that occasionally they touched, and his booted calf by her elbow. Mostly, though, she was aware of Collier Pembroke finger-combing her hair.

She arched her back, leaning her head into the stroke of his long, artistic fingers. No wonder animals enjoyed being petted.

"You've lovely hair," he murmured gently, working through a tangle. "Despite that you clearly get a great deal of sun, it's soft."

Then he said nothing for a long while, and she listened to his breath mingle with the breeze in the cottonwoods.

Laurel considered explaining her mother's theories about healthy diet, or how she and her sisters used rainwater to wash their hair. Her throat tightened under the stroke of his hands, but for once she managed a proper response. "Thank you."

"You're quite welcome."

"Your hair is beautiful, too," she told him.

"Ah." He sounded embarrassed. When she looked up at

109

him, her shoulder bumped his thigh and he inhaled, surprised.

She quickly faced forward again. "I'm sorry."

"No need." He sounded oddly breathless. "And thank you."

For? Oh. Because she'd said he had beautiful hair.

"I know we've decided many details of our ... partnership," said Collier, as he began to twist a length of her hair. "But I am afraid that we've not yet approached a matter of particular delicacy."

Delicacy? "I don't need your money," she assured him. "Other than whatever you want to invest in cattle."

His fingers stilled. "No, Lorelei. Not money."

She wasn't sure whether to be annoyed or amused when he called her that without an audience. "What, then?"

"Hairpins, please."

She held up her handful, and he slid a pin free.

"I mean the matter of marital relations."

"Families?" But then she figured it out. "Oh! You mean—"

"Rather," he agreed, sounding embarrassed.

Well, he should be embarrassed! Wasn't their only option plain? "I didn't figure there would *be* any!"

"I assumed as much," he assured her. "Pin."

"It's just business between us, so ... what's to discuss?"

He hesitated long enough that she turned to look up at him again—this time careful not to bump his thigh. Although this way she seemed to be leaning her head rather close to it.

Collier even looked good from *this* vantage point.

"What's there to discuss?" demanded Laurel again.

He cleared his throat, averting his eyes. "Alternatives."

"I don't understand."

"No, I imagine you wouldn't."

Although he didn't seem finished with her hair—she still held three pins—Laurel pushed herself up onto the seat again to see him more directly. "I dislike feeling stupid, Cole."

"You're not stupid. And I am being vulgar even to mention this. Some men would not. But as this is a business partnership, oughtn't we be as thorough as possible from the start?"

Yes. They ought. She folded her arms and waited.

"Men have certain . . . urges." His overly bright gaze—the color of cottonwood leaves—dodged hers when she tried to capture it.

Well, she *knew* that.

"Since we shall not have a true marriage, however, you should be aware that I may seek the solace . . . that is, pay visits . . ."

"To whores?"

He flushed. "Miss Laurel!"

Her hand itched to slap him at the very idea, but he'd approached it so darned tentatively, she wasn't sure she had a good enough excuse. "No, you will *not* be visiting the third floor of the Sheridan Inn. Not and be married to me!"

"I *shan't* be married to you, not wholly—and how does a lady like yourself know what happens on the inn's third floor?"

She had her ways—namely her sister Victoria. "I won't have folks saying I can't keep my husband satisfied."

"You *won't* be keeping me satisfied," he reminded her. "For two or three *years* you shan't be keeping me satisfied."

"Well . . . neither will you be satisfying me," she reminded him.

"Because you won't let me."

Did he *want* to satisfy her? The idea left her hotter and damper than the August afternoon merited. Rather than argue yet again that they would not really be married, she said, "If I can go that long without . . . marital relations . . . then so can you."

"But *you*," noted Collier, "are a woman. Or so rumor holds."

Then she slapped him.

The crack of Laurel's barehanded palm across Collier's cheek echoed off the trees and startled the horse.

He suspected the beast was laughing at him.

Laurel looked as shocked as he felt. Then she set her jaw,

perhaps against any startled urge to apologize. "I'm not a man!"

Belatedly realizing what he'd spoken in frustration, Collier fully understood the slap. "Of course you are not," he offered quietly. "I was wrong to imply otherwise, even in jest."

"You weren't jesting. You just said what other people do— that I'm not content to be female. Well, maybe I do want to do what men do. Do you know what it's like not to even be allowed to put my own nickel into the fare box on the trolley? The driver takes it from my hand and drops it in, every time! And I *like* to drive horses; I'm *good* at it. If that hurts your feelings, too bad. But it doesn't make me a man."

Was that what had gotten into him, that she'd driven the buggy better than he? Collier wasn't sure. Staring into her flashing eyes and flushed face, some of her hair still streaming loose over her shoulders, he felt certain of only one thing.

"You are most definitely not a man," he assured her—and covered her mouth with his.

At first Laurel went so stiff that he could have been kissing a doll. Then, with a suddenness that startled him, she looped her arms boldly behind his neck and kissed him back.

Fully. Enthusiastically. She was most certainly not a man.

She opened her mouth, too, as if to draw him into her, and he did his best to comply by flirting his tongue across hers. It felt decadent, unrestrained, hotter than the August afternoon.

Since Collier was already sitting with one leg tucked, he easily laid Laurel back onto the carriage seat as they kissed. His hands wove into her hair, holding her head still for his plunder. Pins pinged to the phaeton's floor, likely out of the box too. They didn't look. Their mouths were otherwise occupied, wet and hungry and not at all polite. *Wild.*

Good Lord. He'd thought kissing her by the water hole had been erotic. Even without wet clothing or the rush of danger, this surpassed it. Laurel's body cushioned his as he shifted more firmly atop her. She sighed throatily into his mouth. To his shocked delight, she even spread her legs beneath him, to hold him with her skirt-bound thighs as well as her arms.

At that, he rocked against other parts of her too, hard and hot and hungrier than he could remember. He wanted to strip off his suit coat, but did not dare rear off her for even a moment, lest he break the spell his Lorelei had cast. Instead he fumbled one hand at her ankle—her cowboy boot—and then slid it under her skirt and up her stockinged leg as far as her knee, then to her garter, then to the softness of her thigh.

She might appear tough, but parts of her were quite soft.

Laurel stretched under him, arching her back happily. When the joy of plundering her mouth grew frustratingly inadequate—it was hardly the way his body *truly* wanted her—Collier trailed his lips down her stubborn jaw to a perfect, ladylike ear. Then he nibbled on that until she whimpered. Amenable, was she? More kisses down her neck, into the collar of her dress, had her writhing beneath him. "Oh," she said in a gasp. "Oh, Cole."

For once he did not mind being called that.

His hand, under her skirt, found the hem of her drawers and slid inside, farther up her thigh. She arched again—then ran one of her hands down his spine to his flank and cupped his buttock.

This time, he thrust against her. Their eyes flew open, and they stared at each other, flushed and flustered and half-blind with need. At least, he was.

Her surprise reminded him who she was—and who she was *not*—to him.

He wanted desperately, painfully, to ignore that. But he'd already been stripped of the standing of a gentleman. If he stopped behaving as one, too . . .

So he rolled off of her, although it meant falling with a jarring thud into the footwell of the phaeton's box.

Laurel peeked over the edge of the seat, dark hair streaming down around her face, toward him. "Collier?"

He drew one knee up, hoping to disguise just how basely

he and his body were behaving. He could at least spare her that.

"My apologies," he said in a gasp. "Quite unseemly of me."

"Oh, my!" She covered her mouth and began to laugh. "Oh!"

He closed his eyes, trying to fight the heat still surging through his blood. "Amused, are we?" He sounded sulky.

"And right after I insisted that we could both go three years." She vanished over the seat edge, but he heard a snorting sound, as if perhaps she were laughing even harder.

At least he no longer had to keep his knee raised. Laughter had a particularly powerful influence in that area.

"It hardly answers the difficulty," he pointed out as haughtily as he could from the floor of the Coopers' buggy. "If we're merely business partners, though joined by marriage . . ."

"Oh." Her face appeared over the seat's edge again, more concerned. "I see what you mean."

Slowly he braced himself into a sitting position. "Although I enjoy such . . . diversions, they lack a certain . . ."

She waited, curious. He could not believe he was sitting by a creek in Wyoming, speaking like this to a rancher's daughter.

"Completion?" he suggested.

She nodded, understanding. She had sat up herself.

"And that is why I'll need to look elsewhere," he insisted, proudly veering back to the topic. "Discreetly, of course. I've no intention of having people say you do not keep me satisfied."

"Even if I don't?"

"I doubt it shall be through any lack of ability."

"And what do *I* do?" she demanded. "If you do visit the chippies for your needs, how do I deal with mine?"

"Women's needs," he assured her, "are not as powerful as those of men. All the experts agree on that."

Laurel Garrison bit her lip. "You poor thing."

* * *

114

Collier managed to return Miss Garrison to her parents' ranch safely, then even to coax the recalcitrant Firefly back to town, but his thoughts lingered elsewhere. As he saw it, his indiscretion by the creek left him with only two choices.

One was to remove himself from this ludicrous deal he had driven. The other was to indeed marry the girl, but recognize that celibacy, despite their best intentions, might not win the day. There could be worse fates, he supposed, but for a few minor inconveniences.

Only a rotter would deflower and then desert a girl—particularly one who, despite her rough edges, seemed as basically decent as Miss Laurel Garrison. And should he, in a moment of weakness, father a child . . .

Collier had no intention of deserting or ignoring any child he sired. But neither could he imagine dragging Laurel Garrison to England with him, nor—*Lord forbid*—staying in Wyoming. So they must guard against that possibility at all costs. And without putting too much faith in self-control.

Discomfited, but desperate, he approached his cousin.

"You can speak to me about anything, dear." Alexandra patted the striped cushion on the settee beside her. "My husband and son are off at that ranch of theirs. We could plot a murder or have an affair, you and I, and nobody would be the wiser."

"I fear I went off married women some time ago," Collier teased, sitting. "And I never went *on* relatives."

Despite her prim expression, Alexandra's mossy eyes laughed at him. "Never fear. My marriage with Mr. Cooper is quite . . . satisfactory in that area." Now he *knew* she was trying to shock him. Well, he did mean to ask something shocking.

Her pretty lips flattened, though, when she added, "And I vowed upon Stanley's death never again to have relations with another Englishman. So you are quite safe."

Lord Stanley was her first husband.

Collier cleared his throat. "I seem to remember another vow as well. Pardon my boldness, but . . . did you not say,

115

before you remarried, that you would never again risk child-birth?"

He silently cursed himself when her eyes took on the haunted expression that he also remembered. "I did."

He need not ask why. He had lost count of her attempts to give her first husband an heir, and the resulting miscarriages, but he suspected she had not. "But when you remarried . . ." he prompted.

"I insisted Mr. Cooper agree to a childless marriage."

Collier could not imagine marrying—a true marriage, not pretend—under such a stricture. Had Cooper wanted Alexandra so badly as to forsake all hope of immortality?

Collier could not conceive of such love.

"We succeeded for some years, but Alec . . . surprised us," Alexandra said, explaining their young son. "Had I insisted upon seeing a doctor, I doubt Mr. Cooper would have stopped me. He is a man of his word, for all his charming foibles."

Good Lord. "Then however it was you attempted to prevent . . ." There were no polite words for this conversation. "It did not succeed."

"That is the risk one takes," she agreed, too easily for his comfort. "No attempt is failsafe but one, I wager: keep your trousers buttoned in Miss Garrison's presence."

"Alexandra!" But he felt his cheeks warming. He, who had often courted the reputation of a rakehell, was *blushing?*

But she was speaking of Laurel.

"Several techniques *have* proved adequate, otherwise," Alexandra assured him. "If that is what you meant to ask me."

Collier nodded. To his relief she did not ask why he wanted to know. She simply told him what she knew.

And it proved remarkably comprehensive.

Chapter Ten

In late August, Collier invited Laurel to dine with the Coopers again—and, once there, to commit to marriage.

He had no intention of forgetting himself in her company again without the protection of a ring of her finger. And they had discussed their agreement thoroughly. Either they committed to it, or they dismissed it.

When he suggested they sit on the veranda together, to enjoy the afternoon sunshine, Laurel looked at the porch swing with some suspicion. But when he then faced her and went down on one knee, her pretty blue eyes widened into something akin to panic.

"What are you doing?" she whispered through clenched teeth, perhaps so that anybody watching would think she smiled. She spoke quietly, since the house windows were all open against the heat. "Get up."

"It's well past time to get this part done with," he insisted, also low and without moving his lips. "Marry me."

She blinked down at him—then laughed.

Collier frowned. This was not the expected reaction.

117

Laurel covered her mouth for a moment to regain her composure. Then, eyes dancing, she leaned closer to him, clenched her teeth, and said, "This is how you ask me?"

Then she began laughing again.

Good Lord. After a long, stunned moment, Collier gave up his fragile hold on dignity. He laughed, too, and even leaned back against the house's brick wall, one leg folded beneath him, until he could stop. Never would he have risked being seen so, back home—but this was Wyoming. Between mortification and humor, he preferred humor. Thank heavens he was marrying a woman who . . .

That is, *pretend* marrying.

Not that she had accepted yet.

The screen door slammed shut, and Benjamin Cooper looked out at them. He seemed relieved to note that Collier was sitting a good two feet from Laurel's swing, although the fact that Collier was on the ground raised a dark eyebrow. "Someone tell a good joke?" he drawled.

Laurel caught her breath. "Collier just asked me to marry him, but he muddled it up."

Cooper's usually cheerful voice deepened as he fixed Collier with a serious stare. "He what?"

Laurel clutched at her pleated, organdy middle. "He—"

Collier widened his eyes at her, and she recovered her senses. "Oh, never mind that part. Just go inside so he can do it properly, with all his ten-dollar words and such."

Ten-dollar words? Well, really!

Cooper looked at Laurel, and he seemed confused. "You're agreeable to this?"

"Ought she not tell *me* first?" demanded Collier.

Cooper shook his head and turned back to the house, then leaned back out. "You're proposing to *marry* her?"

"Yes."

"You've even got a ring?"

"As a matter of fact, I do."

Laurel looked worried. "Oh, not a ring, too!"

Definitely not how he'd anticipated it. Collier rolled his eyes at her, and she squeezed her lips shut.

"Never thought I'd see things come to this," mourned Cooper, but he went back into the house. It wasn't as if he could not listen from the parlor or living room.

"Now *do* be serious," insisted Collier, resuming the proper position of a knight pledging fealty. When her eyes danced, he waited sternly until she recovered herself.

"My only Laurel," he began honestly enough. "You cannot have failed to notice, these past months, the extent of my feelings for you."

She cocked her heart-shaped face, more serious.

"You have come to symbolize a certain . . . hope to me," he continued, just as honestly. "Perhaps my only chance at a future, when I've despaired of regaining my past. I only trust that, in return, I may somehow add to your future."

The next two or three years of it, in any case.

"Will you do me the honor of marrying me?"

She continued to stare at him, her lips parting into something of an *O*. He took that chance to slip the new ring from his pocket and offer it for her approval.

Her eyes widened. "I swear!"

Again not what he'd expected. "Laurel!"

She covered her mouth, clearly recognizing her error in etiquette, but her eyes stayed wide. "Cole, it's *huge!*"

He frowned at the ring, which he had bought very carefully. "Alexandra's is larger than this." *Oh.* He raised his voice. "And hers is not at all ostentatious."

Lest she, too, were listening.

"But what am I supposed to do with it?"

"If you agree to marry me . . ." He waited.

"Oh! Yes, you knew I would. But what . . ."

He had not realized she was quite this backward. "You wear it," he instructed, and tugged her glove slowly, one finger at a time, off her left hand to demonstrate. Her strong, callused hand beneath it did little to counter the sensuality of so innocent a disrobing. "The third finger is traditional."

119

"No! I mean—" She scowled as she thought. "It's too big and fancy. I can't wear something as fine as this."

She seemed so honestly distressed that he rose to sit on the swing beside her so he could lean near her ladylike ear, her glossy brown hair, and murmur, "It's glass."

She closed her eyes for a moment and shivered. Then she frowned, as if confused. "It . . . what?"

"I hope you don't mind too terribly," he insisted, still very quietly "But for a pretend marriage . . ."

"Oh!" She nodded. "That was very sensible."

"If I think anybody suspects, I'll say you're wearing a counterfeit for insurance purposes, that the real one is in our safe-deposit box." He'd heard similar stories told about other jewelry within his family's circles.

"We have a safe-deposit box?"

"A pretend one," he whispered. She smelled like the mountain. "In Denver."

"Oh." When her eyes drifted closed again, he realized why. He quickly leaned back from her ear.

Laurel drew a deep breath, blinked, then squinted at him. "But . . . glass means it's even *more* fragile, doesn't it? I can't do chores and swing ropes wearing this."

Good Lord. She hadn't meant to question its worth, but its practicality?

"Perhaps you can tie it around your neck," he teased.

She actually brightened. "There's a thought!"

He groaned. "Could you please *try* not to embarrass me?"

Only when she turned away from him, not quite before he caught her hurt expression, did he regret that request.

"Ain't never heard such foolishness," accused Papa, pacing the parlor of their ranch house.

When Mama cleared her throat, from where she had sat for Collier's announcement, Papa scowled her into silence. She caught Laurel's gaze and mouthed the word *sheep*.

Under other circumstances, Laurel might have laughed. Today she felt ill. True, Mariah's beau had been a low-down sheep farmer. For that reason Papa had refused to give his blessing. But what if he refused now, too?

If she loved Collier, that would be one thing. Mariah had eventually defied their father for love, and Laurel had more grit than Mariah did! But she didn't love Collier—even if she loved his kisses, and his voice, and his golden hair and bright, lively eyes.

And this marriage was just pretend. Unless she and Collier kept a healthy distance from each other when alone this winter, it might even end in divorce. At least, once alone, they needn't whisper to each other!

"I realize I've not had a chance to prove myself to you," said Collier evenly. While Papa paced, the Englishman seemed as cool as the lemonade they sipped.

"Haven't you?" challenged Papa, as if Collier's chance had already come and gone since his arrival in Sheridan.

Laurel said, "Papa!"

"Don't work," her father reminded her, pointing in accusation at Collier with two fingers. "Don't make himself useful. Jest wears his fancy duds and plays games on horseback and wastes time in places he best not go."

Oh? For a horrible moment Laurel wondered if Collier had already turned to ladies of the evening for succor. The seductive, feverish feelings he'd awakened in her had kept her awake for more than one night, since their impropriety by the creek. If such temptations really were worse for him . . .

But he leaned nearer her and whispered, "The Buffalo Bill." By which he meant the saloon at the Sheridan Inn.

She nearly melted again. He had to stop doing that!

While she recovered, helped by several thirsty gulps of lemonade, Collier said, "If you've been asking around, you also know that I am not excessive in my drinking habits, nor have I involved myself in gambling or other vices."

"Drink's bad enough," accused Papa.

"Even Uncle Benj drinks," Laurel pointed out, though Collier laid a quieting hand on her arm.

"Cooper ain't your father."

Mama interjected, so he would not have to. "It is true we keep a temperate house. Except for medicines." But her eyes began to laugh again. Only last year, little Audra had gotten lit up on some "painkiller" when having a tooth pulled. Now, whenever the younger girl got too priggish, all Laurel had to do to rile her was call her a booze hound.

Outside of Papa's hearing, of course.

"The allowances that I receive—" Collier started.

"Remittances."

Collier's gaze turned steely. "Call it what you will; the larger part is an inheritance through my mother. I can count on a yearly income that, though moderate, will remain steady—steadier than were I a clerk or a farmer. Perhaps more significantly, I am second in line to the estate of Brambourne."

That was more significant than being able to feed and clothe her? Not that Laurel meant to count on him for that.

Papa folded his arms and shook his head at her, as if trying to figure this whole thing out, and she felt ill again despite Mama's silent support. "Never knew you to hanker after nobility and such."

"My family is not *noble*," Collier corrected. "Though it's a common misconception here. We are in fact—"

But at Papa's scowl, he said, "No matter."

"You're right, Papa," clarified Laurel. "I never was one to hanker after society. I'm still not. But Collier's different . . . and I hanker after *him." If in the wrong ways.*

Her father glared at both of them, then released his breath in a long-suffering sigh. Laurel took great hope in that sigh. At least it wasn't a no.

Then he asked, "Where you two thinkin' to live?"

She glanced at Collier. This was the tricky part.

"My inheritance is not such that I could soon purchase a residence," Collier admitted. But he was watching her, waiting for her to take over.

"We're going to prove up my claim and live there."

And despite that they had done relatively well till now—that they had convinced Uncle Benj and Mama, and that

Laurel even wore an embarrassingly fancy glass ring—Papa's eyes narrowed to murderous slits, focused wholly on Collier.

"Git," he said.

Collier sat back, as if insulted. "Pardon?"

"Git out of my home!"

"Oh! I thought . . . Yes. Well." He cleared his throat. "Please hear me out."

But Papa had already dismissed him to turn his outrage on Laurel. "That's what this is about, ain't it?"

"Papa!"

"Oh, Laurel, it's not," said Mama. "Is it?"

"Knew you was stubborn," accused Papa. "But I never thought I'd see the day when one of my girls—"

He stopped himself before Laurel found out what he never thought he'd see. Collier, maybe because of all his education, seemed to fill in the rest of the sentence even so, and his silvery eyes went molten. He slowly stood. "I will do you the courtesy, sir, of not assuming you to mean what a more vulgar man might by that."

What? But even though Laurel looked questions at Collier, he was too busy returning her father's glare to stop and whisper more explanations to her.

"You," said Papa, "are either a skunk or a fool."

"In England I might call you out for that."

"Well, we ain't in England." Papa glared at Laurel.

She stared helplessly back, waiting. But despite swallowing several times, her father said nothing. Finally he looked at Mama. "Talk to her."

Then, with a dismissive wave of his hand, he stalked past the lot of them, snatched his hat off the hook in the front hall, and slammed out the front screen door.

"Oh, my," murmured Mama, wilting slowly back in her chair. "Can't one of you fall in love with a rancher?"

Laurel decided not to say that after they married, Collier would be a rancher. She was too busy watching him get slowly angrier than she'd ever seen him.

"I told you Papa might take it badly," she tried explaining, but he turned his glare on her. *Well!* Only when she glared right back did he seem to recover his more gentlemanly manners.

"I—" He took a deep breath, released it, then faced her mother. "My apologies for bringing such discord into your home, Mrs. Garrison. This was not my intention."

"I don't suppose it was." Taking her own deep breath, Mama sat up again. "So what, exactly, *was* your intention?"

"To do the parents of my intended the courtesy of asking for their blessing in person."

"Mmm-hm." Mama turned to Laurel. "How about you?"

"Well . . ." Laurel looked down at her engagement ring, but unlike Papa, Mama wasn't going anywhere. "I won't say this has nothing to do with the claim," she admitted slowly. "It's all part of the future we've worked out—our cattle ranch, and . . . and eventually a house, I guess."

She looked at Collier, who said, "There's no house?"

"There's a claim cabin," she reminded him. "But I might someday want a house."

"Oh. Then as soon as our profits allow, absolutely," he agreed slowly. "You should have a house."

Once he left her? But Mama was still listening.

"And each other," Laurel added. "*We're* part of it, too. Making something on our own."

"Mmm. And what happens should Collier inherit? How happy would you be off in England as Lady Brambourne?"

Aware of Collier watching, Laurel barely managed to keep from grimacing. "Not very happy, I guess. But we wouldn't have to live there. Not all the time. Would we?"

Mama waited, so Laurel turned to Collier. "Would we?"

Only then did she remember that—unless death came suddenly to his older brother—they would no longer be married by then.

"I am sure that we could reach a compromise," he said.

Which relieved her all the same.

"Seems you still have some rough spots to work through," said Mama. "A long engagement might be wise."

"We thought to marry in late October," said Collier.

"Do couples have such short engagements in England?"

"Ah," countered Collier. "But we are not in England. I assure you, our reasons are not improper. I do not want Laurel wintering alone on the mountain any more than does her father. And I do not want to see her lose her claim."

Mama took a sip of lemonade, then asked, "Have you ever been through a Wyoming winter, Lord Collier?"

"No, ma'am." He smiled. "Not nearly as many as you."

To Laurel's relief, her mother smiled. "Touché."

"Then you approve?" she asked, but Mama shook her head.

"Not really, Laurel. I don't disapprove the way your father does, but if this is even partly about keeping the claim, I don't want to see you ruin your life for it."

Collier blinked. "Pardon?"

"You either, Lord Collier. You seem like a nice enough fellow." She grinned. "For a Marmaduke."

"Mother!"

"But you are both very young." Mama leaned closer to them, intent. "Neither of you can see the future. And yet you're ready to risk tarnishing it with regret, marrying in haste like this. How could I approve of that?"

"But if we do marry?" asked Collier, and Mama sighed.

"I will, of course, wish you the best that luck and love have to offer. But consider yourself forewarned."

And she took another long sip of lemonade.

"Will . . . ?" But Laurel couldn't ask her mother to tell Papa for her. If she was adult enough to marry—especially to pretend to marry—she was adult enough to do this. "I'll go tell Papa. About October."

When she stood, Collier did too. "I shall go with you."

"No. I should do this alone. But thank you." And she kissed his cheek. It was the first time, she realized then, that she'd kissed any part of him but his lips. He'd shaved very cleanly, and he smelled as wonderful as ever.

But she had to go face her father.

When Laurel went onto the front porch, Victoria—at the

125

corner—pointed toward the woodshed, so that was the way Laurel went. Papa sat on a stump, sharpening a knife on a whetstone, Kitty on one side of him and Elise draped over his shoulder on the other. "Angle it right," he explained. "Keeps its edge."

She felt a pang inside her. He hadn't shown *her* how to sharpen knives since she turned twelve and started riding sidesaddle. Would he draw away from his other girls the longer their skirts got? Had he already done it with Audra?

Then again, Audra had always been a little lady.

Papa slanted his gaze toward her, then paused in his rhythmic scraping to murmur something to Elise.

"Look what I found!" she exclaimed, trotting to Laurel's side to pull her prize from her pocket. It could have been anything from a lizard to a snake to a frog.

But it was a woolly-bear caterpillar.

Normally banded with black only on the ends, and brown in the middle, this one was nearly black. *Sign of a hard winter?*

It would be even harder if she didn't somehow put things to rights with her family.

"Very pretty," said Laurel carefully, accepting the fuzzy critter into her palm. It curled protectively into itself. "Are you going to keep him?"

"I want to watch him turn into a moth," insisted Elise.

"Well, you make sure to feed him lots of grass and leaves until he does." When Laurel returned the caterpillar to Elise, the little girl dropped it back into her pocket. Luckily Mama had learned about checking pockets when Laurel was little!

"Kitty, may I please speak to Papa alone?" she asked.

Kitty looked worried, her eyes big behind her spectacles, but she nodded and ran after Elise—maybe to show their find to Mama and Collier. Laurel hoped Collier wouldn't embarrass her by yelling or something.

"I won't be wintering alone now," she said, while Papa resumed blade sharpening. "I mean to marry him."

"So I figured." He looked up from the knife, annoyed. "Best

get Mariah and rustle up some outlaws and Indians fer your sisters while you're at it."

"Collier's not bad man, and you know it."

"A skunk or a fool," he insisted, and started drawing the knife over the hone again. "If he's the skunk, Laurel Lee, then you're the fool. And if he's the fool . . ."

She winced away from what was coming, even before he said it, even without him looking up or stopping his work.

"Then you ain't who I raised you to be."

What truly hurt was that he was right. She and Collier *were* doing wrong. They were using marriage for their own ends . . . and worse, she wanted to do it.

"I hope you'll be at the wedding." Her voice wobbled.

"I hope you won't," he said, still not looking up.

So she fled back to the house.

"Elise," Mama was chiding as Laurel reached the veranda. "Leave the poor man alone."

"Not at all," insisted Collier as amiably as ever, but Laurel heard tension in his voice. He did not, she guessed, like caterpillars. "They're . . . charming."

She took a deep breath, then straightened her shoulders and headed inside. "If we're getting back to town with time for me to ride home, we'd best go," she told everyone. "Give me hugs now."

They did. Even Audra came down from her room, where she'd been reading—as always—to congratulate her. Only Kitty was clumsy enough to ask, "Are you crying, Laurel?"

"Of course I'm not!" Her eyes stung, was all.

Still, Collier looked more closely. "He made you cry?"

"I do not cry." But she was learning to read Collier better lately. His icy calm meant anger. "And don't you dare go all protective on me, when he's just trying to raise me right."

And failing.

Still, he hesitated, ignoring Elise's stubborn tugs on his coatsleeve. So Laurel leaned closer to him, and his scent of soap and saddle leather. "If we don't leave now, I swear that

127

I'll undo everything. The only chance of this happening is to leave. Right now."

So he circled his arm around her and led her out to where Firefly stood, waiting, with the Coopers' phaeton.

Collier helped Laurel up first, as though she could not climb into a buggy on her own. Then he swung gracefully up beside her. "We will let you know of further plans," he promised his future in-laws, while Elise bounced on her toes begging to be in the wedding and Kitty hugged Audra's waist, simply watching.

Laurel waved, too. Everything *would* be fine. *Really!*

But she felt particularly bad driving right past Nate Dawson, astride his cow pony, as they left the ranch.

Chapter Eleven

Collier wondered if his and Laurel's impending wedding influenced Benjamin Cooper's decision to winter in Sheridan. Alexandra certainly had not.

"Really, Mr. Cooper," she fussed as they oversaw the extraction of their belongings, to be moved to their newly rented house all of three blocks away. The Irish workers they'd hired kept getting in the way of the Garrisons, who were moving back into their home for the start of the school term. "How you find this town preferable to San Francisco for the winter is beyond me."

Then she gasped. "Be careful! That is fragile."

"Aye, yer ladyship," agreed the hulking redhead toting a large basket of what Collier suspected to be china.

Cooper raised his voice over the bustle. "Just you fellows remember—you'll get a fine bonus if nothin' gets cracked." Then he added to Alexandra, "Now see, darlin', the folks we're employin' right here? San Francisco has enough high-class types to keep your natural order in balance. Sheridan *needs* us."

Alexandra deliberately looked away from his teasing, just in time to start at young Alec racing down the stairs two at a time. "Kitty and Elise are here! Kitty and Elise are here!"

"Oh, bother." Alexandra sighed. "Not yet."

Her husband drew her into the parlor and kissed her cheek. "You just let us workin'-class types do the fussin'. Deal?"

"Please speak to your son," she insisted sternly.

"Always glad to do that," he called back as he left.

When Collier moved to follow, Alexandra extended an arm. "Do stay. We are most certainly *not* 'working-class types.' "

But even as she said that, young Alec—a carpetbag slung over his shoulder—towed Kitty Garrison into the parlor, saying, "And we'll live at the Wrights' old place all winter. If I'm good, they might let me attend school with you!"

"It has nothing to do with behavior," chided Alexandra. "We employ a perfectly good tutor. What *are* you carrying?"

"It's Kitty's things," said the boy proudly. "I wouldn't be much of a stand-up fellow if I let her carry them herself!"

"Ah," said Alexandra, then waved a hand. "Do go on then, children. Quietly." And the two continued toward the kitchen, Alec explaining, sotto voce, his father's promise that while in Wyoming, he could wear long pants like the other Western boys.

Alexandra covered her eyes. "You see what I put up with." She looked out from under her self-imposed blinder only when the smallest Garrison girl charged past them, clutching a basket and calling, "Carry *mine*, Alec! I'm a girl, too. Carry *mine!*"

Then his cousin pressed her hand over her eyes more firmly.

Glancing toward the foyer, Collier saw two more Garrison ladies fending off assistance from the movers. "Excuse me."

Alexandra sighed as he left.

Victoria was asking one of the men how long he'd been in the States, and from where in Ireland he hailed. Audra, the

130

fair girl, noted Collier's approach with clear relief.

But as Collier reached them, a voice behind him flushed the workers with the simple announcement of, "Burnin' daylight."

Then the rancher trundled into sight under the weight of a large trunk. He scowled to see Collier. "Pembroke."

"Mr. Garrison," returned Collier, then hesitated. Just because the rancher insisted on doing his own labor hardly recommended the habit. But . . . this was not England.

So he actually said, "May I help you with that, sir?"

"Nope," drawled the rancher. "Wouldn't want you to break a sweat." He started up the stairs like a Tibetan Sherpa.

Had Collier just been insulted?

"Excuse me." Thaddeas Garrison carried another trunk by him, far more sprightly than his father. Did they save on tips?

Then a voice he recognized far better called, "Make way for the Garrison women!" Laurel, a satchel in each hand, marched in the front door, followed by her mother, who carried a fishbowl.

Laurel stopped when she saw Collier. Mrs. Garrison kept the water in the bowl by spinning around, then circling them both.

"Cole! You aren't at the Wright place already?" Laurel dodged a mover even as Collier swept her out of the man's way. Today she looked more like the cow-wrestling Laurel, in a simple blouse and dark skirt, her hair pulled back into a ponytail.

"Lordship." The mover nodded with deference as he passed.

For the second time that afternoon, Collier heard himself say, "Let me help with those."

But she'd already dodged to the stairs. "I can do it."

"You're not moving back in with your family, are you?" he asked, stepping closer to the banister to look up at her. If she had given up on the ranch . . .

"Golly, no. I'm just helping." She vanished around the landing, and he wondered at his discontent—even before Garrison and his son clumped past for another load.

"Take care, dearest," cautioned Alexandra from the archway to the parlor. "I hope you shall civilize Laurel, not that she will tarnish you."

"Gold does not tarnish," Collier reminded her.

But the age-old saying had little power against the sense that he was somehow not a "stand-up fellow."

Laurel couldn't have attended the fall roundup even if she weren't getting married. But being engaged to maybe the only man in town who wasn't involved either didn't help.

"That would be where the cowboys gather the local cattle, yes?" asked Collier, strolling with her through her parents' tree-lined in-town neighborhood. They saw each other at least once a week—to keep up appearances as much as anything. "To identify which belongs to whom, take them to market?"

His voice sounded as thick and delicious as ever, but it was a voice that had never yelled at cattle or maybe anybody.

Around here, babies knew "roundup" before they knew some colors and relatives. "Papa said it's rough, and too busy, that I'd only be in the way."

She'd seen them as a child, but not as a lady.

"Perhaps it's for the best," suggested Collier. But before she could resent his dismissal, he asked, "Is this a good time to purchase cattle for your homestead?"

"No, it's the worst time. If someone doesn't get his price at market, maybe then."

"And how long do the fall roundups last?"

"First snowfall." She didn't like how he nodded, as if that solved everything. She didn't even like that he enjoyed walks. No self-respecting cowboy walked anywhere he could ride.

Laurel wondered if this was what cold feet felt like.

"We've much to accomplish before then," assured Collier.

Now that she could keep her claim, she herself certainly did.

If only the darned wedding did not keep interfering.

Proving Herself

*   *   *

One Sunday in early September, Laurel's mother and sisters would not let her go home until she'd faced the petty details.

"Ask Collier," Laurel pleaded. "He's the one who knows about society things. *He* should do it."

Especially if he didn't want her embarrassing him.

But, as with so much, tradition forced this on the woman.

"I want to be a bridesmaid," decided Elise, leaning her head into Laurel's side. She leaned back, scowling, when Laurel said, "I wasn't thinking to have bridesmaids, baby."

"It's too soon for a big wedding," agreed Audra, a stickler for propriety. "It's really too soon for any wedding."

"Luckily," said Mama, "it seems more townspeople than not are forgiving Laurel and Lord Collier's brief engagement."

"Because he's British?" asked Kitty.

"Because at least he's not a *sheepherder*," clarified Laurel, making a face at Mariah, which Mariah made back.

"Most folks know about Laurel's claim," said Victoria from her authority as a newspaperwoman. "It's kind of like the soldiers going off to fight the Spanish last spring."

At the time Laurel had thought couples remarkably foolish to rush such a decision. Now look at her!

"Besides," added Vic. "They want to see a royal wedding."

"He's not royal, and we want a private wedding," insisted Laurel, but Vic didn't even seem to hear her. She was asking, "How long were you and Papa engaged before you married, Mama?"

"Why look! Here comes Alexandra," announced Mama, and rose to greet their guest at the door.

To Laurel's relief, Lady Cooper provided a voice of reason.

"Of course they shall have a private wedding," she agreed. "As none of the groom's family will be able to attend, it is the only fitting decision. In fact—and I do hope I am not intruding, Elizabeth—Mr. Cooper and I hoped you might allow us to hold the wedding at our residence, freeing yours for the reception."

She did not add, *considering your husband's misgivings*;

133

the younger girls weren't supposed to know about that. But Laurel felt as if she'd just shed a very heavy weight.

Mama looked relieved herself. "That's a kind and excellent suggestion," she said, and even took the Englishwoman's gloved hand. "Thank you."

"Laurel's marrying Lord Collier at the *Wrights'* house?" Victoria made a face toward Mariah, but not in insult. Colonel Wright had tried to force her and Stuart off their claim. Since then, his reputation had fallen as sharply as had his business.

"Ironic, huh?" Mama smiled. "Alexandra, do you have any suggestions for our announcements?"

And it began again. Laurel stayed firm on her decision to have no bridesmaids, since Collier, an outsider, would not have ushers. But the others triumphed everywhere else. They would decorate in white and orange, but only if Laurel called it "apricot." Mother insisted she could get orange blossoms even in late October. Victoria's friend Evangeline would play piano, as she had for Mariah. And the wedding cards would be simple but silver-edged.

Laurel had already begged her mother to see to her dress, so she needed only to visit the seamstress to be fitted. But on her traveling outfit she balked. "We aren't going anywhere."

"Of course you are, dear," insisted Lady Cooper. "A wedding journey is customary."

"I can't leave the claim, so we'll do without custom."

"Homestead laws aren't *that* strict," protested Mariah.

"No. I . . ." Laurel stood, suddenly suffocating in orange blossoms and apricot. "I shouldn't even be wasting the afternoon on all this. I need to be taking care of my claim!"

Her sisters looked as if she'd just spoken Sioux.

Mama said, "Well, that is something for you and Lord Collier to decide." Which would require another trip to town, probably a whole dinner to go with it, and in the meantime she wasn't smoking meat or canning vegetables or finishing her horse shed . . . or helping with the roundup.

Because of honeymoons and wedding cards and being female!

"All right," she declared suddenly. "We will." And she marched out of the parlor, through the kitchen, and to the pantry, where her mother kept their newfangled telephone. Laurel had used it only once before, but she felt desperate.

She lifted the receiver, then jiggled the cradle. "Hello, Lolly?"

"Laurel!" answered a disembodied voice. "You're visiting your parents? Isn't that nice!"

"Would you connect me to the Coopers' house, please?"

"Really, dear, it's more proper for Lord Collier to ring you. He hasn't said his vows *yet*, you know. And are you sure you want to set such an example for your sisters?"

Laurel glanced out the pantry door, where her youngest sisters—and Victoria—were watching, and felt a pang of guilt. Was there nothing women were allowed to do anymore?

No wonder she liked things better on her mountain. "I could walk there before you finish putting me through."

"Well, really!" But Lolly connected them. The Coopers' maid answered, then fetched Collier. Then a comfortingly familiar voice asked, "Hallo?"

"You aren't planning a honeymoon, are you?"

As long a silence as answered her question, she began to fear they'd been disconnected. Then Collier said, "Laurel?"

As if anybody else would telephone him about their honeymoon! "We can't leave the claim for that long. There'll be too much to do if the snows haven't come, and if they have, I don't want to risk not getting back."

"You're telling me this on the telephone machine?"

"Cole, please!" The word shuddered out of her, more forcefully than she'd expected. It was all too much to handle, and she felt clumsier than ever, and she just wanted it done with.

She used her booted foot to shut the pantry door, careful not to catch Elise's fingers on the jamb.

"Why don't I come over there," he soothed.

"No! Then I'll never get to leave." That had to be why she wanted him to keep his distance. It wasn't that she would

135

want to be alone with him, or kiss him. They had an agree-ment. "It's just that . . . it's all *cards* and *colors* and *flowers*."

"And this presents some sort of difficulty?" Clearly he didn't understand either. Why had she even called him?

"If you came over here and did one overly proper thing, right now, I might just kick you."

"Then I shan't come over," he agreed firmly. Her laugh shuddered out of her as uncertainly as had her *please*.

Then, when he said, "Shall we take a wedding journey come the spring thaw?" she suddenly wished he *had* come over, because her need to kiss him overwhelmed her need to protect herself.

Which frightened her more than it should.

"As long as it's not during the spring roundups." Relief soft-ened her voice to almost a whisper.

"God forbid," he murmured back.

She realized she was smiling. Then she remembered the *fall* roundup, and sobered. "What are you doing with your afternoon?"

"I've been reading about your American stock market," he told her. "What are you doing?"

She laughed again, embarrassed. "I'm hiding in the pan-try."

"Ah," said his voice from the receiver. "Is someone threat-ening you with those dreadful girl-shoes again?"

"No," she protested, pleased that he'd remembered her tastes on that subject, and that he clearly did not take the subject as seriously as her father sometimes did. "Nothing like that."

"Then don't you have a frontier to conquer?"

"I guess I can, now." No wedding journey until spring.

"Crisis averted, then."

"Yup." And she felt amazingly better. A little lonely, yes, but nowhere near as overwhelmed. Because of his . . . help.

It occurred to her that she was courting trouble. "Cole?"

"Lorelei?" he teased back.

Suddenly she did not know what she wanted to tell him. "Thank you."

"You are welcome, dearest. Do send Alexandra home with the details, please. I should like to arrive to my wedding on time."

Dearest. That was probably for Lolly, but she replied, "Yes, milord."

He laughed. "I never expected to hear *that* from you!"

"Well, don't expect it. I was joshing!"

"So I assumed."

Then Laurel just stood there in the dark pantry, the telephone receiver cradled to her ear, and listened to a *whuff* sound that she guessed was him breathing.

She jumped at a sudden clicking. "Hello?" asked a gruff voice. "Hello? How does this confounded contraption work?"

"Mr. Davis?" she asked, recognizing his Minnesota accent.

"Eh? Is this Lolly?"

"No, it's Laurel Garrison. We—I was using the line. I'll hang up so Lolly can put you through. Good-bye, Co—Lord Collier."

She heard the smile in his voice. "Good-bye, Miss Garrison. And you, Mr. Davis."

Setting the receiver back in its cradle, Laurel felt odd inside, sort of lonesome and happy at the same time.

And scared. Very scared.

This wedding would be complicated by more than orange blossoms and apricot decorations!

While Laurel saddled Snapper to ride home, Mariah shooed the other sisters out of the stables. "This is *private*."

"Is it?" asked Laurel, wary.

"We haven't had much time to talk." Mariah held Snapper's halter while Laurel smoothed the saddle blanket, then lifted her sidesaddle onto the gelding's back.

"We never did talk a lot," she noted carefully.

"That's not true." And Laurel guessed it wasn't. There'd been a time when they were each other's best playmates. They'd been inseparable . . . until they started to grow up.

137

While Laurel wanted to play Indians by the creek, Mariah went gooey-eyed over the Sears Roebuck catalog and started curling her hair, even on weekdays. She even started wearing . . .

But now Laurel looked at her sister's not-as-waspish waist more closely. "You're not wearing your corset."

Mariah blushed. "Laurel Lee Garrison!" But when Laurel only quirked a brow—*See why we don't talk?*—Mariah smiled, secret and soft. Laurel hadn't seen such pleasure in her sister before, even when she talked about Stuart MacCallum.

And Mariah did go moon-eyed when she spoke of Stuart.

"I'm going to have a baby, Laurel," she confessed.

Laurel felt everything inside of her go still. "A baby?" Her sister and a sheep farmer! It was . . . it was . . .

Actually, it was scary. "Does Papa know?" Laurel tightened the cinch, making sure Snapper wasn't holding his breath.

"I don't think so. Mama and I thought we should wait. Stuart knows, of course, and he's terribly excited. And I wouldn't be surprised if Vic's figured it out."

"You're . . . ?"

Again Mariah nodded, so happy that another laugh bubbled out of her and she didn't even seem to notice.

"Well, congratulations! That's wonderful, I guess."

Mariah blinked those big gray eyes of hers, the edge of her giddiness starting to fade. "You *guess*?"

Yet again, Laurel had somehow blundered across the line of propriety. "You do want to have babies, right?"

"Well, of course I do. What woman wouldn't want babies?"

Laurel winced. "Not for a long time I won't. Maybe never."

"Oh, you'll change your mind," said Mariah in her know-it-all way. "Actually, that's what I came to talk to you about."

"Babies?"

"No! But . . ." The older girl blushed.

Despite her need to get back to the claim, Laurel wondered what could make her sister so uncomfortable. "But what?"

Mariah took a deep breath. "You seemed so upset about

138

the honeymoon, I thought maybe you had concerns. I wanted to, well, assure you."

Laurel waited. "Assure me?"

Mariah blushed even more. "Oh, mercy! I just wanted to say that if you have, well, *questions*. About the wedding night. That you don't wish to discuss with Mama. Then you should feel free to, well . . . ask me."

"Oh! You mean about—"

Mariah nodded. Well, of course Laurel wouldn't need to know about that with Collier. But she had to admit a certain amount of curiosity.

"You like it, then?" Their mother had assured them that many women did—with the right man, of course. But Laurel only had to watch some dogs or horses to wonder about that.

Mariah covered her face with her hands for a moment, then sat down on a bale of hay. When she lowered her hands, however, there was no mistaking the naughty glow in her eyes when she said, "Yes. I like it very, very much."

And this was Mariah. The good girl! The lady!

Looping an arm over Snapper's neck, her cheek against his side, Laurel asked, "How much? Is it as good as kissing?"

"Is Lord Collier a good kisser, then?"

Now Laurel blushed. But really, he was a fine kisser. All she had to do was remember their time by the water hole, or in the buggy by the creek, and she could understand why Mariah blushed.

Did Stuart touch Mariah in such intimate places as Collier had touched *her*? Laurel decided she didn't want to know that much.

"You kiss while you're doing it," Mariah confided, still blushing. "At least . . . we do. Mostly. Oh, Laurel, you must never let Stuart know I've been telling you these things!"

"I'm not certain I can ever face Stuart again!"

But Mariah laughed. She was, after all, the woman of experience. "Perhaps I said too much. I just wanted to reassure you that, if you're worried about your wedding night, you oughtn't be. Everything will be fine, if you love him. It's like joining your souls by joining your bodies."

If she loved Collier?

Laurel quickly turned her face into Snapper's neck. She *didn't* love Collier. She was only pretend-marrying him. And she would never find out if he was the sort of man who would kiss her while they "became one," and that was all for the best. *Really.*

"Laurel?" Mariah stood again. "You do love him, right?"

Laurel wished she could lie more easily. "You've no idea," she whispered into Snapper's black mane.

Luckily, that was enough for Mariah. But the conversation left Laurel strangely unnerved as she rode back to her claim. Or maybe the feeling came from what she rode back through. Leaves, though turning colors, still hadn't begun to fall. Squirrels, their tails especially bushy, seemed more active than ever. And a honking noise drew her attention skyward, to watch the uneven *V* that was a flock of geese, already heading south for the winter.

If she weren't marrying Collier Pembroke, she would soon be bidding farewell to her homestead.

Laurel guessed that had to be enough for her, too.

Collier's family did not attend the wedding, because Collier had not yet told them of it.

Oh, he saved one of Alexandra's silver-edged wedding cards for them, and bought an extra copy of the *Sheridan Times* to clip their announcement. His family need not suspect that the ceremony had been anything less than appropriate. But he did not want them interfering. Most likely they would not have come anyway.

But a greater reason was that he did not fully trust Laurel to go through with it.

He found it remarkably easy, readying to marry her. His name appeared in the society column as glowingly as if he were the crown prince. He had occasion to brush off his best coat and top hat. And once married to Laurel, he would even have a family again.

Of sorts. If only a pretend family.

It should sustain him for the two or three years he needed to prove his worth and return to England, in any case!

The morning of the wedding dawned cold. The thermometer that Benjamin Cooper and his son had installed outside the kitchen window had shown a hard freeze for several days, but the skies stayed reassuringly blue. All in all, Collier felt rather optimistic about the day.

Even the decorations, which the Garrison girls had set out the evening before, looked cheerful. Apricot had been a brilliant choice, not being any one of the colors in that silly rhyme about "Blue, love will be true; red, wish herself dead; yellow, ashamed of her fellow . . ." etc. He'd once noted to his younger sister that the only two auspicious colors in the entire list were blue and pink—all the rest meant something unpleasant. Choosing a color unburdened by such superstitions was just the ticket.

Unless Laurel knew enough about the color spectrum to have realized she was combining yellow and red, and thus was both ashamed of him and wished herself dead.

After a sharp rap on his bedroom door, Benjamin Cooper opened it. "Well, don't you smell fine."

Collier said, "Perhaps it's the orange blossoms." Mrs. Garrison had brought bouquets of them off the Burlington Northern, straight from New Orleans, two days previous.

"You look ready to do this," noted Cooper.

Did he expect Collier to abandon the wedding? "I am."

But Cooper made a clicking noise, quirking the side of his mouth under his mustache and inhaling through his teeth. "Well, then, son, I got something I'd better show you."

Despite a pang of foreboding, Collier followed the rancher into the hallway and to the round window with its view to the west. Even standing within a foot of the glass, Collier felt cold shimmering through it. "What should I look for?"

Cooper folded his arms and ducked his head, as if waiting patiently. "The mountains."

So Collier squinted, leaning closer to the icy glass to better see . . . the smudge of grayness where the Bighorn range should have been. "Is that fog?"

"That's snow, son. Comin' this way." Cooper cleared his throat, and when he cast his gaze upward toward Collier, he even had the grace to look sympathetic. "And if Laurel has a lick of sense about her, she isn't."

"Isn't?"

"Heading out in the middle of a snowstorm, even if it is to marry a prize like yourself."

Collier looked back out the window, digesting this news. "It's already come as far as her homestead?"

"Yep. Though even if it hadn't, I wouldn't advise her to try outrunnin' it."

They both knew how good Laurel Garrison was about following people's advice. "And if she were to try?" Collier had to force himself to turn away from the fascinating, looming storm.

Cooper's eyes narrowed with honest anger. "You'd best pray she doesn't, son. 'Cause if she gets caught out in weather like that, could be she won't be marrying anybody. Ever."

Chapter Twelve

When Laurel opened her eyes on the cold morning of her wedding, something about her cabin felt wrong.

Maybe it was marrying a man she didn't love. Maybe it was lying to her friends and, even worse, her family. Maybe it was the fear of becoming "Lady Laurel."

Lord Collier had assured her that she would not have to sport the title. But he should tell that to Lady Cooper, who'd been protesting her fancy handle for ten years now. And when it came to cowboys . . .

Likely "Lady Laurel" would follow her to her grave.

She huddled, warm under her quilts, blowing little clouds of breath, and thought, *I don't have to go through with it. Papa always said if you find yourself in a hole, the first thing to do is stop digging.*

But if she quit on this particular grave, she would lose the claim. *And* all the money her folks had spent on the wedding. *And* the esteem of a man who she'd come to rather . . . like.

She just had a bad case of the jitters, was all. Maybe she should have spent the night in town, as everyone had asked

143

her to do. But, dang it, this was her last night alone in her own cabin, on her land, the reason for doing this in the first place.

Her last night alone for the next few years, anyhow.

She would not be hurried out of it. She'd promised she would set out near daybreak. The ride wouldn't take her but an hour, going easy. Since the wedding wasn't until afternoon, she still had plenty of time to be bathed and powdered and dressed up like one of Elise's china dolls.

But everything surely did seem still outside. The bird cries sounded distant and infrequent. No bare aspen branches scraped together; no pines rushed like a creek.

Something wasn't right!

Laurel swung her feet to the dirt floor, hugging her quilts closer while she yanked her boots on over the stockings she'd worn to sleep. The ground outside had frozen hard over the last week. The inside would freeze once she let the cookstove die out. But when she and Collier returned—that was an image she had trouble envisioning—they could fire things up again.

With her boots on, wearing her cocoon of quilts and blankets, she shuffled to the window to scrape off frost and peek out at the quiet clearing. It looked normal, just more hushed.

Well, *something* felt wrong. And not just her conscience.

Moving to the stove, Laurel pulled off her nightgown only long enough to throw on a boy's woolen union suit, a pair of dungarees under her heaviest skirt, and two flannel shirts. Only then did she pull on her coat, hat, scarf, and mittens and step outside to see just what was wrong. The morning seemed dark; it wasn't just the slow sunrise that cast a shadow across the basin. Snapper nickered at her from his corral, in the shelter of the shed she'd built, so she doubted dangerous animals roamed about.

Then what seemed like a mere handful of white, like feathers, blew past her from behind. Slowly Laurel looked over her shoulder at the mountains—and the mountains weren't there.

"Damn," she exclaimed. The honest-to-gosh curse slipped out of her on a puff of white breath. The first snowfall, and it had to be a storm? On her wedding day?

Laurel had grown up in Wyoming. She knew that the smart thing to do would be to make sure Snapper had feed, carry in a good load of firewood, string a rope to the shed, then go back inside to sit this out. She'd be a fool to get caught between here and town, should this blow into a blizzard. Her family knew that, knew better than to ride out and check on her.

"Well," she told Snapper, wiping a wet blob of snow off her cheek with a mittened hand. "I guess I can get married as well in another few days as today, right?"

No matter what the family and the newspaper and those fancy cards Lady Cooper had printed up said.

No matter what the Good Lord Collier was expecting.

Who knew? Maybe this was the sign she'd needed to re-think this whole plan. What she ought to feel was relieved.

But she stood there in the snowy clearing and wasn't quite sure *what* she felt . . . except cold.

"We can hardly sit here not knowing," protested Collier half-way through breakfast. He couldn't eat anyway.

The girl had faced down a longhorn cow. What made him think she would not try to face down a snowstorm?

"Point of fact." Cooper gestured with his spoon at the dining room window, beyond which snow fell steadily like powder from an upturned box. "That is exactly what we've got to do. Takes a lot more gumption to stay home and let the world sort itself out than it does to charge off to do the sortin'. That's why I've always figured the women of the species outdistance us menfolk in courage. The least we can do is learn from 'em."

"Mr. Cooper," chided Alexandra, low. "Your spoon is for eating, not conducting an orchestra."

"You are right as ever, my darlin'." Cooper put down the spoon. Rather forcefully.

145

"All the same, I should like to go wait at her parents' home," declared Collier. "In order to know all the sooner."

"*All the sooner* might be week's end," warned Cooper. "They can ring us on that telephone box as soon as she turns up."

Collier folded his napkin. "The Garrisons are decent people. I doubt they would protest putting me up, should the storm keep me from managing three blocks back."

Even the house beside theirs was blurry, through the white.

"Go ahead," conceded Alexandra. "And you," she added, when Cooper pushed his own chair out. "But you had best hope she isn't riding down today. The groom ought not see the bride before the ceremony, on their wedding day."

Cooper blinked at her. "*That's* why we should hope she isn't out in this storm?"

Alexandra narrowed her eyes, clearly swallowing back a less-than-ladylike retort. Fortunate Cooper. If she'd been Laurel, he'd likely be wearing her tea. "Yes, dearest," she said, voice dripping with sarcasm. "That is the only possible reason to hope she is not out in this storm. Why else?"

The way her husband advanced on her, it would be a few minutes before Cooper left. Collier could not sit still that long, so he went to the front hall and put on his chesterfield, galoshes, gloves, muffler, and his beaver hat.

"The benefit of bein' in town," announced Cooper when he showed, shrugging on an incredibly heavy coat of some thick, curling black fur, "is that if we *do* get turned around some, we're bound to hit a fence or a house. The trick"—he pulled a cowboy hat low on his head, then tied it down with a muffler—"is to not stop until you've reached shelter, savvy? Even if you fall down the creek bank and break your leg, you'd best drag yourself along till you hit a fence, then follow it to a house. Else we'll have to thaw you out to fit you in the coffin."

Collier thought that, as usual, the older man was talking mainly to hear himself talk. Then Cooper said, "Here goes nothing," and opened the door.

Good Lord! This was October? Collier actually took a step back, instincts he'd thought long civilized out of the Pembrokes warning him to stay inside.

Then his civilized blood triumphed over that instinct, and he lowered his head and pushed out into the storm.

Snow had already collected to about six inches, though Collier could not hear it beneath his boots—the wind howled too loudly. Fighting that wind, he could see Cooper ahead of him, and trees or lampposts up to ten feet off. Cooper was right; with picket fences on one side of the walkway, and curbs on the other, they could navigate the three blocks to the Garrison home.

But Laurel would be riding through open country.

As he stumbled along, Collier found himself following Cooper's advice—and not just to keep moving. He prayed Laurel had the sense to stay home.

The Garrison house seemed even more tense.

"Hail, the camp!" called Cooper, as soon as he pushed open the front door into their foyer—so that nobody would think, for one hopeful heartbeat, that Laurel had arrived safely, Collier guessed. Victoria and Audra hurried over to help the men shed their snow-packed wrappings and coats, and to collect frosty hugs from their "uncle." "Thought we'd pass the time where folks make a decent cup of coffee, if you don't mind the imposition."

"Of course we don't mind, Benj," insisted Elizabeth Garrison, going to her husband's partner for her own hug—one that lasted longer than Collier felt was seemly. "We can use the distraction."

"Can we?" asked Cooper facetiously.

"Yes." Mrs. Garrison's return smile seemed wan. "We can."

Then she surprised Collier by enfolding *him* in a brief hug, as well. "Don't worry, Lord Collier. If any of my daughters can handle herself in a snowstorm, it's Laurel."

"Then you think she *is* in the snowstorm?" His voice came out a touch higher than he'd expected.

She did not rush to correct him.

147

"Nothin' drains that girl's good sense faster than bein' told she *cain't* do somethin'," complained Jacob Garrison, appearing in the doorway to his den. He shook his white head, glaring at Collier as if this were all his fault. "Even by God."

"And yet you told her she mustn't stay alone on the claim." Immediately Collier regretted his words. This was her *father!*

Garrison squinted at him, then shook his head in dismissal. "Rather a live foolish daughter than a dead clever one."

"You go in with him, Benj," insisted Mrs. Garrison. "I'll get you that coffee and telephone Alexandra to let her know you arrived safely. Would you like anything, Lord Collier?"

Garrison vanished back into his den, though not before Collier heard him mutter something about *lord.*

"Tea?"

"I'll make you some."

"Oh, and Lillabit," called Cooper, and coughed. "The boy and I might could use a dose of medicine—ward off the grippe."

Mrs. Garrison smiled more honestly and mouthed what looked like, *In your coffee?*

Cooper waggled his eyebrows at her, then vanished into the den. Collier hesitated, then followed the lady of the house as far as the doorway of the kitchen.

"And how do you take your medicine, Lord Collier?" she asked. "In a shot glass, or with some soda?"

Only then did he remember what she'd said about having a temperate household—except for medicine. "You . . . imbibe?"

"That would dishonor my husband. But Mr. Cooper does."

"Today, at least," decided Collier, "I believe it would be fitting for me to honor your husband as well."

Only when she smiled in approval did it occur to Collier that he did, in fact, feel as if he owed the older man something.

The man was Laurel's father. Collier was only her pretend fiancé. If she was out in this, then to some extent, it was at least partially his fault. He *was* responsible for having upended

148

their lives. For the pies and cakes he now noticed covering almost every available inch of table and counter in the kitchen.

For goading their daughter, a young woman of whom he was surprisingly fond, into betraying their trust and her future.

Perhaps he could use that medicine after all. But instead he stepped into a kitchen for the first time in a year. "Please, Mrs. Garrison, call me Collier. The title is merely a courtesy."

Then came the waiting.

Collier spoke to Thaddeas and exchanged pleasantries with each Garrison girl, except shy Kitty, as the morning passed. Audra played piano. Victoria recited. Elise showed him several dolls, her new wedding frock, and a small silver ring she'd received for her birthday. "It used to fit on *this* finger," she explained with childlike solemnity, "and then I moved it to this finger, and then to this one. When I'm too big for that, I'll put it on my pinky. And if I ever get too big for that, Daddy says I can wear it on a chain around my neck."

Like Laurel and her glass engagement ring? The memory pained him worse than he would have expected. *Lord.* He'd asked Laurel not to embarrass him. . . .

"Or"—and she giggled—"in my nose!"

They were a nice family, he admitted to himself. Rough at the edges, certainly, but good-hearted, creative, kind. They'd done nothing to deserve his deceit. Were Collier a true gentleman, he would end this. If Laurel arrived safely—rather, *when* she arrived—he would take her aside and tell her.

He did not look forward to robbing her of her homestead, nor to becoming a man who jilted local women. But if he did not accept those consequences, was he a true gentleman? Or had he degenerated into no more than a remittance man, after all?

Collier's heart stilled when, at midmorning, Garrison came into the house carrying a snowy girl. When his wife unwrapped a shawl to reveal stringy yellow hair—when Collier realized the shivering creature was not his fiancée, but their pianist—his fear became nausea. He sank into an empty chair, watching Mrs. Garrison drape the girl with blankets from the warming oven and feed her hot, sweet tea, and he wondered at the painful clutch in his stomach. It isn't Laurel, he told himself firmly.

But it could have been. Or it could yet be worse.

"I wore the m-mittens M-Mariah gave me," whispered the waif. "I didn't mean to cause trouble."

"And you didn't, darling," assured Mrs. Garrison, ignoring the child's stringy hair. "But there'll be no wedding today."

After this new visitor had been washed, dried, and dressed more appropriately, Thaddeas introduced her to Collier as Miss Evangeline Taylor. As soon as he bowed to her, she fled. Ever after, he only caught glimpses of her from safe distances.

Perhaps the Little Match Girl saw a truth in him that the others did not—that he had used Laurel for his own gain.

And maybe the regret she saw was nowhere near enough.

When the clock was nearing noon, the back door blew open and a round furry lump staggered in wearing cowboy boots under its snow-encrusted skirts. The stillness in Collier, where he'd felt fear, expanded until his heart felt hollow.

She fumbled awkwardly at her wrappings, until Victoria and Mrs. Garrison hurried to her side to help, pulling off a snow-covered bearskin, a scarf, and under that a hat, and under that a shawl, and under that a coat. Only then did they reach Laurel, complete with brown hair and red cheeks and nose. She wore gloves under her mittens, and a second coat under her first. When she beat her skirt, Collier wondered how many of those she wore.

"Brrr!" She swung her arms, stomped her feet, and slapped her hands across herself to bring up the blood, her eyes bright with the adventure. "Can you believe that snow? Papa, I gave Snapper an extra ration of oats. Oh, thank you, Mama," she added, when Mrs. Garrison draped an oven-warmed blanket over her. "Do you have any coffee? Yes. Thank you."

Then, as Mrs. Garrison helped her raise the mug to her lips without spilling it, Laurel's blue gaze found Collier's.

"Cole! You're here!" Then she noticed the others were all staring as he was. "What's everyone looking at?"

Everyone began to talk at once.

Several of them yelled.

Chapter Thirteen

Laurel had expected a much better welcome.

It all sounded a mite garbled—even with cotton in her ears and a shawl wrapped around her head, she'd been disoriented by the continuous howl of icy wind. But she caught the gist.

Papa called her a fool, and Thaddeas seconded it. Uncle Benj accused her of turning him gray before his time. Mama fussed as if Laurel had walked in from the storm stark naked.

Collier just kept staring. That unnerved her most of all.

She took another shivering gulp of hot, sweet coffee. For this she'd ridden almost eight miles through a snowstorm?

"A danger to horse and self," Papa accused. Those were fighting words. She'd had Snapper since he was born!

"I did not endanger my horse! You've said yourself, Papa, that God gives the critters a heavy coat for a reason. The wild mustangs are weathering the storm just fine, I guess, and so did Snapper. I did everything right!"

Unappeased by his scowling skepticism, she turned her defense to Uncle Benj, who, if doubtful, at least looked sympathetic. "I *did!* I had my compass. I had three different tins of matches, so even if I lost some, I'd have others. You saw how I bundled up—and that's not counting the pack I loaded onto Snapper. If I got lost, I could've built a lean-to for us and kept warm for a couple of days with the coal oil I brought along. I was careful!"

Increasingly desperate, she turned to her mother. "I *was!*"

"Drink some more coffee, baby," murmured Mama, neither agreeing nor disagreeing. So Laurel took another shuddering sip of the deliciously hot liquid. The warm blanket wrapped around her made her want to shiver all the more, somehow.

Collier still said nothing at all. Her sisters—and the mousy Evangeline Taylor, of course—kept their tongues, too.

"Horses fall," Papa reminded her darkly. "Startle. Buck. Lose the horse, you lose your pack. Break an arm, knock yer head on a branch, could be you wouldn't light them matches."

Oh. "Well, Snapper *didn't* fall," she insisted . . . but not quite as emphatically. He had stumbled once or twice. "Or throw me. And I'm here just fine, just like I promised."

Everyone just kept staring—even the one she'd come for.

"I keep my word," she insisted to him, her fiancé.

But Cole turned and stalked silently off to the parlor.

Papa shrugged on his buffalo coat and wrappings, then headed out toward the stables, maybe to check on her horse. Thaddeas sank into his chair, shaking his head. "You little idiot," he said again, echoing Papa's accusations. "Will you never learn?"

It was Uncle Benj who finally enveloped her in a big, welcome bear hug, blankets and all. "My darlin' Laurel, don't you *never* do anythin' like that again." His voice sounded muffled against her hair. "I doubt my old heart could stand it."

But after that one embrace, he stepped to her mother's side as if to give *her* support.

"I should go talk to Collier," said Laurel, looking toward the hallway. His reaction particularly annoyed her. Not that

153

he had a whole lot of reason to care, she guessed, beyond seeing their partnership through. But still, she'd kind of thought . . .

Hoped . . .

He was the reason she'd come. Him . . . and the ranch, of course.

"Not yet, you won't," insisted Mama, pushing Laurel down into a kitchen chair. "You eat some stew while I fill the bathtub. Then you will take a hot bath so that you don't catch your death. Then you will put on warm, dry clothes, and *then* you can talk to your Collier. It's not like either of you are going anywhere soon. The wedding's been postponed."

"Postponed!" And after she'd ridden all the way here?

"The judge telephoned earlier to say he'd come when the weather cleared and no sooner," said Mama. "*He* saw the sense in waiting it out."

This was not how Laurel had thought it would go at all.

Collier still stood in the parlor, watching the snow out the bay window, when Laurel came to him. She smelled of soap and of pine, as if she'd perfumed the water with it, and her hair hung long and thick down her back. She wore a red woolen dress with a gored skirt, and as she met his gaze straight on she looked . . .

Uncertain? Lovely. Blessedly, miraculously alive.

She did have a beauty about her, a health no cosmetic could imitate. No blush could give her face that warmth; no dye could streak her hair such deep colors. Her stride was perhaps too long, her gaze too direct—but at least what he saw, she was. And Collier had come within hours of turning her into something else.

"May we have some time in private?" he asked Benjamin Cooper, still not lifting his gaze from the hesitant Laurel.

"Long as you remember you're not married yet," Cooper warned them. He absented himself from the room, though, ushering Kitty and Audra with him.

"You're acting like you're mad at me," accused Laurel. She

stood not a foot away, and yet those mere inches felt like miles.

"Dogs get mad," he corrected. "People get angry."

"Then you're *angry?*"

He nodded slowly. He supposed he was.

"I took some risk, but I took it for you!" She flushed, then frowned and kicked at the carpet. "I mean . . . because I promised I would. We made a deal."

"That is what angers me." Before she could argue that, Collier put a steadying hand on her arm. "Could we sit? Please?"

Immediately she looked wary. She'd worn indignation better.

"I need to speak to you of something important. Privately."

She glanced toward the archway to the foyer, then the doorway to the kitchen. But apparently realizing, as he had, that they'd find no better privacy today, she sank onto the settee.

He sat beside her and inclined his head toward hers so that he could murmur his explanation very low. "I am having second thoughts about the wedding."

She spun on him as if he'd bitten her. "You what?"

"Please hear me out." When she only glared, he leaned closer and spoke in her ear. "I'm thinking of what's best for you."

She shivered. Was she still suffering from her cold ride, even after the hot drinks, hot bath, hot blankets?

"Oh, come here," he invited grudgingly. And he drew her into his arms, held her against his own warmth. She resisted, stubborn and rigid at first, then slowly relaxed into his embrace. They made a surprisingly good fit. "Laurel, had you been hurt or killed trying to get here, it would have been my fault."

She stiffened again, if only to draw back. "Yours?"

"Had I not made this inappropriate offer, you would have been safe in your cabin, or with your family in town. And that may be the least of the risks to which I've exposed you. Your mother was correct. You ought not burden your future with what we know—what we've *agreed*—shall be a failed marriage."

As she faced him to whisper back, her cheek brushed his coat's shoulder. "If we annul it, it won't have been a marriage at all, just business. And that could still work. I know it could!"

He sometimes forgot how innocent she was. "I doubt we will manage an annulment, Laurel."

"Well, maybe you can't, but I have something to say about that too, you know! Just like I had a say in coming here today."

"And even if we did manage it," he assured her, "Nobody but ourselves would know. As far as your family are concerned, you would forevermore be the former Mrs. Pembroke, deserted and eventually divorced. I do mean to have children someday. Sooner or later, I would need to officially cut our ties—and that is selfish of me, unforgivably so. Today when I feared it too late, saw how many people we might hurt, I understood *how* selfish."

Laurel watched him from his shoulder, a crease between her eyebrows. But all she said, very softly, was, "We made a deal."

"What?"

Her blue eyes narrowed. "We, Lord Collier, made a *deal*. You act as if you're taking advantage of me, but that's hogwash. You want something from me? Well, I want something from you, too. My ranch. As for the future, well, I'd rather be a divorcée with her own prospering ranch than a poor spinster who never could prove up her homestead because she started too late, with bad land and no backers. You would be amazed how folks overlook a little notoriety in a person who runs a successful business."

He had to smile. "Perhaps."

"Do I want to do it without you? Sure I do! If I were a man, I could. But if I were a man, nobody would be scolding me as if I had no right to make decisions and take risks with my own life."

Well. That was an intriguing perspective!

156

"If you won't marry me, I can't make you. Well . . ." The smile that turned up her lips worried him. "Not without making up some fib about you taking advantage, and I've put my folks through enough without a shotgun wedding. But don't you dare jilt me and pretend it's for my own good, because that's just . . ."

She scowled at the very idea. Collier could think of several apt words, but suggested her own. "Hogwash?"

She nodded sharply. "You promised."

He felt they'd missed something important. Certainly he was wrong to wed with no real intention of permanence. But he was not misleading her. And he doubted he could fight his own worse nature *and* her determination. "You are correct," he admitted finally, leaning his forehead against hers. "We have a deal."

She relaxed against him, warm and soft and alive, and smiling brightly. "So as soon as the weather clears?"

"As soon as the weather clears." Something moved at the corner of his eye, and he watched. Both of them saw when little Elise again peeked around the corner.

"That little wretch," murmured Laurel, her voice low in her throat. Collier thought he could get used to holding her like this. Not that he should.

"I am very glad," he whispered, "that we kept our voices down."

She nodded, her rich dark hair sliding against his shoulder.

The next time Elise's head slanted into view, both Collier and Laurel were staring straight at her. "Elise Michelle Garrison," scolded Laurel. "What do you think you are doing?"

Instead of fleeing exposure, Elise stepped into the room and rocked on her heels. "I just wanted to see him kiss you."

"What?" demanded Laurel, stiffening again.

But Collier—in light of maintaining their charade—said, "Excellent suggestion, Elise." And he ducked his head to press a gentle kiss onto Laurel's warm, alive mouth.

She relaxed into his shoulder again. By following the tilt of her head, he found himself levered more fully over her. He turned his head to better slant their mouths, his lips opening.

Hers did, too.

Damn, but he appreciated her not freezing to death!

"So you aren't angry with me?" whispered Laurel breathily. Their noses touched. Her eyelashes almost brushed his.

"With myself," he clarified, and covered her mouth again.

A sharp whistle startled them apart. Looking around, Collier quickly saw Benjamin Cooper filling the doorway to the kitchen.

"Like I said," noted the rancher, "you ain't married yet."

Laurel pressed her lips together and ducked her head, but she hardly looked chagrined. "No, sir."

"Just be glad it was me, not your daddy, what interrupted you." Cooper shook his head. "I doubt a bucket of water would do y'all *or* that furniture of your mama's much good. Lord Collier, we'd best be gettin' you home."

"Home," echoed Collier blankly, his lips still tingling. His side felt cold without Laurel snuggled up against it. *Good Lord!*

Cooper crossed the room and drew him up by the elbow, as if helping an intoxicated mate find his way. "Snow's deeper, but I don't guess the walk back will be too much worse than the walk here." His gaze narrowed. "Might help you cool off some, too."

Collier glanced back at Laurel, with her dark, gleaming hair spilling over her shoulders, her blue eyes sparkling, her lips redder than usual. He very much did not want to go back to the Coopers' home. But staying the night here could prove disastrous.

"Yes," he said. "I had best accompany you, at that."

Cooper did not sound particularly pleased as he said, "I figured you'd see it my way."

When Collier reached back to take Laurel's hand, it did not feel quite so tough as it sometimes did. Perhaps because of how fragile he knew the whole girl to be, after having risked losing her to the weather. "Until the wedding then, Miss Garrison," he murmured, and kissed her knuckles.

He wished her engagement ring were real. Perhaps, for a moment, he wished everything about this were real. That showed how badly worry had drained him. He no longer thought straight.

"Until the wedding," she agreed softly.

It took almost more willpower than he had to let her hand slip from his. "I'll make my good-byes to your family, then."

As he left the room, Elise dove onto the sofa beside her sister and exclaimed, "That was a *good* kiss, wasn't it?"

Unfortunately, he did not hear Laurel's answer.

"Oh!" whispered Mariah when Laurel stepped out into the hallway in her wedding gown two days later. "It's *beautiful!*"

Which just made Laurel feel guilty. Mariah had always dreamed of a fairy-tale wedding, but once she and Stuart had set themselves to it, they hadn't left time for fineries. Mariah had married in her best blue dress—the one she wore today! Instead it was Laurel marrying a British lord, draped in white silk and lace with a floor-length tulle veil.

She did like her wedding gown, she supposed. Mama had kept it simple, limiting herself to a yoke of beaded lace that matched one long, flaring panel of lace and beadwork that opened off one hip to sweep down the side of the gown until it pooled into the generous train. Who wouldn't feel pretty in such a dress?

Who wouldn't look like a lady?

But Mariah should have had it, not her. Not for a wedding that was just pretend, anyhow.

To even think that made Laurel's stomach cramp, and she had to swallow. Hard. Especially after taking Collier to task the other night, she had to go through with this. Didn't she?

She turned to the full-length mirror. "I don't look silly?"

"No!" Mariah sounded indignant at such a question.

Mama reached carefully into the knot of orange blossoms and styled curls that they'd created of Laurel's hair and tucked a blossom more carefully, saying, "He won't know what hit him."

Laurel stared at herself a little longer. She liked the idea of Lord Collier not knowing what hit him—more than she should.

Her other sisters seemed equally impressed by Laurel's bridal gown when she swept carefully down the steps. Even Thaddeas grinned broadly and said, "Well, who are you?"

"Shame on you," chided Mariah. Somehow getting married had given her the authority to scold a brother ten years her senior. "Acting as if you've never seen her pretty before!"

"Not gussied up like this," insisted Thad, but he kissed Laurel's cheek by way of amends. "It looks good on you."

"Thank you," said Laurel. But it *wasn't* her; it was the dress. The rest was pretend, as she and Collier had agreed.

Why that should sadden her now, she had no idea.

All Papa did was nod once at her, his gaze admiring despite his continued reservations about her wedding. "Best be gettin' you there afore you take mind to skip out," he drawled, and claimed her mother's best cloak to drape over her shoulders. "Have a hard time findin' you in all this snow."

"I'm not skipping out, Papa," she assured him, embarrassed to have folks dressing her like a doll, as if she were unable to do for herself, but not embarrassed enough to push him away.

Her father sighed, as if disappointed.

"Jacob Garrison," scolded Mama, and Papa kept his peace.

Lace and satin were draped across the Coopers' parlor and hall, which was abloom with white roses and orange blossoms. When she saw Uncle Benj and his wife in their party best, Laurel felt better about her own fine gown. Surely Collier would expect elegance.

Alexandra bustled her and Papa off into the upstairs sitting room, instructed them to come down the steps when the music began, then left them alone together. If Laurel weren't wearing gloves—special ones, with a slit up one finger especially for a wedding ring!—she would be chewing her fingernails by now.

"Not too late to change yer mind," Papa reminded her one last time, despite Mama's warning.

"I gave my word."

"Don't count until after the vows."

"I'm not changing my mind, Papa," she assured him—but then she wondered, What if he relented? If her father agreed, here and now, to let her stay on her claim alone, would she still marry Collier? Even after giving her word, would she?

But she didn't ask. Papa didn't offer. And the piano music began. "Here goes," said Laurel, as Papa gave her his arm.

Then he hesitated, touching her cheek with his free hand.

"Papa?"

"I hope you know what you're doin', Laurel Lee," he drawled.

Then he led her to the landing and down the stairs, to marry a man she did not love.

Collier looked so blindingly handsome in a fine Prince Albert coat and high polished boots that she nearly forgot that she didn't love him. But she'd do well not to forget.

Maybe the marriage would be pretend, but the ceremony seemed even less real. Despite her fears, Laurel managed the "I will" as clearly as Collier, but she felt suddenly shy when he ducked to kiss her afterward. While she'd kissed him before, it had not been in front of her family! Still, even embarrassed, she could do worse than be kissed by the bright-eyed Collier Pembroke.

"Hold steady, Lorelei," he whispered. "That was the worst."

But she wasn't so sure.

The afternoon blurred after that. They bundled over to her parents' house for a small reception with friends and neighbors. Shaking hands and accepting kisses wore on Laurel faster than she would have guessed. And she noticed that Collier winced, almost imperceptibly, every time someone congratulated her.

Finally she elbowed him and asked why.

"It is not done. The groom gets the congratulations, not the bride. The honor was not conferred upon her, but upon him."

"Well, it's done in *Wyoming*," she warned him. *Where we have more important things to do than read books on etiquette.*

"I am pleased that you think it such an honor to wed me."

Then he had another hand to shake, she had another kiss to bear, and they both received more congratulations. At moments like these, she felt glad it was all pretend. She did not have to worry about the fact that, because of the storm, they'd moved their wedding from a Wednesday—"best day of all," according to the rhyme—to a Friday, "for losses." She did not have to concern herself over the meaningful glances folks exchanged, wondering—she guessed—just how soon the first baby would come. She needed only finish out the day and tomorrow they'd go home to her claim.

But she and Collier had one more obstacle to clear.

They could have spent the night at her parents' house, of course, or at the Coopers' residence. Instead, after changing into street clothes, they followed local tradition and went to the West's finest hotel north of Denver.

"Who is that?" asked Laurel, as Collier walked her through the lobby of the Sheridan Inn. Three men stood in the hallway that she had heard led to the Buffalo Bill Saloon, watching in some amusement. To judge from their fancy suits, cloth-topped shoes, and forward manner, they weren't local boys.

"Those," said Collier tightly, "are remittance men."

"Are they friends of yours?" She turned around as they walked, because Collier was leading her onto the elevator after the bellboy and their two bags whether she wanted to go or not.

One of the Englishmen winked at her, or else at Collier. She wasn't sure which. Either way, she narrowed her eyes in threat, even as the elevator man closed the grilled cage in front of her.

"Not friends exactly," he admitted.

"Oh! Is that the one you knocked down, protecting my honor?"

Looking down at her, Collier smiled. "I did not knock him down, and how would you know?"

"I have my ways of finding out," she said mysteriously.

"Your sister Victoria," he teased, showing his dimples.

She grinned back up at him. At the very least, this marriage would, as Mariah had said, be ornamental.

But it would also present challenges, and the first was their big, quiet hotel room.

"So," she asked, falling loosely into a chair. "How shall we amuse ourselves?"

Only then did she think better of the question.

Her new husband's golden hair might make him look like an angel. But his slow, full smile was devilish.

Chapter Fourteen

Laurel stood, unsettled by Collier's smile. They had a deal! True, he'd expressed doubts at their ability to keep that part of the bargain, but it was a bargain, even so!

It hadn't occurred to her that maybe she ought not trust him. Now they were alone together. Soon they would be alone in her claim cabin. Worse, as her legal husband, he had a *right* to . . .

To her relief Collier sank gracefully onto the mate to her chair. "We do what we agreed to do, Lorelei. We pretend."

She ignored the endearment. "But not when we're alone."

"No." He exhaled slowly. It *had* been a very big day, what with getting married and all. "Your virtue is safe with me for now . . . unless you wish to renegotiate our agreement."

And risk babies? Permanence? England?

A shiver ran through her at his smoky look. It was only now twilight. They'd not even pulled the bed down from the wall . . . not that she should be thinking of beds.

"Not hardly," she assured him.

When a knock startled her, she spun to face the door as

164

she might a bear. Collier laughed. But he also reached for her as he stood and crossed toward it. "C'mere."

When she hesitated, he turned those eyes to her again—shiny but dark in evening shadow—and his dimples deepened. "Please."

So she did. He took her hand, slid an arm around her waist, and then he opened the door.

The bellman from the lobby held a tray with a tall bottle and two crystal glasses. "Sorry to disturb you folks," he said. "These were sent over by Mr. Benjamin Cooper."

Cole stepped back from the door, drawing Laurel with him, sliding his other arm around her. His warmth and solidity tempted her to relax into the casual embrace, even as she questioned such public intimacy.

"Please put them on the table," Collier instructed, then ducked his head so that his breath scalded Laurel's ear. *Ohhh!* Knees suddenly weak, she leaned more heavily into him. "This is our wedding night," he whispered. His lips brushed her neck. "Do pretend to enjoy it."

Wasn't she?

Somehow, as his lips sneaked across her jawline, she could not form words to challenge his assumption.

"I'll leave you alone now," promised the bellman. When Laurel opened her heavy eyes, he'd returned to the doorway.

"One moment," insisted Cole, and slid a hand from around her. Laurel had to swallow back an instinctive protest at how much colder she felt. When he offered the man a tip, Collier's forearm brushed near her breast. She shivered. "Here you go."

"Thank you, sir." The bellman didn't look to see what he'd gotten. "I'll make sure nobody disturbs you folks."

Collier's "We'd appreciate that" sounded smoky.

When the door shut, Laurel needed deep breaths to gather her strength. Then she spun out of his embrace. "What was that about?"

"That," he answered easily, shrugging out of his dress jacket, "was how newlyweds would likely behave."

165

"Not in front of someone else."

Returning to the table to drape his coat on a chair back, then lifting the bottle, Collier slid his gaze back to hers. "You've really never been in love, have you?"

"Have you?" she challenged, then remembered his lost fiancée. Well, he shouldn't have riled her.

"Not in its purest form," he assured her. "You?"

"I haven't had the time."

But he found that amusing, too.

"It's a good year," he said instead, apparently about the bottle. "Your uncle has fine taste." Then he set about removing the stopper, a process he managed so competently that it drew her curiosity despite herself.

"Is that wine?" she asked finally.

"Champagne." He raised an eyebrow. "You've never imbibed?"

"The only spirits my father tolerates—"

"—are for medicinal purposes," he finished. To judge by his dimples, he found that funny. "Well, you married to escape your father's yoke. If I'm not to take your innocence the usual way, allow me this: let's celebrate with a toast."

"Papa never had me in a yoke! He just . . . worries."

"Now his worrying shan't keep you off your ranch. Ahhh, here we go." With a loud pop, the cork flew from the bottle and bounced off the ceiling. Laurel retrieved it while Collier poured champagne into the goblets, where it fizzed and bubbled.

The cork smelled tart but not unpleasant. Uncle Benj would not gift her with something downright immoral. Would he?

And she and Collier had accomplished quite a bit today, even if it wasn't what the rest of Sheridan thought they had.

Collier offered her a crystal goblet, an inviting half smile hovering on his full lips, his eyes livelier than ever. Sometimes the unfair beauty of this man overwhelmed her, as if she'd momentarily forgotten it. His hair caught the glow of the electric lights, and his shirt looked crisp and starched.

"Perhaps just a sip," she agreed, accepting the drink. She'd boarded the train, as far as trusting him went. Might as well give up the notion of jumping off.

Her fingers brushed his as she accepted the glass. The champagne looked even better up close, full of bubbles. Bubbles danced on her nose, making her want to sneeze.

"To success," toasted Collier. "However we define it."

Not very romantic, but then, this was business.

"To success," Laurel agreed. He touched his goblet to hers with a gentle clink, and they each took a sip.

Champagne tickled *inside*, too, and she coughed. Then, looking up at him through her lashes, she returned his friendly smile. "I thought it would be sweeter."

"Oh, no," he assured her. "That would ruin it. Take another taste, and hold it on your tongue a moment."

She did. The champagne hopped around her mouth like a grasshopper, then slid down her throat, and that *was* better.

"You like it?" Cole prompted.

She nodded. They both took another sip.

Then he said, "Let's do another toast, European-style."

"European?"

For a moment, as he extended his own goblet, she thought he meant her to drink from *his* glass. The idea tickled as much as the champagne. But he drew his hand around hers, so that their arms circled as they tipped their own glasses toward their lips.

"What shall we drink to?" he asked.

"To the claim," she decided.

He hesitated barely a moment, then nodded. "To the claim." And they each took another fizzy sip.

Laurel began to feel warm inside, which seemed odd, since the champagne was cold.

"And to Brambourne," Cole insisted then. "May our lands get proper stewardship on both sides of the Atlantic."

That seemed fair—especially with that extra bit—so Laurel said, "To Brambourne," and they drank again.

Then, since she liked this custom, she said, "To family!"

At that Cole hesitated. Did he not like his family?

"May we finally prove ourselves to them," she added.

Now he nodded. "To proving ourselves."

After that sip, Laurel giggled.

Collier widened his bright, bright eyes. "You find something amusing, Mrs. Pembroke?"

Being called *Mrs. Pembroke* seemed even funnier. Less funny was how Cole pried her goblet gently from her hand. "Wait!" she protested, reaching after it.

"I think you'd best pace yourself," he advised. "It needs to last us all night."

"Except for when we're in bed," she argued, then flushed, hotter than ever before, and not just because of the champagne.

Though maybe partly because of that.

"Not that we'll be doing anything untoward in bed," she added stiffly. "Maybe we should take turns. With the bed. I'm guessing you don't want to sleep on the floor."

He parted those full, soft lips of his as if to argue, then shook his head instead. "I'm nowhere near ready to sleep," he assured her smoothly. "Are you?"

She shook her head. *Nowhere* near.

"Hmm." He looked around them. It was a regular room, nothing special except for their bags, electric lights, his dress coat hung over the back of a chair.

His face brightened. "Do you play cards?"

She nodded. "Whist is fun."

"Well, we can start with that," Cole agreed, and pulled out a chair for her. It was the chair that already wore his coat. Laurel, pleasantly dizzy now, sank into it. She liked the feel of his coat behind her. It smelled nice, like him. Collier pushed the chair in with her on it. He was very good at that sort of thing.

"It's early. I'll go down to the bar and get us a deck."

"Take me!" She sounded like Elise. "I've never seen it. It's supposed to be very impressive. For a bar."

Collier frowned, though his eyes sparkled like champagne. "I am not taking my wife into a saloon!"

She scowled at him.

"Especially not tipsy. Every temperance lady in the state would be beating down this door by morning, with good cause."

"And Papa," she guessed with a sad sigh.

"We do have certain appearances to uphold," he reminded her, sounding as prim as Audra for a moment, and she nodded.

"Mustn't ruin our appearances," she agreed. "Goodness knows how important the way things look is."

"Are you quite all right?" He cocked his head to look more closely at her. "Other than being tipsy?"

She nodded.

"Just in case." He took the champagne bottle with him. "I'll be right back with playing cards."

She wondered if he would kiss her good-bye. Their being married and all. But instead he went to the door. "Right back."

She nodded. With one last look he left—with the champagne.

There was still some left in the goblets. If she were home, maybe she wouldn't like this floating, spinning, so-very-relaxed feeling. If something went wrong with the horses, or a wildfire lit, or a bear attacked, she would be in a bad place, floating and spinning. But stuck here at the inn for the whole evening . . . the whole night . . .

She needn't worry about anybody needing her, even herself.

Once she'd emptied her and Collier's goblets she stood and wove her way to the gabled window to look out at the quiet blanket of snow. Sheridan's street lamps glowed in the darkening evening, only a mile or so south of the inn. The mountains loomed to the west. In town, her family was likely in the living room, maybe listening to Audra play piano

169

or Victoria read out of the paper. She wondered what Uncle Benj and Lady Cooper did of an evening.

Then she wondered if they thought of her; would they think she and Collier were . . . becoming one?

Body and soul, Mariah said. She'd made it sound nice. In fact—Laurel went to the stretch of wall that hid the Murphy bed and, grasping the brass-rail handle, pulled it down just a few inches to peek at its neat muslin coverlet. How many married couples had been in this room, and done . . . that?

It was like a whole new part of the world that she'd never really considered before.

When she heard Collier's step outside the door, she let the bed close again and leaned against the wall, innocent as she could be. *Babies*, she reminded herself firmly, thinking again of Mariah and Stuart. And then, *England*.

Babies were one mistake she did not intend to make, no matter the fun of floating and spinning.

Collier had brought the champagne bottle back with him, as well as the cards. "I trust nobody got the wrong idea," he admitted, his smile quirking one dimple. "It is early yet."

She nodded and came back to the table to watch him open the deck. The cards looked brand-new. He pulled out her chair for her again, then sat and shuffled the deck with surprisingly deft hands. "Whist it is," he said, but his eyes were dancing.

Then he smiled more devilishly. "What shall we play for?"

Get Laurel Garrison—rather, Laurel Pembroke—tipsy, and she became a lot more fun to be around. It wasn't long before Collier had set about corrupting her at cards, too.

Whist would have amused them for only a short time.

"They're all red," she insisted, showing him her cards.

He tipped the hand back at her, barely looking at it. "But some are hearts, and some are diamonds. It's a flush only if you have all five of one or the other."

She scowled, as if she suspected him of cheating her out of an anecdote—the only thing he'd talked her into wagering.

A terrible card player, she had already told him about her sister's marriage to MacCallum, the time she saw a grizzly, and the cattle drives she'd once ridden on as a small child.

Collier had no intention of cheating. At least, not to win.

She had a cute scowl. "How do I know you aren't simply changing the rules as is convenient to you?" she demanded.

"You cannot win with all one color. My word as a gentleman."

She looked none too convinced—and, he thought, not just because they'd both had far too much champagne.

"Oh, ask your uncle Benj, you silly get," he muttered, annoyed by her distrust. *She* was the one immediately benefiting from this arrangement of theirs, after all. He'd arranged for ten head of cattle to be transferred into her name, and tomorrow they would move into her "claim cabin." *He*, however, might need to spend months, even a year pretending to be respectably married before he reaped any true benefits.

Although he would enjoy sending on to England the wedding portrait they had taken before coming out to the inn.

"What's a get?" demanded Laurel.

He scowled. How terribly déclassé of her. "Where did you hear that word?" He'd had quite a bit of champagne himself.

She laughed a gaspy, uneven laugh. "You just said it, you . . . you get!"

Oh. Now he laughed, too. "It's an insult. Like calling someone a bastard. *Not* something one says in polite company."

"Oh." She upended the champagne bottle, frowning when the very last splashed out. "Am I not polite company?"

By the standards to which he'd been raised, not really. Especially not sitting alone in a hotel room with him, pickled. But for Wyoming, she was perfectly acceptable.

And they were married.

"I sound lower-class when I drink," he explained. "Because I generally go to lower-class places when I do."

"Like where?" She sounded fascinated.

Collier had already loosened his cravat; now he unbuttoned the top two buttons of his shirt. For a moment he

171

looked at his cards—one pair of fives. He couldn't remember who'd gone last, anyway. So much for poker.

Putting down the cards, he pushed back from the table, stood unsteadily, then went to the wall and, with a firm pull, drew down the bed. Rolling onto it felt *much* better.

Lower-class places, eh?

"Taverns, mostly," he clarified, staring woozily at the ceiling. "When I was at school we would sneak out to this horrid little place called the Boiled Hog, and we would spend our allowances on terrible ale, god-awful stuff really, just to be refractory. Some of my friends paid for female companionship as well, but I never got so drunk as to take that risk. Not at the Boiled Hog, thank you. And a good thing. Percy got the pox from one redhead there." He frowned. "A shame, really."

"Smallpox?" asked Laurel, and he turned his head on the bedspread to see if she really didn't know.

She really didn't.

"It's a sickness one gets by bedding someone who is already diseased," he explained. "Molls are particularly prone to it."

"Molls?"

He considered all the many euphemisms they could use— *fallen frails, soiled doves*—then just went with the plainer word she'd once used herself. "Whores."

Laurel considered that, seeming uncomfortable. Well, if she did not want to know, she ought not have asked. His gentlemanly side protested, true. But he could usually silence his gentlemanly side with enough alcohol.

He'd agreed to partner her, not parent her.

"You know quite a bit about . . . iniquity, don't you?" she mused. "For a high-class British gentleman."

What she did not understand about high-class British gentlemen loomed so powerfully that Collier laughed. Loudly. "A fellow needs a few hobbies," he defended.

She laughed too, then leaned over the table, scattering cards. "So you were sent away to school?"

"Mmhm," he agreed, remarkably sleepy all of a sudden.

"Weren't you terribly lonely?"

He'd missed his mother at first, and his siblings, and their nurse. But not his father the viscount. Being ignored hurt far less from a distance. "Not terribly. This is worse."

"This?"

"America," he clarified. "At least at school people spoke the same language as I. I knew that, in case of an emergency, I could send for someone. Here . . ."

"We speak the same language here," she protested.

He grinned. "Not really, no."

"Oh." She thought about it. "I guess it must be lonely at that, being sent away from your own country."

"At least I have a wife now," he teased, unwilling to wallow in self-pity for once.

"Just don't get used to it," she teased back.

"Nor you," he agreed.

"If we had more champagne, we could toast to our plans again." She sighed, clearly disappointed.

"Since we've not, shall we call it a night?" He was sleepy.

"Where are you going to sleep?" Her question surprised him.

"Perhaps the bed?" He winked conspiratorially. "That's what I should do in England. You won't make me homesick, will you?"

"Oh." But her expression did not admit agreement.

"Oh?"

"I . . . it just seems rather rude, is all. But I can sleep on the floor. I'm tough." She said this last with some pride.

"On the floor? Hardly!" He hoped she wouldn't require he actually sit up to argue this. "It is a very large bed."

"You really mean for *both* of us . . ."

There she went, thinking he meant to get into her bloomers again. Not that he would mind. He'd rather come to like her sun-warmed edges, and she did clean up quite nicely.

Seeing her in that wedding gown today, he'd had a hard time reminding himself that it was all a charade.

173

"I promise to keep my pants on," he told her. But from her expression, she suspected even that. *Bloody hell.* With great self-discipline, Collier sat up. "Lorelei," he said.

"Stop calling me that."

"We are married. Even if we do not consummate it, we will spend time alone. We will have to learn to trust each other."

Still she hesitated. Likely she'd been warned men were after only one thing. Not completely wrong, as far as warnings went. But he was no stranger, out to ruin her.

Not that he doubted he could seduce her, if he tried. If he really wanted to. But really. He *had* promised.

Being drunk, he wondered how important his promise was. He had a package of "French letters"—what the box called crepe rubber condoms. He would not sire what could yet be the future heir of Brambourne. Certainly not in godforsaken Wyoming.

Then something else occurred to him: he had promised to respect her virtue numerous times. *She* had not.

"Or perhaps it's not that you distrust me," he guessed aloud, delighted by the thought. "Perhaps Laurel Garrison . . . Pembroke . . . does not trust *herself!*"

"Don't be a . . . a get," she said.

"That's it, eh? You fear that if you lie down in the same bed with me, you won't be able to keep your hands to yourself."

"Cole!"

He nodded wisely. "It's understandable, really."

Humor lit her eyes, despite her exasperation. "You may be pretty, Mr. Pembroke, but you're not so irresistible as that!"

Pretty? In fact, he challenged it. "Pretty?"

She flushed, but did not recant. "As if you didn't know."

"Girls are pretty," he protested. "Gardens can be pretty. Mediocre sunsets, a full moon, flowery china service." He flung out one arm, to encompass all the fragile, effeminate things that the word might describe, and as he began to fall forward anyway, he went ahead and stood. "Men are not pretty."

She did not say, *Well, you are.* Her scowl said it for her.

He went to the table, planted a hand on either side of her, and suggested, "I'm . . . handsome."

Arching her back to better see him, she shook her head. "Beautiful, maybe." Then she blushed. But she did not look away.

He leaned so close his nose almost touched hers. *"You,"* he admitted, "are pretty."

Her eyes widened, as if she'd not expected a compliment. Well, she *was* pretty . . . in a wild, Wyoming way. When her lips parted slightly, more as if to taste the air between them than in invitation, Collier considered proving that.

"But I did promise," he told her now, and turned stoically back to the bed. He enjoyed falling back onto it. *Good bed.*

She simply sat and scowled at him. Her eyes were beginning to droop. She was tired too.

The part of him that was drunk insisted that this was her problem. But the rest of him remembered the vows he'd just taken. *"Please* come to bed," he said, suddenly wondering how many other bridegrooms made the same plea on their wedding night.

The thought amused him.

"You promise not to try anything untoward?"

"I doubt," he admitted, "that I am in any condition. But I shall leave my clothes on, just in case. Except perhaps for my shoes." Besides, to disrobe he would have to stand again, and he did not see that happening soon. But it could not hurt to claim an extra measure of shining British integrity.

"It's been a long day," admitted Laurel. "And I *am* tired."

He waited.

"Move over to the far side," she decided, and he groaned. More moving. But she glared, so he complied.

"You, however, may turn off the lights," informed the part of him that was drunk.

Since she had to stand anyway.

She rolled her eyes at him, stood, and wove as far as the doorway to turn off the electric switch. The room fell into darkness, broken only by faint light through the gabled window, likely the inn's lights reflecting off the snow.

He felt the bed sink as Laurel crawled onto her side. "If you forget our bargain, I will kick you," she announced.

"You could just say, 'Get off of me,' " he pleaded wearily. "I promise, that would be enough for any honest gentleman."

Even drunk. Even from his wife.

"Get off of me," she said quietly into the dark room, although he was a good foot from her. Practicing, he supposed. He wondered if she would need it. "Get off of me."

Then she giggled and added, "You get."

He considered the more delicious ways he could shut her up . . . but fell asleep before he could enact a single one of them.

Waking up was another matter.

Chapter Fifteen

Laurel woke deliciously, and on top of Collier.

She'd pillowed her face into his neck. When she breathed, golden hair tickled her nose. Wrinkling it in protest somehow brushed her lips across his collar. His jaw scratched her cheek. For the first time since they'd met, Collier had stubble.

He jerked slightly beneath her, as if she'd tickled him. His arms held her firmly against his broad chest, and one of his legs wrapped around her, shoe and all, heavy and confining but wonderfully warm and hard. And as far as hardness went, well . . .

She was starting to notice something uncomfortably hard against her thigh, not quite in the right place to be his hipbone. But she squirmed a little to shift off, because it was sort of jabbing at her. When she did that, Collier groaned. The sound rumbled through his body, and that felt nice, too.

"Laurel." His voice sounded rough from a night's disuse. When he spoke, his breath tickled her neck. "Good morning."

The words sounded as if he was smiling.

It occurred to her that, delicious as it felt to wake up

wrapped around Collier Pembroke, this was what they had agreed not to do. Well, part of it. "Did you do this?"

And yet she could not quite force herself to pull away from him yet. He felt better than a quilt . . . except for the hard part. When she shifted again, he grunted. "Did I— *Ah!* Mmm. Did I do what?"

"You were supposed to stay on your side of the bed."

Now he took a deep, waking-up breath, which lifted her slightly. When he sighed it back out, she sank along with his chest. "And I believe I did just that."

She looked at the shadowy room, and he was correct. *She* had moved onto *his* side. "Oh," she said, in a small voice.

"I apologize, however, for not immediately putting you back in your place. Thus." And he rolled so that she found herself lying on her back—on her side of the bed—with him on top of her.

When finally she realized that what she was feeling was not his hip, she felt very warm. *"Oh!"*

"But if I had, I may have felt the need to do this," Collier whispered down at her, and his beautiful face came closer, and then his lips touched hers, tentative, beseeching.

And she liked that very much, despite how hot she felt.

"And if you did not protest," he continued, the weight of him pressing her into the feather mattress, "I might have been tempted to do this." He kissed down the front of her throat, the morning roughness of his cheek chasing his soft, full lips.

He even looked beautiful waking up, she thought, weaving a pleased hand into his thick, golden hair.

"But, of course, I would realize how uncomfortable you must be," Collier whispered, "having slept in your street clothes. So it would only be gentlemanly of me to do this."

And, to her pleasured amazement, he began to release the buttons down the front of her dress. She ought to protest. Call him a get, or kick him. Instead she closed her eyes and savored the feel of a man's hand—Collier's—working down to her belly button, her release from her gown's bodice. She felt even hotter now, especially where Collier hadn't reached yet.

Her stomach cramped in a surprisingly nice way.

She felt very hot, for someone whose clothes were being *opened*. The steam-heating at the inn must be awfully efficient.

"And, then, lady permitting," continued Collier, his rich voice caressing her even as his hands did, "I would do this." He straddled her, one solid thigh by each hip, the hardness in his pants pressing urgently in the middle. He cradled her face, then drew his hands down to her collar and off her shoulders, drawing her bodice with them, opening the front more fully to his view.

Laurel was having a very hard time catching her breath in this heat, but she felt glad Collier was sliding her bare arms out of each sleeve for her, so she wouldn't be trapped by them.

He leaned down to kiss her jaw, up to her ear, where his breath sent little hot shimmers of happiness shuddering down her. "Would you like to know what I might have done next?"

She turned her head to kiss his neck.

His sigh purred his approval, but still he waited for her permission. "I mustn't overstep my place."

"Yes, please," she whispered back, sacrificing air for a continued demonstration.

"I believe," he decided, "that I would finish this part." Levering himself back off of her—all but where he straddled her—he began to unlace her camisole.

She watched his hands drawing the ribbons from eyelets, then lifted her gaze to his face. He had such thick, dark lashes, what with his eyes half-closed like that. The movement of his chest showed that he was breathing more deeply than she'd guessed, especially since she still felt faint from *lack* of air.

"And then . . ." As with the bodice, he parted the camisole by gliding both hands down and outward, drawing them right over the curves of her now naked breasts. Laurel's breasts responded as eagerly as she did. If she could only breathe!

"Oh, Lord." Collier leaned down to kiss one breast, then

the other. Laurel thought she might melt—if she did not faint first. "Oh, Laurel, I was mistaken." He sat back, gazing full on. "You are not merely pretty. You are absolutely beautiful."

She had never thought anybody would say something like that to her, much less someone so beautiful himself. And yet . . .

Flushing hotter than ever, Laurel felt her breath jam in her throat, and panic overrode the delight of Collier's lovemaking. She thrashed beneath him, trying to get free of his legs, and to his credit he rose quickly onto his knees. "Lorelei?"

But she was lunging over the side of the bed to throw up.

That, Collier would later decide, had still been a high point to their first day of married life.

Guilty of allowing her to drink to excess, he did manage to assist. He'd been around any number of drunks. He dampened a towel to clean her face and let her breathe its coolness. Opening the window to let in some icy fresh air helped as well.

Both of them.

Once he felt fully recovered, Collier slipped downstairs to fetch wine from the empty saloon. Hair of the dog, as it were. After petting and fussing over her, where she lay huddled, it even occurred to him to retie her camisole. This was not a proper time to be admiring her womanly endowments, and without them covered, he did not have that kind of self-control!

Laurel blushed again when she realized what he was doing, and he kissed her cheek. "Later," he promised against her temple.

She shook her head vehemently. "Not later! We have a deal!"

Her protest felt icier than the fresh air. "But earlier . . ."

"You ambushed me earlier!"

Collier could argue that it was he who had awoken with her on top of him, that he had given her any number of chances to stop him. But since he was no longer drunk, he found himself being a gentleman again. She was stopping him *now*.

"My apologies." He could bring up the topic—and explain French letters—at a better time. "For my lapse in control."

"Well." She tugged the towel off her face. "I lapsed too."

She did at least attempt fairness, though grudgingly.

Luckily for appearances, Laurel had initially woken quite early. She eventually recovered enough for them to complete their morning itinerary, going to the Coopers' residence to collect Collier's most necessary luggage and his thorough-bred.

By then Laurel was no longer ill, merely cross.

"We'll need to borrow packhorses," she decided, seeing what Collier considered necessary. "We can't get a wagon that far."

No access by wagon? "Packhorses?" he repeated.

"Packhorses," she confirmed. "Or mules."

That took some doing as well. During much of it, Benjamin Cooper kept glaring at Collier, either because he thought Collier had deflowered his favorite "niece," or because he suspected Collier was at fault for her bad mood—or both. By the time they left, Collier felt glad to escape town even for the snowy foothills, both he and Laurel leading a mule. He rode his thoroughbred mare, Foolish Pride, which Alexandra had persuaded him to accept as a wedding gift. Laurel, of course, rode her shaggy, surefooted little mustang. And each mule was loaded high with only some of the clothing and mementos Collier had brought on his exile from England.

The ride to Laurel's cabin was not completely unfamiliar—he had gone as high as the water hole. But with landscape evened out by snow, it seemed like wholly new territory, treacherous and slippery. They had to dismount and lead their horses carefully through a gulch, over knee-high in snow, or to edge around rocky spots. Collier could not remember feeling this cold since a hunting trip he'd once taken in the Scottish Highlands.

But when they reached Laurel's cabin, gratitude was not

what Collier first felt. Laurel had been desperate to keep *this?*

Cabin was a misnomer, one that had led to his envisioning hunting lodges or snug farming cottages. Laurel's shack was made of cheap lumber, covered with ugly black paper, and if it was even fifteen feet square, then Collier was a gypsy king.

He was supposed to live here? For *years?*

What had he done?

"You unload the mules," called Laurel through the muffler that wrapped her mouth and nose. Only her eyes showed, watching his reaction sharply. "I'll fetch some hay for the stock."

Unload the mules?

Ah. Indeed. He supposed, manual labor or not, he could not ask *her* to do it; it was his luggage. Dismounting at the corral, Collier studied the knots holding the packs onto the long-nosed, long-eared beasts. With a nod of triumph, he untied one. *Voilà!*

After hovering a moment, the tarpaulin-wrapped load began to slide off the animal's opposite side.

Collier grabbed futilely for it, but managed only to grasp an edge of the tarp, helping unwrap the load as it scattered into the snow. Startled, the mule let out an ungodly screech and bucked around the corral, returning twice to kick one particular offensive satchel.

Collier decided right there that he hated mules—and that they should hire help.

Laurel managed not to laugh. She helped him gather the loosest items to carry into the shack. But the view inside hardly improved Collier's spirits. When Laurel said, "Best finish with the stock," he went with her, if only to escape.

But each time he carried another load of luggage in, the place just looked worse. By the time the animals were fed and watered, and Collier—with Laurel's help—had carried everything in, he knew he was not imagining the squalor of this place.

What, in God's name, had he done? This was his punishment for pretending marriage . . . and for not managing to see the place before taking vows. Clearly he had committed weightier sins than he would have imagined.

"It will warm up some, once I get the stove going," Laurel assured him, drawing her muffler off her face and setting about starting a fire in what he assumed was the stove. He'd seen her mother's stove, due to the Garrisons penchant for gathering in their kitchen. One could fit eight of these into it.

Slowly he pushed his own wrappings off his face. His breath misted as he looked around. *Good Lord.*

She had an uneven table with an oil lamp and, in the corner, a small bed whose log posts still wore their bark. When he looked closer, he saw that the mattress lay across a system of ropes. Even the small size of the bed did not hearten him. Solving the issue of marital relations with Laurel might at least ease some of the . . . well, provide a silver lining to . . .

Then he decided that this was too bad for even the best of sport to redress.

Other than the lopsided table and the bed, he saw no furniture. No chairs, only wooden boxes and nail kegs. No wardrobe, only pegs on the wall. Rather than sit on a box, he sank weakly onto the quilt-covered bed, wincing when he heard the mattress crunch beneath him. *Hay. The girl sleeps on hay.*

Now he was the one who felt like throwing up.

"Well, this is it," said Laurel cheerfully from the stove. Her mood had improved in proportion to how high they rode. "I—I know it may not seem like much, right off."

Gentlemen never said, *Lord, what a hellhole* about someone's home, no matter how meager. Gentlemen found something, *anything*, to compliment.

Laurel looked at him, then turned back to the fire she was building. "We can fix it up some," she added. "Eventually. Once we begin to turn a profit."

Collier searched the four walls around him with growing desperation. *Something!*

Good Lord—the floor is dirt.

"It's weather-tight." Laurel's voice rose slightly. This was *why* gentlemen found something to compliment, so as not to make people feel the way she was clearly starting to feel.

Anything!

"There's an outhouse, out back." She dropped a stick of firewood, then picked it up again. "If you . . . that is . . ."

An outhouse. "Did you build that yourself?"

Laurel nodded, then raised her chin with pride. *Ah*. He had married a woman who could construct an outdoor lavatory . . . when the whole country looked like a lavatory from here.

Collier swallowed back his growing disappointment. With one heavily gloved hand, he tested the mattress again. Still hay.

"How very . . . capable of you."

"I added that second window, too," she said quickly, pointing. "And I reshingled the roof. The squirrels had gotten into it something awful. Vic and I filled the chinks at the bottom of the walls with rocks and sealed them with daub. I've only seen one snake inside since we finished."

Collier stood again, no longer trusting the mattress.

Laurel's eyes narrowed as if he'd insulted this place. He had not. He *wanted* to. This was not the sort of place where either of them should live, and he wanted to lash out at its ugliness. But he did not, out of respect for her. But all she said was, "Best take off your coat. Otherwise it won't warm you if you have to go back out."

Collier did not plan to go back out—if he did, he might never turn around! But he supposed he had an outhouse to tour, for later. He removed his gloves and his chesterfield overcoat. It looked as unsuited for the peg where he hung it as he felt.

Lord, but it was cold!

"Well," he said. "Perhaps I'll unpack, then." Even if he had no idea where to put most of what he'd brought. He was stuck here, after all. He would not likely be welcome at the Coopers' residence, should he flee . . . and he had nowhere else to go.

He wondered darkly if Laurel kept any "medicine."

"We can build shelves," she assured him—and he felt himself relax into the relief of a marvelous idea.

"Better yet, I shall buy us a cupboard," he said. "Or an armoire. And a proper bed."

"Oh, we don't need any of that."

"I insist," said Collier.

"You would do better to put your money in savings, in case an emergency comes up."

"No," repeated Collier fervently. "I *really do insist*."

She scowled at him, and then at her cabin. "I suppose we could use chairs," she conceded slowly. "But the rest . . ."

"You've noted yourself how many clothes I own. It would be hoggish of me to take all your lovely pegs. Assuming we can get it here without a wagon, a cupboard is simply essential."

"But not a bed," she said.

"Absolutely a bed."

"I *like* my bed."

"You can't mean that." Collier could have bitten his tongue when that slipped out.

"Well, I *do*, Mr. British Nobleman, Looking-Down-Your-Nose Pembroke!" She planted her hands on her hips. "My bed smells like the mountain. Not to mention that I built it myself. But maybe you wouldn't understand that, because I guess there isn't a single thing you've done by yourself in your whole life."

"Well, *that* is uncalled for." And untrue. Just because he did not create things with his hands did not mean he did not have accomplishments!

"Maybe you should get yourself that bed, though," continued Laurel, working herself into a temper. "Otherwise we'll just have to take turns in mine, because I'm sure as shooting not going to risk sleeping in it with you."

Oh, bloody hell! "Are you quite through?"

She frowned down at the dirt floor. "I don't know."

"I am doing my very best not to insult your . . . home."

Her expression argued that his very best had not been much.

"I will admit it is a shock to me. Did you think it would not be?"

"I *like* it," she insisted. Proudly.

Collier looked around the shack again, then decided perhaps he should stop doing that. It never got better, even trying to see it through her eyes. "Just because it . . . surprised me," he managed, "does not mean that I shall not make do. Especially with extra furniture, perhaps a new stove."

"I like my stove."

"It is more like a stovelet," he noted.

"Well, I bought it on my own, and I *like* it."

He felt bloody cold for October. If they were to have separate beds, perhaps they could have separate stoves.

Unsure what else to do, he began to put his boxes and satchels in some rough order, deciding what he could take out and what would stay packed. One of the first things he dug out was a thick sweater, which he put on. He made sure he knew where to find his books, as he would likely be doing a great deal of reading up here. And as for his Union Jack—

"What's that?" asked Laurel, as he unfolded the banner of dark blue crossed with red and white.

"It's the flag of Britain. It combines the crosses of Saint George, for England; Saint Andrew, for Scotland; and Saint Patrick, for Ireland." And it was beautiful.

"Why do you have it?"

That seemed unusually thick of her. "Because I am British."

"But . . . you weren't planning to fly it, were you?"

The idea appealed tremendously. This little shack might be a hovel for now, but at the very least, he could proclaim his presence by flying the flag of his birth.

Laurel looked ill at the very thought.

Unwilling to risk one more argument today, Collier silently and reverently folded the flag and put it back in its protective wooden box. This was a battle he would choose for another day—among what he feared was a rising mass of battles he had never expected.

Laurel wasn't sure whether to feel angry at Collier or sorry for him. He looked so rueful, going through his belongings as if they were all he had left in the world. They weren't! He was half owner of this cabin now—a cabin she felt sure would prove its worth to him as the winter continued and they remained snug and tight. He owned ten heifers, earmarked and out on the range, that with any luck would produce calves come spring.

He had her.

But of course, that part of the marriage was just pretend.

After making sure the cabin was warming up, she put her coat and wrappings back on to look around her claim, to see if everything had weathered the storm well enough. She did not invite Collier to come along, and he did not suggest it. She liked doing it herself. She dug down through the snow to harvest some frozen carrots. Then she spent some time leaning on the top pole of the corral, watching the two horses—little shaggy Snapper and Collier's fine thoroughbred mare—and the borrowed mules.

When she went in, Collier was still sorting his belongings.

"Whatever is this?" he asked, holding up a cigar box with what looked like two cigar butts stuck inside it.

Laurel wished he did not sound so . . . fastidious . . . when he said that. "It's our wedding present from Elise. Two cocoons."

"Cocoons."

"Mmm-hm. She caught some caterpillars, and fed them until they made themselves cocoons. In the spring they'll be tiger moths. We should put them someplace dark and dry, but not very warm. Maybe the woodshed."

Collier slid the box across the table from him.

"She's only six," defended Laurel.

"A candy dish would likely be out of her range," Collier agreed, with a quirk of his lips.

187

"I think it's a wonderful gift!"

So much for the hint of a smile. "Is there anything I can say or do today that would not insult you?"

She hadn't been that touchy, had she? If so, she guessed she could blame it on how sick she'd felt this morning, or perhaps on how . . . Well, what he'd done to her, as they woke up.

It hadn't bothered her at the time, of course. It had felt *good*—and exciting, like the best possible dare. But as much as she liked him talking to her like that, touching her like that . . .

Well, she felt all the more rankled at having to stop. And of course they *had* had to stop. Yet . . .

Being sick the morning after her wedding embarrassed her. But she felt even more embarrassed by how badly she'd wanted—still wanted—to do what she and Collier had agreed not to.

Maybe *that* was what riled her. If men's urges were even more powerful than women's, then she supposed she should have more sympathy for her husband. So she sighed, letting as much animosity as possible vanish on that long release of breath. "I'm not certain. I seem to be in the mood to be insulted."

Collier—beautiful even in the shadows of the late-afternoon cabin—managed a wan smile. Honesty, at least, they could try.

But before she could learn where that honesty could take them, Laurel heard Collier's thoroughbred neigh. Loudly.

Was someone coming? She did not know the mare well enough to recognize whether she was frightened or merely interested, but Laurel went to the window to check the corral, just to be sure.

The other horses seemed disturbed, too—milling, jumpy, looking continuously toward the back of the cabin.

A bear, she guessed, going cold. Maybe a mountain lion.

"Best get your coat." She went to the door for hers.

"What's wrong?"

"I don't know yet." She made sure, after wrapping up, not to put on her gloves. It was harder to use a rifle with gloved hands. And she was taking her rifle.

They stepped outside in time to hear a different horse's bugle, not from the corral—familiar despite the fact that she'd never heard a wild horse so close before. They weren't facing a grizzly. "Oh!"

"Oh *what?*" Collier had a rifle too—she'd not realized he'd brought something so useful. "What is wrong with the horses?"

Laurel stood frozen, not doing anything she should. She knew she was failing him. And yet when the wild stallion trumpeted through the clearing, she couldn't even lift her rifle.

Collier's thoroughbred bugled back, and then the mustang stallion charged into view from the woods. Laurel caught glimpses of movement, from his harem amidst the trees, but mostly she saw him, rearing up, kicking down the top rail of the corral—

He was doing what wild stallions did—stealing mares. And yet he was beautiful.

"What the hell?" asked Collier, over their horses' protests as the paint stallion cleared the lower rail into their midst. Large for a mustang, he had a long, shaggy coat, and his mane flowed brown in some places, white in others. When he stretched his neck to trumpet again, Laurel felt his power.

Any rancher worth her salt would have shot the bandit horse. She could get a twenty-five dollar reward. Worse, he was after her stock! And yet she couldn't.

Laurel dropped her rifle and ran to the corral for her lariat. She shook out the loop and swung it over her head, once, twice, praying she would not miss—and sent it neatly sailing over Snapper's head, just in case. "Whoa, boy!" she called to her panicked gelding. "Whoa! You stay here, boy. You hear me? Whoa!"

In barely a minute it was over. The stallion bullied the mare into a beautiful leap over the lower rail, then galloped back into the snowy woods, pushing the thoroughbred ahead of him with the borrowed jenny kicking after for good measure.

For a moment the ground seemed to tremble as the rest of the ghostly band of horses followed this new plunder.

The other mule, a jack, brayed his indignation after them.

"Whoa," called Laurel to her panicked gelding. She walked along the rope, burning her cold, bare palms. The wild horses hadn't paid her any never mind since she'd been here, but Snapper wasn't a mare. Laurel didn't think he would run off. But she'd had him since she turned twelve. The idea of losing him made her ill.

She could have wept in relief when he came to the fence rail to blow a distressed greeting at her. She lifted the loop from his head.

Only then did the full weight of her selfishness hit her, and Laurel turned to face Collier.

He stood there where she had left him, his rifle pointing toward the dirt, staring after his vanished thoroughbred. She considered riding after it, but that would be useless, foolish. The wild horses knew this mountain. They could get where Snapper and the mule never could, and faster.

Collier finally turned from the woods to her, and his bright eyes reflected far more at her than she wanted to see.

Betrayal. Confusion. Helplessness.

But he said none of it. He was a gentleman, after all.

Instead Collier turned and went back into their cabin.

Chapter Sixteen

This was not Collier's home.

He did what he could to make it so. Over the next weeks, he and Laurel made two more trips into town before steady snow created too many drifts and sinkholes to risk more. It was enough to pay for the jenny they'd lost and replace Collier's lost saddle horse with a gelding. And it was enough to pack in more essentials . . . even if Laurel implied they were luxuries.

They now had ladder-back chairs and lumber for shelves. A tarpaulin covered the dirt floor—except where they'd cut out a large circle around the stove—to protect new rugs. And they owned a proper feather bed . . . or Collier did. No amount of arguing or pleading convinced Laurel to try it, even alone.

But even these fundamentals of civilization hardly made the twelve-by-twelve claim shack into a home. Certainly not for a man who had once dreamed of inheriting a three-hundred-year-old Tudor manor.

A wife did not make a home, either. Not a pretend wife.

191

Yvonne Jocks

As beautiful as Laurel had looked in her bridal gown, and as glorious as waking in her arms had once been, their union was still a charade. And as one week became two, then four, he felt growing relief that neither of them had forgotten it to the point of doing anything irreversible.

At least, no less reversible than the marriage itself.

Because this *wasn't* his home.

And he would do well not to forget that.

Collier woke slowly to darkness, the wind creaking against the shack's walls, and water being poured near his head.

During his bachelor days, very little woke him until well after dawn. But this sound, he recognized. He rolled over in his soft bed and pillowed his head on his elbow, to better watch the curtain they'd hung to surround Laurel's little stove-let. When pulled, it allowed several feet of privacy—enough for a person to get dressed or wash in the warmest part of the house.

Except it hung barely a foot from Coller's bed, and Laurel tended to light a lamp on the table, also within the curtain's circle, creating an unintentional shadow-play every morning.

Collier had been waking early quite a bit.

He was proper enough to let her know he'd woken, the first time. He'd cleared his throat, even sleepily greeted her, and she'd merely gone still, then whispered, "Go back to sleep."

"Aren't you cold?" he'd asked that first time. Her silhouette, floating within arm's reach, looked cold.

"And now I'm self-conscious. Be quiet and go to sleep."

He'd obeyed one of those two injunctions, in any case.

Every morning, after stoking the fire, Laurel set their wash-tub on the floor and put water on the stove to heat, then pulled the curtain. And every morning Collier leaned slightly off his bed to sleepily watch one trim, stockinged foot vanish upward to where her silhouette unrolled it off a shapely thigh, then return bare. Then the other. He watched the hem of her nightgown slowly rise, showing naked ankles, until all he could see of it was in silhouette as Laurel lifted it over her head.

At this point, her silhouette became a work of art. Collier lay back and watched, deliciously frustrated, as she stepped into the empty tub, then dipped her washcloth into the heating water and began to clean herself, letting the tub catch the drips.

The water swished in its pot and dripped off the rag with a plunking noise into the tub. Collier could smell the pine and soap on its steam—the smell of her.

Laurel's silhouette ran the washcloth over her arms, then up and down her legs, across her belly and other places. Sometimes her elbow or hip hit the curtain, emphasizing just how close she really stood.

And Collier watched, telling himself, *we have an agreement, we have an agreement*, and aching with his desire to drag her into bed with him. Finally her silhouette would towel itself dry, step from the tub, and dress for the day. By the time she drew the curtain again, hooking it away from the stove, Collier had closed his eyes so that she would not suspect him of such ungentlemanly behavior. At least, he hoped she did not suspect. Sometimes she stood near his bed, as if watching for signs of wakefulness, for what seemed like several minutes.

Then she would wrap up and go outside, and sometimes that brief wash of cold through the door was the only thing that kept him from resorting to vulgarity for his relief. Soon Collier would either get up to wash and shave while she was out, or he would sink back into sleep, just as she'd instructed him.

But when he did, he usually dreamed of a marriage that was complete in every way . . . with neither of them sleeping on straw.

Laurel welcomed the chance to get up and out before Collier woke. Not that she particularly admired a man for sleeping in! But . . .

Clearly she could admire a man *as* he slept in.

She wouldn't have guessed herself to be such a terrible voyeur until marriage presented her with the regular temptation of Collier in his nightshirt, lying in bed, every morning. He was her husband, if a pretend one, which somehow made it more permissible to look, if not touch. Didn't it?

So most mornings she did.

He looked so very fine for mountain life, and Laurel felt guilty. When she tried to apologize for not doing more to save his mare, he'd told her not to martyr herself and replaced Foolish Pride with an ordinary, dapple-gray gelding. When she said she'd not meant to mislead him about the cabin, he insisted that the cabin was fine, though his eyes said different.

Now Collier's hair fell over his face when he slept, giving him a boyish look she rather liked; it made her fingers, which knew only too well how soft that burnished golden hair felt, itch to smooth it back. His solid jaw and the dusting of whiskers across his normally smooth cheeks reminded her of just how manly he could be, beautiful or not. His lashes fanned thick across those high cheeks—oh, what some women would give for such lashes—and his full lips parted slightly as he breathed.

She knew what those lips tasted like, too, and her longing to test those memories could also be called an itch. At such moments, standing barely a foot from him, his bed surely softer and warmer than hers, his arms even warmer than that . . .

Well, Laurel sometimes wanted to ignore their agreement of celibacy as much as she guessed Collier did. So she fled that longing, hurrying outside into the cold to do her morning chores.

Reminding herself that he wasn't outside doing them with her provided a more sour kind of deterrent. Oh, he offered to help now and then. She turned him down, same as she'd rejected his suggestion that they hire help—on a homestead! He had argued harder for the hired help than to do the work himself.

Proving Herself

No, this wasn't his world, no matter how he tried to gussy it up to look that way. He dressed fancy every day, despite that they saw only each other and she was hardly impressed by his suits. He wrote letters for eventual post and read books, while she was out feeding and watering their horses or dragging home dead branches for firewood. When he did go riding, in the woods near the cabin where the ground was more even and the snow not too heavy, it was for pleasure, and he still used that silly saddle of his. He usually took his Scottish rifle and his binoculars, and twice he brought home game. He'd even cooked it when she refused—though she'd had to show him how. But darned if only an hour after being up to his elbows in rabbit guts, Collier did not set their table with china on top of a white linen cloth and ask if she did not mean to dress for dinner.

And he would have thrown out the rabbit skins if Laurel hadn't kept them to cure for herself.

Maybe that, too, was part of the problem. Not only was Collier unsuited to her world, but Laurel couldn't forget how unsuited she was to his. All the more reason not to amend their original agreement of celibacy. He'd told her of the "French letters," both annoying and impressing her with his preparation. She also knew how to keep track of her cycles with the calendar. But though the marriage was legal, Laurel had to keep it pretend in her home. She had to know they could end it in a few years.

A baby would trap them into worlds where they did not belong. And even if there was no baby, if she grew too fond of her ornamental Englishman her heart might do the same thing.

"Hello, the camp!" called a familiar voice from outside.

Collier put down his copy of Dante's *Inferno*, eager to greet Benjamin Cooper, of all people. After only a month of marriage, he felt eager to greet practically anybody, even Laurel's father, who'd come by a week before to make sure their cabin was weather-tight . . . and to glare at him.

195

Laurel, outside already, welcomed her uncle Benj first. But that gave Collier time to put a pot of water on the stove before they came inside with a wash of late-November cold.

"Figured I'd see if you two could still be reached up here," Cooper said as he put a full flour sack on the floor.

"You shouldn't have risked it," Laurel protested. But her "uncle" interrupted her by pulling down his muffler and whistling through his teeth.

"Whoo-ee! Well, will you look at this place. Jacob told me Lord Collier here had been doin' the local merchants a good turn, lately. Howdy, son."

"Cooper," greeted Collier, shaking the man's mittened hand in honest welcome. "Let me help you with your coat."

Cooper arched an eyebrow. "Your bride has a coat on, too." But Laurel, beside him, was already shedding her wrappings.

"I have learned," said Collier, trying to keep his tone pleasant, "that my bride is a remarkably self-sufficient woman."

He sensed Laurel's searching gaze on him, but he dared not try to decipher it. Did she *want* him to take her coat? Or would that, like so many of his offers, insult her with implications of feebleness?

"That she is," agreed Cooper. "But it doesn't mean she couldn't use some pamperin'. Now let's see what you've done with this place." He turned slowly around to catalog the changes.

"It's a little crowded," said Laurel. Was that his fault?

"Some might call it snug," drawled Cooper, but paused when he noticed her bed still sitting in its corner.

"We use that one as a sofa," said Laurel quickly.

"Yes," added Collier. "It's a comfortable place to read. Good window light."

"I would be loath to think that either of you was strainin' your eyesight, trying to read mail with poor lighting." But Cooper had that same sharp look of intelligence in his gaze that had first warned Collier never to underestimate him. "Especially since I brought a load of it up with me."

Reaching into his coat, he produced a large packet of newspapers, magazines, and letters, tied with string.

"Collier subscribed to some magazines," explained Laurel. Did she think him overextravagant again? Or were cowboys not great readers, what with all the time they spent breaking broncs and branding beeves?

"Well, it looks like some of 'em are subscribing back," said Cooper. "I feared I would have to strap bits of it all over that Appaloosa of mine, to get it all through the snow, which, by the way, I do not recommend. It took more shovelin' than an educated fellow like myself or Collier here—*or* a lady—ought to face."

Collier's "Thank you" was more heartfelt than polite. To have news of the world outside this snowy wilderness meant more to him than he ever once would have guessed.

And besides, the more it snowed, the more he found himself stuck inside. With Laurel. Watching the sway of her hips as she worked. Smelling her piney scent when she passed. Picturing the shadow-play she gave him every morning.

Collier could use every distraction possible. However, since they had the even rarer treat of company, he put the mail aside for later. In fact, he placed it on Laurel's bed, to continue the charade that it was, indeed, a sofa.

"Please sit down, Uncle Benj," invited Laurel.

"We could have our tea early," Collier suggested.

"It doesn't have to just be tea," explained Laurel, but her uncle, sitting, stopped her with a broad grin.

"I am intimately acquainted with the custom, darlin'. And yes, I would indeed appreciate some coffee for my tea."

Only getting into each other's way a little, Collier and Laurel poured drinks and warmed some of their breakfast biscuits to have with precious marmalade. Cooper regaled them with news the whole time. Laurel's sister, Mrs. MacCallum, was expecting a child in the spring. After pleading to attend the local school, Alec Cooper had found acceptance more difficult than he'd expected, although, as his father proudly informed them, "The boy's making a good go of it." Victoria

197

Garrison had published another editorial, this time in favor of the eight-hour workday for miners and factory workers—and yes, they had a copy in their mail. Apparently Jacob Garrison's cowboys were now "joshing" him by checking their watches whenever he rode up, pretending that they were counting the minutes until quitting time.

Not that Collier could imagine anybody *joshing* his father-in-law—except perhaps the man's partner or wife.

Cooper looked more sympathetic when he said, "I'm sorry to report that nobody's seen mane nor tail of your mare, son."

Collier rather enjoyed the rancher's surprise—and Laurel's—when he said, "As a matter of fact, I have."

"You?" asked Laurel. But when her uncle glanced toward her, she fell silent and took a sip of coffee.

"Often I'll ride as far as the ridge, past the beaver dam," Collier explained. "I've seen the wild horses three times now."

Wrapped in extra blankets he would sit for some time, watching through his binoculars as the beautiful animals foraged through the high snow, easily a mile away. He'd noted how the pinto stallion, as well as one of the older females, kept discipline in their ranks with a system of charging, biting, and chasing the miscreants away until their behavior improved.

Even among animals, banishment made a cruel punishment.

Sometimes something startled the horses and they would gallop away, back toward the shelter of the trees, their flying manes and tails mingling with a spray of white snow.

"Foolish Pride has survived so far. She's with them."

"Well, who would have guessed," marveled Cooper.

Collier, after another sip of tea, added, "For all the good it does me. I've never gotten close enough to get a clean shot."

"You *wouldn't!*" protested Laurel.

Collier only quirked an eyebrow at her. He'd not decided just how far he would go to retrieve his mare. But, as with the topic of seduction, he would not promise never to even try.

Cooper looked from one of them to the other; then he

stood. "Well, now, I'd best not be stayin'. It's an even longer ride home, has been my experience, and the sunlight sure has been fickle of late. And I doubt anyone will get through again until we get a good, hard crust. But you know your daddy's watchin' for your stove smoke every day, don't you? If he don't see it when the day's clear, I reckon he'd reach you if he had to." He snapped his fingers. "He'd pop up here on willpower alone."

"He shouldn't. I didn't take up homesteading to put other folks in danger!"

And God forbid you be obliged to anybody, thought Collier. But now was certainly not the time for that discussion, either.

Laurel and Collier put on their coats to stand on the stoop and watch Cooper leave, perhaps their last contact with the outside world until the snow crusted over. When Collier wrapped his arms around Laurel from behind, she stiffened.

Some days, he wondered if he'd *frightened* her that morning at the inn. "Just keeping up appearances, darling," he assured her. When Cooper twisted around in his saddle for one last wave, Collier raised his hand in return. "Do smile."

Whether she did or not, he couldn't see. But he could read her feelings when she pushed back inside.

Collier followed, latching the door. "May I take your—"

"No! I can take off my own coat," she insisted.

Well, that answered that. "As you like." Shrugging off his own, Collier hung it on its peg.

Laurel began to clear the tea dishes with sharp, angry moves, still wearing her coat.

"What is wrong?" asked Collier, snatching a delicate piece out of her reach. Menial though it might be for a Pembroke to wash dishes, better *he* do it and keep them whole.

In any case, she too was a Pembroke . . . to a degree.

They really should hire help.

"Nothing is wrong," Laurel insisted, emptying the contents of her mug back into the coffeepot with a splash.

"You're clearly upset." He moved the marmalade closer to his plate. He had not finished.

"Why didn't you tell me about the horses?"

Collier blinked at her, startled by her vehemence. "You knew about them before I did." And had not bothered to warn him.

"I mean, why didn't you tell me you've been stalking them?"

"I haven't been stalking them. I've been observing them."

"With a rifle."

"Yes. With a rifle. Now please let me take your coat," offered Collier calmly, but before he could reach for her, she wrenched the damned thing off and threw it onto her bed.

"I can take off my own coat," she repeated. "Of all the many things you could do to be helpful around here, taking my coat isn't one of them."

Ah. So that was what had her out of sorts. He folded his arms, perhaps to protect himself from her anger. "If you feel I am not doing my share on your homestead, then by all means, tell me what needs doing." *That you will let me do.*

"This isn't about that! It's about making me look bad in front of Uncle Benj."

Collier had to sit down now, even if she was still standing. Since she had not just entered the room, it was technically excusable. "How could I manage so unlikely a thing?"

"By making it look like we don't talk to each other."

They *didn't* talk to each other. They exchanged courtesies—commented on meals and the weather, and occasionally made small requests of each other. But the wedding was once their shared topic. Now wed, they found that discussing anything else of import led so often to arguments—or to teasing, perhaps even more frustrating—that they'd taken to avoiding it.

Which could hardly be good.

"If you must know," admitted Collier, "I did not tell you about the horses because you said you feel responsible. I saw no reason to bring up a painful topic."

"You brought it up to Uncle Benj."

"No, *Uncle Benj* brought it up." Collier took a deep breath—this was his job, as the gentleman. "But I apologize for having contributed. I assure you, I can think of very little in this world less likely than Benjamin Cooper thinking ill of you. The man loves you more like a daughter than a niece."

Slowly Laurel sank into a second chair. She still had that stubborn lift to her jaw, but Collier suspected that somehow the situation had been defused.

"You know," she offered tentatively, "Papa has brothers back in Texas. So I have real uncles. But I've never met them."

Ah. Now this was more like it. Conversation with tea. "A shame," said Collier. Carefully—as if Laurel might leap up and begin hurling crockery—he drew his bread plate back toward him.

"We've always had Uncle Benj. Even if he's not related by blood, he might as well be, as much as he loves all of us."

"He seems particularly fond of you," Collier noted.

"Do you think?" Laurel smiled at a memory, and Collier paused in sipping his now-cool tea to savor the smile. He'd seen too few of them lately. "Maybe it's because I look like my mother. He's very fond . . . You know, I even used to try to talk like Uncle Benj. Like when he talks cowboy—'waddies' and 'purt near' and 'reckon.' That was before I knew he did it so the other men wouldn't think he was putting on airs. Anyway, Mama used to look at Papa and say, 'Jacob, I swear she's yours.' "

Laurel laughed.

Collier could not imagine such a jest going over at Brambourne. Such topics were not a source of humor in his set. Particularly not when there truly was a resemblance.

And now that he noticed, there was that. Dark brown hair. Blue eyes. Laurel looked like someone other than her mother. She looked a great deal like Benjamin Cooper.

"And?" Collier cleared his throat. "And your father?"

"Oh, you know Papa. He would just glower at her, the way he does." Thinking of happier family times seemed to have

201

soothed Laurel considerably. She even reached across the table and stole a piece off Collier's biscuit, then popped it into her mouth. "Why do you only put marmalade on it one piece at a time?"

He smiled at her brass. "Because that is how it is done."

"Mmm." She nodded knowingly. "In England."

And New York City. And Denver. But Collier did not want to argue anymore. He never had wanted that. He only wanted things to feel normal. Like home.

"Oh!" Laurel leaped to her feet and claimed the lumpy flour sack that had sat by the door during the entire visit. She hefted it onto the table. "It's heavy! Shall I open it?"

Collier spirited a piece of china to safety. "Do."

So she did, exclaiming with mixed joy and annoyance. Cookies and candies. Flour and white sugar, lest they run low. A large pat of butter, and a bottle of milk. Tinned peaches and tomatoes. Dried apples. Nuts. And another jar of marmalade for Collier. "They shouldn't have," she said more than once. "We really didn't need any of this."

Just as they did not *need* chairs. That she could not see how much finer the world was with feather beds and butter was beyond him. The same philosophy, in fact, went toward good table manners, and a gentleman taking a lady's . . .

Coat! Collier leaped out of his chair and across the room—luckily, a short trip—to snatch her coat off the mail that Cooper had brought, a gift even more precious, in his eyes, than the food. "Thank the Lord it's not snowing," he murmured, testing a newspaper with his fingers. "They're not wet."

"I guess they would have dried if they *got* wet," said Laurel. *The little barbarian.*

But before he could argue that—or decide if he even wanted to—Collier noticed familiar handwriting on a rather fat letter. He forgot all else, even what Laurel said about Thanksgiving.

The sight of a mother's handwriting could do that, even to a son full-grown and married.

Chapter Seventeen

Laurel went to the feed-store calendar and began to count. The days had already begun to blur into each other. Was this Tuesday or Wednesday? Surely Uncle Benj would not have made so harsh a journey on Thanksgiving itself! "Collier?"

No response.

Likely she'd angered him, flippantly dismissing his magazines. She regretted that, the same as she regretted so much between them. Something about him made her want to behave badly, just like around her father.

Well, not *just* like around her father.

She looked up from the calendar, ready to apologize, and saw how intently he was reading a letter—a letter with fine, feminine handwriting, on what was clearly quality paper.

Laurel's first thought was, *Lady Vivian*. The surge of dismay she felt at that—a frightened kind of cramping—surprised her more than she would ever have expected.

"Cole?" Her voice came out higher than before.

Collier looked vaguely up. "Yes?"

What day is it? That was what she'd initially wanted to

know. Instead she asked, "Who's the letter from?"

"My mother. She sends her love—I'll read you that part, once I finish." And he sat down on her bed to keep reading.

Oh! His mother? Collier had spoken very little of the woman who had allowed his father to send him away, but of course he would be hungry for news from her. Laurel went back to the gifts of food that Uncle Benj and her mother had sent up for their Thanksgiving, trying to put everything onto shelves very, very quietly, so as not to disturb Cole's reading.

Did his mother really send her love to a woman she'd never met? That was, of course, kind of Lady Brambourne. But Laurel had to wonder if the woman would welcome her so enthusiastically did she know what Laurel was really like, instead of just what she looked like in silk and lace and orange blossoms, for the wedding photograph, and what Collier may have told her.

Setting the butter and milk on the windowsill, where they would stay cold but maybe not freeze, Laurel wondered what Collier *had* told his mother . . . and if any of it was the truth.

Finally her pretend husband put the letter down. He seemed pensive. It made his jaw look even stronger.

"Is something wrong?" she ventured.

Collier blinked, then became his usual, pleasant self again. "No, nothing at all. Did you have a question for me?"

"What day of the week is it?"

"Tuesday." She'd thought he would know. Collier did not keep a journal, but he did add to his pile of letters home on a daily basis. "Is that important?"

"Thanksgiving is the day after tomorrow," she explained. "Uncle Benj brought us food for a Thanksgiving dinner."

Starting to reread the letter, Collier said nothing—as if he'd traveled far, far away from her. Well, that was what he wanted to do, wasn't it? That was his goal in their agreement.

"Do the British celebrate Thanksgiving? I mean, of course they wouldn't have the Pilgrims, and Squanto and all."

"Hmmm?" Again, Collier looked up. "Oh. Well, no, not in the same sense you Americans do. But we do observe the harvest, and give thanks in most of the churches."

You. We. They really *were* two different peoples. In the quiet that remained after Uncle Benj's departure—and their own argument—Laurel felt lonelier than ever. She went to her bed and sat down beside Collier. "May I read it?"

"Here. I'll read you the passage I mentioned." He flipped over several sheets. " 'It was naughty of you to do something as consequential as to wed without your father's or brother's blessing. The viscount is quite put out with you, as is your younger sister, who takes your secrecy as a personal affront. Was your intention—' Wait; it's a bit beyond this."

"Was your intention what?" persisted Laurel, and Collier slanted bright, amused eyes toward her.

"Inquisitive, are we?"

She liked it when he teased her like that. It helped soothe her loneliness. "Well, I *am* Victoria's sister."

"If you must know, she writes: 'If your intention was to spare us the long journey, rest assured that we are quite capable of such expeditions, were they planned with sufficient care to our schedules. I place blame firmly on you, for you wrote so enthusiastically of our new Mrs. Pembroke that you have quite convinced me of both her excellence and your mutual fondness. You've convinced Agnes as well, which may explain her resentment of your secrecy. Please give Mrs. Pembroke our love and warm welcome, and be a good husband to her. Agnes begs her new sister to write and tell her of your ranch.'

"Then she writes more about Edgar and father."

Laurel watched him pocket his letter. "Agnes thinks I'm her new sister?"

"She's always wanted a sister," agreed Collier.

"But I'm *not!*"

He frowned. "You've enough sisters already, I daresay?"

"It's not that! But if it's only a pretend marriage, then she's only a pretend sister, and she doesn't even know it. She doesn't know a thing about me—nothing real—but she's hoping for a friendship like in a Louisa May Alcott book."

"Jane Austen," suggested Collier.

"And in two years we'll just end up hurting her."

Collier considered that. "It might be three years."

Now she did kick him, though lightly.

"What the devil—"

"We should feel bad whether it's two or three or ten years. Think of something to spare Agnes's feelings."

"Pardon?"

"You came up with this solution for us."

Collier parted his lips, inhaling as if to make a comment, but wisely held his tongue. If he said anything about how poorly this had worked out . . .

Well, Laurel wasn't certain if she would kick him again or weep. Or both. They'd barely been married a month. Surely they would find some sort of balance between bickering and . . . well . . .

Getting too fond.

"I can't write her," decided Laurel.

"You must!"

"It's not fair for two people to become friends, maybe grow close, when they're only going to be ripped apart. It's mean, and I can't believe you want to do that to your baby sister!"

Collier said, "She's fifteen."

"Audra's almost fifteen, and I wouldn't wish it on her."

"You *must* write her, Laurel. You are older; it is not her place to send a letter until you've given her permission by writing first." More etiquette foolishness, she guessed. "Just take care not to invite close friendship. Keep your note distant, polite. Acknowledge her without encouraging her."

Distant. Polite. Did he know who he'd married?

"I'll make spelling mistakes." She softly bit her lip.

"If you like, I shall correct them for you."

"My handwriting isn't as pretty as your mother's."

"*Laurel!*" With an air of defeat, Collier slumped backward across the bed, propping his head on the wall behind them. "Are you being this intractable on purpose, or merely to goad me?"

206

Looking at him beside and now rather beneath her, on *her* bed, Laurel thought again how pretty a man he was—especially when he stopped being so proper. She did goad him, didn't she?

Was it to shake the propriety right out of him? If so, she was playing a dangerous game. She suspected that only Collier's propriety was keeping him from sliding in next to her one night and renegotiating their bargain with persuasions she'd so far shown little ability to resist.

In her bed. Right here. Where she sat. And he lay.

Oh, dear. "I'll go check on the horses," she decided, standing. By the time she had reached the door and put her coat back on, Collier had moved to the table again.

"I'll catch up on the news," he said just as decisively.

"Good idea," said Laurel. She put on her hat, her gloves, and her muffler, opened the door, then shut it again.

The newspaper that Collier had picked up made a noise as a gust of cold air hit it, and he looked up. "Something wrong?"

"How long ago do you think Uncle Benj left?" she asked.

"Perhaps an hour. Why?"

Laurel nodded. Going downhill would be more slippery, but he'd done the digging on the way up. So he should be halfway back to town by now, maybe more. And that was good. Very good.

"Why?" asked Collier, standing.

"It's started snowing again," she explained. "Hard."

And one good snow was all it would take to completely seal them off from town for who knew how long. Alone. Together.

Collier had thought the snowstorm on their scheduled wedding day had been a blizzard. The storm that swept down on them the day before Thanksgiving proved him mistaken.

Like a living thing it tore at the claim shack until he felt certain it would fly apart around them. Without his clock, they could not have told day from night, so thoroughly did

207

snow eclipse the sun. The wind shrieked like banshees, desperate to claw their way in—and this, with the protection of the woods!

When first Laurel began to dress to go outside, he could not believe it. "You're *mad!* One cannot see a foot out there!"

"Someone has to see to the horses," she reminded him.

"Then for pity's sake, let me." At least he, with more weight on him, would be less likely to blow away!

Laurel gave him an odd look. "*Now* you want to help?"

"I never said I would not do what must be done."

"Well, I'm the one who knows how." And she wrapped on her muffler. "They're used to me doing it, too. You saw the rope I tied between here and the shed and the corral—that'll get me there and back. It'll just take me longer than usual."

"Are you *enjoying* this?"

Those fiery blue eyes, the only part of her face now visible, widened. "Not enjoying," she protested through the scarf. "But I won't let a storm best me, if that's what you mean."

She reached for the door, but Collier caught her coated arm.

"How long ought I wait before coming to look for you? Should something happen."

She stared at him for a long moment. "You don't."

As if that should be obvious? "The hell you say!"

"Even if I got lost, it wouldn't do any good for you to do it too. Then folks would find us both frozen to death."

Collier stared at her. "You cannot be serious."

She patted his bare hand with her mittened one. "If I'm not back, don't come looking until the snow stops. Now hurry— I'm steaming up my scarf." When she unlatched the door it slammed open, as if thrown in by a giant hand. Snow burst in like blown sand against Collier's face. Laurel yelled something. When he shook his head, she slapped the door with one arm, and he nodded.

He'd not been the one who'd wanted to homestead, nor to ranch. His was not a family that fed and watered their own horses.

But closing that door against the storm, with his wife still out in it, had to be the least gentlemanly thing Collier had ever done in his life. Compared to that sense of impotence, the humility of sweeping up the grainy snow before it melted did not even signify. And then the helplessness he felt when she finally did return, safe and whole, and he could not hold her . . .

Perhaps that was when, finally, he began to give up.

Laurel refused to let him help with the horses throughout that entire first blizzard. She said she would show him what to do once the weather cleared, but no sooner. She assured him the horse shed, off the corral, was holding, and that their unseen cattle should be fine as well. Herd animals, their stock would have banded with others', wandering the range together, staying in front of the wind. The larger "outfits" would put out hay, for which the smaller outfits paid them a percentage—no longer did they count on the cattle's ability to forage through the snow.

"High as the grass got this summer, they'll do fine," insisted Laurel cheerfully, as if all the demons of hell weren't howling around them. "Especially the longhorns. The more they mix with the blooded stock, though—like Herefords and the Angus—the more helpless they seem to get."

She pronounced *Hereford* badly—only two syllables. In the face of her condemnation of lineage, Collier did not correct her. Was he as helpless in her eyes as a well-bred *Her-e-ford?*

Certainly he was no rancher. He cared little whether the cattle survived, and even felt ambivalent about the horses. If anybody should survive these storms, it should be the humans—particularly one young, dark-haired, blue-eyed human with a stubborn jaw and ladylike ears. But he imagined the scorn with which Laurel would greet such a thought, so he stayed silent.

Several days after frozen hell descended, Collier woke to an otherworldly silence and the discovery that they had, indeed, survived. But Laurel did not manage the time to teach him about feeding and watering the horses before the next blizzard arrived.

Then the next.

By then, he'd begun to reconcile himself to the fact that, although he might have careful lineage, his wife—like the longhorns—had the survival skills. Well, it *was* her ranch.

And her country. And her world.

Collier began to wonder why he'd ever thought to fight that.

Something was wrong with Collier. Laurel noticed it the first morning he didn't bother to shave.

"Do you mind terribly?" he asked when she commented. "It seems an increasing waste of effort, otherwise. Certainly we've better things to do with the water."

They melted snow for their water, slow but hardly grueling. Still, Laurel guessed it was a trial to someone who'd grown up having his baths drawn for him. So she shook her head.

"No. That's fine." It wasn't any of *her* never mind if he shaved or not. In fact, it gave him an attractive, mountain-man look, and she had to make an extra effort to keep her distance.

But he looked increasingly less like her Collier.

By Christmastime, his hair had grown down past his collar, so long that if she reached out, she thought she could draw it into a tiny golden tail. She didn't, of course, tempting though his wavy hair looked; even overly long and catching on scruffy golden whiskers, it was not hers to touch. They had a bargain.

But it seemed unlike him. He became more inclined to take a drink than he had their first month of marriage, too. He rarely took more than one a day; she didn't worry that he was turning into a drunkard. But the regularity of it unsettled her. She wished they could get into town, so she could ask advice from her mother, or even Uncle Benj. Collier would like a trip to town, she thought. There would be plays and lyceums, musicales . . . and servants.

210

But they were truly snowed in. And all they had was each other, which was clearly not enough.

The day before Christmas dawned clear and bright. "Come see!" Laurel called, after enjoying the dazzling sunlight for several minutes. Surely it would do Collier's heart good to finally escape the cabin. "It's *beautiful* out!"

"I won't see beauty," he noted, "until the lot of it melts."

He was going to hate two-thirds of the year around here, then. "Well, I'm trying for the creek to make sure any stock that gets this far can find water. I'll take fishing line, too— maybe catch some trout for Christmas dinner. Fresh meat would be good."

Collier, reading, paused before answering, "Would it?"

She smeared soot under her eyes, to protect against snow blindness, then grinned at her reflection in the mottled old mirror and added two black stripes across each cheek. "Look, Collier! I'm on the warpath!"

He cocked his head at her, then frowned—not as if he disapproved, but as if she reminded him of something long ago. Then he shrugged the moment away. "You'll take your rifle?"

"I always take my rifle," she assured him. "Fusspot."

His lips turned upward, but it was a quiet, even smile, without dimples, and she did not fully believe it.

"Come outside," she urged, wishing they'd found a better balance between them. She even went to his side and drew three lines across his forehead with her sooty fingers. "Be an Indian!"

"What does the thermometer say?"

Her shoulders sank. "Seven below."

"I believe I shall stay in, thank you." He hesitated, then added, "Unless you need my help?"

"No, I'm fine. I just thought you might . . . well, never mind." Before she'd thought about it, she kissed his whiskery cheek.

Collier raised his eyebrows. Since she had no real excuse for the gesture, she simply grinned and backed away. "Last chance. You haven't seen anything until you've seen rainbow trout in a cold-water creek."

"I shall accept my blindness," he assured her dryly.

So she went alone. It took some effort to get as far as the creek, but that was fine. Days like this reminded her of getting out of the cabin to play when she was little. She'd dressed warmly. She had the rifle, just in case the wolves they'd heard lately came down from the higher mountains and threatened her. And she really did think a good meal of trout, cooked in the last of their butter, might be just what Collier needed to lift his spirits. She would set the table with his silly linen tablecloth and china for the occasion. Perhaps she'd dress for dinner.

Just this once.

She broke the ice carefully, as she'd been taught. Falling through would be deadly in this kind of cold. The current was still running in this mountain-fed stream. Even if a body didn't die of shock, she could get swept under more ice, too. And Laurel could imagine no worse death than drowning. So she took plenty of care. Only after she'd cleared the broken ice out of the way and tested the edges for soundness did she settle in to fish.

She had to take her gloves off long enough to bait the hook with a piece of salt pork, but she doubted it would take long. She could see the trout darting past the hole in the ice, their scales reflecting the crystal water and freezing, midday sun. Barely had she tossed in the hook than one of them bit, and she pulled out a fish almost a foot long.

She whistled as best as she could through her muffler. Then she unhooked the fish, tossed it onto the ice a few feet up from her, and repeated the process. She warmed her hands under her arms and by blowing on them. It wouldn't do to lose fingers to frostbite, no matter how good the fishing was!

She caught enough fish for Christmas dinner in the first fifteen minutes, then started catching them to salt. The more trout she pulled out of the creek, the more she wished Collier had come with her. He'd proved a decent hunter; she suspected fishing counted as a gentleman's sport, too—and this kind of success couldn't help but lift a man's spirits. And it did seem his spirits that were in trouble . . . hard though it was to imagine anyone's spirit not prospering up here!

She remembered what Collier had said when she went out into the blizzard: *Are you enjoying this?* She guessed she was. Up here it didn't much matter whether you were man or woman, young or old, educated or illiterate. Even at its cruelest, the out-of-doors was the one place where she had never felt judged, or as if she were falling shy of expectations, or unsure what to do next. Maybe that was why she'd needed this homestead so much, this homestead that Collier, for all his blue blood, had won for her. Maybe that was why she loved these mountains.

Laurel had caught almost more fish than she could carry on a line—another reason Collier should have come, being taller! But she had just a smidgen of bacon left, so she figured she might as well drop her hook one last time. Her hands were fine, and her head clear. The ice was still sound, and her rifle lay within reach. She even saw a jackrabbit hop by, so she had no worries of wolves or bears. The day could hardly get better.

Then she saw the shadow moving under the ice.

It startled her something fierce at first. She screeched, the closest thing to a scream that had ever left her throat, and scrambled back an extra foot from the hole she'd broken. It looked like a monster, ready to lunge for her!

Then she recognized a stub of what had once been a branch, reaching from the water as the log rolled, and knew her monster—driftwood! Some broken hunk of tree had washed down the creek, under the ice, and hooked itself on her fishing hole.

The first thing Laurel did was laugh, the noise bouncing off the trees and into the sky. Oh, but this would make a funny story to tell Uncle Benj! Then she figured she'd best encourage that piece of tree to continue downstream, or it might complicate her ice breaking next time. She looked around, found the stick she'd used to clear broken ice, and poked at the log.

At first it stayed fast. But when she smacked at it harder, the stub of a branch that had caught on the ice's edge submerged, and the looming shadow bumped slowly past her fishing hole.

There, thought Laurel, proud of her self-sufficiency.

Then the fishing line that had slyly wrapped around her booted ankle hooked itself to the driftwood and pulled her in after it.

Chapter Eighteen

Laurel's first shock was that it had happened at all.

I was so careful! That was what she thought, even as water closed over her head.

Then the cold struck. And it did *strike,* like being thrown from a horse. Cold like Laurel had never imagined. A hurt so violent that the world seemed to stop—and she almost let it.

Then came fear, a rush of desperation as she thrashed out, grasped with mittened hands at something . . . anything . . . everything. Her arm struck hardness. Cold magnified the pain of that ten times, but she made herself clutch for whatever she'd caught with her forearm—an edge of ice, thick and sharp and slippery.

Something pulled at her leg. Her other boot scrabbled at the rocky creek bottom without purchase. By all rights she should have lost her grip and slipped under. Instead she got her arms *over* the ice cap and wedged herself, as the log had, against its edge with the push of the burning-cold current.

She scrabbled at the ice, grabbing only handfuls of snow that stuck to her wet mittens and made her all the clumsier.

Her clothes were burning too now, as the water soaked through. Worse, something—the fishing line—still yanked on her as the log pulled inexorably downstream, still trying to drag her under.

Laurel hurt too much to think; she could only *do*. Somehow she held to the icy creek edge and kicked her waterlogged, booted foot—the one not dragging at her—to lunge out. Current and line hauled greedily back. Whenever her good foot hit the rocky bottom of the creek, it slipped off its purchase.

That was when Laurel realized she might die.

"Help!" Her voice shuddered out of her, a sort of squawk into the freezing, sparkling air. Her whole body was shuddering violently, as if to rattle her soul right out of it. Now she screamed the word: "Help!"

She heard her scream echo against the peaceful gurgle of water, and the clack of her teeth. "Collier, help!"

But he would not hear her inside. She'd told him she didn't need his help. Now the cabin was too far, the woods too thick.

Laurel tried to draw her caught leg back, only to feel her other toe slip again off the submerged rocks in a grisly tug-o'-war. She was well and truly snared.

"Help!" But she heard only her own shuddering voice.

So she would free herself.

Somehow, holding on to the ice with her elbows and arms, she managed to fumble the icing glove off her right hand. She hated to plunge her burning hand into the water again, but she had to—*had* to! Her leg ached from being pulled. She reached under the ice, felt for the line that held her to the log—and felt nothing.

She tried again, more frantically, thrashing her submerged hand. Then she realized she *was* hitting something, but just wasn't feeling it. When she drew her arm out of the water, she saw where she'd cut it on the line in her senseless fumbling.

It took her a moment to recognize the cuts for what they were, because they were not bleeding.

I don't want to die. The thought racked her again, as painfully as the trembling, as painfully as the strain on her caught leg, her hip. *Not now!*

She couldn't do that to her parents.

She couldn't do that to Collier.

To raise her right hand back onto the ice, Laurel had to fling it with her shoulder, like a useless, heavy thing already dead. Only once she'd steadied herself again did she draw her left hand close enough to use her teeth to drag off that mitten.

She looked at her left hand, still alive, still pink with cold. The engagement ring looked like another piece of ice, sparkling in the sunlight that she'd so foolishly thought benign. It wasn't ice. Neither was it a diamond.

Glass.

Her cold fingers wouldn't move, no matter how she willed them. But she could clumsily move her hand, her arm. Shuddering, whimpering, Laurel bashed the back of her hand against the ice.

She'd thought she'd lost all feeling in her hand until her brittle knuckles smashed against solid ice. She screamed, wept, couldn't do it again. But the ring sparkled at her, whole and taunting, and she didn't want to die even more.

Crying now—she could feel the heat in her eyes, and wondered if the blurring of her vision was steam—she tried again. Then again.

The third time, the fake stone smashed—and a jagged piece of glass remained in the setting.

Now Laurel fumbled under the water's surface with her left hand. It helped that she didn't hurt so badly now—except her hand. Trying desperately to hold on to the ice, still catching and then losing hold with her left toe, she swung her hand blindly at where the fishing line dragged at her. She could feel nothing with it, not even the throbbing residue of the blows. The pain of a thousand knives was fading to a dull ache, and her trembling was subsiding, even if the rest of her got clumsier by the second.

She knew just how bad that was. The sparkling, sunny water, and the crystalline snow, and the pine boughs high over her . . . it all seemed suddenly, remarkably beautiful. She felt as she had on her honeymoon, dizzy and spinning.

No! With drunken, lurching motions, Laurel kept doing the only thing she'd managed to think of: she fumbled at the taut, hidden twine with what she hoped was still the back of her hand.

Stupid. She should have listened to Papa. *Stupid.* And Cole. She'd refused to need him, to need anybody, and now . . .

Would he feel guilty for having gotten her here, when she died? He shouldn't, but he would. That would be her doing, too.

I'm so sorry.

And then, with a sudden, strange stillness, the pulling stopped. Laurel's caught foot touched bottom.

She'd cut the line.

Laurel tried to take a breath, for strength. She realized her wet muffler was freezing over her mouth and nose. Still she managed to roll herself out of the creek, into the snow beside the water hole she'd broken, onto the fish she'd caught. She lay there for a moment, and she no longer hurt.

What a relief, to neither be drowning or hurting. She tried to breathe through the suffocating, stiff wool over her face, and could not. Her stiff, pale hands wouldn't obey her anymore. Only by drawing her face across the snowy ground could she drag off the muffler and draw a breath, shallow even now.

Frostbite was the least of her worries now. Her sudden, overwhelming need just to lie still and rest—that was the worst of them. It seemed so tempting to relax into the spinning, the floating, like drinking champagne.

But she'd been safe to feel that way before. Collier had been there. He wasn't here now. To be safe, she needed Cole.

Laurel used her elbows and knees to prop herself up, then

tried to stand, but either her clothing weighed too damn much or her legs had no strength left. Maybe both. She crumpled back into the snow, on her side, and wondered if her tears were starting to freeze on her face. Her lashes sounded crunchy when she blinked.

It surprised her to see that two of the fish, lying on the ice, were still faintly flopping. Maybe she hadn't been under too long yet. Maybe she had hope . . . if only Collier would come.

Now, even when Laurel tried again to call for help, she had no strength. She had to do something else. *Sleep.*

No. Not alone. Not this time.

Each movement clumsier, each a greater effort, Laurel rolled over in the snow—and stared, nose-to-stock, at her rifle.

Somehow, hands as dead as lengths of firewood, she managed to knock away the rifle's safety. It took her three tries to get a finger under the trigger guard. The first time she tried to squeeze the trigger, her finger just slipped loose again.

Maybe if she rested . . . But she knew better than that. Not alone, she thought again. If this was her last chance to sleep, it shouldn't be alone. She'd done too much alone already.

It took her five tries before she wedged a lifeless thumb past the trigger guard. She did not try lifting the rifle. It pointed at a snowbank, which would be good enough . . . unless the bullet struck a hidden rock, ricocheted, and plugged her.

The thought struck her as funny, but her laugh caught.

The rifle's report, when it fired, startled her. That hurt. It broke the peace of this beautiful, sunny, snowy afternoon . . . and the afternoon *was* so beautiful. There were worse days to die.

Why bother fighting? Collier wouldn't answer a solitary shot. He would think she was shooting some meat. He wouldn't come looking for hours yet, and by then . . .

She couldn't do that to him. Not make *him* find her here, make *him* carry her corpse back to her parents. Not when all he'd done was try to help her—more than she'd ever let him.

Drawing only shallow breaths now, as if maybe her very

lungs had frozen stiff, Laurel fumbled at her rifle with useless, frozen hands, to eject the empty shell so that she could fire again.

Collier put on his coat, gloves, hat, and muffler to go outside—more out of boredom than anything else. Laurel had asked him to come fishing out of pity; he could see that clearly enough. She'd wanted to prove that she could spend the winter here alone. Thus far, with all the assistance she'd needed from him, she was managing that just beautifully.

He went along with it. What else did he have to do? But her pity he wouldn't tolerate.

So he headed out alone. The sunshine struck him, dazzling. Instead of hiding in their shed, the horses stood in the corral, staring out into the woods, looking concerned.

Collier had to whistle several times before they came to him, and that only because he extended a hand with a sugar cube. He fed one to his own ordinary gelding, Llewellyn, and one to Laurel's Snapper. The horses seemed to enjoy the treat, and nuzzled at his hand for more. When no more was forthcoming, they turned back toward the woods, as if staring at something unseen.

Could they hear Laurel fishing? That was the direction of the creek, and she was the one who actually cared for the beasts.

Collier considered following her tracks. Lord knew he could use the walk, after so many days in that tomb of a cabin. He could ask if she needed help carrying her catch home.

Which would likely insult her again.

But he couldn't go back inside. He felt like Dante emerging from hell—from the self-imposed limbo that had swallowed him these last weeks. It would swallow him again, no doubt, when night fell. But during this bright day, he could at least go see the creek. He could walk his wife back to the cabin whether she wanted it or not. He was still that much of a gentleman.

And no matter their bedroom decisions, he was her husband.

Greenhorn or not, Collier had no difficulty following the path Laurel had blazed through the trees. Too late, he realized he'd left his rifle. Hopefully he would not meet a wolf or a grizzly, or they would be dining on Englishman today. Laurel would be very put out that he'd gotten himself eaten in her care.

Against those thoughts sounded the report of a rifle ahead of him. Collier sped his step. Having hunted before, he called out to identify himself. Mustn't get oneself shot. "Laurel!"

Nothing. That seemed odd. Had she been hunting, the rifle would have frightened her prey away far more than would their voices. And if she was fighting something more dangerous . . .

Surely, against a grizzly, she would accept assistance!

"*Laurel!*"

Collier began to hurry. When he saw the darkness of her, crumpled on the creek bank, he ran.

"Oh, Lord. Laurel! What in God's name . . ." But he could see what had happened—the hole in the ice, the fish. He could not tell if the white that crusted her clothing and hair was snow or hoarfrost—but when he fell to his knees beside her, gathered her against him, he saw ice on her lashes, and her moving lips were blue.

"Be still, dearest. I'll get you inside. Lie still now." He tore his gloves off, put them on her hard, pale hands, then unbuttoned his chesterfield. He was trying to open her own coat when he finally heard what she was trying to say.

"Here," she rasped, as if she simply didn't know to stop calling. "C-Cole. I'm here."

Perhaps limbo had been safer, because something inside Collier cracked more painfully than he could have believed.

"And I am here too," he insisted, lifting her out of the waterlogged mess of a coat she'd worn, wrapping her in his own. He pushed her hands into his shirt—they were like ice!—and

221

then stood with her and all her wet weight. Somehow he would get her back to the cabin.

Her face seemed hard and pale too, especially her nose. Her breath came so shallow that he feared it would stop. Was that not how one froze to death? Did one not just stop breathing?

The pain tore at him. Not her. Not her!

Resting between staggering steps, he took a great gasp of air, then covered her icy lips with his, where her head rested on his shoulder, and breathed into her mouth. Perhaps he could *make* her take deeper breaths. Warmer breaths.

He did that every few steps. At one point her blue eyes lifted slowly to capture his gaze.

"B-bargain," she said in a gasp. What, did she think he was trying to seduce her? And her little more than a corpse?

"Be still," he chided, and staggered on. "You little idiot."

"N-not!" When her eyes flashed at him, his heart cracked. Perhaps she would live, at that. It was certainly his Lorelei. "Ev-everything . . ." She had to catch her breath. "Right."

She'd done everything right, had she? "And where stands frontier wisdom of going out alone?" he demanded. He heard a whicker up ahead. They'd neared the cabin. They could do this!

Laurel couldn't seem to draw breath, so he breathed for her again. Her lashes drifted closed, but as he resumed walking, her lips moved. He wanted to weep at her sheer pigheadedness.

"Wait until we get inside," he insisted thickly.

Then they reached the cabin, and he managed to shoulder the door open and carry her into what felt like heavenly warmth, compared to the icy body in his arms. He knew better than to believe her safe now. Perhaps he was no mountain man, but he was well-read. She would be lucky if she did not lose body parts.

Assuming she lived. But she had to.

"You're getting out of those clothes," he instructed, laying her on the floor in front of the stove. Damn their lack of space!

If he'd not insisted on chairs, a second bed . . .

Collier closed his eyes for a moment, forcing those thoughts away for later. Laurel stared up at him, helpless but determined. She'd had something to say, hadn't she?

Her lips moved again, and he had to lean near. Luckily he had experience removing a woman's clothing without looking.

What Laurel finally managed to say made him laugh—uneven and panicky, but laughter all the same. Clearly she'd not appreciated his reference to frontier wisdom.

She called him a get.

Laurel watched Collier through a detached sort of veil, as if this were happening to someone else. He poured a cup of hot coffee, then scooped in more of their sugar than necessary, the way her mother would. Then he fed her little sips between undressing her. She could hardly feel his hand against her face, the cup's rim against her lips.

Compared to dying, the hot, sweet liquid didn't seem so bad. Except that, as it warmed her, she began to tremble again. Worse, she began to burn again, her hands and face and feet.

Collier stripped her of every stitch of clothing, which should have embarrassed her but, through the shaking and the pain, did not. He wrapped her in a quilt off her bed, which didn't seem to warm her at all, and was doing something else too. Water, she realized. He was pouring water into their washtub, as fast as he could warm it on her camp stove.

Her stovelet, he'd called it. Maybe she should have let him buy a bigger one, after all.

With the little washtub either full or warm enough, Cole lifted her from the quilt and into the water. Her arms and legs draped out the sides, and now she tried to cover herself.

"Idiot," said Collier when he noticed. He folded her arms into the warm water, under her breasts. Only then did he

223

drape a blanket over her. "My word as a gentleman: I'll not ravage you in this helpless state."

"G-g-get," she managed to grunt back at him. But her mouth still wasn't working quite right, and the pain crawled from her hands and feet up into her arms and legs, along her bones. Her eyes stung, despite her determination not to cry.

Cole fed her more sweet coffee, then scooped snow from outside and started warming more water. "I'm sorry it can't be hotter," he told her, drying her wet, melting hair with a towel.

Laurel shook so badly that she splashed water out of the tub. Collier tried holding her from behind, despite that he must be getting cold too. He kept breathing on her—on her ears, on her neck, into her hair. That did feel warm, but she trembled too violently to appreciate it. Besides, warm hurt.

Cold—*that* had been peaceful.

"What else is there?" he demanded, scooping water out of the tub in order to replace it with warmer. "*You* are the one who has lived here all your life. What else can I do?"

"N-n-nothing," she said in a gasp. *Oh, God.* Every bit of her hurt.

He gave her another sip of sugary hot coffee, so at first she didn't realize just how angry her answer made him. It was only when he put down the mug and gathered her close again that he said, very clipped, "Bugger that! I will *not* sit back and do nothing, no matter how strong you think you are. You may not have noticed, Lorelei, but you are half-dead. So I suggest you tell me—what else can I possibly do?"

She wondered what "bugger that" meant. More, she wondered at the dangerous gleam in his silvery, reflective eyes.

She didn't dare say nothing. So she said, "W-w-we wait."

As midday became afternoon, Collier remembered what Benjamin Cooper had said about the courage it took merely to wait. Never had he felt so useless . . . and for something so *very* important.

He did everything he could. The warm baths seemed to

help. At least Laurel's hands and feet and nose were turning red, instead of that corpselike white they had been. At least her breathing deepened. But her moans of pain tore at him, especially knowing that Laurel Garrison Pembroke would not allow a whimper to escape her throat unless the pain was, indeed, excruciating.

When warm baths no longer seemed to help, he dried her off—every bit of her, as thoroughly as possible. Finally he saw the nude glory of his wife . . . and he couldn't appreciate her beauty for her trembling, the clamp of pain about her mouth, the barely reined panic in her blue eyes.

She knew how bad this was, perhaps more even than did he.

When she was dry he moved her into his bed, quite certain that feathers would insulate her better than would straw. He warmed bricks on the stove, then put them—wrapped—under the covers with her. Searching his memory for anything he knew about quickening the blood, he tried adding cayenne pepper to some sweetened tea, and made her drink that.

Laurel coughed, panted, and glared at him. But she drank it.

"There must be something," he said for perhaps the hundredth time. "I can go for a doctor."

She shook her head. "Even if you made it to t-town, you wouldn't make it back."

Her speech wasn't quite so slurred as it had been.

"Cooper said that your father watches the chimney smoke. If I put something on the fire to signal an emergency—"

"No," she said. "No, Collier. Please. He might k-kill himself trying to get here. And then what could either of you do? T-take me out in the cold to get me to Sheridan?"

Live or die, it would be in this cabin. In this bed. Alone with him. And he only now began to guess what she'd come to realize.

Laurel closed her eyes and moaned.

"There must be something," he repeated again. But her eyes closed. She'd run out of suggestions.

Collier watched her shivering in his bed. Well, she needed him now, poor thing.

Unsure what else could be of help, he made sure the fire was stoked, then stripped down to his long underwear and climbed into bed with her. Her eyes flared open, their blue a stark contrast to her red nose, but he quieted her by kissing her swollen lips.

She did not kiss him back. She was in too much pain.

"I mean to warm," he explained. "Our bargain is secure."

Then he wrapped her in his arms and with one leg, stopping some of the worst of her shakes simply by weighing her down. Silly though it seemed, he took comfort from her in his arms.

After a long, stiff moment, Laurel closed her eyes, leaned into him, and let him.

Chapter Nineteen

Safe in Collier's strong arms, cuddled against the heat and hardness of him, Laurel finally stopped shaking and slept. But when she woke she was alone again—and she hurt.

Oh, but she hurt! She ached deep inside, as if dying. And when she moved her hands, they felt as sensitive against Collier's soft sheets as if she really had burned them.

She turned her head to find her husband.

"Collier?" Her voice sounded thin to her ringing ears.

Nothing. He'd lit the oil lamp on the table to combat the darkness pressing against the windows. He'd put up the wash-tub, laid out her clothes to dry. But his coat was gone. *He* was gone!

He'd left for help after all! What if he didn't survive the trek into town? He could freeze to death, as she almost had . . . worse, because he was alone in a country he'd never loved. And it would be her fault for having dragged him up here in the first place, for getting hurt. She had to find him, to stop him.

Laurel ignored the slash of pain in her hands to swing herself up and slide her legs out of the bed. Then she fell.

When her tender feet hit the floor, hard despite the padding of one of Collier's rugs, she cried out. The blow to her knees seemed a relief, and she drew her hands to her instead of stopping her fall, let her shoulder absorb the rest of the blow.

It still hurt. Never had she hurt so badly, not even when she'd broken her arm as a child. Now she lay helpless and naked on the floor between the bed and the stove, the world spinning.

Alone.

I got out of a frozen creek, she told herself desperately. *I can get back onto my feet.*

But she'd only gotten to her knees before the door opened with a gust of cold and blowing snow—icy on her over-sensitive, naked skin—and Collier strode back in. Snow dusted his coated shoulders and his armload of firewood.

"Good Lord," he muttered when he saw her. He dropped the wood into its box with a crash and hurried to her side, pulling his muffler down off his shaggy face as he dropped to his knees. "What happened? Let me help—"

But when he tried to gather her into his arms, she screamed at his icy touch. He shrank back. "*What?* What did I do?"

"You're cold," she whimpered, shivering. "And I'm naked." On the floor. In front of him. It began to matter more, the longer she lived.

"Blast. I'm sorry, dearest. You rest a moment and I'll be right with you." Collier draped a blanket over her, then stripped off his coat, muffler, gloves, and hat. After a moment's consideration, he stripped off his sweater, too, so that he wore only his boots, pants, and suspenders over his long underwear.

They'd slept together, practically nude. Laurel cringed, even under the blanket. A drop of wetness on her breast startled her, and she realized it was a tear. She was crying.

Darn it, she *never* cried! But it all hurt so badly!

"There." Collier crouched again beside her. "This may still hurt, but hopefully not as much. Ready?"

She shook her head.

"Really, the bed would be better for you."

She had to swallow hard to make the words come out. "May I please have my nightgown?"

She could not make herself look at him, so she didn't see his face, but she heard his soft curse as he straightened and went to her side of the cabin, then found her flannel night rail. If he was angry, it wasn't at her. "Here you are, dearest."

Kneeling, he put the gown over her head. When it brushed her nose, she yelped again—and he jumped with her.

"I'm sorry, Lorelei. I wish I could do better." He drew the sleeves over her hands carefully, much as her mother would slide sleeves onto a baby, using his hand to open the wrist so that tender fingers wouldn't catch. "I should have thought of this myself."

She shook her head.

"There we are. Ready?"

She nodded, and Collier caught her under the arms, then lifted her back up and onto the feather bed with what seemed like little effort. "There you are, dearest. Let's move you closer to the middle, so you'll not fall again."

She knew she wasn't his dearest—but she liked hearing him say it. She liked his being here. "I thought you'd gone," she admitted. "Just now."

He actually drew back, his bright eyes flaring. "Left you?"

"To go get help."

"I would have the manners to say good-bye first. But I'll not leave anytime soon, even should you want me to."

She remembered the snowflakes dusting his coat, saw the dampness there where it hung on its peg. "It's snowing again."

"Yes. What's this?" The covers caught on her left hand, and he winced again even as she yelped. "I'm sorry, Laurel. You've broken your ring. Quality will out, I suppose."

She shook her head. "No. It saved me."

"What?"

"Please help me sit up."

He did that, bracing her with pillows, careful not to touch her hands as he lifted and readjusted her. She liked his nearness, his arms around her, despite the hurt. She liked how surprisingly strong he seemed.

He'd stayed, and she felt safe now. "I broke the ring on purpose," she explained, her own weak voice a constant surprise. "The fishing line had me, and the glass cut me free."

"You thought of that?"

She nodded.

"In the middle of a frozen stream?"

She nodded.

"You continually amaze me." And he kissed her forehead. To her pleased surprise, *that* did not hurt. "But your hands are starting to swell, so I'd best get these rings off while I can."

"No," she protested. "Not the wedding band!"

Collier cocked his head oddly, his bright gaze searching her expression, and she flushed. She did not know why it should matter, really. But it did, deep inside where part of her was trying to die. She was supposed to *wear* her wedding band.

She liked his flashing smile, even if she didn't understand it. "We'll put it on a string around your neck," he assured her.

Remembering his dismissing the same suggestion for the engagement ring, she asked, "Won't that embarrass you?"

"I fear, my dearest Lorelei, that we shan't make it out of this damned cabin come spring without worse embarrassment than that. I shan't have you lose a finger to mere show."

Considering what it had felt like to huddle naked on the floor, she guessed "show" really was the least of their worries. So she told him where to find her mother's salve. Collier used it to grease her finger, then drew off both rings.

She had to clench her teeth to keep from screaming again.

"Tell me if I hurt you," said Collier, focusing on the rings. She said nothing, tears streaming down her cheeks, until both bands of gold slid free and he said, "There!"

Then he saw her and winced. "Good Lord. Are you all right?"

She nodded.

"The devil you are! I told you to let me know—"

"It had to be done," she reminded him, her voice shaky.

She didn't expect Collier to stand as suddenly as he did, or to pace across the room, spin, and return to her bedside.

"Laurel Pembroke, thus far I've done very little to assert my husbandly rights," he told her. For just a moment, before she realized the foolishness of such thoughts, her stomach cramped in expectation. "But I swear to God, if you do not abandon this idiotic show of strength, I may do something drastic."

Had she really feared he would say something different? "It's not idiotic."

"It is when you so clearly need help." He carefully wiped her cheeks with a handkerchief. "Do you wish to blow your nose?"

She shook her head. "It hurts too much."

With an indulgent smile, he put the handkerchief on the crate that served as a bed table. "Then I'll make soup."

She considered repeating that she wasn't being idiotic. But the more she thought about what he'd said, the more truth she saw in it. She was laid-up, plain and simple. If it weren't for Collier, she would be dead. If he weren't here to feed her, and stoke the stove, she could still die . . . even if she was the daughter of a rancher, and he was a remittance man.

"Thank you," she said, although it came out grudgingly. Could be he heard that, too, because his full lips pulled upward, slightly lopsided.

"Do not thank me," he said, "until you taste the soup."

"I did everything right," she insisted, wondering. "I was dressed right. I broke the ice so carefully. I wasn't too near the edge. It wasn't my fault I fell in."

"Did you think other people who have frozen to death, or drowned, or been attacked by bears, were merely half-witted?"

"Not half-witted, just not . . . competent."

From the stove, he gave her an odd look. "Like me?"

"No! Just . . ." But she wasn't sure what else to say, so she lay quietly and rested. Perhaps Collier had a point, damn it. He'd already been very smart. Now that she had to lie still and listen to him, why did he have to go and get even smarter?

Over the next week, Laurel couldn't do much *but* lie quietly and listen to Collier. He hadn't lied about embarrassment, either. Her hands swelled so badly, they reduced her to infantile helplessness. She couldn't feed or clothe herself. She needed his help for such privacies as getting to the chamber pot and washing herself. And he did help—no complaints and with good spirits. That was how he did the wood chopping, too; and the horse tending, the cleaning, the cooking. Laurel knew she looked horrible—a swollen, blistered wretch of a girl—but he smiled as if she were beautiful and spoke as if she were precious. Never once did he avert his eyes from the horror she had become.

It felt bad to admit it, but she hadn't thought Collier had it in him. Yet every night he climbed back into bed with her, drew her gently against him, and she knew he did. After only a week, his arms felt harder than they'd ever been—and he'd been athletic all along! His lengthening hair glowed even more golden. He became more beautiful than ever . . . because he was more than beautiful. He was competent.

Against that competence, Laurel's affection for her pretend husband deepened into something stronger, something that felt less like pretend and more like something else.

Was it love? Really?

Now?

Now that she was helpless and ugly. Now that she'd entered a false marriage, with the agreement that they would part in a few short years! *Now* she realized her weakness. She might just love this man!

Collier had strengths she'd never guessed, strengths she'd been unwilling to see past his fine clothes and British accent.

No wonder she'd felt safe with him. She was.

Only her heart was in danger.

Collier had not believed he had it in him. Had anybody told him a year previous that he should be laboring at such menial tasks, he might have shot himself.

But now that he found himself doing it, he had neither the time nor the stomach for suicide. The horses needed water, and Laurel needed a warm cabin, and everyone needed food. The chamber pots must be emptied, and the wood must be carried. So Collier called upon his British fortitude to endure until that bright, distant day when their situation would improve.

And in the meantime, something quite unexpected happened.

He began to enjoy it.

Clearly he did not enjoy standing in manure or sloshing slop onto his glove. He disliked spiders crawling onto his hand when he picked up a stick of wood for the stove, and the backache and blisters that came with wood chopping, and how his clothes smelled after a long day of such labors. He resented the ridiculous effort it took to clean their clothes in a snowbound cabin. He had no intention of doing any of it one day—one hour—one *minute* longer than he must. As soon as spring came, he would pack every scrap of clothing down to Lee's laundry himself, to avoid such a nuisance. And yet . . .

He rather liked who he became while doing those things. Chopping wood hurt, but carrying in an armload of freshly split logs seemed a minor triumph. Water buckets were heavy, but the pleasure with which the horses met his arrival, snorting a greeting and nuzzling at his coat in search of their hay, pleased him. He might not enjoy chores. But he took deep satisfaction in knowing that he could, indeed, perform them.

And he took satisfaction in caring for Laurel.

She was in clear pain. Her hands and feet swelled badly

the day of her accident. By the next day her hands and nose had erupted into a rash of small, angry blisters. Were he in England, Collier would have called a physician and retreated to the den with some brandy while someone else treated her. As it was, *he* had to rub the salve gently onto her, then follow her instructions to make what she called willow-bark tea for the pain, and attempt to keep her clean and dry. At least her injuries were no worse. A throbbing pain sometimes woke her, and she seemed more sensitive to the cold, even from a simple opened door. But she'd survived.

Nothing turned black, which she explained would mean lost fingers or a scarred, stumped nose. The blisters faded, and she soon could stand, even to use her chapped hands, if carefully.

Collier felt gratitude for every day that she could sit longer at the table, or pace another round about the inside of their cramped cabin, or help with small tasks as he cooked dinner. He thanked the Lord for things as important as her life and as trivial as her unblemished, healing face. But unlike the gratitude he would feel had he hired a physician and merely waited for the results, he felt more . . . satisfaction.

He could keep a fire going. He could keep horses. He could rewarm a half-frozen woman, and see her survive. Crude skills to have, perhaps, but important. *Human.* And he owed them to Laurel and her idiotic insistence on spending the winter in this shack.

The wind turned warm for two days in early January—Laurel called it a "Chinook." So he wrapped her up and took her out. She protested being carried even more than she did going outside, though he knew cold hurt her, but he insisted. He carried her through the slushing snow to the corral, where she could greet the horses from his arms. And when Laurel turned her face to the trees and the sun, her blue eyes half-mast against the strangely warm wind, Collier watched her face and felt more grateful than ever, because he beheld beauty.

And because she had allowed him to share it more fully

than he ever would have had she not fallen into that damned creek.

Of course, the snow did not melt completely. Barely had the Chinook begun its thaw than another snowstorm hit, tucking them back into their cabin, and they went to sleep to a lullaby of howling wind and sleet rattling against the windows.

They still slept together. He doubted Laurel needed his warmth anymore, but he was neither so crass nor so foolish as to suggest they separate any sooner than she wished!

It was during the storm that the inevitable embarrassment of such an arrangement struck.

Collier awoke with Laurel draped atop him, nuzzling his neck over the collar of his union suit, and he felt so hard against her, under his long johns, that it hurt.

At first he simply gasped. Lord, but she felt good against him, so soft and curved, so eager.

He even whispered her name, in case she wasn't asleep.

But of course she was. At his voice she stilled her slow writhing atop him. Her sigh heated his ear and made him shiver as violently as she had, back in the grips of freezing. With nothing but a little flannel and cotton separating them, he could feel the pillow of her breasts against his chest, the curve of her thigh against his erection, and he wanted her, needed her, more than he'd needed any woman in his life.

And she was asleep.

We have an agreement, we have an agreement, we have an agreement. If he could shovel manure, surely he could resist ravaging a sleeping woman still recovering from frostbite. Especially an innocent woman, his wife in name only.

Carefully Collier found her shoulders and tried to push her gently off him—and she caught her breath.

He could tell the moment she woke. She stiffened against him, so to speak, then rocked tentatively atop his own stiffness. "Collier?" she whispered.

"You," he said, lest she blame him again, "are on top."

"I guess I am." Her admission steamed past his ear and, if

235

anything, he got harder. *We have an agreement.*

"Perhaps you should . . . get off now."

"Am I hurting you?" More words. More warmth across his ear.

"Not exactly." In fact, this was the most pleasurable torture he'd experienced in months, if not years. But much more of it and he would forget his upbringing and hers.

"Oh." Leaving a hand on his chest, she slid carefully, slowly off of him, as if memorizing every plane, swell, and ridge of him as she did. The last time this happened, they'd both been fully dressed, but this time . . .

Collier clenched his teeth so as not to whimper. Well, he had said they would both suffer embarrassment before spring. This would be his turn. He meant to apologize.

But before he could even draw the breath to attempt it, she slid her hand off his chest and down his abdomen to cup him.

He drew breath—all in one great gulp. "Laurel!"

She drew her hand back, not releasing him so much as lightening her touch, and whispered, "I'm sorry. I was just curious. I've never . . . Does it hurt?"

If he said it did, she would probably remove her hand. "Not precisely."

"Oh?" She drew her fingers to the tip of him while he shuddered beside her. "Then why are you whimpering?"

He *wasn't* whimpering. Was he? "I . . ." Then she brushed her fingers across him again, and he lost the ability to talk.

"May I?"

He had no idea what she was asking, knew damned well he'd likely regret it, but heard himself pant the word "Yes."

She slipped her hand in through the flap of his underwear to feel the hot length of him directly with her palm, and now he *did* whimper. Good Lord, but this was unfair. He should stop her. Any moment now.

But it felt so good. Ladies never did such things, only paid women—and paid extra—to have someone . . .

236

Collier felt guilty for thinking of his wife and such women at the same time, but he felt so guilty about every delicious bit else, it barely signified.

"It's like a horse's," she marveled, continuing her exploration. Before he could take too much flattery from that, though, she added, "But not as big. Horses' . . . things . . . are *huge*. I wouldn't want anything that big coming near me."

Faced with either weeping or laughing, Collier choked out a voiceless laugh. That need was nothing against his urge to push Laurel back onto the bed, pull up her nightgown, and show her just how large he was.

Were it possible, he was getting larger.

"What do you call it?" she asked, sliding her fingers down to the base of him, but not quite all the way.

"Mine in particular?" he said in a gasp, eyes burning.

"What?"

He decided not to explain that particular tendency of some men. "Lorelei," he managed. "Dearest. You are not hurting me, but you are . . . teasing. Unless you've—ah—rethought our agreement, I should prefer to continue this c-conversation outside of bed."

Perhaps not at the moment would he prefer it, but soon and perhaps for days.

When she slid her hand from him, he almost wept, both from relief and disappointment. At least he could breathe again. Perhaps he should move to her little straw bed.

He heard Laurel fumbling on the crate that made their bed stand. Then her hand splayed gently onto his chest again, and again he moaned. "Laurel," he tried to warn . . . or rejoice.

It wasn't over after all.

This time she slid her hand to his shoulder, down the arm that lay opposite her, to his hand currently digging its fingers into the mattress. This meant her lying slightly atop him again. The gentle, pendulous weight of her breasts brushed across his chest as she reached his hand.

237

"Collier," she said unevenly. "I've rethought our agreement."

And he realized, as her fingers entwined with his, that she'd just put her wedding ring back on.

Chapter Twenty

Collier went very still. "You've what?"

"I've rethought our agreement. I want to . . . have marital relations. With you."

And she slid more fully on top of him, as if to insist. She even found his hardness with her thigh again, and sighed the sweetest, shyest little sigh.

Oh, Lord!

Of course, Collier knew better than simply to accept that. Likely she was speaking from some misplaced sense of gratitude, or she'd been shaken by her brush with death, or she simply felt so much better, compared to how she'd felt a week ago. . . .

Perhaps she'd forgotten their very good reasons for keeping this marriage celibate. Or possibly she was simply curious—as she should be, the way she'd questioned him, fondled him. The way her thigh was moving against him even now.

Well! Point of the matter being, any real gentleman would roll out of bed, light the lamp, make tea, and discuss the matter.

239

But drunk wasn't the only situation in which Collier tended to behave in a less-than-gentlemanly manner. He found Laurel's free hand and used his body to roll her onto her back, then kissed her until she writhed happily beneath him. "Lovely."

"Oh, good." Laurel sighed and wrapped her arms behind his neck and kissed him in return.

And Collier set about consummating their marriage.

Laurel could not remember feeling so excited. Not when Snapper was born. Not when she filed for this claim. Never.

"When do we take our clothes off?" she asked when Collier's lips detoured to her throat.

He levered himself off her just a little, as if he could see her. "Impatient, are we?"

He sounded so amused that she drew a hand from where she'd made a ponytail of his thick hair to feel across his whiskered cheek and find a half-hidden dimple. "Yes," she whispered.

Then he kissed her again, and she enjoyed that too. "You do know," he warned, "that the faster we go, the sooner we finish."

"Oh." She hadn't known that. And it didn't make sense. Why couldn't they just keep doing it for as long as they wanted to, or until they tuckered out, one or the other? "Why?"

"Trust me," he said teasingly into her ear. His whiskers tickled, and his breath made her stretch, arching her back under him.

"Yes, Collier," she whispered. "Yes. I trust you."

He stilled on top of her. "You do?"

"Mmm-hm." She stroked her palms down his back, pleased at how much of him she could feel through his underwear. He had a lovely, muscled back, but such narrow hips. And a firm little butt. When she felt that, he began to press against her with his . . . thing . . . even though he was the one who protested.

"Stop it." He caught her wrist and moved her hand off of his behind. "Dearest, I want you to concentrate for just another moment. Will you do that for me? Please?"

He kissed her, hard and deep, as if to make the offer more tempting. She could barely remember what he was asking when his lips lifted from hers, but she knew she'd do anything he asked.

"Yes. Why? Why can't we just—"

"Because you had to go and trust me."

"Well, of course I trust you. I *married* you."

"Yes. But are you quite certain you want to do this?"

Would she have said so otherwise? "Yes!"

"As you wish." And he kissed her again, rocking against her with his hardness, caressing a dexterous hand down her shoulder, onto her breast. Oh, she liked that! The only thing she didn't like was not being able to explore him as much as she had.

Except his back. She did love feeling along his flank.

"When do we take our clothes off?" she asked again, and he laughed on top of her.

"Whenever we wish," he assured her. "May I?"

Perhaps he felt her nod, because he reached down, caught the hem of her nightgown, and pulled it clear up over her head, lifting her up with one hand when he had to. He also had to swing his leg off of her, so as soon as her hands slipped free of the flannel sleeves, she sat up and said, "Now you."

He sat up too, wrapping them in a quilt, their knees framing each other's. Together they undid all the buttons down the front of his union suit. He was faster, because he knew them better in the dark. The most difficult part of pushing the underwear off his arms was how his hands kept returning to her breasts.

Oh, his hands felt good on her breasts.

Once she'd stripped him, Laurel wished they'd lit the lamp. Instead she had to use her hands to explore the wonders of the male form, which had Collier moaning again.

She liked exploring all of him—his smoothness in some

places, his light dusting of hair in others, his hard muscles, his soft touch. But his maleness fascinated her most of all.

He seemed drawn to her breasts. When he ducked his head to kiss one, suckling and laving its tip with his tongue, she moaned, so deeply did that sensation shudder through her.

He sat back immediately. "You shivered. Are you all right?"

In answer, she kissed him. The shiver had been nothing like the ones racking her for days. This shiver had been hot.

Reassured, he turned his attentions to her other breast, which caused more shudders, and freed her hands to explore other parts of him, too. "What *do* you call it?" she asked again, filling her hand with him. He might not be as huge as a horse, but certainly he seemed larger than necessary for the job at hand. "You didn't answer me."

He laughed, which she didn't understand, and kissed her again, leaning her back into the bed over the brace of his arms.

"I heard a cowboy call it a dingus," she said. "On a horse, I mean. He didn't know I'd heard him. But that's a silly name."

"Yes," he said under his breath, pushing the topic of their discussion harder against her belly. "No dignity whatsoever."

"So?"

So he told her: a Latin word, two more "vulgar" terms, as he put it, and several that just made her laugh.

"As the party with more experience in these matters," he cautioned her, "I must warn you that laughter may not be the best reaction in such a situation."

But having beautiful Collier's hands all over her—his *mouth* all over her—made it easy to laugh. "John Thomas?" she said in a gasp. He kissed her, but he laughed as he did, right into her mouth.

"Oh, and you ladies are so much more demure," he fussed pleasantly, rolling onto his back, his strong arms taking her with him. *Ah!* Now this had possibilities! It freed her hands to slide all over his chest, her legs to straddle his . . . and still released his hands to caress her breasts.

"At least we don't have silly names for parts of our body." She slipped a hand downward to see how the rest of him worked.

It seemed a very long time before Collier argued that. "You," he insisted, "are just too innocent to know such names."

Then he told her some of them—and slid his hand between her legs to demonstrate.

"Oh!" Well, she certainly didn't want to laugh. She hadn't realized that was considered a part of her body! It felt . . . felt . . .

"None of which," purred Collier, his fingers seeking impossibly deeper, "I should be telling a respectable woman."

She squirmed on his hand, urging him to do more. "Good."

"Good?"

"I n-never cared about being respectable. I—oh!—only did it for my f-family." When he slid his fingers free, she felt wet.

He laughed again, which made him rock beneath her, and she liked that, too. "Well, my dearest, bed is one place you need not worry about being respectable. At least, not with me."

And who else would she be in bed with?

For a brief instant, quick enough to feel a blinding pain, Laurel remembered that they were to be married only a few years. She tried to banish that thought, and when she couldn't manage it alone, she enlisted Collier's help.

"Can't we do it now?"

"You're not liking like this part?" And it did feel . . .

"I'm liking *this* part." And she shifted so that she straddled the hardest, hottest part of him with the wettest, achingest part of her. Oh, that could help her forget anything.

"Patience, Lorelei." Cole grasped her hips with his long, strong hands and lifted her off him, but before she could protest the betrayal—or hit him—he then settled her back in a slightly different way, shifting his hips, and she realized— *Oh, my!*—just what he'd done. His most intimate part pressed between her legs, and when she squirmed, he slid into her a little bit.

Oh, my, oh, my, oh, my! She hadn't expected to have this much say over things. She'd thought it was something *he* did to *her!* But instead, when she stiffened, everything stopped. And when she took a breath and opened her legs wider, she let herself slide more firmly onto his thick hardness. His hands still on her hips, more to guide than to control her, Collier panted, hard and voiceless, while she experimented. She marveled at how such a tight place in her body seemed to make room for him—barely—and at the tingling, trilling sensation that bubbled up her spine and down her legs from where they'd joined. Every time she thought she'd taken as much of Collier as she could, she would relax and shift her weight and, surprisingly, slide another inch downward.

Finally she did have all of him inside her. And his hands slid up to her breasts. "Yes," he whispered worshipfully.

"Oh," she whispered. "I thought it was supposed to hurt."

"Didn't it?" He sounded drunk as he drew his hands down to her hips, then up again, and leaned up to kiss her.

This time, when his tongue filled her mouth, it seemed particularly naughty—knowing how thoroughly *other* parts of him were filling her—and she met it greedily with her own. She managed only a "Nn-hnn" as a denial.

And then he began to move beneath her, and she still didn't hurt, but, oh, she certainly began to want more again. It felt vaguely like riding, but awkward, more frustrating.

"Here, dearest," coaxed Collier after a moment of that. She protested with a mew of complaint when he rolled her onto her back again and took the position of rider. But he whispered, "Only until you understand better," in her ear, and the heat of his breath and the scratch of his whiskers sent shivers though her.

Then he began to withdraw from between her legs, and she grasped his legs with her own, grasped his buttocks with her hands, and tried to stay him. Not yet; she wasn't used to it yet! "No!"

"Shhh," he said, his voice laughing, his breath still shivering across her ear. "Trust me."

And she wasn't sure she could. But then he slid back into her, filled her again, and the swift, sure sensation of it rocked gratifyingly through her. "I trust you," she said quickly.

He kissed her, and kissed her again, and again, and while he did he pushed slowly into her, drew out of her, pushed in again, over and over until they'd created a rhythm together, better than dancing, more erotic than even the deepest kisses. She strained against each thrust, hungry, aching for . . . something. Something flirting with her. Something teasing at her. Just *this* was more thrill than she'd ever known, and should be enough, so she wasn't sure what more she could want—until suddenly, like a flash flood, something even more ecstatic rushed through her.

Then she screamed out in sheer joy.

Collier muffled her with more kisses, perhaps laughing, but she barely noticed for the euphoria that shuddered through every bit of her, every finger, every toe, every strand of hair. *Yes*, she wanted to yell. *Yes, yes, yes!*

Why wouldn't Collier let her yell?

His own movements quickened; then he stiffened and groaned on top of her, poured himself into her, hot and hard, and finally lay there, trembling.

"Oh, my Lord," he murmured, and it really did sound like a prayer. "Yes, Lorelie. Yes."

Just what she'd wanted to say.

"Cole," she said in a gasp. Her body tingled all over, as if she could leap out of the bed and fly, as if she could melt right into the bed. Or right into him. "This is *wonderful!*"

He kissed her again, deeply, more tenderly than before. "I am pleased you find it so, darling."

"Why haven't we been doing this all along?"

He began to laugh again and wrapped his arms around her. He rolled onto his back so that she was on top of him again. "I apologize for being derelict in my duties," he assured her.

"Well, I hope you don't plan on being derelict anymore!" She leaned down and kissed him again, loving the feel of his lips on hers, his special taste, his special smell. She loved being naked with him, and she loved him. Whether she'd meant to or not.

"Not in the least, my dearest," he teased, petting her hair out of her face as if he could see her.

"Can we do it with the lamp lit next time?" she asked.

"We can do it any which way you like." That intrigued her.

"Is there more than one way?"

He laughed but eased her off him. She wasn't so happy about that. "You, Lorelei, are no lady."

For a moment she felt cold. He'd known she wasn't a lady—not like his Lady Vivian was. He'd known that!

"What's wrong?" he asked more quietly. He drew her into his arms, kissed her cheek, her healed nose, and she tried to relax. Why would he have meant that as an insult, when everything else had been so nice? "Are you sorry—"

"Have you done that with Vivian?" she asked.

"Ah." He cleared his throat. "I've done that with Vivian only once, the night we became secretly engaged."

Oh. Well, she shouldn't ask the question if she didn't want the answer. Yet she kept on asking. "Was *she* ladylike?"

"A gentleman never speaks of such things," he said.

She kicked him. Lightly. He answered the attack with another kiss. "You would not want to suspect that I might tell her about this, with you, would you?"

Which was completely true, damn it.

"However," he whispered, nuzzling her ear, "I *will* confess that I have never had such fun in bed with a woman in my life as I just had with you. You are marvelous. You are beautiful. You are exciting in ways I'd never guessed I'd like so very much."

She felt herself blush and guessed Lady Vivian must not have been very good after all. "That was just my first time."

"I know," he agreed, cuddling her tighter against him.

"Will I get better with practice?" she asked.

"If I survive it, I imagine you might."

She liked the sound of that, and snuggled into his chest. She didn't know what the future held—she doubted she wanted to. But for now, deciding to do this with Collier had to be the best decision she had ever made.

"Thank you," said Collier, as if reading her thoughts. "Thank you, Laurel, for being my wife like this."

She supposed that "no, thank *you*" would not be the ladylike response, so she giggled instead.

He kissed her. "Go to sleep."

"Why?"

"So that we can rest up and do this again."

Ooooh! She closed her eyes and pretended to sleep, as she used to when she was a child.

Before she knew it, she was waking in the most delicious way with Collier all over again.

Across the next day they consummated their marriage twice more—passionately, blissfully, delightfully—before Collier remembered the French letters.

The birth control they'd forgotten.

He debated telling Laurel of their mistake. *His* mistake. But it seemed unfair to worry her needlessly. Instead, after he'd returned from feeding the horses, he pulled her into his lap and said, "Now that we're getting the hang of things, perhaps we'd best discuss how to be sure nothing comes of it. In the future."

In hopes that they still had that choice.

Laurel looked confused—well, she kissed lasciviously about his ear at first, as if deliberately to taunt him into more love play, but *then* looked confused. What a beautiful young woman—and bold, and capable, and adventurous. The miracle that she had allowed him to . . . That she *wanted* him . . .

Collier kept himself from thinking of the consequences—beyond the possibility of conception, at least. He would not darken this joy with fears of a future they could not control.

Instead he asked, tentatively, "Our bargain not to have children . . . *that* still holds. Doesn't it?"

He tried to imagine living his life in Wyoming or dragging Laurel to England. Neither idea appealed.

"Oh! Of course it does." She nodded quickly, and even forgot to return to his ear. "This is just . . ."

He waited, uncertain, and she ducked her head. "For now."

From your beautiful lips to God's ear, Lorelei.

"Then we'd best start keeping that from happening," he said. "Soon. Begin as we mean to end, don't you say?"

She nodded, so far not looking panicked. That relieved him. Only one of them should be panicked at a time.

"So why don't I get out the box of French letters I told you about, and you get your calendar, and we will show each other what we know. Agreed?"

Laurel stroked his whiskers. "Show each other . . . how?"

"I doubt the calendar will be too amusing," he admitted. "But I rather hoped that the others we might demonstrate."

She bolted off his lap, quick as that, for the calendar. He made her show him before he would open the box of condoms, and could have prayed his thanks when he saw that— if her mother's system was sound—she was unlikely to have conceived this week.

Then he opened the French letters, and they both laughed at them, but then they began to kiss and laughed less, and soon they had returned to the bed together to wait out the snowstorm.

Best purchase Collier had ever made, that bed.

The following week brought a hard freeze, air so cold and fast that Laurel called it an "Alberta clipper." Collier was able to walk on the snow to go about his chores, instead of walking in it. Mostly. Occasionally he fell through.

"When you can jump up and down on it and not fall through, maybe we can go to town," said Laurel. He hesitated to take her out in the cold weather, even for such a treat as that . . . except for how quickly they were going through the French letters!

He'd never met such an adventurous woman, in or out of bed, and they did indeed celebrate their marriage, their youth, and their survival both in and out of bed. And against the wall. And over the table.

Once he gave up being proper, it seemed, Collier gave it up fully. Impropriety was so much more fun, and the bright side to the horse feeding and slop emptying!

Sometimes they lay in bed for hours, petting and exploring and loving each other with leisurely grace. Other times they chased each other, naked, about the cabin until one of them would win, pinning the other down and having his or her wicked way. Always they slept, deep and exhausted, entwined with each other as tightly as possible.

Falling asleep with Laurel, waking with her, lying with her, laughing with her, Collier sometimes thought this was all he could ask for in life.

But he knew better than to believe it just yet. Not in this insulated little world of theirs, where he could play at being a mountain man and she could work toward recovering enough to be a rancher. Sooner or later the outside world would intrude.

And they must not do anything irreversible until they knew how they would feel when that happened.

He just did not realize they might be tested so soon.

Collier awoke with a start, to Laurel punching him in the arm. "Cole. *Cole!* Someone's coming!"

"What?" He caught her offending fist, kissed it, then pillowed his head more comfortably on her bosom. He loved her bosom. He loved a great deal about her, especially sleeping.

She persisted. "Lord Collier!"

Inhaling slowly, deeply, he opened his eyes. "How would you know there's someone—"

A solid knock at the door interrupted him.

"The horses," whispered Laurel, glancing frantically at the window. "We slept late. It's midmorning!"

Considering how late it had been before they'd finished their latest, most enjoyable battle of the bed yet—she'd been named queen by time they fell asleep—this news hardly surprised him.

"I'll go ask them to wait." Then he climbed out of bed, drawing the uppermost quilt with him. Lord, but it was cold!

"It's Papa!" she guessed, eyes wide. "And we're naked!"

"Perhaps it's Cooper," he reassured her, wrapping the quilt firmly around him.

But Laurel dove fully under the remaining covers anyway before he reached the door, unlatched it, and drew it open.

Good Lord. It *was* her father.

Considering everything Collier had recently enjoyed with the man's daughter, this *was* rather awkward.

Jacob Garrison, hand still lifted to knock again, looked startled. Then he dropped his gaze to Collier's bare feet—and by the time that gaze climbed the quilt, back to Collier's unshaven face, it had narrowed to something far more dangerous.

"Our apologies," said Collier as primly as he could. Considering. "I fear we slept in. If you will allow us a moment to put ourselves in order, we will happily invite you inside."

Garrison did not agree or disagree. He just stared.

Collier began to shut the door.

Garrison stopped it with a firm hand. "How's the girl?"

Collier considered taking offense . . . until it occurred to him how poorly equipped he was—or had been—to care for Laurel, and how close she'd come to not being at all well.

"She's safe," he assured his father-in-law. "Merely hiding."

Laurel's muffled voice called, "Hi, Papa!"

Garrison did not look happy. But he shook his head, turned around, and headed for the corral.

Collier shut the door, latched it, then slid slowly down, quilt and all, laughing. Partly at the irony. Mainly from relief.

"Cole!" Peeking out from the foot of the bed, seeing that

the door was indeed latched, Laurel struggled from the covers and began pulling on clothing. "It's not funny!"

"Of course it is."

"Get dressed! He's had a cold trip, and we should be giving him hot coffee, not sitting around!"

That did spur him on to find his cleanest pair of long underwear, then start the extended process of dressing for the winter. Pants. Shirt. Boots.

"How can I face him?" asked Laurel more than once, dividing her attention between putting stockings on her beautiful, bare legs and putting coffee on the stove. "After we've . . . we've . . ."

There was no way her father could guess all that they'd done. At least they had that . . . if Collier wanted to live.

"We *are* married, Lorelei," he reminded her. He combed his too-long hair, then tied it back with string. "Most people believe we've been doing that for far longer than we have."

Though perhaps with not as many variations.

"I know." She faced him. "Do I look all right?"

Except for the faint flush of whisker burns on her cheeks. He decided then and there that, as soon as he got the chance, he would shave. "You are the most beautiful woman I've ever seen," he assured her, which made her blush. Then, so that she wouldn't have to go into the cold, he went to the door himself and called his father-in-law back in.

He saw that the man had managed to bring a one-horse sleigh with him and grinned. A trip to town it was!

Garrison entered, stomping the snow off his boots, and took off his hat. "Laurel Lee," he greeted stiffly.

She threw herself into his arms, cold or not. "Papa!"

Collier liked seeing Garrison's arms enfold her as tightly. But he hoped Laurel did not smell too much of her husband.

Or of sex.

251

Chapter Twenty-one

"Fell in the creek," Papa repeated, when Laurel explained why he'd seen only Collier's tracks outside the cabin.

"Yes, sir." Here was where he would say he'd told her so.

"Actually," interceded Collier, from where he poured coffee at the stove, "she was more dragged in. Pure accident."

His loyalty warmed her. "Cole carried me home."

"Laurel knew how to treat her injuries," Collier insisted.

Papa looked from one of them to the other. Then he held out a callused hand. "Best see."

She put her right hand in his—ooh, it was cold! He looked at it, turned it over, and nodded. "No scarring."

"No, sir," she agreed, feeling guilty on her own, since *he* wasn't putting it on her. "But the cold makes me ache something awful."

"It will," warned Papa. "Some time, yet."

Collier put a mug of coffee in front of him, and another in front of Laurel, then sank gracefully into the chair beside hers. "I gather you've had the same difficulty then, Mr. Garrison."

Had he?

Papa looked none too pleased to turn his gaze back to Laurel's husband. "Never fell in no creek."

And that was all they got out of him on the matter.

He'd brought a two-person sleigh—a Christmas present from Uncle Benj—so that they could ride back to town with him, spend the day, and hopefully return before the weather changed, if it changed.

As soon as they'd had their coffee, they dressed to go out.

"Cooper certainly is generous when it comes to Laurel," Collier noted, a thoughtful note in his voice.

All Papa said was, "Best I drive."

They both insisted on tucking and wrapping Laurel so thoroughly beside her father that she could barely breathe. At least the cold didn't make her hurt . . . except her nose.

The sleigh ride had to be the fastest, easiest trip to town Laurel had ever made from her claim cabin. The hard, thick crust on the snow evened out every obstacle, from coulees to fallen logs to all but the biggest rocks. And the little black gelding seemed so eager, she felt sure even Collier would have no trouble driving him home. Collier rode beside them on Llewellyn, clearly enjoying the outing as much as she was.

"This is wonderful, Papa," Laurel said, snuggling closer to her father's familiar warmth. "Thank you for coming to get us."

He said nothing, just nodded. That was familiar and safe too.

Still, she found herself watching how well Collier rode, despite that silly saddle of his, more than any other scenery. Now that they'd left the cabin, the thought of everything she and her new husband had done together made her blush—especially since Papa had probably guessed.

But she must truly be a hoyden, because she didn't regret a bit of it. Simply knowing that this marriage wasn't meant to last the way other folks' were made things different.

Still, she guessed she'd enjoy every bit of it while she could.

As they reached the outskirts of town, Collier rode closer to the sleigh and called, "I'd best get a shave and a haircut before I risk frightening my cousin, much less do some business."

"Business?" asked Laurel.

"Check the mail, see to my accounts," he clarified. "Do you mind, dearest? I ought not be but an hour or so."

Dearest. Sometimes it felt real. "Not the hair," she insisted, and his eyebrows rose. Even with half his face covered, he looked beautiful, what with those bright, eager eyes of his.

"Pardon?"

As long as she was wringing every bit of enjoyment out of this marriage as she could, why not make her preferences known? "I like your hair this way. Please don't let them cut it."

Collier made a sweeping bow to her from horseback. "As you wish, Mrs. Pembroke."

She wasn't certain if Papa snorted. But she definitely sighed as she watched Collier urge his horse on ahead of them, toward South Main.

"Ain't mistreatin' you," clarified Papa, in that way he had of asking things without really asking at all.

"No, sir. Collier's wonderful."

"Wonderful," he repeated, clearly unconvinced. But that was all right with her. He didn't have to like her husband any more than he liked Mariah's. He just had to be polite.

She could certainly count on her gentleman husband to be polite in return.

Laurel expected to be mobbed by her sisters when Papa sent her ahead into their in-town house while he saw to the horse. She'd forgotten it was a school day.

But Mariah was there, and she was clearly in the family way.

"Mama fetched me," she explained, while they hugged as tightly as the baby under her apron would allow.

"Oh, my," said Laurel, standing back to look at her older sister's round figure with widening eyes. "Oh, my goodness!"

"Only three months to go," said Mariah happily.

"And as healthy as she's ever been," agreed Mama, enveloping Laurel in the kind of accepting, concerned embrace only a mother could give. "And how are *you*, my little homesteader?"

"I'm fine," insisted Laurel, as the door opened and Papa came in, stomping snow from his boots. "Really. It's wonderful!"

Mariah widened her eyes with playful interest, then glanced toward Papa and looked quickly away, biting her lip. Some things they just didn't discuss around their father.

Papa's glance, noted Laurel, shied just as surely from Mariah. Maybe he didn't know how to react to his daughter's condition . . . or feared his true reactions would just cause trouble.

At least that was one difficulty Laurel and Collier would not have to face!

Papa did tattle on her, though. "Fell in the creek some weeks back," he accused, shrugging off his coat.

"No!" exclaimed Mariah. "Good heavens!"

"Then you'll need a warm bath," said Mama firmly, as if it had just happened. "And I know just what to put in it."

"It's been weeks," Laurel assured her. She'd been paying more attention to the calendar lately, after all. "Almost a month. Really, I'm already feeling much better."

"Your father nearly froze in a blizzard once," insisted Mama, "and it took some time for him to fully recover—though he denied it, too. I know you're a full-grown married woman. You don't have to have the bath if you don't want it—"

"A hot bath?" challenged Laurel. "In a full-body tub?"

Mama and Mariah laughed with her, and Laurel realized they'd all three been young wives on homesteads during hard winters. The realization startled her. She'd always felt so different. She *was* different. Wasn't she?

"There's plenty of time before lunch," insisted Mama, leading the way into their bathroom. "Your sisters and Thaddeas will be here, and the Coopers."

"Collier will be back by then," said Laurel. "Wait until you see his hair!"

"Is it shorter or longer?" asked Mariah. Soon Laurel was in the tubful of blissfully hot, sudsy water, while Mariah sat on a chair beside her—with a curtain drawn modestly so that she mainly saw Laurel's head and shoulders, of course. It seemed they had more to talk about in this one late morning than they had the whole previous year. In particular, Laurel found herself fascinated by the swell of her sister's belly.

It wasn't as if she'd never been around a woman in the family way before. Some of her earliest memories were of falling asleep with her head resting on her mother's big tummy, already understanding that she had another sister or brother in there. She'd been twelve when Elise was born. That was quite old enough to understand.

And yet, that had been her mother. This was her sister!

"Does it hurt?" she asked, scrubbing soap into her hair.

"Not at all," said Mariah. "I don't even feel sick anymore."

"But it's got to feel different. May I touch it?"

When her sister nodded, Laurel swished her hand free of suds, dried it on the towel Mariah offered, then put her splayed hand on her sister's belly, as she might a mare in foal.

It moved, and her eyes widened yet again. Just like with Mama or a foal. It really *was* a baby!

"My belly itches," Mariah admitted. "And my back hurts some. But nothing awful. Not like when I was feeling so sick, or two months ago, when my, well . . ." Glancing at the door, she whispered, "My bosom hurt terribly. I wouldn't let Stuart touch me."

Laurel flushed, thinking of all the wonderful things Collier did with *her* bosom. Time to rinse her hair. "But that . . . passed?"

"Oh, yes." Now Mariah blushed.

Laurel felt relieved. Not that it should matter to her. She herself wouldn't be having a baby, maybe not ever. And that, unlike the lingering knowledge that she and Collier's marriage was finite, still did not bother her.

She had, after all, seen mares foal!

"Why all the interest?" teased Mariah. "Do you and Lord Collier have news?"

"No! Goodness, no. Collier and me?" Laurel shook her head. "We've no intention . . . that is, not anytime in the next few years."

Or any of the years after that. It wasn't exactly a lie.

"Oh." Mariah ducked her head. "What about everything else?"

Laurel stared at her sister's deepening blush. "You mean . . . ?"

Mariah nodded, golden curls bouncing, and Laurel couldn't keep from smiling at the thought. "Oh, Mariah! If I'd known it was that much fun, I might've ruined myself long ago."

"Laurel Lee!" But Mariah laughed.

"It *is!*"

"Well, yes. Of course it can be marvelous fun. But it's so much more than that, too!"

Laurel watched how dreamy her sister's gray eyes got and wasn't sure she understood. Collier's making love to her the way he did—kissing her and filling her and drawing her to such ecstasy that she couldn't hold it in—amazed her, every single delicious time. She felt important with him, and beautiful, and happy.

That had to be what Mariah meant. But when Laurel said, "Of course. Much more," that felt like lying, too.

And she did not really like lying.

"I'm so glad." Mariah sighed. "Now it's so clear, what Mother used to tell us. You know, about the importance of being in love. The rest is wonderful, of course, but without the love, it would just be . . . ."

Laurel waited, uneasy and fascinated at the same time.

"Just carnal," Mariah decided. "Temporary. With Stuart, I know it won't matter how long we need to wait after the baby's born before . . . you know."

"It won't?" challenged Laurel, and again her sister blushed.

"Well, it might. But he'll be patient, because what we have is so much more than that. And that's what makes . . . the rest of it . . . so much better. Don't you think?"

Did she? Maybe, for Laurel and Collier, it was just carnal. It was certainly temporary.

Laurel started lathering herself again with her mother's special soap, harder than ever. What she and Collier had been doing wasn't just anything, and she resented her sister for that angelic glow, and that round belly, and for acting as if, once again, she could do everything better than Laurel could.

Everything womanly, anyhow.

It was all foolishness, just like the stupid shoes. The only womanly thing Laurel had ever liked, she'd found with Collier. And she planned to keep doing it with him at every chance, and enjoying it too, whether he loved her or not.

For as long as she could.

But somehow, that thought just made her madder.

"Are you all right?" asked Mariah, and she looked so concerned that Laurel felt guilty. Here her sister sat, giving up her day to spend time with her, and Laurel blamed her for being better at marriage—when Laurel's had been a sham to begin with.

"I'm fine," she insisted, fibbing some more. "I just want to be dry and dressed when Collier gets back."

Everything would make more sense with Collier there.

Or at least the difficulties would be easier to ignore.

Had Collier gotten the mail *before* going by the barber's, he might have cut his hair after all. But appearances made the man. So he went to the "tonsorial parlor" right off, indulging in a bath as well as a good, professional shave. It amused him how little surprise the barber showed at his scruffy appearance. Apparently Collier was not the first man to come into Sheridan without having shaved in weeks; nor would he be the last.

Neither did the barber hesitate to accept Collier's refusal

to have his hair trimmed, despite long hair not having been fashionable on men for over seventy years. "Women," was all the man said when Collier explained Laurel's preference.

A dark-haired cowboy, who had entered the shop shortly after Collier, made more of a fuss. "So, Marmaduke," he challenged—as if Collier would truly want to fight with a straight razor at his throat. "You do everything your wife wants?"

The implication, of course, was that Laurel emasculated him. Considering the last few weeks, Collier deliberately misconstrued his meaning.

"I have not," he answered, "had any complaints thus far."

The barber laughed, and the cowboy stalked out without waiting for his own turn.

"I mean that in the most proper sense," Collier clarified.

"Well o' course," agreed the barber. But he insisted on giving Collier a nickel discount for having so thoroughly amused him.

A new suit of clothes came next. Only once he felt cleaned and pressed—truly like himself for the first time in months—did Collier go by the bank, then the jeweler, and, of course, the druggist. By the time he gathered the pile of mail waiting for them at the post office and saw the familiar, authoritative handwriting on a letter postmarked from England, it was too late to reconsider his hair.

Good news rarely came from his father.

Collier found a seat right there in the store—Louk's, where the post office was kept—and unfolded the letter to discover what nasty turn was about to befall him this time.

Displeased by your secrecy . . . Impatient, he turned the page over. Part of his pleasure in marrying Laurel had been the realization of exactly how making his own decision would displease the "governor."

Edgar wanted to visit with you. . . . Collier read somewhat more slowly there. Was it possible . . . could it be that he and his family could, as the Westerners would put it, "mend fences" after all? The very thought of returning to England, to

259

Brambourne, caught his imagination and shortened his breath.

But his father refused to divulge what Edgar wanted. So Collier began to skim again, until . . .

Docking in New York City on March tenth. Then he realized, with growing dread, that he oughtn't skim this letter after all.

He started over, reading more carefully, but it was the same letter. It still scolded him for marrying without permission. It still hinted at a matter of personal business with Edgar. And on the third page, it still said that the Viscount of Brambourne and his heir—as well as the Baron Tentrees with his wife and their daughter, Edgar's fiancée—would arrive in the United States at the beginning of March.

Good Lord. These United States!

The only balm to his panic—and Collier did recognize his panic—was that they were not, apparently, coming to Wyoming.

We shan't manage to tour your new ranching interests, wrote the viscount, unaware of how this particular slight of Collier's life would benefit his second son. *We shall be in Denver from Easter through mid-April. Your presence is expected*.

There was no explanation of why they would cross an ocean and more than half a continent to get as far as Denver, but could not manage Sheridan. There was no request of Collier and Laurel's presence, just an expectation.

For one long, glorious moment, Collier considered crumpling up the letter and throwing it into the stove that heated this little store. The hell with Father and his expectations.

But then he looked more closely at the store, one of Sheridan's better-established businesses. Small chunks of ice floated in a puddle inside the doorway, where snow off customers' feet collected and then melted. Everyone wore coats and hats, most of them worn from years of use in harsh weather. A matron counted out payment for a purchase with red, chapped fingers. Her baby stood clutching her wet skirts, his nose running.

Proving Herself

Sheridan boasted of itself as the "Denver of the Northwest." They claimed an opera house, four churches, three schools, three newspapers, and a population of . . . what had Cooper told him? Somewhere around five thousand people. Denver itself likely had something closer to a hundred thousand.

Collier suddenly *wanted* to go to Denver, no matter why. He wanted to stay with Laurel at the Windsor; he wanted to abandon the tedium of menial chores that had become their daily routine. He longed to attend the opera. He hungered for the chance to dine in real restaurants. The only thing he wanted more than that was to return to England itself.

When last he'd looked into the matter, London was nearing a population of five million. Sheridan, for all its quaint attractions, was little more than a burg.

As the woman with the red-nosed baby approached the door, Collier stood and opened it for them. She looked startled—he wasn't certain why, as these Westerners did tend to treat ladies with at least an attempt at propriety—but she said, "Obliged."

Collier did not bother to sit again. He was unsure he could remain still. The matter of business with Edgar beckoned him. They'd once had an agreement. And he had managed Brambourne for two years, after all! If he had even a slim chance of returning, he had to go. *They* had to go.

Collier thought of Laurel and felt sick again. Oh, he did adore her. Her spirit, her strength, her incredible body. But Father would not. Edgar would not. The Baron and Baroness Tentrees and their daughter . . .

Oh, dear. Collier began to wonder if the Lord was all that good, after all. Because any chance he had of returning to Brambourne would likely rest on convincing his family that, should Edgar refuse his inheritance, Laurel would make an able lady of the manor and a laudable mother to future heirs.

Even if it *was* all pretense, mere months after the marriage was hardly the time to begin insinuating a possible divorce. Besides, no matter what the viscount meant to discuss, Collier had a bargain with Laurel.

But they had a great deal of work ahead, before his little rancher was ready for such a meeting.

Everyone arrived for lunch before Collier did. *Everyone*.

Laurel's sisters surrounded her as they hurried in from school. Audra, who had just turned fifteen, looked amazingly grown-up, with her strawberry hair pulled back into a knot and her skirts hanging primly down to her ankles. Laurel guessed she might make a fine schoolmarm yet. Victoria wanted to know how the claim cabin was holding up, and to repeat the latest news about all their friends. Kitty just stood quietly, waiting her turn, until Laurel scooped her up into a big hug and spin. Elise, pulling on Laurel's skirt, wanted to know if the cocoons had hatched, and why she'd been gone so long, and where Collier was.

"He had business to conduct," explained Laurel. But he'd also said he wouldn't be but an hour or so—and that was two hours ago! He'd also called her *dearest*. Had that been as false as his schedule?

Thaddeas strode in, solemn and welcoming, and Laurel gladly accepted her hug from him, too. She assured him that she was fine, the claim was fine, Collier was fine.

"Where is this newest brother of mine?" he asked, and she had to confess that she wasn't sure.

"But he should be back any minute."

"I'm sure he will be." Thad gave her another hug. But he looked slightly dangerous as he said it. Had Collier been courting her, he would have just lost his visiting privileges.

But Collier wasn't courting her. He'd already married her. He'd already . . . well . . . quite thoroughly! Things one oughtn't think of around one's older brother, any more than around one's father!

Uncle Benj arrived with as much noise as usual, sweeping Laurel into the kind of hug she'd given Kitty, dismissing her thanks for the sleigh with his usual bluster. Little Alec shook her hand solemnly to welcome her back. And Lady Cooper looked expectantly about her. "I trust Collier is about here somewhere."

Every time someone commented on him, Laurel felt more fearful. What if he had gone by the Sheridan Inn and was even now getting drunk with the remittance men? What if, tired of chores and of her, he'd boarded a train and left town?

Then Elise called, "Here he is!" and ran for the front door. Laurel sank into the seat nearest her, weak with relief.

Collier had never looked so beautiful as when he strode into the foyer of her family's in-town house. He answered each greeting with that easy charm, shook Thad's and Benj's hands, kissed Alexandra's, and scooped the persistent Elise up into his arms.

But his bright gaze seemed to be searching. He smiled when it reached her.

Oh, heavens. She'd grown accustomed to the scruffy Collier, the man with whom she'd been sharing her bed, her dreams, her body. This was *Lord* Collier again, clean-shaven and neatly pressed. For a moment she thought he'd cut his hair anyway—and somehow that scared her. His being Lord Collier again scared her.

Then she realized he'd merely pulled it back into a little golden tail.

"Forgive me, dearest," he said, sinking to his knee beside her chair, putting Elise down to take Laurel's hand in his. And though he looked and smelled like aristocracy—except for the tail—he sounded like the Collier she lived with, loved.

Only now that she recognized her fears of desertion—just like when she woke alone in the cabin—did she realize just how desperately she'd been loving him.

"You said an hour," she accused softly, and his bright eyes widened. Had he not expected her to care?

"I know," he assured her, kissing her hand as he had his cousin's. She wanted a different kind of kiss, but with her family milling about, she couldn't have it. "It was beastly of me not to at least telephone when I realized I would be late. I received some news from home—nothing grievous," he assured her quickly. "Nothing we cannot discuss later. But I fear I let it distract me far more than I should."

Nothing grievous. That was good. But now that she was relaxing into the surety that he'd returned to her, Laurel noticed a nervous edge about her husband. Maybe the news *wasn't* grievous. But it surely was eating at him all the same.

Mama appeared in the archway to the formal dining room. "Collier!" she greeted, coming to his side to kiss his cheek as he stood. "What perfect timing. Dinner is just now ready."

"I hope I did not delay—" he began, but stopped when she pointed a commanding finger at him.

For a small woman, Mama could put a great deal of command into a single pointed finger. "That would be *less* than perfect timing. I believe I said your timing was perfect."

"Ah, darlin' Lillabit," teased Uncle Benj, coming up behind her. "Is this here scamp impugning your veracity?"

"I should not dream of it," insisted Collier, slanting his amused gaze down to Laurel. He still held her hand. When she squeezed it, he squeezed it back. Everything would be all right, grievous news or not.

And yet she held him back just a moment, as the others started into the dining room and he helped her to her feet.

As if she couldn't even stand up on her own!

"What kind of news?" she asked. "What's there to discuss?"

"Really, we needn't—" But he must have understood how she was glaring up at him, because he mouthed the word *Ah.* "My father and brother wish to see us in Denver next month. I would like to make that our wedding trip. Dinner smells delicious."

She felt as she had when she'd fallen in the creek. His father and . . . what?

"Laurel!" called Elise impatiently, and Laurel heard their father chide her poor table manners.

"Shall we?" pleaded Collier, more tugging than escorting her toward the dining room.

Stunned, she followed. "Your father and brother?" she hissed as he bent to help her into her chair.

Pushing it in for her, he murmured into her ear, "And Lady Vivian."

His Lady Vivian?

Then he sat beside her, and Papa bowed his head to say the blessing, and Laurel couldn't say a darned thing.

But as soon as they got to the *Amen*, she kicked him.

Chapter Twenty-two

Laurel took the news no better than Collier had expected—even discounting the kick. As soon as her younger sisters left for school, she drew him aside into the marginal privacy of the front foyer.

"Easter's too soon," she protested. "We'll likely have snow through May! Even if we make it to the station, the trains might not be getting through!"

He tried to remember how amusing he sometimes found that stubborn streak of hers. "I would prefer we plan on going and have the weather detain us, than plan on poor weather and find ourselves unprepared in fair."

She sighed. "What sort of preparations?"

That seemed a good sign. "I should like to order a week's worth of proper dresses for you before we leave town today."

"As in . . . seven?"

"Unless weeks have changed since last I counted." But she had that mud-throwing look about her again. He'd best not push his luck, so he leaned nearer to murmur, "Please, Lorelei. We've maintained appearances for *your* family."

He did not understand the way she searched his face then, but at least she grudgingly conceded. "Seven new dresses, for mercy's sake. And what else?"

He *did* adore her, barbarian or not—so much so that he wrapped her in his arms and kissed her until she relaxed that clench of her jaw. It had been entire hours since they'd done this, and he'd missed it. She tasted so sweet, and felt so soft against him, that he almost forgot where they were—

Until her brother cleared his throat. "Time and a place, Pembroke," scolded Thaddeas Garrison darkly from the doorway, his arms folded as if to bar any possible protest.

"Quite," said Collier, less embarrassed than he perhaps ought to be. "My apologies."

"Mmm-hm."

"Really, Laurel," admonished the rather round Mrs. Mac-Callum, passing through from the kitchen. He supposed Mr. MacCallum was to be congratulated, for Mariah was clearly in the pudding club. "Whatever could you have been thinking?"

Collier had no idea why his wife then advanced on her older sister—though why ever it was, he quite understood the older sister retreating to the safety of her parents, in the parlor.

Just in case everything fell to bits, though, he penned his reply to England, to post before they left that afternoon.

Father. Thank you for your gracious invitation. Mrs. Pembroke and I cannot commit to a date, due to the capricious nature of Wyoming's winters. However, we shall make every effort to be there before Easter.

His father would dislike such guarded promises, but it was the truth. After consideration, Collier added, *It all depends on the Chinooks and the Alberta clippers.*

Resp. your son, Collier.

Laurel didn't want to go to Denver. She didn't want to meet the viscount, and Edgar, and certainly not Lady Vivian. And she sure didn't want Collier meeting up with Lady Vivian!

But it was important to him. And, as he had pointed out, they'd maintained appearances for *her* family, hadn't they? She didn't like wondering where the pretense ended and the reality of his affection began—which "dearests" he'd really meant, or even whether he'd answered the door wearing only a quilt specifically for show. But her family believed her happily married.

The least she owed him was to do the same for his.

"A viscount is more important than a baron," she repeated determinedly as they rode out to the ridge together. She'd been forcing herself out into the cold during the week following their trip to town. "So I always address your father before Mr. Tentrees."

"Yes," agreed Collier slowly. "Except that he is *Baron* Tentrees. You'll have little call to speak to either first, in any case. They will address you."

"Don't speak until I'm spoken to?" she challenged, aware of the dare in her voice. Well, it was a foolish notion, no matter whom she'd married.

"Only for a week," he pleaded. "And when you are alone with the Baroness Tentrees and her daughter—"

"Vivian," clarified Laurel darkly.

"*Lady* Vivian," he corrected, "speak to the mother first."

" 'What a lovely day, Baroness,' " she said, to practice.

"Your ladyship," he corrected.

"You're joshing me." And it wasn't particularly funny.

"Here." Collier reined in his dapple gray, so Laurel did the same with Snapper, and they both dismounted, hitching their horses to a tree branch, just in case. "Best that we continue on foot. You have the coffee?"

She patted the canteen under her coat, where it was warming her nicely. "You have the binoculars?"

He lifted the case by its leather strap, and they proceeded from there toward where the trees began to clear out, proof of how rocky this particular ridge was.

Laurel didn't have to ask about the tarpaulin and blankets, since Collier wore them rolled and tied to his back. They'd decided against the bearskin, even if they were downwind from where they hoped to see horses. The wind could change, after all.

Collier leaned closer to her, pressing his muffler-wrapped mouth to her scarf-covered ear so that he could quietly ask, "Are you certain you're all right?"

She nodded, torn. On the one hand, she loved his concern for her health: it still made her feel safe, cared for. But she was a rancher herself now. Even if she hadn't seen any of her earmarked cattle since winter descended on them. A bit of achiness in her bones shouldn't slow her down.

"Then I'll go ahead." At the edge of the treeline he sank to a crouch, then crawled through the snow to where the ledge dropped off into a high valley.

Laurel watched, holding her breath. She did want to see the horses he'd been watching. And this hard crust, which allowed them to wander more easily, wouldn't last much longer. To her relief, Collier stopped before reaching the very edge. He shrugged the blanketing from his back and spread it out—tarp first, to keep them dry, and then the blanket. He rolled onto his back long enough to dust the snow off his front, then rolled back onto the blankets to lie with a view of what she assumed were wild horses. Then he beckoned to her.

Laurel hunkered down and scuttled through the snow to her husband's side. Immediately he drew the edge of the blanket over them both and held her close. "Still all right, then?"

Her hands throbbed. But as Papa had said, that would last for a while. And lying here with him was more than all right. "I'm fine," she insisted. "Where are they?"

He pointed. She squinted and, yes, there they were, partially hidden in the pine timber, pawing through the snow to graze. There had to be at least twenty horses in this particular band . . . and one looked to be taller than the rest, and snow white. It was Foolish Pride. Thoroughbred or not, she was surviving the winter!

269

"Here," Cole said, handing her the binoculars.

As she drew them to her eyes, the view seemed to lurch, and then, suddenly, the horses appeared *much* closer. Shaggy, snowy, wild mustangs of all different colors and ages, bays and roans and sorrels, paints and blacks, long forelocks and manes, tails held close against the cold. *All the pretty little ponies.*

"They're beautiful!" she exclaimed quietly, delighted. "Oh!"

"Aren't they?" he agreed. "Look farther north, and up."

She did, and after a few tries she brought the paint stallion into focus. He stood on a higher rise than his harem, keeping an eye over them all. He had an intelligent face, a bit of Arabian slope to his nose. His particolored mane was quite handsome.

"He guards them," Collier explained. "But there's a mare who seems to be in charge otherwise. Brown, with a bald face."

Laurel spent a few more minutes admiring the stallion, then returned her magnified attention to the rest of the band.

"Oh! There she is. One white sock."

"That's the one. Everyone's behaving themselves today; I imagine because it's so cold. When she's displeased with another horse, she chases it out and it must wait for her permission to return and join the others. It seems quite distressing."

"Really? I'd think it would depend on why she chased them off in the first place. Maybe they'd rather be on their own, without all the rules."

"*You* would think that," teased Collier, and she snuggled closer against his warmth, then handed the binoculars back. She liked the way his bright eyes caressed her face—well, what he could see of it—before he accepted the glasses. What she could see of his high cheeks, over his muffler, were still clean-shaven. He hadn't gone back to being scruffy. But bits of burnished gold hair curled out from under where his scarf wrapped around his neck, just for her.

"I suppose *you* would want to go back to the herd," she

said, resting her chin on mittened hands to better watch the distant horses. How could people want to kill them just for being wild?

"I'm afraid I would," he agreed. That made her feel sad.

"How does a horse ask to get back into the band?" What Collier had learned, simply from observing the horses through his binoculars, impressed her. He'd always been a good horseman.

He even drove well, if Firefly wasn't at harness.

"He lowers his head very near the ground and makes a kind of chewing motion. I don't know why, but that's usually when the mare turns her shoulder to him. Once she's not facing him flat-on, that means he has permission to rejoin them."

And some of us, she thought, *go to Denver.*

She wondered how the viscount might signal permission to return to England, ending his second son's exile. The thought made her ache inside far worse than the cold ever could.

But it was what Collier wanted. So she took a deep breath, then said, " 'What a lovely day, your ladyship.' "

" 'Indeed, Mrs. Pembroke,' " pretended Collier back at her, even as he watched the horses. " 'The view of the mountains is exquisite.' "

"I'm not a ladyship?"

"I'm not even a lordship," he reassured her. "Not unless . . ."

"Not unless what?"

That he said nothing worried her with the same fear that had lodged deep inside her since he'd announced his family's visit. "Not unless *what?*"

"It's not likely," he admitted finally. "But if Edgar renounced his claim, then I might yet become the heir."

"And eventually the viscount?" He nodded. "And then you'd be a lordship."

"Then I would be everything I've ever wanted to be." His rich voice deepened with a touch of wistfulness.

Everything he'd ever wanted to be—in England.

271

"Don't concern yourelf," he assured her, putting down the field glasses on their blanket. "Were it to ever happen, I doubt it would be before our own agreement . . . that is to say . . ."

"Before our two or three years are up?" she clarified, aching even more.

"But I'm afraid for now we still have to convince them that you would make a proper viscountess."

Laurel considered that. "Do you think . . . could I really convince them that I would make a proper viscountess?"

She didn't blame him for his glance of surprise. Up until now she'd begrudged him every ounce of cooperation. "Certainly," he assured her. "You're hardly a washerwoman or a barmaid, Laurel! You're the daughter of one of the most prosperous ranchers in Wyoming. You already know basic etiquette." His smiling eyes took on a teasing gleam. "Even though you ignore it half the time."

There's nothing wrong with washerwomen or barmaids, either, she thought stubbornly. That was what her mother would say, and probably what she should say too.

Instead she watched his pretty eyes, and how his hair fell over his forehead from beneath his hat, and she dared wonder, for the first time, Could I convince you?

Not that she wanted to be a viscountess. She didn't even want to leave Wyoming. But neither did she want to lose Collier.

Chances were, he wouldn't return to England. He'd said so himself. But she could understand his wanting to hope. If he were to rethink their agreement a few years from now, if she had even the *chance* of his rethinking it, perhaps extending it indefinitely . . .

"All right, then," she decided, covering her uncertainty with a determined tone. "What will the viscount be expecting from your perfect wife, then? Other than my calling him 'your lordship.' Assuming he's spoken to me first."

She must have gotten that part correct, because Collier drew his muffler down off his face to show his full, lopsided smile—dimples and all—and then reached up and slid her muffler down off her face as well. Then he leaned close enough to touch foreheads with her, in their little cocoon of warmth on this snowy ridge.

"I know what *I* expect from my perfect wife," he whispered, and pressed his lips to hers in a delicious illustration.

She sank back onto the tarp, hearing snow crunch beneath it, and didn't protest at all when he rolled onto her. She laughed when he used his teeth to pull off his mittens, then began fumbling under their blanket and coats and clothing. She knew full well that the temperature was somewhere around the zero mark. But they had remarkable ways of keeping each other warm.

"I'm already practiced at this part," she said happily, offering her mittens up to him so that he could pull those off with his teeth, too. He complied, like the gentleman he was.

"Mustn't lose one's edge," he whispered. "Viscountess."

Viscountess. *That* made her feel a little cold. She'd spent her whole life disappointing her father with her unladylike behavior. How would she possibly impress a viscount?

But when her and Collier's bare hands finally found hot, bare skin under layers and layers of clothing, she knew she had to try. And not just for him.

She'd gotten herself out of a frozen creek. She'd managed to keep her claim, despite Papa's setting himself against her. Surely she could prove herself—*Oh* . . .

She pretty much lost the ability to think as Collier mounted her, filled her, began to move inside her. But she managed to clutch at one thought, as surely as she was clutching at him.

To keep him, she guessed she could do anything.

She had to.

Collier could not explain Laurel's sudden enthusiasm, but he welcomed it. She would need every bit.

Not that he had lied. Her father might be nouveau riche, but she'd been raised well enough, for a Wyoming girl. He hardly need worry that she would blow her nose on her sleeve, or curse, or slap the viscount on the back and call him "pard."

Amusing though that image was.

But when he considered everything that she ought to do, rather than simply what she might avoid, the task sometimes seemed overwhelming.

"Take shorter steps," he chided gently at least once a day. "There is nowhere to which a lady need hurry."

"Nowhere?" Laurel protested finally, folding her arms. That was that just the sort of thing that she ought *not* do in Denver. Rather than scold—she was only being Laurel, after all—Collier took her hands in his and unfolded her arms for her.

"*Nowhere*," he insisted, looking seriously down at her.

Her eyes began to dance up at him. "Not even if the hotel were on fire? Or would a lady simply stand there and look pretty until she went up like a torch?"

"One would hope that in a fire," Collier said, ducking his face closer to hers, "nobody would notice either way."

Then they were kissing again, and embracing again, and no longer caring how ladies and gentlemen behaved.

"So I shouldn't speak too loudly," she clarified perhaps a week later, lying with her head pillowed on his bare abdomen while they both recovered from another bout of marital relations.

He was stroking her hair, drawing his fingertips across its sleek darkness. "Certainly not. That shows deficient breeding."

"Should I whisper, then?"

"Hardly. Exclusivity is quite rude."

She turned her head to better see past the length of his chest to his face. "Do you swear you aren't making this up?"

"My word as a gentleman."

She considered that. "Do you swear you're a gentleman?"

He stopped petting her hair and brushed his fingers across her cheek instead. Lord, but she'd become precious to him. Especially now that she might . . .

The thought seemed too radical to entertain. But what if she found she enjoyed society? What if mixing with people like the Baroness Tentrees encouraged her to experience England?

Was it possible that his little rancher might yet bloom into a wife not only worthy but *desirous* of British citizenship?

Oh, he doubted it. Likely such thoughts ran counter to their original bargain. But it made a lovely dream.

He sighed. "Unfortunately, my dearest, I am not always a gentleman around you."

"Unfortunately?" she challenged, and caught his finger between gentle teeth, then began to tease it with her tongue. He had shared many things with her that he had never, never thought he would reveal to a proper wife.

At moments like this, it hardly seemed unfortunate at that. But once they reached Denver . . .

Damn, but he both dreaded and anticipated the trip in equal measure. One moment he could not wait to escape this box. The next he hoped to be completely snowed in. With her.

Since he had no answer, he opened his own mouth, dampened two fingers, then reached out and drew them slowly down Laurel's chest, down her abdomen, across her belly, and lower. She arched into the sensation as a cat might arch into a particularly satisfying caress. Then she turned her face away from his face and in the direction of his feet—and important points between—to thank him in equally salacious ways.

Collier had no idea what he was doing with so uninhibited a woman as her—outside of this, of course!

That should have been enough warning.

Laurel guessed she'd hoped her mountains would rescue her by snowing them in. February and March passed with the sort of intemperate weather that bolstered such selfish optimism. A Chinook turned their good, hard crust to slush again; then a blizzard packed it down into shoulder-high snowdrifts.

Then, the third week in March, an Alberta clipper froze everything so solidly that they could have skated to town—and the freeze lasted. So Collier and Laurel loaded their sleigh, tied Snapper and Llewellyn behind it, and drove away from the only home they'd known together.

"Only for a week, right?" Laurel asked, huddling closer against Collier's side, under the carriage rug, as he drove.

"Only a week," he assured her. "You won't lose your claim."

And her claim *was* the important thing, wasn't it? Even if he did still think of it as only hers? Laurel wasn't sure anymore . . . and that uncertainty scared her.

They stayed the night with the Coopers—not because they weren't welcome with her parents, but because the Coopers had more space. It gave them time to settle the horses, dine with her family, have alterations made on her new clothing, and to buy her a finer trunk. Heaven forbid Collier be embarrassed by Laurel's *luggage*, after all.

The arrangements did not, however, allow Laurel to seek comfort from Collier in the most pleasant, most primal way she knew how. By unspoken agreement, neither she nor Collier wanted to insult their hosts with less-than-polite behavior.

Besides, their minds were on other things.

By time they rose in the wee hours of the morning to catch the five twenty-five to Denver, Laurel felt so nervous she could barely eat.

What if she embarrassed him? What if she spoke before she thought, and angered his father? What if she proved to him only that she wasn't suited to be his wife?

Collier's spirits, however, improved with every passing minute. The way Laurel felt whenever she rode into the foothills, Collier seemed to feel as they left for the train depot.

Collier saw to the luggage and the tickets, and they waited together in the steamy warmth of the stove-heated depot. He looked so competent as a traveler, and so handsome . . . especially with his hair still long, and pulled into its little tail.

That concession to his winter as a mountain man, he had

made for her—and it meant a great deal to her. But . . .

Again her stomach clutched. What if she embarrassed him?

After the train chugged into the station, the temperature dropped and the noise increased as disembarking passengers filled the depot, many just to grab a cup of coffee before climbing back onto their second or third-class cars. Collier ushered Laurel across the frozen platform, which was shadowy against the pressing darkness of early morning, and gave her a hand up the wrought-iron steps onto the train. As if she couldn't climb stairs alone, as a lady.

Then again, in these shoes . . .

The interior of the Pullman palace car stunned her. Burnished walnut and mahogany. Plush seats of velvet and brocade. Polished brass and silver. Mirrors. Oriental carpet. The ceiling even boasted painted frescoes. It looked more like a parlor than a train—and a fine parlor indeed!

Several passengers glanced up from newspapers or needlework to note Collier and Laurel's arrival. Laurel couldn't shake the feeling that they were noticing the quality of their coats, which the colored porter politely took to hang in a small wardrobe by the doorway—and then the quality of their traveling suits.

"Second class would have been fine," she murmured once Collier led her to their seats and settled beside her to await the train's departure.

"Not for you," he assured her. But when she narrowed her eyes in challenge—had she wanted first class?—he had the grace to duck his head and smile a little, complete with dimple. "Father may meet the train," he explained more honestly.

May *meet the train?* "You mean he might not? You cabled him we're coming, right?"

"Yes, but he's an important man." Collier did not look any more satisfied by his answer than she felt. "And he may just want me to know how little importance I hold."

How little importance? Collier? "But he's your father."

"I apologize," he said. "I ought not have spoken so."

Laurel began to wonder about some other things. His father had been in the country for a month. He'd crossed an ocean and over half a continent, and yet he could not come the extra four hundred miles to Sheridan? It was not as if Sheridan were some whistle-stop! They had the inn! Or was that, too, simply a means by which to show his power over his son?

"But, Collier—"

"Please, Lorelei. Please pretend I did not say that."

Collier sounded so miserable that Laurel did hesitate.

With a long whistle, one more called "All aboard!" outside, and a great lurch, the train began its departure from Sheridan. Her home. Where she wanted to be. Laurel had been to Denver before, with her family. But she'd never dreaded it like this!

"Look." Collier pointed. "I made certain we had seats on the west side, so that you can watch the mountains when the sun comes up."

And she looked at him, so golden and beautiful and so kind to her—and so desperate to impress his family—and her heart almost broke. So instead of asking more about his father's motivations, Laurel held her tongue and slipped her hand into Collier's.

He squeezed it tightly.

And for the first time Laurel stopped wondering merely if Collier's family would like her.

For the first time it occurred to her that she might intensely dislike Collier's family.

Chapter Twenty-three

The British-financed Windsor Hotel, five stories of granite and sandstone, dominated downtown Denver. Its spacious lobby and twenty-foot ceilings echoed with culture—as did the genteel clack of billiard balls by the adjacent wine room. This was the world to which Collier had been raised and educated, not the world of incessant cold and daily drudgery.

So why did he find himself murmuring, as they approached his father's rooms, "'Half a league onward'"?

Laurel, on his arm, stopped right there in the hallway. "We're going into the Valley of Death?"

Ah. "You know Tennyson."

"I know that poem. Victoria recited it at school." She considered him a moment. "I have *some* education."

"I never doubted it." In fact, she looked every inch the American heiress. She'd changed from her traveling suit into a sleek day dress of cinnamon-colored batiste, enhanced with lighter lace bands and insets. Her dark brown hair, drawn neatly up with Alexandra's borrowed Lalique combs, glowed with the same good health that lit her blue eyes. And winter had faded her suntanned skin toward a somewhat more ladylike complexion. "In fact, you are everything I could have hoped for in a bride."

"But it's not really—" Whatever she'd meant to say, Laurel ducked her head and tried, "They might not think so."

For a mere second son? He could have done far worse . . . even from their viewpoint. And from his, he was beginning to wonder if he could possibly have done better.

"If anybody can convince them, it is you. Oh!" And he drew a small box from his pocket, one he'd been holding since the day before. "I almost forgot. I brought your engagement ring in for repair. They could not quite match the original; I hope you shan't mind the difference."

"It's smaller," she said—exactly what he had hoped *not* to hear. But then Laurel smiled widely up at him, her heart-shaped face as beautifully unpretentious as ever, and he did not doubt her approval. "I like this one much better. Thank you, Cole."

They stood together in the corridor, glancing both ways as if to hide some desperate dealings, as Laurel removed her glove long enough for Collier to slide the ring onto her finger.

"This one seems sparklier, too," she noted, turning her hand slightly to catch light in its facets. *Interesting.* Collier would not have thought that she, of all women, would so easily see the difference between cut glass and a real diamond.

She surprised him in so many ways.

"Perhaps it's the lighting," he suggested smoothly, helping her put her glove back on. The family would see the diamond when she removed her gloves again to dine, or for tea—no sooner. To show it off would be coarse . . . and, considering the type of ring Lady Vivian would likely wear, foolish.

"Ready?" he asked, taking a deep breath.

"Nope," she admitted just as honestly—but without any plea to back out of this appointment either. "You?"

How could she make him smile, against so serious an occasion? But she did. "Not at all," he assured her. "Shall we?"

" 'Into the valley of the shadow of Death,' " she misquoted.

"That would be the Bible, dearest." He considered that. "I suppose it's better than 'the mouth of hell' though."

She nodded, and Collier knocked.

The Viscount of Brambourne's hotel room, while fine, was still a hotel room all the same. It had a sitting room off the viscount's bedroom, larger than that off hers and Collier's, but hardly a palace. And Collier's father, while a distinguished, strong-jawed man in a fine suit, was still a man.

My father could take him, she thought grimly.

She recognized Edgar easily from his resemblance to Collier—likely their beauty came from their mother. And the three Tentrees—rather, the Fordhams *of* Tentrees—struck her as a matched set of china dolls, mother, father, and daughter.

Before Laurel could see more of Lady Vivian than pale blond beauty, Collier squeezed her hand, and the viscount was commanding her attention. "So this is the wife."

She belatedly realized that Collier had presented her.

The viscount looked her up and down. Was her hair neat? Was her dress nice enough? If so, both were thanks to Collier, not her. And in any case, she'd been spoken to.

"Good afternoon, your lordship."

"Rather chill for me." He turned to Cole. "I see no reason to have hastened a marriage before receiving proper permission."

Laurel wasn't sure she understood the insult—beyond that it *was* an insult, and a rebuke. When she glanced at her husband, the tightness in his jaw showed he did understand.

Either way, Edgar Pembroke, Senior, was doing little to impress her with anything but his poor manners—even the way Americans defined them!

"As my letter explained," said Collier, "the scheduling of our wedding was a business decision regarding her ranch."

"Our ranch," she interrupted. *Oops.*

Collier squeezed her hand. "Of course, dear. Our ranch."

"Yes. Well. We'll speak more of that in private." And that

was clearly all the greeting the viscount would give his second son or his new daughter-in-law. Collier bowed slightly and said "Father," then turned toward his brother.

Edgar, blond and handsome as Collier—if lankier—was more pleasant. "So this is my new sister! Mrs. Pembroke, you are even lovelier than your photograph."

When she extended her hand, he pressed it between his own and kissed her on the cheek quite gracefully. "I trust you are enjoying Denver," he said. Collier had explained that statements were considered more polite than flat-out questions.

She could have said, *We just got here*, or, if she were really honest, *I'd rather be home*. But she said, "Thank you, Lord Edgar. I usually do enjoy Denver."

Again, Collier showed his approval with faint pressure on her hand while Edgar moved his attention to his brother. "And good *Lord*, look at you! How long has it been?"

"A year and a half." Had Cole been counting the days?

"So it has." Edgar had the grace to look uncomfortable. "Water under the bridge, hey? Shake hands, shall we?"

When they did so, the older brother's eyes widened, and Laurel had to swallow back a laugh. Chopping wood tended to strengthen a man's grip, at that.

Then the Tentreeses stood. Collier turned with Laurel to make those introductions. And between giving and receiving proper responses, she finally faced the woman he'd meant to marry.

Golly. If this was what Collier chose on his own, Laurel didn't have a snowball's chance in Texas of keeping him.

Lady Vivian wore what Laurel guessed was the latest fashion from Paris. Her perfume glided across Laurel's nose just as the most expensive scents probably should. Even up close she looked china-doll pale, the most ladylike pallor Laurel had ever seen. Her yellow hair was so carefully dressed it seemed permanent, unlike Laurel's, which was held up not only with hairpins but with prayer. But Lady Vivian owed her poise to more than clothes and hair. She had a lady's posture, a lady's expression, the kind of daintiness Laurel guessed would require assistance through doors and in and out of carriages. Or chairs.

A short woman herself, Laurel felt like a draft horse.

"Charmed," Collier told Lady Vivian with a bow.

"Such formality from an old friend," she scolded. "Do shake hands, Lord Collier, as a brother should."

Laurel hoped he took particular care with the lady's bird-like bones. She noticed that he addressed his "Congratulations on your forthcoming nuptials" to Edgar.

The honor was conferred on the groom, not the bride, Laurel remembered. People really did care about these things!

"May I present my wife," said Collier, as he had to her parents, and now Laurel had to smile and say something inane.

She chose, "I'm pleased to finally meet you, Lady Vivian."

"And you," said the china doll. "We shall be sisters ourselves, shan't we, Mrs. Pembroke?"

She seemed awfully reserved—but so did Uncle Benj's wife sometimes. If Laurel didn't know Vivian had jilted Collier, she didn't guess she would have hard feelings toward the woman.

And considering how she'd benefited from Vivian's loss, maybe she should drop *those* hard feelings, too. "Yes, we shall."

For at least another couple of years. And maybe . . .

But this sure wasn't the time to plot to keep Collier.

The ticking of the clock on the mantel seemed to be increasing in volume. The room's heat stifled her; she longed to rush to the window, throw it open, and hang out into the air. Even if it would be city air, it would be cold. She could at least *see* the mountains beyond the chimneys and the telephone wires, if she just went to the window.

But when the viscount said, "Please join us," she sank onto a settee beside Collier. She was doing this for him, after all. Nothing else mattered, did it?

At least, nothing in Colorado.

Collier said, "I hope you were able to spend time in New York before leaving for the West." Laurel recognized it as one of the four rules of proper conversation—pay compliments, ask after others, be positive, and smile.

Unsure about the first three, she made sure to smile while Edgar began to tell them about New York City.

Had Collier feared Laurel would embarrass him? After dinner and an evening's company with his family, he knew better.

He was an idiot to have doubted her. His family—unfettered by his mother's usual tempering influence—embarrassed him. Laurel was his quiet little rock against a tide of pettiness.

Little of the conversation focused on him or his past year, nor on Laurel and Sheridan. Considering how much he and Laurel had to hide, this was perhaps a fortunate slight . . . but a slight nevertheless. Before leaving England, he'd grown used to being treated as the informal overseer of Brambourne. That had changed with his exile to the American West. These were no longer his peers; they were, by all accounts, his betters. He felt the gulf between what he could have been and what he now was, more by what they did *not* discuss than by what they did.

Instead of asking after Laurel's family, or Collier's plans, they discussed their own travels so far—San Francisco and Los Angeles. Thus far they had not been impressed by the United States. Despite what Collier had so carefully taught Laurel about polite conversation, they said so.

"Their railway travel!" admonished Tentrees. "Could it be more dreadful? The rushing and the pushing."

"I must own that I dislike it immensely," agreed his wife. "The conductors must pound on the doors before opening them, and they barge through demanding to see tickets far more often than is necessary. And those nasty vendors, pestering one to buy their wares despite the most cutting looks!"

Collier knew from their long ride today that Laurel enjoyed train rides. But she smiled politely and said nothing.

"What I find distressing," offered Edgar, "is how one must live at the table d'hôte morning, noon, and night. Thank goodness the Windsor is British enough to provide even sitting rooms, or we should be gathered in their lobby even now."

"They charge extra for it, though," reminded their father. "That would be the Scots' influence."

"And their style is abysmal," agreed Lady Tentrees. "Even once we insisted they bring in flowers, they did not know the fashion of dyeing them until our Vivian explained it."

Looking around him, Collier realized that the room boasted a large crystal vase of white roses—which, likely because of the purple water, were taking on a lavender blush.

"Her favorite color," explained Lady Tentrees.

"Service was no better at dinner," Vivian noted, to murmurs of agreement. "The waiters turn worse the angrier one becomes. It is as if they fear that by waiting on one, they might appear rightly subordinate. I doubt the saying that 'gold cannot tarnish' should have any meaning at all, for that sort."

Laurel's hand was starting to squeeze his. Collier knew the others had noticed the vulgar familiarity of their clasped hands, but counted the loss of appearance a fair price for his ability to reassure his wife. Now he began to wonder if, rather than reassuring her, he was reining Laurel back.

"The manner of the lowliest shop girl indicates perfect equality," mourned Vivian, then covered her mouth with a gloved hand. "Oh! Beg pardon, Mrs. Pembroke."

"My wife," Collier corrected her, only years of training keeping his tone polite, "is the daughter of a cattle baron, and a landowner in her own right."

"Papa hates to be called a cattle baron," Laurel corrected him, her voice low. "He's just a rancher."

"Just a rancher on one of the largest properties in Wyoming," noted the viscount.

Laurel seemed startled, as if she'd forgotten he was there. "Yes, your lordship. But he owns only half of the Circle-T. Your niece's husband, Benjamin Cooper, owns the other half."

Oops. His father's face reddened. "You will refrain from discussing that woman in my presence."

Collier squeezed Laurel's hand. He would explain how Alexandra's marriage had disappointed her family—later. *Please* . . .

When Laurel simply nodded at the viscount, Collier could have kissed her. Had it been proper. Which it was not.

But as soon as the viscount indicated that he was tired of everyone's company for the night and should like to retire, as soon as they maneuvered their way through all the proper good nights and rest wells, Collier all but dragged Laurel back to their own room, then gathered her tightly against him and kissed her with all the gratitude he was humanly capable of conveying in a kiss.

Thank the good Lord that, unlike Vivian, he had no fears of Laurel breaking under the strength of his ardor.

She blinked dazedly up at him as his lips released hers and he took the first truly deep breath he'd had in hours. "Did I do all right, then?"

"You were perfect. You were the true lady in that room, my dearest. If gold truly cannot tarnish, then the company this evening was no more than a clever reproduction."

"Fool's gold." She smiled shyly. "That's what folks call iron pyrite, what they think is gold but isn't. Fool's gold."

"Compared to you, Vivian and Edgar are iron pyrite." And he kissed her again, and somehow, between starting and ending that kiss, they'd sunk to their knees on the drugget carpeting.

What a lovely turn. Unlike at the Coopers', Collier felt no compunctions against making love in a well-built hotel room.

"Compared to you, too," she assured him loyally, arching into his touch as he ran his spread hands down her cinnamon-clad back, over her petticoat-pillowed derriere, then back up the neat darts of her bodice to other pillowy regions. "Mmm."

She couldn't say anything more for several minutes because he was kissing her as erotically as he wanted to make love to her—and undoing her buttons as quickly as he knew how.

Which was rather quickly.

"I don't understand," said Laurel, which surprised him. But when he paused to blink down at her, she laughed a husky, honest laugh. "Oh, I understand *this*," she insisted, pushing his coat off his shoulders. "But . . . what did your father mean about seeing no reason to hasten our marriage. Does he think I'm that ugly?"

"You are not the least bit ugly, my darling," Collier assured her, opening the bodice of her gown, then detouring his attentions to her camisole-covered breasts. That meant laying her onto the carpet and kissing across her chest long enough to dampen the embroidered silk to near transparency. She did have such marvelous breasts.

"Then what—oh, yes, like that! What did he mean?"

Hmm? Oh. "That you're not in the pudding club." When she snorted, he defined that as pregnant. Then, since she liked expanding her vocabulary in the most unladylike of ways, he offered, "Gone. Looking in seduced circumstances. Knocked up."

She laughed. "Knocked up?"

He paused in his enjoyment of her womanly attributes to grin down at her. "Think about it." And, by way of illustration, he thrust gently against her, certain she could feel his arousal even through their clothing.

"Ooh. He thought you'd married me because you had to. Well that *is* rude." She considered that. "And not in a good way."

"What could be rude in a good way?" he challenged, covering her more thoroughly. His demonstration of "knocking" had reminded him of just how marvelous the "up" part would be.

"Mm. Like this." Rocking beneath him, she drew her skirts high enough to free her stockinged legs, wrap them around his, and neatly roll him over onto his back.

"That *is* rude." He stretched under her. "*Ah.* And that."

287

She'd already drawn back on her knees to undo his trousers. Over the last months she'd gotten quite as good with that as he was with the fastenings of a lady's apparel.

Passing footsteps provided an erotic naughtiness to their love play. But they could not have chosen a worse time for someone to knock on the door. "Oh, bloody hell," he muttered, propping himself up on his elbows.

"Shhh," ordered Laurel—and, rude little minx that she was, she slipped a greedy, gloved hand into his trousers' flap, to do more rude things to him . . . in a very good way.

Laurel, he mouthed silently at her, widening his eyes as much with his hot, hard reaction to her touch as with rebuke.

Again the knock at the door—then a familiar voice, pitched just right to be heard inside without disturbing other residents of the hotel. "Collier? It's Edgar."

Bloody hell. Collier supposed he should find out what—

But Laurel shook her head fiercely, scooted back down to straddle his shins—then bent down over him and took him into her mouth. Instead of answering Edgar's summons, Collier found himself stretching his mouth wide in a silent cry, then quickly biting the heel of his hand to keep from giving it voice.

She was being *remarkably* rude. He doubted he'd ever been part of anything so wantonly, wonderfully rude in his life.

"Viv and I hoped to discuss something with you." But with Collier's continued silence—and Laurel's, beyond a tiny, happy slurping noise—Edgar clearly decided they'd not yet gone to their rooms. Were they in the bedroom, rather than the floor of the sitting room, near the door, Collier would have heard no more. The rushing in his head as he clenched his throat against the pleasures shuddering through him did not help.

"P'raps they went out for fresh air," he heard Edgar say.

Then Viv, "Or the bar." Viv was there too!

Laurel began to lick him then, tiny licks up and down the length of him that reduced his breath to tiny little gasps.

"Not with his wife," protested Edgar.

"Oh?"

Laurel sat up at that and glared at the door. Clearly, despite her enjoyment—an enjoyment obvious from both her enthusiasm and her still-damp sheer camisole—she, too, could hear to the hallway. This, of course, was Collier's chance to push her off of him, call excuses through the door, and make himself quickly presentable.

He did not. Instead he slid both hands into her thick, soft hair and drew her firmly back down to what she'd been doing.

Laurel giggled around the girth of him, another beautifully novel sensation, and his voice escaped in a squeak, which made her giggle harder—though she did that silently.

"Did you hear something?" asked Viv from outside the door.

Collier's eyes were tearing.

"What? No, nothing. Let's send a note, then, and he'll come to my rooms later, hey?"

Then Collier heard nothing at all, because Laurel was clearly trying to get her bloomers off under the layers of her brown skirt, wiggling her behind in an adorably distracting way even while she gamely continued her hot-mouthed torture.

Gaining confidence in their privacy as relative silence ticked past, Collier decided to reassert himself. When Laurel sat up to move back over him, he caught her hips and rolled her over onto her back, sliding a thigh—still clothed in neatly creased trousers—between her legs, to tease her in return.

She opened her mouth in clear protest, even as she rocked under the thickness of his leg. *Naughty, heavenly mouth.* But Collier wanted what she did, too much so to taunt her as the little barbarian deserved. Drawing his other knee between her legs and spreading them wide with his own, he slid his now thoroughly wet hardness into her thoroughly hot welcome.

Then he set about finishing, as painstakingly as possible, what the little minx had started.

Writhing and straining beneath him, biting her lip so firmly he feared she would make it bleed, Laurel grasped at his hair, pulling the tie loose from his queue, then weaving her fingers deep into it. Collier tugged her camisole up over her breasts and tried reminding her of just how cruel she'd been just moments earlier. And during it all he continued to thrust.

Filling her, loving her, wholly.

When she began to whimper, he took pity on her and covered her mouth with his to muffle the cries that began to stammer out of her. When the ecstasy clawed him and he finally shuddered his seed into her, she silenced his own howl of joy in the same way.

He poured himself out, more of him than he knew existed—never had he found release so violently in his life—and by the time he'd sunk onto her, completely exhausted, he truly feared he could not move.

Good heavens. What had he done, marrying this girl?

Even as he wondered that, he managed to drop his head just far enough to kiss across the fine, soft hair at her temple. It had fallen from its coif, of course, in rich, dark waves. And Laurel's skin, flushed pink with his lovemaking—had he ever thought it unladylike?

He now understood his need to buy her a real diamond, even if it used most of his latest remittance. This was no longer a counterfeit marriage, no matter what they'd said or planned. Whatever they did in the future, it was real right now, and he could not have felt more fortunate. Or more fearful.

Because the only thing he wanted as badly as to stay married to Laurel was the one thing she'd protested from the start.

Another knock sounded at the door, this one more tentative, and Collier stiffened atop his wife. *Again?*

But this time nobody called. Instead a folded paper slid under the door, and footsteps continued away from them.

For a long time Collier just stared at the bit of stationery on the carpeting.

"Can you reach it?" asked Laurel finally, her voice thick with satisfaction.

"I fear," he said, panting across her damp skin, still on her, still in her, "that I cannot move at present. Even were I willing."

"Want me to?"

"Please do."

So she reached out an arm still sleeved in cinnamon batiste—neither of them had actually shed anything except perhaps her skivvies—and caught it with her fingertips, drew it back to them and, one-handed, managed to bully it open.

" 'Collier,' " she read. " 'Please see me as soon as possible, regarding . . .' Oh."

"Hold it steady and I can read the rest," he offered. But when he saw the words, he wondered if she'd stopped from an inability to read Edgar's handwriting, or an unwillingness.

Please see me as soon as possible, regarding the future of Brambourne. We need you back.
Resp., E.

"Oh," he said. Something of an understatement.

We need you back.

It was the one thing he wanted as badly as he wanted Laurel.

England.

Chapter Twenty-four

"I *do* have to see what they want," insisted Collier, stripped to his waist and washing himself at the cherrywood stand. Laurel sat on the bed and watched him.

Actually she was admiring him: his bare back and shoulders and chest, how he could be so broad in some places and so slim in others. Was it any wonder she couldn't keep her hands off him?

Remembering what they'd done on the carpet, in this oh-so-posh hotel, she felt warm for more reasons than the flannel nightgown she'd changed into behind the dressing screen while Collier washed other parts and put on neatly pressed trousers.

"And I'll thank you not to distract me again," her husband ordered sternly, turning to point at her.

Laurel widened her eyes in an attempt at innocence. After all, he was the one who had started things, kissing her like that. After hours of suffocation, biting her tongue and smiling like a fool, Laurel had felt desperate to collect her reward, to remind herself of why she'd come here.

Which was him. And, oh, he had reminded her!

In the washbasin mirror, she saw that he'd smiled despite his pretense at severity. A real lopsided Collier smile.

"Never distract you again?" And she hugged her flannel-draped knees up to her chest. It seemed a terribly big bed to be alone in while he went to see what his brother wanted.

The future of Brambourne.

He dried himself off. "Not tonight, at least."

"Not at all tonight? Couldn't I distract you a little when you get back from the summons?" Likely she was a hoyden, at that. But when misbehaving felt as good as Collier did . . .

Well! She still felt warm and tender and satisfied from that. And she'd rather savor those sensations than the fear that had nibbled at her ever since she'd read his note. *We need you back.*

We. That meant Lord Edgar *and* Lady Vivian, right?

They needed him back. In England.

Collier sighed as he slipped into a fresh white shirt, hiding his sleek muscles. "It is an opportunity, not a summons."

"Oh." An opportunity to return to England. Away from her.

"How promising an opportunity, I shan't know until I get there." He tucked the shirt into his pants, then combed his burnished hair and tied it back into its neat tail.

"They never mentioned your hair," said Laurel, watching Collier's gaze capture hers in the mirror, then refocus onto his work. Actually, the Englishers hadn't talked about him much at all, considering that he'd been gone for over a year.

"That means they detest it."

"Oh." She considered that. "They didn't mention me, either."

"Of course they did, dearest. Edgar admired your beauty, Vivian called you a shop girl, and Father noted that I've not yet knocked you up." When he turned back to her, dimples crescented his cheeks and his eyes shone bright, reassuring her of how little the poor opinions of others mattered. Especially theirs. What mattered was his. And he'd said . . .

"Not yet?" she asked, and fear chewed a little harder.

"I meant to say, at all," he assured her. "I've not forgotten our bargain. I fear we've shocked the druggist with our number of purchases."

"We keep forgetting to use them." She sighed. "The letters." Even this evening. She'd enjoyed it even more for the oversight.

Collier paused while adjusting the drape of his suit jacket, then turned back to her, more serious this time. "I should like to discuss that later. If you are willing."

Laurel swallowed. Hard. Was he angry that she forgot? Did he think she meant to trap him into staying married permanently?

Or was there the chance that he *wanted* more?

She wasn't sure which likelihood frightened her more. If he was returning to England and wanted babies with her, then it meant he wanted them together . . . but not in Wyoming.

They should not have forgotten the French letters so often.

"All right," she agreed bravely. "When you get back."

"Thank you, darling." Collier started toward the door to the sitting room, then stopped himself, came back to the bed, and leaned gracefully across it to kiss her. Laurel liked that very much. It felt so wonderfully . . . married. She had to use every bit of self-control she had left to keep their kiss chaste, to let Collier go instead of seducing him onto the bed, trying to keep him there so long that he'd never find out what Edgar offered.

After she'd spent the evening experiencing British society, her supply of self-control was running dangerously low.

To Collier's surprise, not just Edgar but Vivian waited in the antechamber of the rooms beside their father's.

"Good Lord," he exclaimed as his older brother closed the door behind them. "Do you mean to court scandal, or are you—"

But he bit back the rest. He was no longer the overseer of Brambourne. He'd lost whatever right he'd had to bully his older brother out of the messes Eddie regularly created.

Then Vivian, from her chair, said, "You were not so afraid of scandal two years ago, Collier," and he went quite still.

Edgar knew about Vivian. Did Father, Tentrees? Would they . . . ?

Collier tamped back panic with the realization that they had little ammunition left against him. Would they deprive him of his family, the land of his ancestors? Make him shovel manure or live in a one-room shed? Father might yet reduce his remittance, but most of that came from his mother's inheritance. Tentrees was unlikely to call him out. And they could not make him marry Vivian, because he was already married.

Laurel to the rescue again.

Rather than making excuses, Collier said, "Two years ago I knew what was to be gained. Tonight you must enlighten me."

"Have a drink," offered Edgar, indicating the chairs with a sweep of his own hand. "Courvoisier? Or perhaps absinthe?"

Trust Edgar to find absinthe in Denver.

Collier accepted the offer and the chair—the one farthest from his affianced sister-in-law. "The brandy, please."

"I must apologize, Lord Collier," said Viv softly, "about having broken our agreement. You must believe how dreadful I felt. But what else could I do? They'd sent you away to this horrible wilderness, and I had nobody. And . . . well . . ."

Collier felt as if he were waiting for the ax to drop.

"My marital prospects are limited," she reminded him. "Since I am not . . . not"—she ducked her head in a way he'd once found charming, but now saw as merely high-strung—"pure."

He rose and strode across the room. "Good Lord, Viv!"

Edgar handed him the Courvoisier, and Collier took a longer draft of it than was wholly polite. "This is hardly the place!"

"Don't mind me," said Edgar. "Vivvie and I have no secrets."

Again Collier wondered what he had to lose. He suspected he could take Edgar, if it came to fisticuffs. Maybe. "May I remind you, Lady Vivian, that you were not pure two years ago either."

He took another sip of the brandy, awaiting the worst.

Viv's eyes widened. "I most certainly was! Merely because there was no . . . Oh! It is too lowly even to discuss."

There had been no blood when he'd first bedded Laurel, either. Heaven only knew in what childhood fall from a tree, or a horse, or a rock his wife had lost the proof of her virginity. But he'd known. With Vivian he'd resolved to overlook his doubts—as long as she carried no other man's child, and stayed faithful afterward, who was he to scorn her?

But if she was blaming *that* for her engagement to Edgar!

"No use, Vivvie," said Eddie now, remarkably cheerful for a man whose future bride had just been insulted. And, according to her, deflowered by his own brother. "I told you he would have noticed the difference. If there's anything Collier knows, it's the horses between his legs, and the women . . . well."

"Thank you." Lady Vivian turned firmly away from them both.

Collier studied his older brother with some surprise. "Are there no secrets between you, then?"

Edgar, who had his own skeletons, raised his own glass to acknowledge Collier's unspoken question. "None. Which, my dear brother, brings us to the issue at hand."

The future of Brambourne. We need you back.

Collier dismissed his first suspicion as too bizarre, even for Edgar's creative standards. But he had difficulty forming a second suspicion, and so waited for them to enlighten him.

Rather than say more, Edgar offered his fiancée a gloved hand. "Lady Vivian? Perhaps you . . ."

With a nod, Viv rose and went to Collier's side, pale and golden. Once, Collier would not have put any thought into how a lady achieved her beauty, only that she did. Now he wondered if Vivian were one of those women who took small doses of arsenic to keep their complexions.

If so, Edgar faced yet more hurdles in siring an heir.

"It's simple, really," she said—then kissed him.

"Perhaps I should leave you two alone," suggested Edgar.

But Collier caught Viv by the shoulders and pushed her firmly away—to full arm's length. While her lips parted further in dismay, he took several steps back for good measure. *Lord!* His first suspicion, bizarre or not, had been correct! "*I'll* leave."

"Collier!" protested Vivian.

Edgar looked from one of them to the other, amused. "I say. Is that how I looked when you first tried it on me, Vivvie?"

"You," she reminded Edgar, turning so sharply that her skirts swayed, "had a reason for rejecting me so rudely."

She thought *that* was rude? It took every ounce of Collier's gentlemanly breeding to not wipe his mouth on the back of his gloved hand. "As have I," he told her coolly. "Like Edgar's, my interests are otherwise engaged."

His brother reared back, one eyebrow quirked. "Oh, really?"

"I *am* married," Collier reminded them. That he'd left his wife's side to meet these two seemed increasingly foolish.

"Oh, that." Viv sank back onto a chair without any help. "I understand your animosity at our engagement, Collier, but really! You need not have been so drastic as to marry, much less *her*."

"It had nothing to do with your engagement," Collier insisted. At least, it no longer did. Somehow his values had indeed changed—so very, very much. "I love my wife."

And he only felt foolish for not telling the wife first.

"What remarkable fidelity," noted Edgar. "You really *are* going native on us, hey, Leatherstocking?"

"Good evening." And Collier made a cold bow to them.

He hadn't reached the door before Vivian said, "You could be back in England by summer, Lord Collier. To *stay*."

And he stopped. He loved—*loved!*—Laurel. But Wyoming . . .

"Return to England how?" he asked.

And at the knowing look his brother and future sister-in-law exchanged, he felt caught as surely as Laurel had been when the creek dragged her into its freezing current.

He merely faced a different class of danger.

Their room did not, Laurel found, overlook the mountains. Unable to sleep without Collier, she opened the window anyway. Even with a view mainly of telephone wires, trolley lines, and chimneys, lit by so many lights as to cheapen the waning moon, the icy cold felt fresher than the steam-heated air of the hotel.

It felt more like home, even if it didn't smell of it. And this was Denver! What must flatland cities smell like?

Laurel wanted to go out—just around the corner, to see the Rockies that dominated Denver's horizon. But it was late . . . and she was a lady. More of a lady every day, darn it. And less . . . herself.

Since she must be squandering coal, or electricity, or whatever the Windsor used to power its steam radiators, Laurel reluctantly closed the window and climbed into the large, soft bed to await Collier. Funny how in the mountains, often miles from another human, she never felt alone. But in a posh city hotel, with more people living within a mile than she guessed populated all of Sheridan, she felt horribly lonely.

She would feel better when Collier returned, of course. He was the reason she'd come—that and the deal they'd made.

The deal didn't include her worrying what he would say—about babies or England—when he got back. Watching her covered feet, moving under the blanket like gophers, Laurel guessed she ought to stop thinking of it as a pretend marriage at all.

But, oh, those awful people. Carpeted rooms with dyed flowers. Gloves and girl-shoes! She hadn't fallen in love with Collier's suits or etiquette—even if she'd come to love the kindness behind his manners. She hadn't fallen in love with his taste for opulence. She'd fallen in love with him *despite* those things.

Desperate for distraction, she got up again, pulled on her robe, and sat down at the writing table in the sitting room to try, yet again, penning a brand for her unnamed ranch. Thus far she'd used earmarks to blaze hers and Cole's cattle. But come spring roundup, they'd need a brand. Before marrying, she'd considered everything with an *L—lazy, flying, backward, bar, double-bar*—to no avail. Now that Collier might leave . . .

She still had another year or two, she reminded herself. He was honorable enough to see their deal through.

Which was only one reason, out of a mountain of them, that she should let him go anyway. Collier had helped with *her* dream.

But he also wanted to talk about the French letters. Which meant there was at least the chance he wanted to quit them. Which maybe meant something else.

If they *were* truly married, forever married . . .

Feeling like some of those girls back in school who would practice combining initials on their slates, Laurel dipped the pen in the inkwell and began to try variations of the brand including the letters *P*, and *CP*. Or perhaps *BB*, for Brambourne. Maybe that would flatter his self-important father enough to toss Collier at least a crumb or two of recognition.

But then it wasn't her brand at all.

She covered two pages, but nothing worked. Maybe a body had to be out on the range to hit upon a proper brand. Or maybe a person ought to know how much longer she would have a partner.

When the door opened, she all but spun to face it. *He's back*, she soothed herself. *He's back!*

But for how much longer?

"Laurel!" Collier looked odd. Tired. Hesitant. When he came to her side, kissed her cheek—like a husband, *her* husband—he smelled somehow different, too. But the way he

paused, then ducked back for another kiss on her mouth—
that was pure Collier. So was his self-deprecating smile, all
bright eyes and dimples, when he did straighten.

"Whatever are you doing awake?" he asked, shrugging off
his suit jacket as he went into the bedchamber.

"I was waiting for you." Stoppering the inkpot, Laurel followed him. "I can't sleep in this place."

She was perfectly happy to clamber onto the bed now, to
sit and watch him remove his gloves, loosen his tie. She loved
watching him undress, especially the jacket and gloves and
tie. She loved that she got to have the *real* Collier.

"This is the best hotel in Denver," he reminded her on a
laugh. "How could you not sleep here?"

"It's too close."

"As opposed to your cabin?" She felt a lump of uncertainty
deep inside her when he called it *her* cabin.

"In our cabin there's nobody on the other side of the wall."

Raising his eyebrows with curiosity, Collier leaned slowly
closer to the wall opposite of her, apparently listening. Then
he shrugged and came back to the bed, sitting down to un-
button his shoes. "I apologize for keeping you waiting, dearest."

He apologized so easily, and for things that weren't even
his fault. She admired that about him. As difficult as she
found apologies, his showed a kind of quiet courage.

Her fingers itched to reach across the space between them
and untie his hair, to let it fall into little golden waves below
his collar . . . but then they would never talk.

And if they stopped talking, they might forget the French
letters again. And before they did that, she really should
know, even if she feared his answers.

"How did it go?" she asked. "With Edgar."

Bending over his second shoe, Collier hesitated—then
shook his head. "I'm not certain you would want to know."

"I wouldn't have asked if I didn't!"

"No. I suppose you would not. I apologize."

So maybe that courage of his could annoy her some, too.

Especially when it kept him dancing around the topic at hand. Well, she had her own strengths, even if they were nowhere near as diplomatic. "Are you going back to England with them?"

For a long, horrifying moment, Collier just sat there with his elbows on his knees, a shoe still dangling from one hand. Maybe he hadn't decided yet, or didn't know how to tell her.

You can, if you really want to, she ought to say.

We can renegotiate our agreement, she ought to assure him.

Instead she just stared at him and waited miserably until he said, "No, Lorelei. I'm not going back to England with them."

And then she flung her arms around him and kissed his cheek and his jaw and his neck and his mouth instead. "Oh, good!"

"Whoa!" Laughing, Collier caught the bedpost with one hand to keep from falling off under the momentum of her hug. Then he wrapped her in his strong arms, and he really kissed her.

As if she were something special. As if maybe, just maybe, he wouldn't mind being forever-married, too.

"I'm pleased you approve," he admitted huskily as they drew barely apart to catch a breath. Even then, he nuzzled her cheek with his. "It is important for a man . . ." *Mmm.* He'd found her ear. ". . . and his wife to agree on matters of import," he assured her. "For a successful domestic partnership."

She giggled when his breath tickled her neck. He drew back to grin at her, bright and lopsided, and she felt soft inside.

"Do we have a successful domestic partnership?" she asked.

He'd said earlier that he wanted to discuss the French letters and how they kept forgetting them. They'd agreed early on that even if consummating the marriage would not make it permanent, babies would.

Laurel still wasn't sure she wanted babies. But, oh, she

wanted him. And maybe if they were *his* babies . . .

Collier traced the backs of his fingers up Laurel's cheek as if admiring the slope of her face, her eyes. As if she were anywhere near as pretty as Lady Vivian.

But thinking of his former fiancée, some missing impression slipped into place. It didn't make sense. It wasn't possible. There had to be an explanation, of course. What was it?

"I do think," promised Collier, "that we are well on our way."

Either he was lying, or there was some explanation. Or the British saw things even more differently than Laurel had feared.

"Then why," she asked as evenly as she could—despite her inability to breathe, to think, to understand—"do you smell like Lady Vivian?"

Chapter Twenty-five

Trust Collier to marry a bloodhound.

"There is an explanation," he assured Laurel quickly, but with dignity. A gentleman never lost his dignity.

Although, faced with the wrath—and worse, the pain—of his rancher wife, a gentleman came close!

"Lady Vivian was in Edgar's rooms with him." At least that news startled her out of her original suspicion—or what Collier could only assume was her original suspicion.

Though, really—as if he could have done anything with Viv tonight, after what he and Laurel had done. *Well, good Lord!* He doubted he had the strength to do more with *Laurel* tonight!

"Alone!" she asked, wide-eyed.

"With Edgar, of course." Lest she fear some sort of tryst.

"They aren't married yet!"

"They were not, I assure you, doing anything infamous."

"Still, for a real lady, that Vivian has to be one of the most unladylike women I've ever known. You said yourself that *you* once—" *Oops.* Laurel's eyes darkened into suspicion again.

303

Collier began to see the downside to marital honesty.

"Why *do* you smell like her, Lord Collier?" she asked.

So much for *Cole*. But she had cause for suspicion—more than he liked to admit—and as her husband, admit it he must. So he caught her hands in his, not merely for her comfort but for his own safety. "This may sound worse than it should."

She lifted her chin in silent challenge and waited.

"She kissed me," he confessed.

Laurel sat still for a long moment. Then she swallowed. Very steadily, she asked, "Did you kiss her back?"

"Good Lord, no!" The honesty felt good, there.

It relieved him that she took a breath—a deep one. Deep enough to swell the front of her robe, though he ought not be noticing that at this precarious juncture in their evening.

Then she asked, "How did she kiss you?"

"Laurel! A gentleman—" But her expression finished that answer. When it came to one's wife, he supposed a gentleman did not protect the reputation of other ladies, at that. "She just kissed me. It shocked me quite as much as it shocks you."

She scowled—hurt? Angry? "Did she open her mouth?"

Collier looked briefly away, mustering his strength. "Yes."

"What did you do?"

And suddenly he felt relieved to be telling this to somebody. Not just somebody—to Laurel. "For a moment I was too startled to do anything! Then I pushed her away. That's why you smell her on me, see?" He sniffed his hands, then offered them to her as proof, and Laurel smelled them too.

Then she leaned tentatively nearer him and sniffed his neck, his chest, his hair. Collier closed his eyes against the erotic warmth of her, so close to him.

Laurel sat back, sniffed her own hands—and scrambled off the bed for the washbasin. "Yuck! I smell like her too."

Yuck? Collier smelled his hands again, barely detecting the faint trace of Vivian's Parisian scent. But Laurel was washing it off as she would manure or rabbit guts.

Perhaps the Lady Vivian had more in common with such offal than he had ever once realized. "We shall burn the gloves," he offered, also standing. "Laurel, please believe how sorry I am. I should have left the moment I saw Lady Vivian in attendance. I assumed that since Edgar was there—"

"She kissed you in front of Edgar?" Laurel spun to gape at him, water dripping off her elbows.

He caught the towel off its rod and wrapped it gently around her hands. "And I *did* push her away."

She tugged the towel away from him to dry herself in more violent swipes than would he. "Did she fall down?"

Collier drew back. "No!"

"Then you didn't push her hard enough."

He washed his own hands and took the towel from her. "I hope you know me well enough to know there are several things I should never do," he told her stiffly. "One is mistreat a woman—even a woman who behaves as poorly as did Lady Vivian tonight."

Another is to betray you.

But that realization still felt too new, too fragile to offer her yet. When he did confess his love of Laurel *to* Laurel, he would not bury it amid cheap apologies for Lady Vivian. It should stand as more than a distraction.

Distracting though it was.

Laurel was pacing now, scowling—and he loved her. He loved that she *did* believe him. He loved that she did not sulk merely to extort jewelry or travel from him . . . as if she wanted either. He loved that, whether she realized it or not, she'd become a moral touchstone for him, a reason powerful enough, consequential enough, to compel him toward the right decision.

Without Laurel, he might have accepted Edgar and Viv's demeaning offer. Because of his wife, he had to be a better man.

For that, too, he loved her.

"What did Edgar want to talk to you about?" she demanded. "Why did he let Vivian kiss you? Did he end the engagement?"

She looked so hopeful at that thought that Collier found himself smiling—despite the bizarre offer that they had made, and how surprisingly difficult it had been to turn them down.

He just had to keep reminding himself that he had not rejected England, only Edgar and Vivian.

"Come sit down," he entreated, climbing onto the bed and opening his arms to her. He was still mostly dressed, but that was perhaps just as well, if they were to talk. "You're exhausting yourself, and it's been too long a day already."

Laurel eyed him suspiciously. "Will you tell me everything? I need to know everything, Cole. I *need* to."

He supposed any wife would be upset. Had a man kissed *her* . . . !

Even if she'd not kissed the rotter back, and even if she pushed him away so that he fell down—a nice flight of stairs, perhaps—Collier could not imagine accepting it gracefully.

"Every bit," he promised. To his relief, she climbed onto the bed and to him. It felt good to lean back against the headboard and cuddle his wife—his *beloved* wife—to him while they talked. She smelled of soap, pine, warmth, and Laurel.

And he had no fears of breaking her.

"You must repeat none of this, though," he admonished, while she leaned her head against his shoulder to look up at him as he spoke. "Agreed?"

She nodded. "I'm not Victoria. I can keep a secret."

"*This* secret, dearest, is of great import." But when Edgar entertained Viv's scheme, he had made it Laurel's business. And Collier trusted her. That felt as good as she did in his arms. "My brother is unlikely ever to sire an heir."

"Why? Is he sick?"

Was there no end to the improper education he was giving this wife of his? "It is rather more complicated than that. He . . . does not fall in love with women." *As I have.*

306

"Why doesn't he?" He loved how she could look so tousled and innocent, and yet so seductive, all at the same time.

"Because he loves other men." When she stared up at him, waiting to understand, he tried again. "It's not as uncommon as you might think . . . but in England and America it is quite illegal. This is why you must tell nobody—not even my father."

Especially not his father! Considering how badly the Marquess of Queensbury had reacted when he had learned of *his* son . . .

"I know my brother," Collier insisted. "I've known him well enough and long enough to know that this is no foppish whim. It is simply . . . Edgar. I trust you not to condemn him for it."

She shook her head. "But how can love be illegal?"

"Perhaps in the same way our French letters are illegal, though with harsher penalties," he reminded her. "Every time I go to the druggist for more, he and I risk fines or arrest under your Comstock Law. As for Edgar, it's more the practice."

Despite their privacy, he leaned even closer to explain sodomy—and so that he could kiss her hair, breathe her scent.

Laurel's eyes widened. "Men *like* that?"

"Some of them." And some women, from what he'd heard.

She marveled at that, then asked, "Have we ever done anything illegal? Other than the French letters?"

"If we have not," he whispered, "we may yet."

He enjoyed watching her blush, an honest flush of her cheeks, as she imagined the possibilities. Everything about Laurel was honest. Not always as refined as he should have chosen, nor as deliberate. But the only dishonesty he'd ever seen from her, he had suggested in the first place.

Which worried him the more when she said, "But what does this have to do with any scheme?"

"Ah. That." He'd been more comfortable explaining sodomy. "Edgar is as unlikely to lie with Lady Vivian as would you be."

307

Safe in the circle of his arms, she laughed. "Well, that's just silly. We're both girls."

Collier fought back a smile. Another topic, for another day. "He may have difficulty siring an heir. With no son . . ."

This, at least, she understood. "Then *you* inherit."

Viscount of Brambourne. Everything he had longed for. Everything Edgar had ended by breaking their bargain.

"Which neither Edgar nor Father want. Nor Viv, for that matter. So the bargain that they proposed," he admitted, wincing at the sheer impropriety of it, "is that *I* sire the next heir of Brambourne on Vivian, and let Edgar claim the child as his."

Laurel sat up, despite that this meant leaning out of the circle of his arms. "No!"

Lord, but he wished he weren't so exhausted. Loyalty such as hers deserved rewards beyond jewelry or trips. Pleasuring her until she screamed would be a fair start.

"Of course I said no," he assured her, taking her hand.

"Of course you did. Why would they even think you would consider something like that?"

Well, he had stayed to listen.

Laurel jiggled his hand, holding hers, to prompt his reassurance. "Cole? Why would they think that?"

He lifted her hand to his lips again, then admitted, "They made a compelling argument, Lorelei."

"How? If they're childless, you inherit it all."

"*We* inherit it all," he corrected—and she ducked her head against his shoulder again. "Or our son does. Had we a son."

She did not pursue that, so he left that subject for later as well. "But that would be years away. And if they make the offer elsewhere, a pretender could take the estate."

"That wouldn't be fair!"

There was so much about the peerage that his darling Laurel did not comprehend.

"Also, in return for my . . . contributions . . . Edgar promised to invite me home. And I would see my child, or children, inherit."

"Children?" Her eyes widened. "This wouldn't be just a one-time stud service?"

Lord help him for marrying a rancher's daughter—though he doubted she'd learned that term from her father. Now *he* felt like blushing. "Er, no. Another good reason to refuse."

"Why would anyone want children they couldn't claim?"

"To know my line would continue running the estate." When she didn't appreciate the importance of that, he addressed the more personal issues. "I would become a . . . beloved uncle."

He saw no more misgiving in her pretty face than he'd seen when he'd explained other facts of life. She still did not suspect her own questionable parentage.

"But . . ." she began. She'd said that quite a bit tonight.

"I did say no, Lorelei," he reminded her softly.

"They shouldn't have asked," she insisted stubbornly.

No, they should not. Even if there *had* been a chance.

He kissed her for her loyalty. "But they did, and I refused, and the polite response now is to pretend it never happened."

"I'm supposed to go on being nice to her?"

"Merely polite," he assured her. Then, since they were back in civilization, he kissed her cheek and stood to prepare for bed properly—lest there be a fire, and anybody should notice.

"Collier?" asked Laurel as he unbuttoned his shirt. He glanced over his shoulder to where she sat, perplexed, on the bed. "Your *mother* is nice, isn't she?"

What an odd thing to ask. "My mother is a paragon."

"What about Agnes? And your little brother, Acton?"

He stepped behind the dressing screen long enough to pull on a bedshirt. "Acton is a bookish sort, rather like your sister Kathryn. Agnes is . . ." He tried to remember the last time he'd seen his baby sister. It made him sad to think of how long he'd gone without seeing them. "Agnes has a . . . brightness to her."

When he came out from behind the screen, Laurel had crawled under the covers and lay with her cheek on the pillow, watching solemnly for him. Would she ever not be inviting?

Although the spirit was willing, for once the body was weak—no little fault of their mischief on the sitting room carpet! Collier turned down the lights before climbing into the bed beside his wife. He wrapped her in his arms, drawing her tightly against him.

With Laurel beside him, the ache of homesickness dulled somewhat. "Good night, dearest," he whispered into the darkness.

She wriggled slightly against him, as if she could crawl right into him through the nightshirt and his skin. "Collier?"

"What is it?"

"I'm glad you're not going away to England."

He felt her waiting. Did she want him to say he was glad too? He couldn't. He was pleased to be with her, and relieved not to have prostituted himself. But not returning to England . . .

"I'm glad you're glad," he offered finally, holding her.

And he knew he'd let her down.

If only Vivian would behave herself, thought Laurel the next day at breakfast, perhaps she could forgive the kiss.

But she disliked Vivian for so much more than that.

Again the viscount and the Fordhams decided their waiter was dawdling simply to annoy them. When Laurel tried to smile encouragement at the man, she received pointed looks too.

More from the two women, she noticed. Collier did not seem to notice, and even Edgar seemed amiable. They *were* brothers.

When Laurel called a greeting to an elderly rancher of her father's acquaintance, the Englishers stared at her again—though Collier rose to the occasion, standing for the introductions and even remembering that Americans preferred handshakes to bows. "Collier Pembroke, sir. A pleasure."

"Granville Stuart," said the rancher, then presented his

wife, Allis Belle. Collier introduced the rest of the company.

"Congratulations on your nuptials," said old Mr. Stuart—to Collier. Did *everyone* know these rules? Then he turned back to Laurel. "You say hello to your mother and father for us, hear?"

"Yes, sir."

"Aren't you the popular one?" teased Collier as he sat.

Enjoying the brightness of his smile, Laurel almost didn't hear Lady Vivian murmur, "*Who* was *that?*"

It somehow sounded like, *Who do they think they are?*

"Mr. Stuart owns one of the oldest ranches in Montana," offered Laurel, then took a sip of water. "That's all."

It was that easy. Especially when Baron Tentrees, watching the couple leave, said, "I've heard of him."

Vivian's eyes flared at the setback. Laurel sat up taller.

That was when she began to suspect she would not make it through the day without having it out with the Lady Vivian.

After breakfast the gentlemen discussed business while the ladies went through their invitations for the day. Laurel sat in the middle of the room, finding fault with both conversations.

"So you did not know Stuart," the viscount accused Collier. "Tentrees here did. And he's not posing as a cattle rancher."

Posing?

"It may be a small ranch, Father," said Collier evenly. "But as we are raising cattle, I protest your characterization."

"Tell me something about ranching then." And the viscount sat back, folded his arms, and waited.

Edgar, who had taken a position slightly behind his father, raised his eyebrows as if at an intriguing scene in a play . . . especially when Collier did just that. Laurel found herself smiling, and not just from good manners, as Collier explained the American cattle market. Her husband might not have been raised around cattle, but clearly he could learn.

But all his father said was, "So you haven't shown profit."

"At the moment, not a brass farthing," agreed Collier.

The viscount opened his mouth again, but Laurel beat him to it. "It takes two years to show a profit on cattle!"

She might as well have blown her nose on her sleeve, the way every head in the room came up, like horses sensing danger. Ladies weren't supposed to interrupt? Well, she guessed noblemen weren't supposed to belittle their sons, either.

"Thank you, dear," said Collier into the silence. His smile was even, though, without dimples. "But Father has every right to ask how we are investing his money."

His money? The way the viscount nodded told her just why Collier had said that, too. When the older man began to praise how British and Scottish interests were pulling out of the dying market, Laurel made herself turn to Vivian and her mother.

"Mrs. Crawford Hill!" The Lady Tentrees lifted a cream-colored card. "If we must attend any of these dreary receptions, I suppose we should attend hers."

"Is she consequential?" asked Vivian.

"For Denver," qualified her mother.

Laurel remembered her own mother, on a visit to Denver, turning down an invitation from someone with that name. Hill, like the posh Capitol Hill neighborhood where most of Denver's old guard lived. "I despise exclusivity," Mama had said firmly.

Feeling increasingly trapped, Laurel stood and moved to the window, beside that big vase of silly purple roses. She had to wipe the pane with a gloved hand to better see the Rocky Mountains. Feeling the chill on her face, she could imagine the whispering sound of the snow, wrapping the world in white.

". . . sent you here to make something of yourself." The viscount caught her attention again. "And I've seen little proof of it."

"Father—" protested Edgar gently.

"The cattle boom is over; he says so himself." Now the viscount spoke to the Baron Tentrees, not even to Collier. "Men make fortunes on the new, on what they know. None of that here."

"Perhaps," said Collier, "we should wait more than four months to judge my success."

"Four months or four years. I can tell when the spark is there, boy, and you've got no spark. Not for cattle."

"But *I* know cattle!" When Collier slanted a gaze of protest toward her, Laurel stared right back. She had every right to speak, whether she'd married an Englishman or not. "And Collier has incredible business sense. And he knows horses, too. You can't have a ranch without horses."

"Mrs. Pembroke." What bothered her was, it was Collier who said that. He said it gently. His mercurial eyes were asking for her cooperation, not ordering it. But . . . *Mrs. Pembroke?*

Edgar came to her rescue. "She's quite correct, you know. I've seen Collier play polo. He's a smashing rider; always has the best string. Several of my friends have commented on it."

"I *had* the best string," Collier said. "In England."

And he'd had a thoroughbred mare, but Laurel had lost it.

"Polo!" dismissed the viscount. "A mere diversion."

Then Edgar and Tentrees both began to argue about London polo clubs, tournaments, and something called a Westchester cup. Collier told them about a ranch in San Antonio, and the Baron Tentrees laughed at what he'd seen of scrawny cow ponies.

Collier said, "You've not seen them do cutting work, then."

Laurel would have enjoyed more of that particular discussion, had Lady Vivian not caught her ear with the question, "Should I know who Mrs. Margaret Tobin Brown is?"

"Only to avoid her, dear," assured her mother. "She's dreadfully coarse. You saw her at the opera."

"Her?" And Vivian giggled. "Nouveau riche."

"And *Irish*," added Lady Tentrees.

Vivian nodded her resolve. "Then I shall write only the briefest of apologies and dispose of her invitation at once."

And Laurel said, "Given the choice, I would prefer to accept Mrs. Brown's invitation than Mrs. Hill's."

The men were still debating horses. But both ladies blinked.

"Then it is lucky for our reputations," said Vivian, "that you *have* no choice." And with a superior smile, she dropped the invitation into the wastebasket.

At least Laurel did not have to wonder if that had been deliberate. Even the Lady Tentrees said, "Vivian, really."

Laurel walked to the wastebasket, reached in, and withdrew the card. "Mrs. Brown's parties are always more interesting."

"Have you ever been to one?"

"No, but my parents have." *Once.* From what Victoria had gathered, their father had spent most of the time in the furnace room with Mr. Brown, escaping the to-do. But Mama had enjoyed herself. "Then again, my mother is part Irish herself."

The Lady Tentrees's eyes flared. "Oh, my God."

"I understand you much better now," said Lady Vivian smugly. "But you still"—and she snatched the card from Laurel's hand—"have no say in the matter. I am the daughter of a baron, and I am the one marrying the heir to Brambourne. You only married Collier."

Laurel was only vaguely aware that the men seemed to have stopped debating polo, horses, or anything else. "Dearest," called the Baron Tentrees in disapproval.

His wife turned back to Vivian. "You must remember your responsibility as the party of breeding," she insisted, low. Then she turned the facade of a smile to Laurel. "Please excuse our manners, Mrs. Pembroke. Americans do not always follow the same . . . protocol . . . for deciding their social engagements."

That wouldn't have soothed Laurel even if Vivian's slur— *You only married Collier*—weren't rushing through her head.

"First off—" And Laurel took the invitation back. She had younger sisters. She knew exactly how to firmly catch Vivian's skinny wrist, then pry the card from her helpless hand. "Why don't I write our apology to Mrs. Brown. I don't trust you to

314

follow American protocol. And second—" Here she leaned closer, still holding the British vixen captive with one strong hand. "If you value my husband so little, you can keep your skinny, blue-blooded lips off him! *Eh?*"

"Oh, my God," said Lady Tentrees again.

"You may," said Vivian, "have no choice in that either,"

The tramp had grit. Laurel hadn't expected that. But Laurel's scuffles sometimes left *boys* crying, in her wilder youth. If she couldn't take on a skinny piece of taffeta like this, she guessed she wasn't frontier material after all.

"Maybe I don't have say over what he does," she conceded. "But that works both ways. You push me too far, and I'll stop giving a *damn* about your etiquette."

Only then did she release Vivian's wrist and turn away.

Vivian asked, "Should I notice the difference?"

So on second thought, Laurel picked up that crystal vase full of its silly purple water and sillier purple roses, turned, and dumped the entire thing over the tramp's head. *Goodbye, fancy hairdo. Good-bye, fancy gown. Good-bye, poise!*

"You might," she said, into the moment of silence that preceded Vivian's horrified shriek. And then, snatching a hotel key off the table by the door, she stalked out of the room.

The only thing that kept her from laughing out loud was the stunned expression on Collier's face before the door closed.

315

Chapter Twenty-six

Collier stared at the door through which his wife had vanished for a long, silent moment—silent but for Vivian's angry screeching of, "How dare she? *How dare she?*"

Then, slowly, he stood. "Perhaps I'd best—"

The viscount cleared his throat. "Quite. Rightly so."

"And I'll . . ." Edgar shook his head, then strode to Vivian's side, where the Lady Tentrees, rather than comforting—or drying—her daughter, was quietly demanding some sort of explanation. God only knew for what. Laurel and Viv had been hissing at each other like cats, and Collier was glad not to have heard most of it. But, Lord help him, he could guess parts. And if it included Edgar . . .

"We may not attend lunch," he excused, heading for the door.

"Perhaps dinner, then," suggested the Baron Tentrees. Like the viscount, he'd not moved an inch toward the ladies.

Oh, to be so fortunate.

Striding toward his room, Collier wondered how a gentleman even dealt with something like this—especially with Laurel.

Perhaps he should claim some responsibility. He'd brought her here knowing full well of her mud-throwing tendencies, and warned nobody.

But when he strode into their room and found her packing, he somehow defaulted to asking, "What the bloody hell was that?"

"You heard her," accused Laurel, not pausing as she toted one pretty gown after another from the wardrobe to her new trunk.

"I heard nothing to warrant either a tug-o'-war over some invitation or your upending roses on my future sister-in-law." The water had been purple! Had Laurel planned such destruction?

"She said, 'You only married Collier'!"

Actually, Collier had heard that part. But he did not remember Vivian curling her lip, wrinkling her nose, or waggling her shoulders when she said it, per Laurel's demonstration.

"You did only marry me," he pointed out.

Laurel stared at him, her mouth falling open. "*Only?*"

Perhaps he should move the washbasin out of her reach.

"She was tactless to phrase it that way, but I'm not the heir. If you thought to defend my honor, your concern was misplaced. And if you let on to Lady Tentrees about Edgar—"

Were there any consequences that could encompass such a betrayal? Collier could have fallen against the doorjamb with relief when Laurel stared at him, clearly insulted.

"I told you I wouldn't say anything about that, and I didn't! I . . . I guess I let on about the kiss," she admitted. "But it's up to Vivian to explain that."

If anybody could equivocate her way past her parents' questions, it would be Viv. In the meantime—

Collier actually looked more closely. "Why are you packing?"

"Because I won't stay here with these people."

Bloody hell. He stepped forward to take an armful of clothes away from her, but at her glare he returned to words.

"Of course you shall. We have the most of a week left for our visit."

"You can stay. You *should* stay—they're your family. Though not the good ones."

"Are you trying to be rude?"

She considered it, then nodded. "Yes. I've decided it's easier."

"Well, you are succeeding admirably. You do realize, don't you, that children do what is easiest. Adults do what is right."

"Then your brother is not marrying an adult."

"Neither, clearly, did I."

She hurled a wadded lump of cloth at him, perhaps to illustrate her resolve toward a life of rudeness. At least it was nothing injurious like a shoe. Or a knife.

Collier drew a deep, uneven breath. He'd also heard an admonition to remember one's responsibility as the party of breeding. That policy, as ever, had merit.

He picked up the wad of cloth—*ah, a glove*—and, as she was simply dropping her clothing in higgledy-piggledy anyway, he tossed it after the rest. "Laurel, stop this. Let me get your coat and we shall take a ride. Once you've calmed down—"

"I don't want to calm down," she said. "I want to go home."

"Are the two mutually exclusive?"

"I think they might be." But after admitting that, she stopped with an armful of muslin, as if she'd been roped.

Good Lord, he was beginning to think in Western metaphors.

"Darn it," she protested, frowning. "Now I'm not as angry!"

"Then is it safe to come within spitting distance?"

He'd been thinking of cats. But when Laurel's eyes flared and she said, "I don't spit," the coarser image fit as well.

"Until today I hadn't thought you doused ladies, either."

"She's no lady."

Since she'd not warned him away, Collier risked crossing the room, moving the muslin from his wife's arms to the trunk's jumbled contents, then taking her bare hands in his.

She seemed less dangerous that way.

"You are quite right, dearest," he assured her. "She is not. I was speaking in general terms."

"Then why are you angry at *me*?"

Was he angry? Possibly. Frustrated, certainly. Embarrassed. Awed. He wasn't sure he'd recovered sufficiently from the shock to decide more. "Were I angry, it might be because, by your little spectacle, you implied you are no lady either."

"Then the British have a different definition of ladies."

"You used the word 'damn.'" He'd heard that part, too.

"Fine. Then I'm not a lady. You knew that from the start." She tried to pull her hands from his, but he held on.

She glared at him.

He let go. "You'd been making great progress, though."

"Progress at being someone I'm not. Someone I don't even want to be. I only tried because . . ." But she did not finish that. Whatever she'd meant to say darkened her eyes with something almost like pain, then vanished. "I'm a rancher."

Again he asked, "Must the two be mutually exclusive?"

"If a lady accepts meanness like I've seen from those people without protesting, then yes. No stand-up rancher would."

"You're saying a stand-up rancher would pour roses over a la—a woman's head?"

"No. A stand-up rancher would leave. If I'd done that right off, likely I wouldn't owe the hotel for staining their settee."

How could a woman who so bravely suffered mud, cold, manure, and frostbite turn coward in the face of a few mean-tempered society mavens? "Oh, Laurel. I promise you that Lady Vivian is one of the least stellar examples of British womanhood ever I've seen. Once you come home to meet my mother—"

She stared at him. "You want me to meet your *mother*?"

Oh. He hadn't yet mentioned his changing expectations for their marriage to *her*, had he? And he did still love her. A simple lapse . . .

Well, it had been a splendid lapse. As far as lapses went. *But still!*

"I believe it is tradition, even in America, for a man to bring his wife home to his mother."

She lifted her chin. "Not his pretend wife."

"That . . ." He cleared his throat, sure this was *not* the arena in which to be making such declarations. Or renegotiations. "I do want to discuss that further. But the question at hand is my father. And the Fordhams. And that spectacle of yours."

"Why is what I did a spectacle, and what Vivian did is not?"

"You mean last night?" When she nodded, he said, "I believe the telling difference would be the presence of spectators."

Laurel clearly did not appreciate his wit. "Well, if your father's the question, my answer is to go home where he and his friends won't bother me and I won't bother them." And damned if she did not return to her travesty of packing. "You can't think any of them want me to stay now."

"What anyone wants is immaterial. What's *proper* is for you to apologize, Vivian to accept, and everything to return to some semblance of civilization."

Laurel stopped in the middle of the room with another armload of Lord knew what, and said, *"Apologize?"*

"You humiliated her."

"And she deserved it. You said so yourself."

"Nevertheless, you must apologize. You needn't mean it. Surely she'll not mean a word of her forgiveness. You can each go back to plotting the other's undoing as soon as formalities have been observed. But you must see that a public apology is essential. That's how it is done."

Perhaps he'd misused the word *must.* "Maybe in England."

He dragged a hand over his hair, then cupped the back of his neck in frustration. "And Lord forbid you should ever behave as if you were in England."

"If that means saying I'm sorry without meaning it, then yes. Does that mean you haven't meant it whenever you've apologized? Around here, Collier, that would be lying."

"And you never lie to get what you want?" he challenged. Apparently Laurel woke other passions in him—like anger.

Collier felt hot. He felt unbalanced. He wanted nothing more than to raise his voice, slam that damned trunk closed, grab Laurel by the shoulders, and make her understand what she'd done.

That was why, when she said, "Maybe that was a mistake, too," he had no choice but to leave.

"I haven't the time or patience for this," he declared, his words clipped. "I will go see to Edgar and make certain that your childishness hasn't ruined him."

Perhaps she recognized her mistake, because now it was she who caught his arm. "Collier! I meant the lying part, not anything else. Don't go all British on me now."

Would that be so bad? "I expect you here when I return."

She reclaimed her hand. "Is that what you expect? Or do you think I'll apologize to Vivian and let your father treat you like dirt and go be bored to tears by Mrs. Crawford Hill, too?"

Collier closed his eyes, summoning his composure. It did not answer his summons. So all he said before leaving was, "Grow up."

"*You* grow up!"

Perhaps there was something to be said for removing oneself from the source of one's anger, rather than counting on one's good breeding to keep one from doing violence to . . . one.

Rather than immediately return to his father's suite, Collier went downstairs to the formal saloon. It boasted a huge mirror, even more decorous than that in the Buffalo Bill Saloon.

It also boasted the heir to Brambourne, sitting at the end of the nearly empty bar.

"Collier!" Edgar raised a glass. "Have a drink."

"It's barely noon," said Collier, going to his side.

"Not in England." And Edgar took another sip.

On second thought, Collier turned to the bartender and asked for a brandy. Then he took the stool beside his brother's. "Edgar, if Laurel in any way implicated you during her little tantrum, I shan't forgive myself."

"Really?" challenged his brother, raising an amused eyebrow. "Even if it means I'm disowned, and you're the heir?"

Collier could only stare, sickened by the weight of what he'd brought about—until Edgar winked. "Well, she didn't. Though thanks ever for sharing with her. I hope you won't marry often."

He wasn't implicated? Collier accepted the brandy that the bartender placed beside him with relief—and annoyance. "Bastard."

"Ah-ah-ah. Wishful thinking." And Edgar raised his glass in a toast. "Here's to women. They do keep life interesting." He took a pleasured sip. "Especially yours."

Interesting? "So how goes the fall of Rome?"

"Father and the baron left. I doubt it matters where *to*, as long as they escaped the ladies. Vivvie's in a right proper snit." Edgar grinned. "And purple, besides."

Collier blinked. "You mean, not just—"

"Oh, by no means just the gown. Her hair, her face, her hands. I—" A chuckle escaped Collier's brother. He cleared his throat, flattened his lips, and said in a somewhat tighter voice. "I doubt purple shall be her favorite color in the future."

Collier tried to swallow back the humor as well. But the laugh snorted out of him anyway, like a muffled choke. "So much for making a good impression, eh?"

"Oh, your Mrs. Pembroke *indeed* made an impression," Edgar assured him. "Lord only knows when it will scrub out. Vivian *did* admit to kissing you, but only that—said she kissed your cheek, and your shop girl overreacted. So no worries about Tentrees demanding pistols at dawn for that other business."

"I suppose I have that to be grateful for." Collier sighed.

"Trouble at Paradise Ranch, is it?" Edgar grinned. "Pard?"

"You are nowhere near as amusing as you think you are."

"But as long as *I* am amused, it's of no other consequence. Do tell me where you found the girl, Collier. She's splendid."

"She's ill-mannered and childish."

"But at least," offered Edgar, "she is not pretending to be

someone she's not, hey? Like others among us."

Maybe that was a mistake, too. "Apparently not any longer."

"Eh?"

But Collier had no intention of discussing his marital difficulties, pretend or otherwise. What he intended to do was calm down. "Shall we play a game of billiards?"

"You're on," agreed Edgar. "What shall we play for?"

"Brambourne?"

"How about ten quid?"

Collier shrugged. "It'll do."

An hour later and ten pounds richer, Collier felt as calm as he would get. He would not take offense. He would try to see things from Laurel's position. He would neither tell her to grow up nor demand to know what she'd meant by suggesting he do the same.

He would take her out someplace where they could see the mountains. If all went well, they could even, finally, discuss their future together . . . assuming she truly regretted only that they'd lied, and not that they'd married.

But Collier knew he was getting ahead of himself in that.

When he entered their room and saw her trunk missing, he realized just how far ahead of himself that had been.

For a long moment he stared at the space where her trunk had been. Then he strode to the wardrobe to look. Laurel's belongings were gone. All she'd left was a note on the writing table with his first name penned on the front.

Dearest Collier:

I am sorry I embarrassed you. If I had thought I would of done that—

"Would have," he corrected absently—then stiffened in dismay. *Good Lord.* He *was* a snob! How superior had he behaved at other times?

If I had thought I would of done that then I would not of come. That is why I am leaving, mainly, but to go home

323

too. This does not seem fair to you, and I am sorry for that. I do not know what else to do. Enjoy your family. Mine is not perfect either. Please wire me through Papa when you will return to Sheridan.

She'd written the word *please* again, but crossed it out.

Collier glanced at the dustbin by the desk and saw a handful of crumpled pages. She had used up most of the hotel stationery, both on earlier drafts of the letter and what looked like . . .

Oh. He supposed those were brands.

She'd signed the note, *Love, Laurel Pembroke.*

Then she'd added, *P.S.: I will find the money to replace the stained settee and wire it to you let me know how much.*

Collier had not married a writer. But for purposes of communication, her letter sufficed. She was going home.

Alone?

Collier stood, grabbed his coat, pocketed the letter, and strode for the stairs. Perhaps he could catch her before she left—hopefully the hotel. If necessary, the city.

Anger was no longer his concern—especially when he learned from the doorman that Laurel had, indeed, left in a hansom cab the man had personally hailed. Oh, he was still angry . . . but for more than their childish words or her scene before his father. As Collier hailed his own cab, fear far outweighed anger.

What if she hired an unethical driver to take her to the station? What if she was set upon by some lowlife on the train? She might purchase a second-class ticket, or even immigrant class, and who knew how well ladies were protected in such cars?

When he reached Union Station, only to learn that he'd just missed the train to Sheridan—and that she had, indeed, purchased second-class passage—fear won out.

"Damn," he said—right there on the platform, without even looking to see if there were women or children about. Standing in a fall of heavy snowflakes, staring down the empty track, he knew he'd failed as a husband. Even a pretend husband.

Damn it to hell.

He went back inside to ask after the next train to Sheridan.

"Long as they're gettin' through, that'll be eleven forty-three tonight," said the station agent.

"Getting through?" repeated Collier.

The agent glanced toward the platform, where snow was already filling in Collier's footprints. More to worry about.

What if her train was snowed in? What if she'd not taken enough money for the dining car?

What if, as this solo departure of hers might yet imply, she'd given up on him and their pretend marriage completely?

Collier sank onto a wooden bench and drew the letter from his pocket. She'd called him "Dearest Collier." She'd apologized, twice—he ached to think she felt guilty for something that was equally his doing. And she'd signed it, "Love, Laurel Pembroke."

Not just Laurel. Laurel *Pembroke*. And *Love*.

For once, he truly hoped she was not merely being polite. There was something to be said for taking her at her word.

Resigning himself to return to the hotel, Collier first went to the Western Union desk.

He had to send a telegram.

The train had barely cleared Denver before Laurel regretted her impulsiveness. Sort of. But she also felt a twinge of relief. She'd burned her bridges with Collier's family. If she stayed, she'd likely argue with him again. She wasn't sure she could bear that.

I expect you here when I return, he'd said, as dictatorial and British as she'd ever seen him. As if she were a child. *She* wasn't the one so desperate for her father's approval that she would debase herself, as he did with the viscount.

That still upset her, no matter how far north the train got.

She made the best of her journey home. She bought a sandwich from a vendor on the platform in Fort Laramie, and chatted with a parson. Much of the time she just watched the mountains, or how brightly her new engagement ring sparkled when she moved her hand. It made her think of Collier's smile.

A smile she might not see again anytime soon.

By the time the train finally reached Sheridan, well after nightfall, Laurel's regrets ached more than her back. Maybe she didn't need Collier to escort her, feed her, protect her, see to her luggage. But she sorely needed him, even so . . . and she'd left.

"That your only trunk, Lady Pembroke?"

Marveling at the warm air—another Chinook—Laurel stiffened at the familiar drawl. She'd figured on getting herself home.

The last thing she expected was to be met by Nate Dawson.

The cowboy carried her to a buckboard waiting by the platform, as if she hadn't assured him there was nothing between her and Collier the very day she agreed to start courting.

She flushed, hotter than even the Chinook merited. "Thank you, Nate—I mean, Mr. Dawson. But you don't have to—"

"Boss sent me to fetch you, ma'am. Reckon I'd best do it."

"Papa? How'd he know I was coming home so soon?"

"Best ask the boss." With a grunt, Dawson deposited the trunk into the bed of her father's wagon. Then he extended a bare, callused hand to help her in. "Your ladyship."

Ladyship? She hopped up and settled onto the familiar seat on her own. Dawson swung himself into the driver's side, where her father normally sat, and collected the reins.

Collier, she thought. *Collier must have wired ahead.* But why hadn't her father or her brother come for her?

She guessed she would have to ask "the boss" that, too.

"I'm glad to see you, Nate," she ventured, and he slanted a wary, squint-eyed cowboy gaze at her as he drove onto Main. "Back when we talked, at Kitty's birthday, I said there was nothing between me and Lord Collier."

"No, ma'am. You said it was nobody's business."

Proving Herself

"Yes, but I implied . . ." She shook her head, trying to make sense of it. If she'd wanted any man back then, it would have been someone like Nate. But she hadn't wanted a man.

Not until she met a man who finally got her to appreciate the finer points of being a lady . . . at least, a lady with the right gentleman. Girl-shoes aside. And *as* a lady . . .

"I . . . " With a deep breath, she just did it. "I apologize for that, Nate. You were a good friend, and you deserved better."

"Obliged." But he had to go and add, "Lady Pembroke."

She glared, and he grinned, and things felt better between them—though not what they'd been. That was fine. She had Collier—who had wired ahead to her family. Didn't that mean he cared?

"Do you know why Papa didn't come for me?" she asked.

"You don't know?" When he saw her confusion, Nate told her. "Miss Mariah's havin' her baby."

Chapter Twenty-seven

Lady Vivian was, indeed, purple. Even powdered and gloved, she looked vaguely corpselike.

"Do *try* the hat, precious," Lady Tentrees was pleading when Collier entered his father's rooms. "You'll feel much better."

She quieted to look coldly at Collier. So did everyone else. Edgar's glare seemed a shade overdramatic, considering his earlier humor, but it might keep the peace with Vivian.

"I should feel better if Father filed a lawsuit," she declared, and looked pointedly at Collier. "But I doubt Mrs. Pembroke has anything I want."

Thank God for that! "We will, of course, replace the frock," said Collier. "And I've already spoken to the hotel manager about the sofa. If you must hire someone to treat your hair—"

"You aren't suggesting I dye it!" protested Viv.

"Then please accept my sympathy for what I cannot doubt will be a trying time for you."

Viv's eyes narrowed, as if she were searching his words for a hidden meaning. He'd had none. His mother had taught him that it was usually better to be kind than to be right—a reason for etiquette that some people had lost along the way.

"And your wife, Lord Collier. I trust we shall be hearing from her soon." If Lady Tentrees truly believed this had come from a kiss on the cheek, Collier could not blame her iciness.

"I can't imagine *not*," added Edgar.

Collier slanted his gaze to his brother, unamused by the reference to Laurel's vehemence, then turned back to the baron's wife. "My wife was called unexpectedly home, and shan't be able to make her apologies in person." *If at all.*

Lady Vivian smiled a little, as if she thought Collier had been the one to send Laurel away. Collier did not correct her.

Instead, after a short bow to the ladies, he crossed the room to where the men stood by the mantel. "Father, may I speak privately with you?"

The Viscount of Brambourne looked slowly about them with a lifted eyebrow, as if to challenge Collier to find privacy without evicting the rest of the company.

"The bedroom would be fine," offered Collier. "Or the hall-way." Since his father would rather have purple flowers poured over his head than discuss anything in the corridor, Collier opened the bedroom door for the older man.

The viscount could have refused. He'd refused private meetings in the past; Collier *was* only his second son. But he seemed intrigued. With a shrug toward the baron, he preceded his son into the bedchambers.

Collier followed, shutting the door. He remembered enough of his upbringing to wait until his father spread a gloved hand and said, "I trust you mean to ask for something."

Did he think Collier wanted money? Or to return home? He *did* want the latter . . . but not if he lost even more in doing so.

"First, I wish to apologize for this morning. It was largely my fault for not interceding earlier."

"Interceding?" Men interceding in the matters of ladies was rarely done—in England. But this was not England.

"Lady Vivian baited my wife. The only difference from the dozens of times before is that my wife took the bait."

"Excusing your wife's petty behavior is no reason to drag me from business," chided his father, and turned as if to leave.

"Second, I too will be leaving Denver tonight. Again, I apologize—this time for the brevity of my visit. But I must return to Wyoming."

"And what," asked his father, "is so important in Wyoming?"

Laurel. Any hope I have of self-respect. My future.

"A bloody cold homestead and over half a year's spotty effort at making something of my life," said Collier.

"Such as it is?" Laurel was right. His father was rude.

Collier stood a little straighter. "Lastly, Father—and it is for this that I requested privacy—I wish to thank you."

"For what, in particular? The remittances?"

"Those as well, of course." *What part of them comes from you.* "Money has provided a useful cushion as I adapt to the frontier. But primarily for sending me away in the first place."

The viscount stared at him, speechless at last.

"You know I'm no rotter. I've been a good son. I advanced the estate, when I was allowed. Some young men in my situation might never have received the opportunity that you gave me, to prove my own"—he could not help smiling—"mettle. I've found many things that I value in Wyoming—more than I was perhaps aware, until this visit. And I never would have done so had you not forced me to 'make something of myself.' So even if that was not your purpose"—and he knew it was not—"thank you."

And he offered his hand.

His father only looked at it. "You fancy yourself a Westerner now, do you?"

"No, sir. I am a loyal subject of the queen. But I live in the West now. What I may become, I've yet to discover." Collier withdrew his hand. The old pain began to well up in him. . . .

But he swallowed it back down. He no longer needed his father's approval to confirm his choices.

Perhaps *that* was what Laurel had meant about growing up. He bowed slightly instead. "Good day, sir."

"Boy," ordered the viscount as he began to turn away.

Collier took a deep breath, then turned back. "I assume you mean that with marginal affection. Sir. But an American might take it as another form of baiting."

"You think making a go with your wife's homestead and your mother's money makes you a man?" Was that *interest* in his voice?

"No less a man than would inheriting my father's estate."

"You don't think Edgar can do it."

That, too, was a question, of sorts. It was one he'd longed for, prior to his expulsion from England. He could easily argue why he, Collier, might better serve Brambourne . . . even avoiding the issue of heirs.

But why should he? Edgar had been born first, and Collier had waited too long to seek his own path, much less find it.

"I think," he said, "that Edgar is willing to learn. And that you might do well to train Acton to the governing of the estate as well, as something of a"—he smiled—*"segundo."*

"Acton," repeated the viscount.

Your third son. But Collier simply stood patiently. To his surprise, his father then nodded.

"Not a bad idea, at that," he said, even more surprising. "Stay an extra night, and we'll discuss it further."

"No, sir. But if you wish to visit Sheridan, they—we—have a fine hotel where you can stay in comfort." Collier bowed.

The viscount sighed. Then he offered his hand. "You really should cut your hair, you know. It looks absurd."

"My wife likes it this way," Collier explained—and took his father's gloved hand in his. For perhaps the first time since he'd graduated, they shook hands.

"You do everything your wife wants?" challenged the viscount, and his lips slanted into an odd expression that Collier slowly recognized as a smile.

A smile that pulled faintly to one side.

"Apparently I do not," he admitted with a sigh.

"Good man." Then the viscount left the room before Collier. One mustn't completely ignore civilized conduct, after all.

Even in America.

When Collier made his good-byes to the others, the Baron Tentrees asked when his train left.

"Tonight, your lordship. But the weather is worsening. I wish to go to the station directly, lest I be snowed in here."

"I forget; does the station have a restaurant?"

"I believe it does . . . or at least a lunch counter." The idea of any of these people—himself included—sitting at a depot lunch counter, with passengers trying to grab quick meals during five- or ten-minute stops, amused Collier almost as much as the baron's questions mystified him.

"Then let me go with you. I never did hear your other thoughts about American polo."

"Father!" protested Viv, from where her mother, looking as tired as a mother with a cranky two-year-old, still tended her.

"Vivian," answered her father evenly, forcing her to actually state her objection or be silent. And, of course, she could not give herself away so boldly as to state her objection.

"I would be honored," said Collier slowly. At the very least it would liven up an otherwise long wait.

While the baron retrieved his coat, Edgar *there-there*'d over his Vivvie—but caught Collier's gaze long enough to wink.

Collier supposed he could thank his father and brother for another prize in having sent him away, as well. Even without Laurel—Lord forbid—Collier was better off without Vivian.

But to say so would be ungentlemanly.

Laurel had seen puppies born, and kittens, and foals, and calves. She'd always found it horrifying and fascinating.

Nothing had prepared her for the birth of Mariah's baby.

And, being a married lady, she got to be there for the whole thing—a privilege Victoria clearly envied.

"What's happening now?" asked Laurel's younger sister, after knocking on the door and delivering another bowl full of clean snow, which Mama was allowing Mariah in lieu of water.

"Same thing as before, but worse." Laurel planted herself between the doorway and Mariah. "She can't walk anymore, not even with Stuart helping. Mama says it won't be long now."

"What does the doctor think?"

"He's reading. He says unless something goes wrong—" Behind her, Mariah cried out again, a wrenching, gritted scream. Laurel and Victoria both winced. "Unless something goes wrong, he says Mama can handle it."

"And she didn't hit him?"

"She only made threats when he wouldn't let her handle it."

Victoria nodded, understanding. "Papa's cleaning his guns."

"*All* of them?"

"His main ones. I think he wants to kill Stuart."

"He always wants to kill Stuart," Laurel reminded her. But the way Vic widened her eyes as she shook her head, this was worse than usual. "Well, as long as Papa stays out there and Stuart stays in here, they should be fine."

And she could not imagine blasting Stuart MacCallum away from Mariah's side with dynamite. When the doctor suggested he should wait outside was the first time Mama threatened violence.

"Laurel!" called Mama sharply. Laurel closed the door in Vic's face and brought the snow to where Mariah sat up in bed in her nightgown, braced against her stocky husband's chest, sweat dampening her forehead.

It seemed odd to see Stuart in the older girls' bedroom— sitting on Laurel and Mariah's bed! But they'd decided months ago that Mariah would stay at her parents' in-town home for the birthing, and it was easier for Victoria and Audra to move than for the MacCallums to displace either Thad or their parents.

The idea of Stuart sleeping with Mariah in Papa's bed, no matter how chastely, did not deserve consideration.

"Here, love," murmured Stuart over Mariah's shoulder, scooping snow into his hand and lifting it to her lips.

Mariah only shook her head, jaw clenched, then threw back her head and screamed—"Mama!" It seemed like the pains were coming so close now she hardly got to breathe against them.

Stuart threw that bit of snow to the side and wrapped his arms around his straining wife, as if he could take on some of her labor. For a moment his brown eyes met Laurel's—more naked than any man's she'd ever seen, except maybe Collier's. She saw then how much he loved Mariah. She saw how his life balanced on this one night. And she saw his fear.

She tried to grin encouragement. Then she turned back to her mother for her own reassurance.

Mama, however, was looking under the sheet between Mariah's legs. That Mariah didn't protest such a violation spoke of just how exhausted and miserable she was. "All right, baby. Now's as good as ever. You want to start pushing? You start pushing."

And Mariah, clenching her teeth, strained back against the brace of her husband and pushed.

Had Laurel ever really thought her older sister lacked grit? Seeing Mariah now, struggling despite exhaustion and pain to have this baby, she knew her sister had more grit than she'd ever imagined. Laurel just hadn't seen it beyond the corsets and the curls and the ladylike shoes. As if, as Collier had pointed out, things had to be mutually exclusive.

Mariah's blond hair hung stringy from sweat, despite that Stuart kept wiping her damp face, and she'd turned red from effort. Tears streamed from her eyes, and her cries grew ragged, and still she gulped breath, arched her back, and pushed again. When she collapsed back against Stuart, she was sobbing.

"I see it," called Mama. "Here—" And she caught Mariah's hand and drew it between the girl's legs.

Mariah's eyes flared wide. "His head!" Stuart looked quickly from Mama to Mariah's delight and back.

"Keep breathing," Mama reminded her. "Now try again, baby. You can do it."

"You can do it, love," repeated Stuart, low, where his cheek pressed against Mariah's hair. "You can do anything."

Then Mariah screamed again, and Mama, busy under her nightgown, said "Yes!" Suddenly she was drawing a red, slimy creature out from the foot of the bed. "It's a boy!" she told them, and lifted the baby to Mariah's sheet-covered stomach, mindless of stains. "You hold him while we clean him up."

"A boy," repeated Stuart. With a gusty yowl the baby started to cry, and Mariah gasped and sobbed and laughed all at once, feeling across him—his grimacing little face, his slow-moving arms—as if she could not believe that he was real and whole and complete. Laurel could hardly believe it herself.

"You did it, Mariah," Stuart murmured. "A boy!"

"You would have loved a girl, too," Mama assured him as she began to wipe the little fusspot clean of the mess that splattered both him and the pulsing cord still connecting him to Mariah. "Laurel, quick, get one of the towels."

Laurel hurried to where they had set a pot on top of the radiator grille, and clean, dry towels in the pot, so that the baby would not get cold.

"Aye," said Stuart prayerfully over Mariah's delighted cooing. "Aye, that I would."

"You can touch him too, Stuart," said Mama with a laugh. Tentatively Stuart reached his large worker's hand out and brushed his fingertips across his son's shoulder.

It was the first time that Laurel, bringing the towel back, had ever seen Mariah's brooding sheep farmer smile.

She guessed he might be a handsome man, at that.

And their baby! He had brown hair, wet and plastered onto his elongated head, and a fierce expression in his scowling little eyes, and waving baby hands, and kicking baby feet, and even a little baby . . . dingus. Laurel had never seen anything so wonderful in her life.

"Well done, Mrs. Garrison," said the doctor, who had put his book down to see to cutting the cord. That, apparently, Mama would allow him. "And Mrs. MacCallum, of course. He looks like a strong, healthy baby. All his fingers and toes, has he?"

"Oh, yes," insisted Mariah, petting the baby's head, pouting in sympathy with his upset. "He's perfect, aren't you, darling?" And as soon as she could, she cuddled him to her chest. "Oh, I know, little man! You have every right to be upset. But you're safe out here. Your da will see to it."

Stuart, resting an exhausted chin on her shoulder as if he were the one who had done the work, stared in dumb amazement.

"Don't get too comfortable," warned Mama. "Stuart, you'd best hold him when Mariah's ready to deliver the afterbirth. Laurel, go tell the others that everything's fine, both with Mariah and little Mr.— Have you two chosen the name?"

Mariah looked over her shoulder at her husband, eyes pleading. His closed his for a moment, then opened them, and he kissed her cheek and whispered, "Aye."

"Garrison," she said. "Garrison Stuart MacCallum."

Mama's eyes danced her approval. "A beautiful name, and just as fine a gesture. Laurel, have Victoria watch your father's face when you tell him—I'll want a full report, and I know she can give the best one."

Then she turned back to the next stage in this miracle. Backing toward the door, Laurel knew it *was* a miracle.

All of it. Not just the baby.

The truth of what Mariah and Stuart had built together shamed her. And the full realization of what she and Collier might have built, but hadn't and maybe never would . . .

That hurt so badly she could hardly stand.

* * *

Garry MacCallum had been born in the wee hours of the morning. By time Audra, Kitty, and Elise woke in Thaddeas's bed upstairs, for breakfast, the adults were exhausted. Though the younger girls begged to see the baby, Mama refused to risk waking the MacCallums; they would have to wait until after school. Laurel and Papa did the cooking. Thaddeas slung a bedroll into his buggy, hoping to catch a nap at his law office. And although Victoria had permission to stay home this once, she couldn't wait to tell her classmates their overnight drama.

As soon as they left, Laurel lay down in Kitty and Elise's room for just a moment—just long enough to catch her breath and decide what to do about Collier, and Denver . . . and what a poor wife she'd proven to be, pretend or otherwise. But when she started awake again, to the noise of little Garry bawling in the next room, the slant of sunlight through the windows told her she'd slept until noon.

Noon!

She sat up unevenly. Blinking down at herself, she saw that she was still wearing the new gown she'd put on in Denver the morning before, complete with a spattering of purple-gray water stains from the splash when she'd doused Lady Vivian.

What had she done?

Her mistakes milled so chaotically through her memory, she feared never grasping them all. Then, somehow, she corralled them into one clear condemnation.

She'd lied.

She'd lied to her family and her friends, cheapening something holy, when she'd married Collier. She'd lied to *his* family when she posed for that wedding portrait. She'd lied to Collier when she'd agreed to pose as his wife—the first time trouble came, what did she do but embarrass and desert him?

And she'd lied to herself. She'd thought she could do this and still have self-respect left, but she didn't. She felt as wrinkled and soiled as this brand-new, ruined skirt, and she didn't know how she would ever put things right again.

337

But she realized, finally, that she wouldn't do it alone.

She found her father in the stables, oiling his saddle.

"Hello," said Laurel, sidling in.

He looked up, blinked at her for a moment, then nodded his own greeting and went back to work.

"Some doings last night, huh?" she asked, timid. But if she saw her behavior as shameful, what would he think?

Papa said, "Yup."

"I'm glad Mariah's okay," she added. Again he paused to look at her, long and hard. When she said nothing, he nodded again—he was glad, too—and turned back to the saddle.

Frustrated with her own cowardice, she finally just spit it out. "Oh, Papa. I've done something terrible, and I don't know what to do about it!"

Papa's hand on the saddle stilled. He looked back up at her. He watched her for a long moment with his steady gray eyes, sturdy and dependable as he'd ever been. Then he cleared his throat and asked, "Anyone dead?"

She stood up straighter. "No!"

When he started wiping the oil off his saddle with a clean rag, she could have wept from relief. Maybe the lack of a corpse meant anything could be fixed, in his view . . . even if he didn't yet know what a poor excuse for a daughter or a wife she was.

"Got a bounty on your head?" demanded Papa as he worked.

She shook her head. "No!"

His eyes narrowed. "Likely?"

"No, sir!"

So he put the rag away, left the saddle where it could dry, and shrugged into his coat. "Best see yer mother, then."

And they went in together.

Chapter Twenty-eight

"Didn't look pretend to me," Papa noted dangerously.

Laurel did not have to look up to know what he was thinking; *Collier, answering the door barefooted in a quilt.*

"It only started pretend," she'd said. "And not even pretend so much as . . . arranged."

"This will be easier," said Mama, "if you don't defend it."

So Laurel tried. But she *had* to defend Collier, even if she couldn't defend herself. Especially when she explained their plan to divorce several years from now.

"Divorced." Papa spat the word. "Widowed, more likely."

When Laurel made herself face him straight on, his disappointment looked like dark fury. On her mother it seemed calmer, sadder. Laurel felt the way she had the morning after her wedding, when she'd thrown up.

"He tried to talk me out of it," she insisted. "But I wouldn't let him."

Then she had to explain how things had changed after she fell in the creek and he rescued her. "We didn't mean for it to happen, exactly, but he was so wonderful, and we just . . ."

"I think we get the idea," assured her mother quickly.

"And now I've ruined it." Laurel was embarrassed to feel tears threatening. She never cried—except, it seemed, for Collier.

"*You* ruined it." She guessed Papa really didn't like Collier, if he couldn't conceive of her being the one at fault.

She told them a little about Lady Vivian. She recounted her indignation, which she now suspected was its own brand of snobbery, and the dumped vase. She admitted how she'd fought with Collier, refused to apologize, called him a liar . . . *her!* And she told them about running away, with no more than a note.

She tried not to spare herself.

Mama said, "Oh, Laurel!" quite a bit.

"What if I can't make this right? What if he doesn't even come back? He never chose Wyoming—he was just exiled here."

"Married," Papa reminded her firmly. Whether he meant he'd make Collier honor his vows, or that Laurel must accept the consequences of her behavior, she wasn't sure.

"He wouldn't desert me," she assured them—and maybe herself. Just in case. "He's too much of a gentleman, and he's too good a man. But staying against his will would be as bad."

Again Papa said, "Married."

Mama was more helpful. "You haven't had *any* indication that you might make him happy?"

"In some ways, maybe." None of which she meant to tell them! "And when I'm pretending to be someone else. But we don't have important things in common. That's got to be bad."

"Ah." Mama looked at Papa. "That must be our problem, dear."

"Figured you'd work it out," he agreed dryly.

"You do so have things in common! There's the ranch, and the family. And you both . . ."

But suddenly Laurel couldn't think of much else. Papa came from a large ranching family, while Mama, orphaned, had been raised by her grandparents. Papa came from frontier stock, while Mama grew up in some kind of luxury back east. Papa was stern and abrupt, while Mama was loving and talkative. Papa's habits were conservative, while Mama worked for such progressive ideals as suffrage and the rights of laborers and immigrants.

Mama held up two crossed fingers. "We're like *this*."

Papa looked annoyed. But when Mama just wrinkled her nose at him, he sighed and looked at a paper he'd drawn from his pocket.

They *weren't* alike, not in any obvious ways—and yet Laurel had never once doubted their love and permanence.

That was when she began to hope again.

She'd never been much for compromise. But doing things alone sure hadn't worked for her. Maybe she couldn't stop being herself, any more than her mother had stopped being a suffragette, or her father a stern old cowboy.

But maybe being more of what Collier wanted didn't have to mean losing herself at all. Especially if she loved him.

"I guess I need to go back to Denver," she said—but that was when Papa slid the paper he'd been looking at across the table, and she saw that it was a telegram.

LAUREL ON 9:15 P.M. TRAIN. PLEASE CONFIRM SAFE ARRIVAL. WILL FOLLOW SHORTLY. SAY I AM SORRY, PEMBROKE.

He was coming back! He would be here—soon!

Maybe she hadn't run out of chances after all.

"Cooper will fetch him," Papa warned before she could insist on going to the depot. After everything she had to make up to her parents, she guessed she could give in on that.

Besides, she had work to do.

Lord knew she'd proved she would make mistakes. It was time to show Collier that she could make an effort, too.

A real one.

Laurel bathed in perfumed water, scrubbing mercilessly at her elbows. While her hair dried, she starched and ironed the

341

most salvageable of her Denver dresses out of her trunk. It was midnight blue cashmere, with black braid and a swagged overskirt, and it took forever to press. Poor Stuart MacCallum almost couldn't leave the house to check on his sheep ranch, until Mama noticed him hovering just outside the kitchen, looking longingly past Laurel and Papa to the back door.

Since she was only wearing her robe—until every swag and braid was straight on the dress—Laurel had to step into the bathroom until Stuart had left for the stables.

She could only guess that Papa let the new father pass.

Even Mariah, barely recovered from childbirth, helped with Laurel's transformation. She insisted on sitting up in bed while little Garry slept in an open, pillow-lined drawer beside her, and using a crimping iron to style Laurel's hair.

"You'll wear Mama's jet earrings," she insisted. "And the matching brooch."

Laurel, never comfortable being fussed over, reread the telegram. *Say I am sorry. Pembroke.*

It was because Collier said he was sorry that Papa had kept the telegram from her—that, and the distraction of Mariah having her baby. Because Collier said he was sorry, Uncle Benj would be meeting his train instead of Laurel. But Laurel trusted Uncle Benj to see the truth of the matter as soon as Collier explained everything, and then he'd be home, and . . .

And Laurel felt torn between fearing to hope and refusing to despair. What *was* Collier sorry for—their fight, or something more permanent, yet to be confessed? She didn't like that he'd signed it *Pembroke*. He'd paid for the word *please* when asking Papa to confirm her safe arrival, but not for his first name.

But she liked that he'd worried about her, even so.

"Didn't Audra used to practice walking with a book on her head?" she asked fitfully. But when she turned her head, she burned her ear on the crimping iron. "*Ow!*"

"Be careful!" scolded Mariah. "Yes, that's how Audra practiced her comportment. And no, don't you dare try it today. Not after all the work I've put into this hairstyle."

After the courage Mariah had shown, Laurel guessed she had some catching up to do to avoid cowardice. So she went ahead and risked asking, "What if he doesn't forgive me?"

At least Mariah wouldn't answer, *Married*, as Papa had.

"Papa and Mama forgave you, didn't they?" she charged.

"Actually . . . when I said I was sorry, Papa said he reckoned I was. And when I said I didn't guess they would trust me much for a while, he said he didn't guess so. Mama just looked sad."

"But they forgave you. There." And Mariah sat back to inspect her work. "All done."

Laurel took a deep, trembling breath. "But Mariah, they love me." She didn't have to explain that Collier . . .

"Oh, sweetie." Mariah opened her arms, and Laurel found herself taking hugs and comfort from a weak, hurting sister she herself should be comforting. But right now Mariah was only physically weak, and her reasons for that lay sleeping in the open drawer.

"I'm sorry," Laurel whispered—and, damn it, wept—into her sister's shoulder. "I'm sorry, I'm sorry, I'm sorry." Now that she'd started saying it, she felt as though she couldn't stop.

She loved her big sister all the more for not asking what she was sorry for, just reassuring her. "It'll be all right. You'll see. Everything will be fine. Just you wait."

But Laurel would believe that from only one person.

And he hadn't gotten in from the station yet.

Laurel was not waiting for him at the Sheridan depot, and Collier felt a stab of disappointment. Whether she was happy, dutiful, or still furious, he longed to see her. He'd missed her more than seemed possible in the day they'd been apart. That she'd not come at all hardly seemed promising.

That Benjamin Cooper *had*—and stood leaning casually against a post with his arms folded and his large cowboy hat sloped down over his forehead—seemed even less so. Especially when Cooper looked up with honest threat in his shadowed blue eyes.

343

"That'll go to my buggy," the rancher drawled to the porter with Collier's trunk. Then he strode over to Collier, his cowboy boots thumping ominously on the wooden platform, and draped an arm over Collier's shoulders in a fatherly way.

Fatherly except for the grim line of his mouth under his handlebar mustache.

"Son," the rancher greeted.

"Cooper," responded Collier more carefully. He didn't shrug off the man's arm—that would be rude—but he did pointedly note the familiarity. "Laurel's . . . all right. Isn't she?"

He'd gotten her father's simple telegram—*She's here*—before he left Union Station. In the end, it had been his train that got delayed for snow. So by "all right," Collier wasn't even sure what he meant. *Not* all right would be if she were still feeling guilty for their argument, or hurt by his angry words, or determined to end their charade of a marriage once and for all.

But when Cooper said, "She's fine," Collier doubted he was encompassing all those possibilities.

"Safe at home with her folks," assured Alexandra's husband. "Funny how the weather works 'round here. You got snowed in, but up here the streets are muddy as the Mississippi. We'll be a while getting there. This is a good thing. Trust me on this."

"Oh?"

"Plenty of time to chat." Cooper swung himself into the driver's seat of his phaeton. Collier had to go around, stepping into the filthiest, slushiest snow he'd ever seen. His foot sank into icy muck. Before he'd made it around the horse, one of his shoes vanished. He had to stop and dig into the mess with a gloved hand to retrieve it; then he tugged it on with a grimace.

Welcome home.

"Perhaps I should purchase boots," he said. "If I'm to survive spring in the Rocky Mountains?"

"Oh, your survival rests on more than that," assured Cooper. He clucked his teeth at the horse, driving away from the

344

station and toward the street. Thank goodness *it* was paved. Enough snow and mud flew before they reached it to plaster a building.

"Pardon?"

"Your telegram asked Jacob to pass on an apology to your wife," explained Cooper. "Musta been a whopper, to send by wire."

Collier thought of all he could have done better. "It is."

"Care to enlighten me before you face her daddy with it?"

That was when Collier realized what this was about. "As a matter of fact, I would not. That is between myself and my wife."

"And her father. You saw to that when you sent the cable."

"Her father allegedly being Jacob Garrison?" It went against Collier's breeding to insinuate such a thing, but damn it, he had to know. Just not for the reasons he would have expected.

When Cooper turned to stare at him, surprise, anger, and amazement registered on his face in even measure. "Allegedly?"

"It's of no real consequence to me either way," said Collier firmly. "Laurel is my wife, if she will have me—"

"Have you after *what?*" pursued Cooper. "Did you tell her you thought she wasn't her daddy's daughter?"

"I did not! What kind of a rotter do you take me for?"

"Well, now . . . Can't see as you'd dare hit her," mused Cooper. "She's mighty vulnerable to other hurts, though."

"Mr. Cooper, I assure you that I would never willingly hurt my wife. I apologized because she seemed upset, to have left so suddenly, and I could not bear—I did not want that. I may not have been as patient with her, or as or appreciative . . ."

Of who she was, and everything that meant. Every wonderful, contradictory, passionate, honest thing.

"I hope," Collier added, more evenly, "to rectify that. If she would allow me."

"Her and her daddy," clarified Cooper, and chuckled.

"Now I'm just plain curious. Whose would she be *but* Garrison's?"

But Collier had known the man was clever. "Yours."

Cooper choked.

Collier waited for him to compose himself. It took longer than he expected. But when Garrison's *segundo* finally spoke, after clearing his throat, it was with a strange kind of denial.

"I'd shoot you for sayin' such a thing if I weren't so flattered by the mere notion."

"You love her," persisted Collier.

"Laurel? Indeed I do. I love all the Garrison girls."

"And their mother."

Cooper slanted his blue gaze toward Collier, then nodded. "I do that. And her husband. Doesn't mean I'm fool enough to overstep my affection with either one of 'em."

"I had no intention of prying," said Collier. "And I meant what I said. It would in no way change my respect or love for my wife. But Laurel *is* clearly more special to you than the other girls, and . . . I'll admit, I am curious about how much a man might sacrifice for the woman he loves. Here in Wyoming, at least."

"So what you figure is, her mother and I fell victim to our forbidden love, and I let Jacob raise the girl rather than rob the family of their respectability." Cooper cocked his head as if trying on the idea for size.

"What I *figure* is that, for the right woman, a man might accept or give up anything."

Cooper nodded his decision. "Well, now. Before I divulge anythin' regardin' this matter, you'd best accept one thing," he said firmly. "Your cousin, Alexandra Ellis Stanley Cooper, is my helpmate, my friend, my companion, my love. Nothin' I say here should be taken to disparage that. Savvy?"

"Understood."

"There was a time, however, before fortune set Mrs. Cooper's beauty before me," the rancher continued as he drove. "Then Mrs. Garrison seemed like the most fascinatin' example of womanhood I would ever be blessed to know. In some ways she still is. Problem was, she gave her heart to that crotchety old partner of mine. And when a creature as pure as Lillabit Garrison gives her heart, it remains unavailable from there on out."

"No disrespect to the lady," said Collier carefully. This *was* his mother-in-law! "But she seems . . . fond of you."

"I'm pleased to hear that, as I am surely fond of her. But if you think our partiality for each other is a pebble next to what she and Jacob share, or a bump on my life's path with Mrs. Cooper, you've not been payin' attention."

Collier waited, certain there was more to come.

"Once we started the ranch, and little Mariah came along, I will admit to some envy darkenin' my appreciation of our new venture," said Cooper. "Rather than risk the partnership, I absented myself to more civilized territory, to do the business that Jacob's not fond of doin'. I spent a good deal of time feelin' sorry for myself, too."

As had Collier?

"It was in Saint Louis that I met a lady who wooed me from my low spirits. She got me to thinkin' toward what was still out there, instead of just what I'd missed, and I will to my last breath be grateful to her for that. By time we parted company, however, this lady was carryin' my child."

Oh? Surely Laurel was *Mrs. Garrison*'s daughter! "You let her go?"

"Keepin' 'em against their will is rarely wise," advised Cooper. "And she was cannier than to stay with a scoundrel like myself. Besides, she was otherwise involved."

Good Lord. "Married."

"In the legal sense," agreed Cooper lightly. "She wanted that baby even more than I did, and meant to raise it as her husband's, so we parted friends. I returned to the Circle-T a happier man for the experience, and found that Jacob had been busy himself. Lillabit had her bustle on backward again."

Collier began to understand. "With Laurel."

"So the whole time my seed was growin' elsewhere—the

lady in question not hailin' from the territories—there was darlin' Lillabit, tendin' her own. Not long after Laurel showed up, I received news that my lady friend—and her husband, of course—had also been blessed with a daughter."

"So since you could not have your own child . . ."

"I may have lavished a little extra affection on Jacob's." Now Cooper took a deep breath, rolling his shoulders. "When I heard tell the other baby died—scarlet fever, it was—Laurel became even dearer to me. And by the time your cousin showed up to perfect my life, the habit was set."

With more cluckings and a "Gee, now!" Cooper turned the buggy off Main and onto a muddier residential street.

So Laurel was not Cooper's daughter, at that. And yet . . .

The man *had* sacrificed. He'd left his friends rather than risk their partnership. He'd let the lady have their baby and her marriage both. And when he'd wed Alexandra, despite that he had no issue, he'd agreed to a childless marriage . . . for her.

Had Collier ever felt superior to the Americans?

"Thank you," he said. It seemed the least he could offer.

"Rumor has it I'm not bashful about workin' my jaw." A smile twitched Cooper's mustache. "And as there was a time I was not above warmin' the bed of a married woman, I don't reckon I'll plug you for the misunderstandin', just this once. Unless you fail to make my Laurel happy every day of her life, of course."

"I mean to make the effort," Collier promised solemnly.

"Whoa." Cooper drew his buggy to a stop at the curb. "I figured as much when you said you'd respect her no matter who her daddy was. Don't forget, I've been around you Englishers some. I know what weight you folks put on bloodlines and legitimacy."

But Collier would rather talk to Laurel than Cooper—which was why it surprised him to look up and see that they were not on Elizabeth Street at all. They had instead stopped in front of the house that the Coopers had rented. "I thought you said Laurel was with her parents."

"I did," agreed Cooper, hopping neatly to the sidewalk. "But you don't want to go there."

"I most certainly do!" With a grimace, Collier stepped down into more slush. He kept his shoes on this time. Barely. "But I am perfectly capable of walking."

"Now, son," drawled Cooper, blocking his path. "I've decided that I like you, and so I'm doin' you a favor. After the day her daddy's had, the last place you want to be this afternoon is at that house. I'll fetch Laurel to you instead."

Really! "I am no coward."

"Never meant to insinuate otherwise. But I'm figurin' on you being smart, all the same."

With everything Collier had yet to discuss with Laurel, to ask Laurel, to tell Laurel, this delay abraded him. He supposed he could push by Cooper and stalk to Elizabeth Street anyway. That was, he thought with amusement, what Laurel would do.

But then he noticed the mountains rising up past the trees—and he had a better idea.

When she saw the buggy driving up in front, through the upstairs hall window, Laurel called, "It's him!"

"Shh," warned Mariah gently from the bedroom, while little Garry made a protesting gurgle.

"Sorry," Laurel called more softly. She touched her white-gloved fingers to the glass and reminded herself to breathe.

Then she took the stairs.

Papa, striding into the foyer from the kitchen, stopped her on the landing with a stern look. A knock sounded. A shadow darkened the front porch, through the door's beveled glass, and Laurel longed to rush the rest of the way down. But it was Papa's house. He could get the door if he liked.

Ladylike, she reminded herself. *Ladylike*.

Papa wrenched open the door.

Alec Cooper, standing in front of his parents, backed up so quickly that the boy bumped into his father.

Laurel descended the stairs more slowly, leaning over the

banister some to better see the veranda. No, she hadn't missed him. The Cooper family was here—but not Collier.

Not Collier!

"Now, darlin' Laurel, you wipe that dismay off your pretty face," commanded Uncle Benj. With a curt, "Excuse us," he shouldered past Papa—who stood very still and threatening—and came to Laurel. He leaned toward her from a mud-safe distance and kissed her cheek, delivering something papery into her hand at the same time. "He's here, and he's safe, and he sent this for you. So don't you fret."

Then he turned back to the others. "Now, Jacob, I know you don't have the manners of that fine son-in-law of yours, but the least you can do is invite my wife and son into your home."

Slowly Papa pivoted back from where he blocked the doorway, still scowling his disapproval at Uncle Benj. "Sent you to fetch his godship."

"Last time I checked, I didn't work for you. Why, darlin' Lillabit, as I live and breathe," he greeted when Mama came in from the kitchen to hug him. "Watch the mud."

"Hullo, Mr. Garrison, sir," said Alec politely. But he sidled a wide circle as he passed Laurel's father, as if still taken aback by the rancher's grim reception.

"Mr. Garrison," agreed Lady Cooper, following with more ladylike steps.

"I think he was figurin' on you readin' it," teased Uncle Benj to Laurel. With a start she looked back at the note in her hand. She guessed if she could do anything, she could do this.

Laurel Pembroke, it said on the outside, in Collier's neat hand. When she unfolded it, the message inside was brief.

We've much to discuss. Please come home. Love, Collier.

Chapter Twenty-nine

He'd signed it with love, Laurel thought.

And he'd said *home!*

She didn't cover her mouth fast enough to muffle her shriek of joy. Upstairs, little Garry started to cry. "Sorry, Mariah!" Laurel called, then ran to the coatrack for her lightest coat. "He's at the claim!"

"He's what?" asked Mama.

"He's at the claim, and he wants me there!"

Papa was nodding his slow, angry nod at Uncle Benj.

"Now that," insisted his partner, "was *his* idea."

"He'll have to come off the mountain sometime," warned Papa, and both Mama and Lady Cooper said, at the same time, "Not the face!"

But surely Papa wouldn't get violent with the man she loved! Not if everything worked out after all. And, oh, for the first time . . .

He'd signed it with love. He'd called the claim *home!*

How could she not hope?

"May I saddle your horse for you, Laurel?" asked Alec

351

eagerly. Of course, she could still saddle her own horse, even dressed up like this. But she guessed she didn't always *have* to.

"Yes, thank you," she said. While Alec scampered out, she ran back to her grim father and wrapped her arms around him in a hug.

"Oh, Papa, thank you! I know you're still angry, and you have a right to be. But if it hadn't been for you, I might not have done any of this . . . so thank you!"

Then she kissed his whiskered cheek and hurried out to the kitchen for her boots. If she heard Uncle Benj cackle, she paid it no mind. She had more important things on her mind.

Home. Maybe he was being polite. But it had to be a good sign, didn't it? If she could be what he wanted, then maybe . . .

Collier must have found another horse. Laurel rode Snapper and led the dapple gray, Llewellyn, through slush and muck that got thicker as they left town. Only the mud kept her wearing her coat in this dry wind—her outer layer was likely a sight. But this was one time she would meet with Collier ready to look the way his wife should—or as close as she could get. Compared to the joy of leaving town for the plains, then the foothills, mere comfort hardly mattered.

When she reined Snapper off the rutted track that led toward the Circle-T, riding across country, he responded with enthusiasm to match hers. Llewellyn in tow, they made for the treeline. The timber, still harboring deeper patches of snow and ice, provided cool relief against the Chinook. The creek rushed by, full and wild. And for the first time in months, the air smelled of more than snow and woodsmoke. It smelled of springtime and hope. Laurel loved these mountains.

But that wasn't the love that drew her to the claim cabin in the pine grove. Not *this* time!

The first thing she saw, when she rode into the clearing, was a British flag flying over her door. She realized that it didn't bother her at all. It meant he was here. Home.

Then Collier hiked around the corner of the cabin, from the woodshed side, with a cigar box in his hands. Or . . . was it Cole?

He wore a muddy duster over dungarees and boots, and what looked like a chambray shirt. His golden hair was drawn back from his handsome face, his eyes bright. When she saw him like that—a beautiful cross of aristocrat and settler—Laurel guessed he could fly the flag of *Spain* over her door and she wouldn't mind!

Catching sight of her, Collier put the box aside and came to take Snapper's bridle. When he did, Laurel all but dove from her sidesaddle into his strong arms, and, oh, he smelled even better than the mountain, and even more like home.

Somehow they could fix things between them. Somehow. Especially now that she didn't have to do it alone.

Collier lost count of the kisses Laurel showered across his face, his neck, his jaw, his ears. Apparently she had forgiven him. That seemed enough justification to kiss his muddy-coated wife back. Happily. Wholly.

Only when Snapper snorted equine disgust at the two of them did Collier straighten from Laurel to tip back her mud-spattered hat and share an appreciative grin. "For shame, Mrs. Pembroke," he chided playfully. "In these parts, one sees to one's horses before engaging in pleasure."

Bold words, considering that the whole of the mountain had become her own personal arsenal of mud grenades. But Laurel just wrapped her arms tighter around him and kissed him again, so ardently that his forehead knocked her hat right off the back of her head. He caught it one-handed while, ever the gentleman, obliging her in the kiss as well. He had missed her! The smell of her, the feel of her, the warmth of her, the spirit of her.

"Is that what one does in these parts?" she asked happily as they drew reluctantly apart, and he looked at her more closely. Her hair was curled and arranged in a way that, even after losing the hat, looked quite stylish. She wore ear bobs.

And she smelled not just of herself but of . . . perfume?

"One does indeed." *Damn.* He had to kiss her some more, hold her some more, breathe her in and reassure himself that she was here with him. Perhaps he'd not wholly alienated her in Denver. Perhaps they had a chance, at that.

Despite what he had to tell her.

Only that thought—the knowledge of the last few obstacles they had yet to surmount—gave him the impetus he needed to grasp her shoulders and slowly, reluctantly, separate them. "Hello, dearest," he greeted. "You look lovely."

"Wait until you see what's under the coat!"

He laughed at the improper images that arose in his mind. But when she tried to kiss him again, he turned his cheek to her, so as not to get drawn back into his favorite enticement.

"I'm afraid we do have matters to discuss," he said when she pouted. "Hadn't we better face them head-on, for once?"

"Matters?" She took a deep breath and nodded, resigned. "Yes. Oh, Collier, I *am* sorry. So sorry!"

"You? Never you . . ." He wanted to kiss her again, her forehead, her cheek, but caught himself, limited himself to an encouraging smile. As distraction, he led the horses to the slushy, muddy corral, where Cooper's Appaloosa already watched with interest. He lifted the loose top log down so that their mounts could step through, then lifted it back into place while Laurel set about unsaddling Snapper—and cataloging her sins.

"I'm sorry I embarrassed you. I'm sorry I said I wouldn't apologize to Lady Vivian. Of course I will. I would apologize to the lowliest whore if I'd behaved that badly, so why not her?"

Collier enjoyed that analogy so much, he almost laughed again. But she looked so very serious that instead he busied himself rubbing Snapper down with his saddle blanket. "We were both out of countenance that day," he assured her.

"And then I ran away."

"I prefer to think of it as shortening your visit."

She rolled her eyes at him, as if to accuse him of dissembling. Collier inhaled the sweet scent of horse, ran his bare hand through Snapper's wiry mane, and wondered how he had ever imagined a life in which only the hired help curried or saddled his mounts . . . and a wife who would expect that.

Even if he did still mean to hire someone to muck stalls and such. Or at least to help.

"I didn't keep our bargain," Laurel insisted. "We had a deal. You deserved better, and I'm sorry."

"As am I," he assured her, stepping back with her to let Snapper go roll in the mud with Llewellyn. "For any number of snobberies and conceits and Lord knows what conde-scensions I've forced upon you, either from myself or my family."

She considered him seriously, then offered a hand. "Truce?"

Truce? He wanted to cup her face and kiss her until they forgot where they were, to thoroughly ruin her coif and pos-sibly lose the earrings, to take her inside and make love until neither remembered past hurts. But he had been distracting them, distracting himself, with the wonder of that for months now. A gentleman could control those baser urges . . . at least for short durations. A gentleman did what truly needed doing.

So he accepted her hand and they shook. And he said, "About that bargain, though."

She pressed her lips together and raised her chin—but did she fear he meant to break the bargain or to keep it? He cursed himself for leaving the slightest of doubts—for either of them.

"Oh, Lorelei." He sighed, brushing his fingers across her cheek. "I should think it would be obvious. . . . But no, that's cowardice. So I shall say it full out."

She nodded cautious encouragement.

"I find myself quite in love with you," he told her.

Her lips parted in . . . wonder? Disbelief? He hoped the first.

"I love being married to you. I want no more to do with our foolish bargain, only because it included an end, and I never want this—us—to end." He took her other hand in his

355

as well. "I've no intention of divorcing you. I want to take you home to meet my mother, so that you can see how poor an example of British society you've met thus far, and she can see what an extraordinary woman I found in the wilds of Wyoming. And I do expect you to see out the visit with me."

Ships left for Wyoming nowhere near as often as trains.

"Oh," she said softly, but he thought—hoped—happily.

"I want you to someday have my babies," he continued, lest he leave any dregs of confusion. "I want to grow old with you. I want to build a life with you to rival anything I could have had in England. And I do hope . . ."

She stared at him, wide-eyed, not helping in the least.

Mettle, Collier. So he dropped the old saddle blanket into the mud and sank onto one knee atop it, looking up at her.

"My dearest Laurel," he said. "You truly have become my hope for the future . . . any future worth having. Please do me the honor of *remaining* married to me. For good."

She said, "Forever married?" so quietly that he barely heard her.

"And longer, if I can arrange it." He lifted her gloved hands to his cheek, felt the nub of her engagement ring under the leather, breathed the freshness of her and her wet, muddy mountain. Her cold, unforgiving, blustery mountain. How could anyone consider separating her from such surroundings?

"Oh," she said again—but still just stared.

"May I please, please take that as a yes?"

Then she laughed and bent to loop her arms behind his neck, as possessive as any lariat but far more enjoyable, and she drew him back up to his booted feet as firmly as if he were a bogged cow. "Yes," she insisted, kissing his cheeks again, his jaw, his ear. "Yes, yes, yes! Now maybe Papa won't hit you."

"Pardon?"

"I'll explain later." And still she held tight. "Oh, Collier, I was so afraid you'd go back to England for good."

"Wild horses," he assured her, stroking her sleek, curled hair back from her face, "could not drag me away." Which reminded him of something else. "Although that does raise another matter. As long as we are clarifying everything."

She drew back. "Should I prepare my calm-lady face now?"

"No, no. You may save that for company." He had asked her properly this time. She'd said yes. Surely that meant that everything else was mere detail. Wasn't it?

Or perhaps he should have learned, particularly with Laurel, never to assume! He did love how she pillowed her head against his shoulder with a relieved sigh, though. He loved standing with her in the muddy corral, an Appaloosa blowing horsey breaths near her shoulder as it investigated the excitement. No matter *what* they might be standing in, she transcended it.

And that was why they wore boots.

"I do mean to make this my home, after all," he explained. "Of course, I realize that it is your claim. . . ."

"*Our* claim," she assured him, ever loyal.

"Thank you. But I must confess to some piracy. As only American citizens can file for free land, and I remain a loyal subject to the queen, I mean to claim this homestead, for England, by force." He kissed her hair. "Thus the Union Jack."

"Oh, really?"

"Although you may fly your flag as well," he added quickly.

"Can mine be on top?" Did she understood her double entendre? Considering how deliciously he had been corrupting her, likely she did. He would make sure of it.

"Perhaps we can take turns," he offered, and kissed her hair. "The correct response is, 'Of course, your lordship.'"

"Oh." She nodded solemnly. "Of course, your lordship. You may lay claim to anything I have."

Oh, my! They'd best leave the corral now, before they risked getting muddier than was seemly, even for Wyoming.

Laurel let him help her as she ducked under the rail.

"In that spirit, I've an idea for a brand," he ventured. When she simply waited, expectant, he went ahead and drew an imaginary *L* on the corral rail, then an *I*. Then he waited.

As he'd feared, she frowned. "*L* is for Laurel, right?" When he nodded, she asked, "What's the *I* for?"

"The Lorelei." Now he was the one waiting. Perhaps it was presumptuous, thinking he could choose their brand. Jokes of piracy aside, it *was* legally her claim.

But then she smiled—a full Laurel smile, beautiful in its honesty. "Oh, Cole! Do you really want to call the ranch that?"

And he began to trust in their partnership—a real partnership—at last.

"How could I not? And . . . as this is to be my home," he continued boldly, backing toward the edge of the clearing, swinging her hand, "you should know that I am set on having a true house. Nothing grandiose, mind you; it should complement the scenery, not do battle with it. But a true building with, at the very least, a kitchen, a bedroom, a parlor, and a den. And a floor—let us just accept that I am a snob about things like that. And a room in back for hired help someday. I thought we could build the whole thing over here." Which was where he was leading her, anyway. "Where that shoulder shelters us from the worst wind, and our front veranda will overlook the basin."

Again she nodded, eyeing the level ground, the nearby trees. She said, "Your remittances aren't *that* good!"

"No, but I included the price of a house in the startup costs I quoted to Baron Tentrees." He might as well confess to everything. Without it he was back to a cozy shack and no real purpose but hers. And her. He supposed he could do worse. . . .

But for the first time since leaving England, he'd begun to hope for far, far better. He had begun to hope for everything. Starting with her. Ending with her. But in between . . .

"Laurel," he confessed. "I do not wish to raise cattle."

She drew back from him, blue eyes widening. "But this is a *ranch*! All I've ever wanted to be is . . ." Suddenly she stopped and pressed her lips together, as if to silence further protests. She took a deep breath and then asked, more evenly, "Startup costs for what? What *would* you like to do?"

Good Lord. He loved her so intensely it hurt.

So Collier told her about raising polo ponies—and how he meant to start with the half-mustang foal his runaway thoroughbred would likely be dropping sometime that spring.

They sat on a boulder, very near where Collier said he would put their front porch. His free hand moved with excitement as he explained his hopes for breeding the speed and refinement of thoroughbreds with the hardy agility of wild mustangs. His other arm was wrapped solidly around her, his hand on her waist. Laurel, cuddling against the safety of his duster-clad shoulder, imagined the wonders he described and felt foolish again.

She felt foolish for ever resisting a nicer house—what did she have left to prove that she couldn't prove living in a larger home? She felt foolish for thinking he meant to forbid her to raise cattle—he was not such a dreamer as to think they couldn't use a moderately more reliable income.

Most humbling, though, she felt foolish because his ideas were better! The viscount had made one decent point the other day. The time to make one's fortune in cattle was passing. That had been Papa's and Uncle Benj's opportunity. But *this!*

Not that Laurel knew a blessed thing about polo—but she knew horses, and Collier knew both. Apparently this would keep him involved with his upper-crust peers on a level *she* could appreciate, one of skill and knowledge instead of mere title or birth order. They could keep their equine stock on her land—The Lorelei!—rather than going months without seeing their cattle as they wandered the range. Collier was already negotiating an agreement with a group of British polo enthusiasts, through the Baron Tentrees, protecting the land and house from forfeiture, in case he did poorly. She might not know much about business, but she recognized in that an incredible vote of confidence.

"May I work with the horses, too?" she asked, increasingly

excited by the idea herself. "Assuming I'm any good at it?"

"I am counting on it. You trained Snapper, did you not?"

"And can I ride along when we go after the mustangs?"

"My dearest wife, you may ride straddle if you wish." He seemed to consider that, then qualified, "For the roundup."

She considered challenging that—she could ride straddle anywhere she wanted, if it came down to that! But then she thought about it, and instead she unbuttoned her coat.

Now that she'd finished ironing the blasted thing, she rather liked her dress. It felt soft. She liked the braid. And she very much liked how Collier leaned back from her, obviously admiring the effect. "Oh my! You look . . ."

That he couldn't find words for it made her blush.

"Is this for me?" he asked, looking her up and down. Then his bright eyes flared, and he blushed too. "That is to say . . . the frock? And the hair?" He leaned closer, inhaling right next to her neck, which tickled. "And the perfume?"

"Well, is this for me?" she countered and reached under his duster to snap one of his suspenders. He must have borrowed work clothes from Uncle Benj, she thought. They were very good work clothes. And oh, did he wear them well.

"I think," he assured her, speaking low—but with an intimacy less seductive than she'd expected—"that it is for both of us. It's time I discover who I can become. With you."

"Collier?" she whispered, despite the fact that this was one of those moments when his sheer, golden beauty overwhelmed her: his burnished hair, bright eyes, long lashes, full lips. This felt even harder to say than an apology—but it was so very much more necessary! "I don't think I've told you that I love you, too."

He went very still for a moment. Then he slanted his eyes, reflecting the blue sky, down toward her and asked, "Are you likely to?"

She elbowed him in the side, making him laugh, which quickly turned into wrestling. She didn't even let him win— he won on his own. The way she went weak, gazing into his eyes, hardly helped her defense. And finding herself pinned beneath him was more than adequate reward.

"I love you," she insisted up at him, and it got easier every time. "I love you, I love you, I love you."

"Thank you, dearest." This time, when he kissed her, it was slowly, deeply, with an affection she'd never imagined. This, she thought, was what Mariah had described. Body and soul. *Love.*

"I've loved you since I fell in the creek, and you had to start doing all the chores," she added, so that he would kiss her again.

"So you were holding out for a laborer at that, were you?" But he did kiss her again, and when she inhaled she felt as though she were breathing him into her, like the mountain air. Maybe they went together, after all. "Perhaps I should rethink the hired help."

She scowled at him, and he kissed her nose. Then he sat back up, drawing her with him. She almost hoped he wouldn't take her back inside, just yet; she wanted to savor the wonder of this, just this, a little while longer.

And they had forever to do everything else.

Maybe he felt the same way. Instead of getting up, he looped an arm around her and looked back out over the basin. She pillowed her cheek on his chambray-clad shoulder and enjoyed how comfortable she felt with him. She should have known they would love each other from the start, considering how easy they were together.

"Being a woman has turned out much better than I used to think it would," she confessed quietly after a while. "I might just ride sidesaddle for the wild-horse roundup after all. If I can ride as well as a man, and do it *sidesaddle* . . . now *that's* an accomplishment!"

"If anyone can do it," he assured her, "it would be you."

"Even getting all gussied up can be nice," she admitted. "Within reason."

"I am particularly attracted to your footwear today," he teased, because she was still wearing her cowboy boots. So she pulled a cloth girl-shoe out of her coat pocket, where she'd been keeping them safe from the mud, and offered it as proof of her willingness to be ladylike. He smiled as he took it from her. He looked at it, turning it in his hand.

Then he drew back his arm and threw the thing far, far away. It arched off into trees still bare, but bright with the promise of spring leaves, and vanished down the hillside, toward the view they would someday have from their veranda.

"Being born second has turned out better than I'd feared, as well," he told her then, quite seriously.

Laurel laughed, delighted, and he grinned his most honest, lopsided grin. Then he drew her against his side again, his arm warm around her, so that they could look toward the Powder River basin and their future together.

The draw of keeping company with a man was sure starting to make more sense. Especially with the *right* man.

"Cole," Laurel asked softly. "On this new house of ours, can we have a porch swing?"

"With this view," he agreed, his voice thick enough to lick off a spoon, "it would be a crime not to."

And while she sat there with her husband, Laurel saw something flutter by that looked suspiciously like a tiger moth.

Dear Reader:

Thank you for reading Proving Herself. I hope you enjoyed Collier and Laurel's story.

My works are, of course, fiction—but I like to think stories like this could well have happened. There were a great number of "girl homesteaders" at the turn of the century. My research (particularly from *Land of the Burnt Thigh* by Edith Eudora Kohl) shows that between the late 1880s and 1908, often more than ten percent of people filing for Wyoming homesteads were women—and a larger percentage of women proved up their final claims than did the men! Once I knew Laurel meant to homestead, it seemed the last man she would fall for—and thus the most interesting hero— would be a pretty-boy aristocrat. Enter Collier Pembroke!

The influx of British remittance men to the Old West (as well as Canada, Australia, and other places) started around the 1870s and continued as late as the 1920s. Something I hadn't fully realized when I started writing *Proving Herself* was just how strong a history polo has in the Big Horn, Wyoming, area! It was in fact introduced by real remittance men—notably Oliver Henry Wallop and Malcolm Moncrieffe—only a few years before Proving Herself takes place! According to *Big Horn Polo: The History of Polo in the Big Horn, Wyoming Area,* graciously provided to me by the author, Bucky King, these men are largely responsible for establishing Sheridan County as a source of the best high-goal polo ponies in the country—a business which is of course more sophisticated than I've likely conveyed in my novel.

My next novel for Leisure, *Explaining Herself,* tells about Victoria Garrison's adventures as a turn-of-the-century newspaperwoman who may learn more than she ever meant to about rustling and train robbery. Look for it in May 2002. In the meantime, I love reader mail! Please write me at: PO Box 6; Euless, TX 76039; e-mail me at Yvaughnaol.com; or visit www.ranchersdaughters.homestead.com.

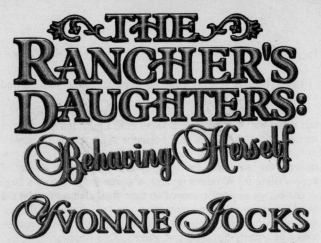

THE RANCHER'S DAUGHTERS: Behaving Herself

Yvonne Jocks

There are so many things that a girl shouldn't do, and for a teacher, there are even more. Miss Garrison is learning them all by doing them. No sooner has the hapless beauty escaped scandal in her Wyoming home by taking a Texas teaching job than she meets up with "Handy" Jack Harwood—a handsome gambler who will surely do her reputation no good. She knows she can get on track, if only she can ignore the unladylike excitement he stirs in her. She'll gamble one last time—on the goodness of Jack's rakish soul and that they are meant to be together. After that, she'll start behaving herself.

___4693-8 $5.50 US/$6.50 CAN

Dorchester Publishing Co., Inc.
P.O. Box 6640
Wayne, PA 19087-8640

Please add $1.75 for shipping and handling for the first book and $.50 for each book thereafter. NY, NYC, and PA residents, please add appropriate sales tax. No cash, stamps, or C.O.D.s. All orders shipped within 6 weeks via postal service book rate. Canadian orders require $2.00 extra postage and must be paid in U.S. dollars through a U.S. banking facility.

Name_____
Address_____
City_____State_____Zip_____
I have enclosed $_____ in payment for the checked book(s).
Payment <u>must</u> accompany all orders. ☐ Please send a free catalog.

Winnie Griggs

What Matters Most

Reed Wilder journeys to Far Enough, Texas, in search of a fallen woman. He finds an angel. Barely reaching five feet two inches, the petite brunette helps to defend him against two ruffians and then treats his wounds with a gentleness that makes him long to uncover all her secrets. But she only has to reveal her name and he knows his lovely rescuer is not an innocent woman, but the deceitful opportunist who preyed on his brother. Reed prides himself on his logic and control, but both desert him when he gazes into Lucy's warm brown eyes. He has only one option: to discover the truth behind those enticing lips he longs to sample.

__4829-9 $4.99 US/$5.99 CAN

Lori Morgan
Autumn Star

Morgan Caine rescues Lacey Ashton from a couple of pawing ruffians, feeds her dinner, and gives her a place to sleep. He is arrogant, bossy, and the most captivating man she has ever met. He claims she will never survive the wilds of the Washington Territory. But Lacey sets out to prove she not only belongs in the untamed land, she belongs in Morgan's arms.

Morgan is completely disarmed by Lacey's innocence and optimism. Like an autumn breeze, she caresses his body, refreshes his soul, invigorates his heart. At last, the hardened lawman longs to trade vengeance for a future filled with happiness—to reach for the stars and claim the woman of his dreams.

___4892-2 $4.99 US/$5.99 CAN

Dorchester Publishing Co., Inc.
P.O. Box 6640
Wayne, PA 19087-8640

Please add $2.50 for shipping and handling for the first book and $.75 for each book thereafter. NY and PA residents, please add appropriate sales tax. No cash, stamps, or C.O.D.s. All orders shipped within 3 weeks via postal service book rate.
Canadian orders require $2.50 extra postage and must be paid in U.S. dollars through a U.S. banking facility.

Name_____
Address_____
City_____ State_____ Zip_____
I have enclosed $ _____ in payment for the checked book(s).
Payment <u>must</u> accompany all orders. ☐ Please send a free catalog.
CHECK OUT OUR WEBSITE! www.dorchesterpub.com

Indigo Moon

Lori Morgan

Chase Hawken's career as a cavalry scout has been legendary, his life a dream. Even when the law turned on him, he took solace in tracking down criminals and bringing them to justice—and he always got his man. But then comes Rebeka, an indigo-eyed beauty who travels with outlaws and stirs feelings he's banished.

Breaking her brother out of jail won't be easy. To do so, Rebeka needs the best tracker in the territory. But the perfect candidate hardly seems willing; Chase even swears that her brother should hang. But his touch speaks of a deeper desire . . . and when together they flee toward the Montana Territory, Rebeka knows that she'll discover not only the man to free her brother, but her heart.

___4792-6 $4.99 US/$5.99 CAN

Dorchester Publishing Co., Inc.
P.O. Box 6640
Wayne, PA 19087-8640

Please add $2.50 for shipping and handling for the first book and $.75 for each book thereafter. NY and PA residents, please add appropriate sales tax. No cash, stamps, or C.O.D.s. All orders shipped within 6 weeks via postal service book rate. Canadian orders require $2.50 extra postage and must be paid in U.S. dollars through a U.S. banking facility.

Name_____
Address_____
City_____ State _____ Zip_____
I have enclosed $ _____ in payment for the checked book(s).
Payment <u>must</u> accompany all orders. ❑ Please send a free catalog.
CHECK OUT OUR WEBSITE! www.dorchesterpub.com